analog's
CHILDREN
OF THE FUTURE

analog's
CHILDREN
OF THE FUTURE
Edited by Stanley Schmidt

The Dial Press

DAVIS PUBLICATIONS, INC.
380 LEXINGTON AVENUE
NEW YORK, N.Y. 10017

FIRST PRINTING

Copyright © 1982 by Davis Publications, Inc.
All rights reserved.
Library of Congress Catalog Card Number: 80-69078
Printed in the U.S.A.

COPYRIGHT NOTICES AND ACKNOWLEDGMENTS

Grateful acknowledgment is hereby made for permission to reprint the following:

Mimsy Were the Borogoves by Lewis Padgett; copyright 1943 by Lewis Padgett, renewed; reprinted by permission of Harold Matson Company, Inc.

Mewhu's Jet by Theodore Sturgeon; copyright 1946 by Theodore Sturgeon, renewed; reprinted by permission of Kirby McCauley, Ltd.

The Witches of Karres by James H. Schmitz; copyright 1949 by Street & Smith Publications, Inc., renewed 1977 by The Conde Nast Publications, Inc.; reprinted by permission of the late author.

Mikal's Songbird by Orson Scott Card; copyright © 1978 by Orson Scott Card; reprinted by permission of Barbara Bova Literary Agency.

In Hiding by Wilmar Shiras; copyright 1948 by Wilmar Shiras, renewed; reprinted by permission of the author.

Weyr Search by Anne McCaffrey; copyright © 1967 by The Conde Nast Publications, Inc., reprinted by permission of Virginia Kidd, Literary Agent.

Meeting of Minds by Ted Reynolds; © 1980 by Davis Publications, Inc.; reprinted by permission of the author.

Novice by James H. Schmitz; copyright © 1962 by The Conde Nast Publications, Inc.; reprinted by permission of Scott Meredith Literary Agency, Inc.

Child of All Ages by P. J. Plauger; © 1975 by The Conde Nast Publications, Inc.; reprinted by permission of the author.

Emergence by David R. Palmer; © 1980 by Davis Publications, Inc.; reprinted by permission of the author.

CONTENTS

Introduction
Stanley Schmidt

"Some of you have been boys," Mark Twain reminded an audience to whom he was about to read an excerpt from *Huckleberry Finn*, "and the rest of you have had a good deal to do with boys."

The same, of course, could be said of girls. One of the relatively few things that all of us have in common is that we have all occupied some version of that peculiar, special position in the world called "childhood." Not many adúlts remember very clearly what it was like (which probably helps account for the popularity of those entertainers who do, such as Mark Twain and Bill Cosby), but even those who neither remember childhood vividly nor have children of their own must recognize that that station in life is indeed unique.

Just how it is special varies somewhat from time to time, place to place—and species to species. The life of a nine-year-old girl in Victorian London was very different from that of her contemporaries in Tahiti or her multi-great-grandchildren in the same city today. Any of those is quite different from the experience of a hatchling snake or a fledgling albatross, or any of the multifarious beings which may begin their lives on the billions of other planets in the universe. Or, for that matter, our own descendants in any of the human cultures which will exist on Earth and elsewhere in the millennia to come.

And yet . . .

There are common denominators. From his own standpoint, the youngest members of virtually any reasonably advanced species or culture must differ from its adults in occupying a special status in society. Among humans, at least, that special niche includes both special restrictions (which children look forward to escaping) and special privileges (to which adults sometimes wish they could return). And those who are relatively new in the world see it from a fresh and perhaps original perspective, relatively uncolored by cultural preconceptions. All of these things change, of course, as the child approaches adulthood—and the line between child and adult is seldom absolutely sharp, though most human cultures provide "rites of passage" to give it some semblance of definiteness.

From the standpoint of the society into which they are born, what is obviously special about children is that it is they who will carry that society into the future, reshaping as they go. That is why adults put up with the temporary nuisances of harboring dependent beings with a somewhat alien view of the world—because their collective future is entirely dependent not only upon a supply of new living bodies, but perhaps even more on that fresh (and sometimes startling) outlook and the potential it represents. Each new life allows its elders to hope, at least for a little while, that *this* one will turn out to have some talent, some wisdom, some compassion that none of his ancestors had before him. It is that possibility that allows the hope that the future will be, on the whole, a better place than the past.

The young heroes and heroines of these stories are repositories of that hope. They are as diverse as the worlds that produced them, and by the time you've met them all you'll realize that "child" is not even a simple world to define. Does it refer to chronological age, physical form, mental set—or all (or none) of these? Some of the characters you'll meet here are practically infants; some are on the threshold of adulthood. Some are literally brand-new; others are—well, I won't say how old. Some are not even human. All are quite special, not just in the general manner of children as a group, but in their own highly individual ways.

I, for one, am by no means ready to relinquish my share of the universe; and I don't think most of the rest of present-day humanity is, either. But if ever someone *must* inherit the Earth, I'd like to think that there will be people like Candy Maria Smith-Foster—and Telzey Amberdon, and the others you're about to meet—waiting in the wings to take our place.

Joel Davis, President & Publisher; **Leonard F. Pinto,** Vice President & General Manager; **Carole Dolph Gross,** Vice President, Marketing & Editorial; **Leonard H. Habas,** Vice President, Circulation; **Fred Edinger,** Vice President, Finance.

Stanley Schmidt, Editor; **Elizabeth Mitchell,** Managing Editor; **Ralph Rubino,** Art Director; **David Pindar,** Associate Art Director; **Terri Czeczko,** Art Editor; **Carl Bartee,** Production Director; **Carole Dixon,** Production Manager; **Iris Temple,** Director, Subsidiary Rights; **Barbara Bazyn,** Manager, Contracts & Permissions; **Layne Layton,** Promotion Manager; **Robert Castardi,** Circulation Director, Retail Marketing; **Alan Inglis,** Circulation Director, Subscriptions; **Rose Wayner,** Classified Advertising Director; **William F. Battista,** Advertising Director (NEW YORK: 212-557-9100; CHICAGO: 312-346-0712; LOS ANGELES: 213-795-3114).

MIMSY WERE THE BOROGOVES

Lewis Padgett

There's no use trying to describe either Unthahorsten or his surroundings, because, for one thing, a good many million years had passed and, for another, Unthahorsten wasn't on Earth, technically speaking. He was doing the equivalent of standing in the equivalent of a laboratory. He was preparing to test his time machine.

Having turned on the power, Unthahorsten suddenly realized that the Box was empty. Which wouldn't do at all. The device needed a control, a three-dimensional solid which would react to the conditions of another age. Otherwise Unthahorsten couldn't tell, on the machine's return, where and when it had been. Whereas a solid in the Box would automatically be subject to the entropy and cosmic-ray bombardment of the other era, and Unthahorsten could measure the changes, both qualitative and quantitative, when the machine returned. The Calculators could then get to work and, presently, tell Unthahorsten that the Box had briefly visited A.D. 1,000,000, A.D. 1,000 or A.D. 1, as the case might be.

Not that it mattered, except to Unthahorsten. But he was childish in many respects.

There was little time to waste. The Box was beginning to glow and shiver. Unthahorsten stared around wildly, fled into the next glossatch and groped in a storage bin there. He came up with an armful of peculiar-looking stuff. Uh-huh. Some of the discarded toys of his son Snowen, which the boy had brought with him when he had passed over from Earth, after mastering the necessary technique. Well, Snowen needed this junk no longer. He was conditioned, and had put away childish things. Besides, though Unthahorsten's wife kept the toys for sentimental reasons, the experiment was more important.

Unthahorsten left the glossatch and dumped the assortment into the Box, slamming the cover shut before the warning signal flashed. The Box went away. The manner of its departure hurt Unthahorsten's eyes.

He waited.

And he waited.

Eventually he gave up and built another time machine, with identical results. Snowen hadn't been annoyed by the loss of his old toys, nor had Snowen's mother, so

Unthahorsten cleaned out the bin and dumped the remainder of his son's childhood relics in the second time machine's Box.

According to his calculations, this one should have appeared on Earth in the latter part of the nineteenth century, A.D. If that actually occurred, the device remained there.

Disgusted, Unthahorsten decided to make no more time machines. But the mischief had been done. There were two of them, and the first . . .

Scott Paradine found it while he was playing hooky from the Glendale Grammar School. There was a geography test that day, and Scott saw no sense in memorizing place names—which, in the nineteen-forties, was a fairly sensible theory. Besides, it was the sort of warm spring day, with a touch of coolness in the breeze, which invited a boy to lie down in a field and stare at the occasional clouds till he fell asleep. Nuts to geography! Scott dozed.

About noon he got hungry, so his stocky legs carried him to a nearby store. There he invested his small hoard with penurious care and a sublime disregard for his gastric juices. He went down by the creek to feed.

Having finished his supply of cheese, chocolate and cookies, and having drained the soda-pop bottle to its dregs, Scott caught tadpoles and studied them with a certain amount of scientific curiosity. He did not persevere. Something tumbled down the bank and thudded into the muddy ground near the water, so Scott, with a wary glance around, hurried to investigate.

It was a box. It was, in fact, the Box. The gadgetry hitched to it meant little to Scott, though he wondered why it was so fused and burned. He pondered. With his jackknife he pried and probed, his tongue sticking out from a corner of his mouth—Hm-m-m. Nobody was around. Where had the box come from? Somebody must have left it here, and sliding soil had dislodged it from its precarious perch.

"That's a helix," Scott decided, quite erroneously. It was helical, but it wasn't a helix, because of the dimensional warp involved. Had the thing been a model airplane, no matter how complicated, it would have held few mysteries to Scott. As it was, a problem was posed. Something told Scott that the device was a lot more complicated than the spring motor he had deftly dismantled last Friday.

But no boy has ever left a box unopened, unless forcibly dragged away. Scott probed deeper. The angles on this thing were funny. Short circuit, probably. That was why—uh! The knife slipped. Scott sucked his thumb and gave vent to experienced blasphemy.

Maybe it was a music box.

Scott shouldn't have felt depressed. The gadgetry would have given Einstein a headache and driven Steinmetz raving mad. The trouble was, of course, that the box had not yet completely entered the space-time continuum where Scott existed, and therefore it could not be opened—at any rate, not till Scott used a convenient rock to hammer the helical non-helix into a more convenient position.

He hammered it, in fact, from its contact point with the fourth dimension, releasing the space-time torsion it had been maintaining. There was a brittle snap. The box jarred slightly, and lay motionless, no longer only partially in existence. Scott opened it easily now.

The soft, woven helmet was the first thing that caught his eye, but he discarded that without much interest. It was just a cap. Next, he lifted a square, transparent crystal block, small enough to cup in his palm—much too small to contain the maze of apparatus within it. In a moment Scott had solved that problem. The crystal was a sort of magnifying glass, vastly enlarging the things inside the block. Strange things they were, too. Miniature people, for example.

They moved. Like clockwork automatons, though much more smoothly. It was rather like watching a play. Scott was interested in their costumes, but fascinated by their actions. The tiny people were deftly building a house. Scott wished it would catch fire, so he could see the people put it out.

Flames licked up from the half-completed structure. The automatons, with a great deal of odd apparatus, extinguished the blaze.

It didn't take Scott long to catch on. But he was a little worried. The manikins would obey his thoughts. By the time he discovered that, he was frightened and threw the cube from him.

Halfway up the bank, he reconsidered and returned. The crystal lay partly in the water, shining in the sun. It was a toy; Scott sensed that, with the unerring instinct of a child. But he didn't pick it up immediately. Instead, he returned to the box and investigated its remaining contents.

He found some really remarkable gadgets. The afternoon passed all too quickly. Scott finally put the toys back in the box and lugged it home, grunting and puffing. He was quite red-faced by the time he arrived at the kitchen door.

His find he hid at the back of a closet in his room upstairs. The crystal cube he slipped into his pocket, which already bulged with string, a coil of wire, two pennies, a wad of tinfoil, a grimy defense stamp and a chunk of feldspar. Emma, Scott's two-year-old sister, waddled unsteadily in from the hall and said hello.

"Hello, Slug," Scott nodded, from his altitude of seven years and some months. He patronized Emma shockingly, but she didn't know the difference. Small, plump and wide-eyed, she flopped down on the carpet and stared dolefully at her shoes.

"Tie 'em, Scotty, please?"

"Sap," Scott told her kindly, but knotted the laces. "Dinner ready yet?"
Emma nodded.

"Let's see your hands." For a wonder they were reasonably clean, though probably not aseptic. Scott regarded his own paws thoughtfully and, grimacing, went to the bathroom, where he made a sketchy toilet. The tadpoles had left traces.

Lewis Padgett

Dennis Paradine and his wife Jane were having a cocktail before dinner, downstairs in the living room. He was a youngish, middle-aged man with soft grey hair and a thin, prim-mouthed face; he taught philosophy at the University. Jane was small, neat, dark and very pretty. She sipped her Martini and said:

"New shoes. Like 'em?"

"Here's to crime," Paradine muttered absently. "Huh? Shoes? Not now. Wait till I've finished this. I had a bad day."

"Exams?"

"Yeah. Flaming youth aspiring towards manhood. I hope they die. In considerable agony. *Insh' Allah!*"

"I want the olive," Jane requested.

"I know," Paradine said despondently. "It's been years since I've tasted one myself. In a Martini, I mean. Even if I put six of 'em in your glass, you're still not satisfied."

"I want yours. Blood brotherhood. Symbolism. That's why."

Paradine regarded his wife balefully and crossed his long legs. "You sound like one of my students."

"Like that hussy Betty Dawson, perhaps?" Jane unsheathed her nails. "Does she still leer at you in that offensive way?"

"She does. The child is a neat psychological problem. Luckily she isn't mine. If she were—" Paradine nodded significantly. "Sex consciousness and too many movies. I suppose she still thinks she can get a passing grade by showing me her knees. Which are, by the way, rather bony."

Jane adjusted her skirt with an air of complacent pride. Paradine uncoiled himself and poured fresh Martinis. "Candidly, I don't see the point of teaching those apes philosophy. They're all at the wrong age. Their habit patterns, their methods of thinking, are already laid down. They're horribly conservative, not that they'd admit it. The only people who can understand philosophy are mature adults or kids like Emma and Scotty."

"Well, don't enroll Scotty in your course," Jane requested. "He isn't ready to be a *Philosophiae Doctor*. I hold no brief for a child genius, especially when it's my son."

"Scotty would probably be better at it than Betty Dawson," Paradine grunted.

" 'He died an enfeebled old dotard at five,' " Jane quoted dreamily. "I want your olive."

"Here. By the way, I like the shoes."

"Thank you. Here's Rosalie. Dinner?"

"It's all ready, Miz Pa'dine," said Rosalie, hovering. "I'll call Miss Emma 'n' Mista' Scotty."

"I'll get 'em." Paradine put his head into the next room and roared, "Kids! Come and get it!"

Small feet scuttered down the stairs. Scott dashed into view, scrubbed and shining, a rebellious cowlick aimed at the zenith. Emma pursued, levering herself carefully down the steps. Halfway, she gave up the attempt to descend upright and reversed, finishing the task monkey-fashion, her small behind giving an impression of marvellous diligence upon the work in hand. Paradine watched, fascinated by the spectacle, till he was hurled back by the impact of his son's body.

"Hi, Dad!" Scott shrieked.

Paradine recovered himself and regarded Scott with dignity. "Hi, yourself. Help me into dinner. You've dislocated at least one of my hip joints."

But Scott was already tearing into the next room, where he stepped on Jane's new shoes in an ecstasy of affection, burbled an apology and rushed off to find his place at the dinner table. Paradine cocked up an eyebrow as he followed, Emma's pudgy hand desperately gripping his forefinger.

"Wonder what the young devil's been up to."

"No good, probably," Jane sighed. "Hello, darling. Let's see your ears."

"They're *clean*. Mickey licked 'em."

"Well, that Airedale's tongue is far cleaner than your ears," Jane pondered, making a brief examination. "Still, as long as you can hear, the dirt's only superficial."

"Fisshul?"

"Just a little, that means." Jane dragged her daughter to the table and inserted her legs into a high chair. Only lately had Emma graduated to the dignity of dining with the rest of the family, and she was, as Paradine remarked, all eaten up with pride by the prospect. Only babies spilled food, Emma had been told. As a result, she took such painstaking care in conveying her spoon to her mouth that Paradine got the jitters whenever he watched.

"A conveyor belt would be the thing for Emma," he suggested, pulling out a chair for Jane. "Small buckets of spinach arrived at her face at stated intervals."

Dinner proceeded uneventfully until Paradine happened to glance at Scott's plate. "Hello, there. Sick? Been stuffing yourself at lunch?"

Scott thoughtfully examined the food still left before him. "I've had all I need, Dad," he explained.

"You usually eat all you can hold, and a great deal more," Paradine said. "I know growing boys need several tons of foodstuff a day, but you're below par tonight. Feel O.K.?"

"Uh-huh. Honest, I've had all I need."

"All you *want?*"

"Sure. I eat different."

"Something they taught you at school?" Jane inquired.

Scott shook his head solemnly.

"Nobody taught me. I found it out myself. I use spit."

"Try again," Paradine suggested. "It's the wrong word."

"Uh—s-saliva. Hm-m-m?"

"Uh-huh. More pepsin? Is there pepsin in the salivary juices, Jane? I forget."

"There's poison in mine," Jane remarked. "Rosalie's left lumps in the mashed potatoes again."

But Paradine was interested. "You mean you're getting everything possible out of your food—no wastage—and eating less?"

Scott thought that over. "I guess so. It's not just the sp—saliva. I sort of measure how much to put in my mouth at once, and what stuff to mix up. I dunno. I just do it."

"Hm-m-m," said Paradine, making a note to check up later. "Rather a revolutionary idea." Kids often get screwy notions, but this one might not be so far off the beam. He pursed his lips. "Eventually I suppose people will eat quite differently—I mean the *way* they eat, as well as what. What they eat, I mean. Jane, our son shows signs of becoming a genius."

"Oh?"

"It's a rather good point in dietetics he just made. Did you figure it out yourself, Scott?"

"Sure," the boy said, and really believed it.

"Where'd you get the idea?"

"Oh, I—" Scott wriggled. "I dunno. It doesn't mean much, I guess."

Paradine was unreasonably disappointed. "But surely—"

"S-s-s-spit!" Emma shrieked, overcome by a sudden fit of badness. *"Spit!"* She attempted to demonstrate, but succeeded only in dribbling into her bib.

With a resigned air Jane rescued and reproved her daughter, while Paradine eyed Scott with rather puzzled interest. But it was not till after dinner, in the living-room, that anything further happened.

"Any homework?"

"N-no," Scott said, flushing guiltily. To cover his embarrassment he took from his pocket a gadget he had found in the box, and began to unfold it. The result resembled a tesseract, strung with beads. Paradine didn't see it at first, but Emma did. She wanted to play with it.

"No. Lay off, Slug," Scott ordered. "You can watch me." He fumbled with the beads, making soft, interested noises. Emma extended a fat forefinger and yelped.

"Scotty," Paradine said warningly.

"I didn't hurt her."

"Bit me. It did," Emma mourned.

Paradine looked up. He frowned, staring. What in—

"Is that an abacus?" he asked. "Let's see it, please."

Somewhat unwillingly, Scott brought the gadget across to his father's chair. Paradine blinked. The "abacus," unfolded, was more than a foot square, composed of thin, rigid wires that interlocked here and there. On the wires the colored beads were strung. They could be slid back and forth, and from one support to another, even at the points of jointure. But—a pierced bead couldn't cross *interlocking* wires.

So, apparently, they weren't pierced. Paradine looked closer. Each small sphere had a deep groove running around it, so that it could be revolved and slid along the wire at the same time. Paradine tried to pull one free. It clung as though magnetically. Iron? It looked more like plastic.

The framework itself—Paradine wasn't a mathematician. But the angles formed by the wires were vaguely shocking, in their ridiculous lack of Euclidean logic. They were a maze. Perhaps that's what the gadget was—a puzzle.

"Where'd you get this?"

"Uncle Harry gave it to me," Scott said, on the spur of the moment. "Last Sunday, when he came over." Uncle Harry was out of town, a circumstance Scott well knew. At the age of seven, a boy soon learns that the vagaries of adults follow a certain definite pattern, and that they are fussy about the donors of gifts. Moreover, Uncle Harry would not return for several weeks; the expiration of that period was unimaginable to Scott, or, at least, the fact that his lie would ultimately be discovered meant less to him than the advantages of being allowed to keep the toy.

Paradine found himself growing slightly confused as he attempted to manipulate the beads. The angles were vaguely illogical. It was like a puzzle. This red bead, if slid along *this* wire to *that* junction, should reach *there*—but it didn't. A maze, odd, but no doubt instructive. Paradine had a well-founded feeling that he'd have no patience with the thing himself.

Scott did, however, retiring to a corner and sliding beads around with much fumbling and grunting. The beads *did* sting, when Scott chose the wrong ones or tried to slide them in the wrong direction. At last he crowed exultantly.

"I did it, Dad!"

"Eh? What? Let's see." The device looked exactly the same to Paradine, but Scott pointed and beamed.

"I made it disappear."

"It's still there?"

"That blue bead. It's gone now."

Paradine didn't believe that, so he merely snorted. Scott puzzled over the framework again. He experimented. This time there were no shocks, even slight. The abacus had showed him the correct method. Now it was up to him to do it on his own. The bizarre angles of the wires seemed a little less confusing now, somehow.

It was a most instructive toy—

It worked, Scott thought, rather like the crystal cube. Reminded of that gadget, he took it from his pocket and relinquished the abacus to Emma, who was struck dumb with joy. She fell to work sliding the beads, this time without protesting against the shocks—which, indeed, were very minor—and, being imitative, she managed to make a bead disappear almost as quickly as had Scott. The blue bead reappeared—but Scott didn't notice. He had forethoughtfully retired into an angle of the chesterfield and an overstuffed chair and amused himself with the cube.

There were the little people inside the thing, tiny manikins much enlarged by the magnifying properties of the crystal. They moved, all right. They built a house. It caught fire, with realistic-seeming flames, and the little people stood by waiting. Scott puffed urgently. "Put it *out!*"

But nothing happened. Where was that queer fire engine, with revolving arms, that had appeared before? Here it was. It came sailing into the picture and stopped. Scott urged it on.

This was fun. The little people really did what Scott told them, inside of his head. If he made a mistake, they waited till he'd found the right way. They even posed new problems for him.

The cube, too, was a most instructive toy. It was teaching Scott with alarming rapidity—and teaching him very entertainingly. But it gave him no really new knowledge as yet. He wasn't ready. Later . . . later . . .

Emma grew tired of the abacus and went in search of Scott. She couldn't find him, even in his room, but once there the contents of the closet intrigued her. She discovered the box. It contained treasure-trove—a doll, which Scott had already noticed but discarded with a sneer. Squealing, Emma brought the doll downstairs, squatted in the middle of the floor and began to take it apart.

"Darling! What's that?"

"Mr. Bear!"

Obviously it wasn't Mr. Bear, who was blind, earless, but comforting in his soft fatness. But all dolls were named Mr. Bear to Emma.

Jane Paradine hesitated. "Did you take that from some other little girl?"

"I didn't. She's mine."

Scott came out from his hiding place, thrusting the cube into his pocket. "Uh—that's from Uncle Harry."

"Did Uncle Harry give that to you, Emma?"

"He gave it to me for Emma," Scott put in hastily, adding another stone to his foundation of deceit. "Last Sunday."

"You'll break it, dear."

Emma brought the doll to her mother. "She comes apart. See?"

"Oh? It—*ugh!*" Jane sucked in her breath. Paradine looked up quickly.

"What's up?"

She brought the doll over to him, hesitated and then went into the dining-room, giving Paradine a significant glance. He followed, closing the door. Jane had already placed the doll on the cleared table.

"This isn't very nice it it, Denny?"

"Hm-m-m." It was rather unpleasant, at first glance. One might have expected an anatomical dummy in a medical school, but a child's doll . . .

The thing came apart in sections—skin, muscles, organs—miniature but quite perfect, as far as Paradine could see. He was interested. "Dunno. Such things haven't the same connotations to a kid."

"Look at that liver. It it a liver?"

"Sure. Say, I—this is funny."

"What?"

"It isn't anatomically perfect, after all." Paradine pulled up a chair. "The digestive tract's too short. No large intestine. No appendix, either."

"Should Emma have a thing like this?"

"I wouldn't mind having it myself," Paradine said. "Where on earth did Harry pick it up? No, I don't see any harm in it. Adults are conditioned to react unpleasantly to innards. Kids don't. They figure they're solid inside, like a potato. Emma can get a sound working knowledge of physiology from this doll."

"But what are those? Nerves?"

"No, these are the nerves. Arteries here; veins here. Funny sort of aorta." Paradine looked baffled. "That—what's Latin for network, anyway, huh? *Rita? Rata?*"

"*Rales,*" Jane suggested at random.

"That's a sort of breathing Paradine said crushingly. "I can't figure out what this luminous network of stuff is. It goes all through the body, like nerves."

"Blood."

"Nope. Not circulatory, not neural. Funny! It seems to be hooked up with the lungs."

They became engrossed, puzzling over the strange doll. It was made with remarkable perfection of detail, and that in itself was strange, in view of the physiological variation from the norm. "Wait'll I get that Gould," Paradine said, and presently was comparing the doll with anatomical charts. He learned little, except to increase his bafflement.

But it was more fun than a jigsaw puzzle.

Meanwhile, in the adjoining room, Emma was sliding the beads to and fro in the abacus. The motions didn't seem so strange now. Even when the beads vanished. She could almost follow that new direction—almost . . .

Scott panted, staring into the crystal cube and mentally directing, with many false starts, the building of a structure somewhat more complicated than the one which had been destroyed by fire. He, too, was learning—being conditioned. . . .

Paradine's mistake, from a completely anthropomorphic standpoint, was that he didn't get rid of the toys instantly. He did not realize their significance, and, by the time he did, the progression of circumstances had got well under way. Uncle Harry remained out of town, so Paradine couldn't check with him. Too, the midterm exams

Lewis Padgett

were on, which meant arduous mental effort and complete exhaustion at night; and Jane was slightly ill for a week or so. Emma and Scott had free rein with the toys.

"What," Scott asked his father one evening, "is a wabe, Dad?"

"Wave?"

He hesitated. "I—don't *think* so. Isn't 'wabe' right?"

" 'Wabe' is Scot for 'web.' That it?"

"I don't see how," Scott muttered, and wandered off, scowling, to amuse himself with the abacus. He was able to handle it quite deftly now. But, with the instinct of children for avoiding interruption, he and Emma usually played with the toys in private. Not obviously, of course—but the more intricate experiments were never performed under the eye of an adult.

Scott was learning fast. What he now saw in the crystal cube had little relationship to the original simple problems. But they were fascinatingly technical. Had Scott realized that his education was being guided and supervised—though merely mechanically—he would probably have lost interest. As it was, his initiative was never quashed.

Abacus, cube, doll, and other toys the children found in the box . . .

Neither Paradine nor Jane guessed how much of an effect the contents of the time machine were having on the kids. How could they? Youngsters are instinctive dramatists, for purposes of self-protection. They have not yet fitted themselves to the exigencies—to them partially inexplicable—of a mature world. Moreover, their lives are complicated by human variables. They are told by one person that playing in the mud is permissible, but that, in their excavations, they must not uproot flowers or small trees. Another adult vetoes mud per se. The Ten Commandments are not carved on stone—they vary; and children are helplessly dependent on the caprice of those who give them birth and feed and clothe them. And tyrannize. The young animal does not resent that benevolent tyranny, for it is an essential part of nature. He is, however, an individualist, and maintains his integrity by a subtle, passive fight.

Under the eyes of an adult he changes. Like an actor on stage, when he remembers, he strives to please, and also to attract attention to himself. Such attempts are not unknown to maturity. But adults are less obvious—to other adults.

It is difficult to admit that children lack subtlety. Children are different from mature animals because they think in another way. We can more or less easily pierce the pretenses they set up, but they can do the same to us. Ruthlessly a child can destroy the pretenses of an adult. Iconoclasm is a child's prerogative.

Foppishness, for example. The amenities of social intercourse, exaggerated not quite to absurdity. The gigolo . . .

"Such *savoir-faire!* Such punctilious courtesy!" The dowager and the blonde young thing are often impressed. Men have less pleasant comments to make. But the child goes to the root of the matter.

"You're *silly!*"

How can an immature human being understand the complicated system of social relationships? He can't. To him, an exaggeration of natural courtesy is silly. In his functional structure of life patterns, it is rococo. He is an egotistic little animal who cannot visualize himself in the position of another—certainly not an adult. A self-contained, almost perfect natural unit, his wants supplied by others, the child is much like a unicellular creature floating in the bloodstream, nutriment carried to him, waste products carried away.

From the standpoint of logic, a child is rather horribly perfect. A baby must be even more perfect, but so alien to an adult that only superficial standards of comparison apply. The thought processes of an infant are completely unimaginable. But babies think, even before birth. In the womb they move and sleep, not entirely through instinct. We are conditioned to react rather peculiarly to the idea that a nearly viable embryo may think. We are surprised, shocked into laughter and repelled. Nothing human is alien.

But a baby is not human. An embryo is far less human.

That, perhaps, was why Emma learned more from the toys than did Scott. He could communicate his thoughts, of course; Emma could not, except in cryptic fragments. The matter of the scrawls, for example.

Give a young child pencil and paper, and he will draw something which looks different to him than to an adult. The absurd scribbles have little resemblance to a fire engine, but it *is* a fire engine, to a baby. Perhaps it is even three-dimensional. Babies think differently and see differently.

Paradine brooded over that, reading his paper one evening and watching Emma and Scott communicate. Scott was questioning his sister. Sometimes he did it in English. More often he had resource to gibberish and sign language. Emma tried to reply, but the handicap was too great.

Finally Scott got pencil and paper. Emma liked that. Tongue in cheek, she laboriously wrote a message. Scott took the paper, examined it and scowled.

"That isn't right, Emma," he said.

Emma nodded vigorously. She seized the pencil again and made more scrawls. Scott puzzled for a while, finally smiled rather hesitantly and got up. He vanished into the hall. Emma returned to the abacus.

Paradine rose and glanced down at the paper, with some mad thought that Emma might abruptly have mastered calligraphy. But she hadn't. The paper was covered with meaningless scrawls, of a type familiar to any parent. Paradine pursed his lips.

It might be a graph showing the mental variations of a manic-depressive cockroach, but probably wasn't. Still, it no doubt had meaning to Emma. Perhaps the scribble represented Mr. Bear.

Scott returned, looking pleased. He met Emma's gaze and nodded. Paradine felt a twinge of curiosity.

"Secrets?"

"Nope. Emma—uh—asked me to do something for her."

"Oh." Paradine, recalling instances of babies who had babbled in unknown tongues and baffled linguists, made a note to pocket the paper when the kids had finished with it. The next day he showed the scrawl to Elkins at the university. Elkins had a sound working knowledge of many unlikely languages, but he chuckled over Emma's venture into literature.

"Here's a free translation, Dennis. Quote. I don't know what this means, but I kid the hell out of my father with it. Unquote."

The two men laughed and went off to their classes. But later Paradine was to remember the incident. Especially after he met Holloway. Before that, however, months were to pass, and the situation to develop even further toward its climax.

Perhaps Paradine and Jane had evinced too much interest in the toys. Emma and Scott took to keeping them hidden, playing with them only in private. They never did it overtly, but with a certain unobtrusive caution. Nevertheless, Jane especially was somewhat troubled.

She spoke to Paradine about it one evening. "That doll Harry gave Emma."

"Yeah?"

"I was downtown today and tried to find out where it came from. No soap."

"Maybe Harry bought it in New York."

Jane was unconvinced. "I asked them about the other things, too. They showed me their stock—Johnson's a big store, you know. But there's nothing like Emma's abacus."

"Hm-m-m." Paradine wasn't much interested. They had tickets for a show that night, and it was getting late. So the subject was dropped for the nonce.

Later it cropped up again, when a neighbor telephoned Jane.

"Scotty's never been like that, Denny. Mrs. Burns said he frightened the devil out of her Francis."

"Francis? A little fat bully of a punk, isn't he? Like his father. I broke Burns's nose for him once, when we were sophomores."

"Stop boasting and listen," Jane said, mixing a highball. "Scott showed Francis something that scared him. Hadn't you better—"

"I suppose so." Paradine listened. Noises in the next room told him the whereabouts of his son. "Scotty!"

"Bang," Scott said, and appeared smiling. "I killed 'em all. Space pirates. You want me, Dad?"

"Yes. If you don't mind leaving the space pirates unburied for a few minutes. What did you do to Francis Burns?"

Scott's blue eyes reflected incredible candor. "Huh?"

"Try hard. You can remember, I'm sure."

"Uh. Oh, that. I didn't do nothing."

"Anything," Jane corrected absently.

"Anything. Honest. I just let him look into my television set, and it—it scared him."

"Television set?"

Scott produced a crystal cube. "It isn't really that. See?"

Paradine examined the gadget, startled by the magnification. All he could see, though, was a maze of meaningless colored designs.

"Uncle Harry—"

Paradine reached for the telephone. Scott gulped. "Is—is Uncle Harry back in town?"

"Yeah."

"Well, I gotta take a bath." Scott headed for the door. Paradine met Jane's gaze and nodded significantly.

Harry was home, but disclaimed all knowledge of the peculiar toys. Rather grimly, Paradine requested Scott to bring down from his room all of the playthings. Finally they lay in a row on the table—cube, abacus, doll, helmet-like cap, several other mysterious contraptions. Scott was cross-examined. He lied valiantly for a time, but broke down at last and bawled, hiccuping his confession.

"Get the box these things came in," Paradine ordered. "Then head for bed."

"Are you—*hup*—gonna punish me, Daddy?"

"For playing hooky and lying, yes. You know the rules. No more shows for two weeks. No sodas for the same period."

Scott gulped. "You gonna keep my things?"

"I don't know yet."

"Well—g'night, Daddy. G'night, Mom."

After the small figure had gone upstairs, Paradine dragged a chair to the table and carefully scrutinized the box. He poked thoughtfully at the focused gadgetry. Jane watched.

"What is it, Denny?"

"Dunno. Who'd leave a box of toys down by the creek?"

"It might have fallen out of a car."

"Not at that point. The road doesn't hit the creek north of the railroad trestle. Empty lots—nothing else." Paradine lit a cigarette. "Drink, honey?"

"I'll fix it." Jane went to work, her eyes troubled. She brought Paradine a glass and stood behind him, ruffling his hair with her fingers. "Is anything wrong?"

"Of course not. Only—where did these toys come from?"

"Johnson's didn't know, and they get their stock from New York."

"I've been checking up, too," Paradine admitted. "That doll"—he poked it—"rather worried me. Custom jobs, maybe, but I wish I knew who'd made 'em."

"A psychologist? That abacus—don't they give people tests with such things?"

Paradine snapped his fingers. "Right! And say, there's a guy going to speak at the university next week, fellow named Holloway, who's a child psychologist. He's a big shot, with quite a reputation. He might know something about it."

"Holloway? I don't—"

"Rex Holloway. He's—hm-m-m! He doesn't live far from here. Do you suppose he might have had these things made himself?"

Jane was examining the abacus. She grimaced and drew back. "If he did, I don't like him. But see if you can find out, Denny."

Paradine nodded. "I shall."

He drank his highball, frowning. He was vaguely worried. But he wasn't scared—yet.

Rex Holloway was a fat, shiny man, with a bald head and thick spectacles, above which his thick, black brows lay like bushy caterpillars. Paradine brought him home to dinner one night a week later. Holloway did not appear to watch the children, but nothing they did or said was lost on him. His grey eyes, shrewd and bright, missed little.

The toys fascinated him. In the living-room the three adults gathered around the table, where the playthings had been placed. Holloway studied them carefully as he listened to what Jane and Paradine had to say. At last he broke his silence.

"I'm glad I came here tonight. But not completely. This is very disturbing, you know."

"Eh?" Paradine stared, and Jane's face showed her consternation. Holloway's next words did not calm them.

"We are dealing with madness."

He smiled at the shocked looks they gave him. "All children are mad, from an adult viewpoint. Ever read Hughes's *High Wind in Jamaica*?"

"I've got it." Paradine secured the little book from its shelf. Holloway extended a hand, took the book and flipped the pages till he had found the place he wanted. He read aloud:

Babies, of course, are not human—they are animals, and have a very ancient and ramified culture, as cats have, and fishes, and even snakes; the same in kind as these, but much more complicated and vivid, since babies are, after all, one of the most developed species of the lower vertebrates. In short, babies have minds which work in terms and categories of their own, which cannot be translated into the terms and categories of the human mind.

Jane tried to take that calmly, but couldn't. "You don't mean that Emma—"

"Could you think like your daughter?" Holloway asked. "Listen: 'One can no more think like a baby than one can think like a bee.' "

Paradine mixed drinks. Over his shoulder he said, "You're theorizing quite a bit, aren't you? As I get it, you're implying that babies have a culture of their own, even a high standard of intelligence."

"Not necessarily. There's no yardstick, you see. All I say is that babies think in other ways than we do. Not necessarily *better*—that's a question of relative values. But with a different matter of extension." He sought for words, grimacing.

"Fantasy," Paradine said, rather rudely but annoyed because of Emma. "Babies don't have different senses from ours."

"Who said they did?" Holloway demanded. "They use their minds in a different way, that's all. But it's quite enough!"

"I'm trying to understand," Jane said slowly. "All I can think of is my Mixmaster. It can whip up batter and potatoes, but it can squeeze oranges, too."

"Something like that. The brain's a colloid, a very complicated machine. We don't know much about its potentialities. We don't even know how much it can grasp. But it *is* known that the mind becomes conditioned as the human animal matures. It follows certain familiar theorems, and all thought thereafter is pretty well based on patterns taken for granted. Look at this." Holloway touched the abacus. "Have you experimented with it?"

"A little," Paradine said.

"But not much, eh?"

"Well—"

"Why not?"

"It's pointless," Paradine complained. "Even a puzzle has to have some logic. But those crazy angles—"

"Your mind has been conditioned to Euclid," Holloway said. "So this—thing—bores us, and seems pointless. But a child knows nothing of Euclid. A different sort of geometry from ours wouldn't impress him as being illogical. He believes what he sees."

"Are you trying to tell me that this gadget's got a fourth-dimensional extension?" Paradine demanded.

"Not visually, anyway," Holloway denied. "All I can say is that our minds, conditioned to Euclid, can see nothing in this but an illogical tangle of wires. But a child—especially a baby—might see more. Not at first. It'd be a puzzle, of course. Only a child wouldn't be handicapped by too many preconceived ideas."

"Hardening of the thought arteries," Jane interjected.

Paradine was not convinced. "Then a baby could work calculus better than Einstein? No, I don't mean that. I can see your point, more or less clearly. Only—"

"Well, look. Let's suppose there are two kinds of geometry; we'll limit it, for the sake of the example. Our kind, Euclidean, and another, we'll call x. X hasn't much relationship to Euclid. It's based on different theorems. Two and two needn't equal four in it; they could equal y^2, or they might not even *equal*. A baby's mind is not

Lewis Padgett

yet conditioned, except by certain questionable factors of heredity and environment. Start the infant on Euclid—"

"Poor kid," Jane said.

Holloway shot her a quick glance. "The basis of Euclid. Alphabet blocks. Math, geometry, algebra—they come much later. We're familiar with that development. On the other hand, start the baby with the basic principles of our x logic."

"Blocks? What kind?"

Holloway looked at the abacus. "It wouldn't make much sense to us. But we've been conditioned to Euclid."

Paradine poured himself a stiff shot of whiskey. "That's pretty awful. You're not limiting to math."

"Right! I'm not limiting it at all. How can I? I'm not conditioned to x logic."

"There's the answer," Jane said, with a sigh of relief. "Who is? It'd take such a person to make the sort of toys you apparently think these are."

Holloway nodded, his eyes, behind the thick lenses, blinking. "Such people may exist."

"Where?"

"They might prefer to keep hidden."

"Supermen?"

"I wish I knew. You see, Paradine, we've got yardstick trouble again. By our standards these people might seem super-dupers in certain respects. In others they might seem moronic. It's not a quantitative difference; it's qualitative. They *think* different. And I'm sure we can do things they can't."

"Maybe they wouldn't want to," Jane said.

Paradine tapped the fused gadgetry on the box. "What about this? It implies—"

"A purpose, sure."

"Transportation?"

"One thinks of that first. If so, the box might have come from anywhere."

"Where—things are—*different?*" Paradine asked slowly.

"Exactly. In space, or even time. I don't know; I'm a psychologist. Unfortunately I'm conditioned to Euclid, too."

"Funny place it must be," Jane said. "Denny, get rid of those toys."

"I intend to."

Holloway picked up the crystal cube. "Did you question the children much?"

Paradine said, "Yeah. Scott said there were people in that cube when he first looked. I asked him what was in it now."

"What did he say?" The psychologist's eyes widened.

"He said they were building a place. His exact words. I asked him who—people? But he couldn't explain."

"No, I suppose not," Holloway muttered. "It must be progressive. How long have the children had these toys?"

"About three months, I guess."

"Time enough. The perfect toy, you see, is both instructive and mechanical. It should do things, to interest a child, and it should teach, preferably unobtrusively. Simple problems at first. Later—"

"X logic," Jane said, white-faced.

Paradine cursed under his breath. "Emma and Scott are perfectly normal!"

"Do you know how their minds work—now?"

Holloway didn't pursue the thought. He fingered the doll. "It would be interesting to know the conditions of the place where these things came from. Induction doesn't help a great deal, though. Too many factors are missing. We can't visualize a world based on the x factor—environment adjusted to minds thinking in x patterns. This luminous network inside the doll. It could be anything. It could exist inside us, though we haven't discovered it yet. When we find the right stain—" He shrugged. "What do you make of this?"

It was a crimson globe, two inches in diameter, with a protruding knob upon its surface.

"What could anyone make of it?"

"Scott? Emma?"

"I hadn't seen it till about three weeks ago. Then Emma started to play with it." Paradine nibbled his lip. "After that, Scott got interested."

"Just what do they do?"

"Hold it up in front of them and move back and forth. No particular pattern of motion."

"No Euclidean pattern," Holloway corrected. "At first they couldn't understand the toy's purpose. They had to be educated up to it."

"That's horrible," Jane said.

"Not to them. Emma is probably quicker at understanding x than is Scott, for her mind isn't yet conditioned to this environment."

Paradine said, "But I can remember plenty of things I did as a child. Even as a baby."

"Well?"

"Was I—mad then?"

"The things you don't remember are the criterion of your madness," Holloway retorted. "But I use the word 'madness' purely as a convenient symbol for the variation from the known human norm. The arbitrary standard of sanity."

Jane put down her glass. "You've said that induction was difficult, Mr. Holloway. But it seems to me you're making a great deal of it from very little. After all, these toys—"

"I *am* a psychologist, and I've specialized in children. I'm not a layman. These toys mean a great deal to me, chiefly because they mean so little."

"You might be wrong."

"Well, I rather hope I am. I'd like to examine the children."

Jane rose in arms. "How?"

After Holloway had explained, she nodded, though still a bit hesitantly. "Well, that's all right. But they're not guinea pigs."

The psychologist patted the air with a plump hand. "My dear girl! I'm not a Frankenstein. To me the individual is the prime factor—naturally, since I work with minds. If there's anything wrong with the youngsters, I want to cure them."

Paradine put down his cigarette and slowly watched blue smoke spiral up, wavering in an unfelt draught. "Can you give a prognosis?"

"I'll try. That's all I can say. If the undeveloped minds have been turned into the x channel, it's necessary to divert them back. I'm not saying that's the wisest thing to do, but it probably is from our standards. After all, Emma and Scott will have to live in this world."

"Yeah. Yeah. I can't believe there's much wrong. They seem about average, thoroughly normal."

"Superficially they may seem so. They've no reason for acting abnormally, have they? And how can you tell if they—think differently?"

"I'll call 'em," Paradine said.

"Make it informal, then. I don't want them to be on guard."

Jane nodded toward the toys. Holloway said, "Leave the stuff there, eh?"

But the psychologist, after Emma and Scott were summoned, made no immediate move towards direct questioning. He managed to draw Scott unobtrusively into the conversation, dropping key words now and then. Nothing so obvious as a word-association test; cooperation is necessary for that.

The most interesting development occurred when Holloway took up the abacus. "Mind showing me how this works?"

Scott hesitated. "Yes, sir. Like this." He slid a bead deftly through the maze, in a tangled course, so swiftly that no one was quite sure whether or not it ultimately vanished. It might have been merely legerdemain. Then, again—

Holloway tried. Scott watched, wrinkling his nose.

"That's right?"

"Uh-huh. It's gotta go *there*."

"Here? Why?"

"Well, that's the only way to make it work."

But Holloway was conditioned to Euclid. There was no apparent reason why the bead should slide from this particular wire to the other. It looked like a random factor. Also, Holloway suddenly noticed, this wasn't the path the bead had taken previously, when Scott had worked the puzzle. At least, as well as he could tell.

"Will you show me again?"

Scott did, and twice more, on request. Holloway blinked through his glasses

Random, yes. And a variable. Scott moved the bead along a different course each time.

Somehow, none of the adults could tell whether or not the bead vanished. If they had expected to see it disappear, their reactions might have been different.

In the end nothing was solved. Holloway, as he said good night, seemed ill at ease.

"May I come again?"

"I wish you would," Jane told him. "Any time. You still think—"

He nodded. "The children's minds are not reacting normally. They're not dull at all, but I've the most extraordinary impression that they arrive at conclusions in a way we don't understand. As though they used algebra while we used geometry. The same conclusion, but a different method of reaching it."

"What about the toys?" Paradine asked suddenly.

"Keep them out of the way. I'd like to borrow them, if I may."

That night Paradine slept badly. Holloway's parallel had been ill chosen. It led to disturbing theories. The x factor . . . The children were using the equivalent of algebraic reasoning, while adults used geometry.

Fair enough. Only . . .

Algebra can give you answers that geometry cannot, since there are certain terms and symbols which cannot be expressed geometrically. Suppose x logic showed conclusions inconceivable to an adult mind.

"Damn!" Paradine whispered. Jane stirred beside him.

"Dear? Can't you sleep either?"

"No." He got up and went into the next room. Emma slept peacefully as a cherub, her fat arm curled around Mr. Bear. Through the open doorway Paradine could see Scott's dark head motionless on the pillow.

Jane was beside him. He slipped his arm around her.

"Poor little people," she murmured. "And Holloway called them mad. I think we're the ones who are crazy, Dennis."

"Uh-huh. We've got jitters."

Scott stirred in his sleep. Without awakening, he called what was obviously a question, though it did not seem to be in any particular language. Emma gave a little mewling cry that changed pitch sharply.

She had not wakened. The children lay without stirring.

But, Paradine thought, with a sudden sickness in his middle, it was exactly as though Scott had asked Emma something, and she had replied.

Had their minds changed so that even—sleep was different to them?

He thrust the thought away. "You'll catch cold. Let's get back to bed. Want a drink?"

"I think I do," Jane said, watching Emma. Her hand reached out blindly toward the child; she drew it back. "Come on. We'll wake the kids."

They drank a little brandy together, but said nothing. Jane cried in her sleep, later.

Scott was not awake, but his mind worked in slow, careful binding. Thus—

"They'll take the toys away. The fat man—listava dangerous, maybe. But the Ghoric direction won't show—evankrus dun hasn't them. Intransdection—bright and shiny. Emma. She's more khopranik-high now than—I still don't see how to—thavarar lixery dist . . . "

A little of Scott's thoughts could still be understood. But Emma had become conditioned to x much faster.

She was thinking, too.

Not like an adult or a child. Not even like a human being. Except, perhaps, a human being of a type shockingly unfamiliar to genus Homo.

Sometimes, Scott himself had difficulty in following her thoughts.

If it had not been for Holloway, life might have settled back into an almost normal routine. The toys were no longer active reminders. Emma still enjoyed her dolls and sandpile, with a thoroughly explicable delight. Scott was satisfied with baseball and his chemical set. They did everything other children did, and evinced few, if any, flashes of abnormality. But Holloway seemed to be an alarmist.

He was having the toys tested, with rather idiotic results. He drew endless charts and diagrams, corresponded with mathematicians, engineers, and other psychologists, and went quietly crazy trying to find rhyme or reason in the construction of the gadgets. The box itself, with its cryptic machinery, told nothing. Fusing had melted too much of the stuff into slag. But the toys . . .

It was the random element that baffled investigation. Even that was a matter of semantics. For Holloway was convinced that it wasn't really random. There just weren't enough known factors. No adult could work the abacus, for example. And Holloway thoughtfully refrained from letting a child play with the thing.

The crystal cube was similarly cryptic. It showed a mad pattern of colors, which sometimes moved. In this it resembled a kaleidoscope. But the shifting of balance and gravity didn't affect it. Again the random factor.

Or, rather, the unknown. The x pattern. Eventually, Paradine and Jane slipped back into something like complacence, with a feeling that the children had been cured of their mental quirk, now that the contributing cause had been removed. Certain of the actions of Emma and Scott gave them every reason to quit worrying.

For the kids enjoyed swimming, hiking, movies, games, the normal functional toys of this particular time-sector. It was true that they failed to master certain rather puzzling mechanical devices which involved some calculation. A three-dimensional jigsaw globe Paradine had picked up, for example. But he found that difficult himself.

Once in a while there were lapses. Scott was hiking with his father one Saturday afternoon, and the two had paused at the summit of a hill. Beneath them a rather lovely valley was spread.

"Pretty, isn't it?" Paradine remarked.

Scott examined the scene gravely. "It's all wrong," he said.

"Eh?"

"I dunno."

"What's wrong about it?"

"Gee." Scott lapsed into puzzled silence. "I dunno."

The children had missed their toys, but not for long. Emma recovered first, though Scott still moped. He held unintelligible conversations with his sister, and studied meaningless scrawls she drew on paper he supplied. It was almost as though he was consulting her, anent difficult problems beyond his grasp.

If Emma understood more, Scott had more real intelligence, and manipulatory skill as well. He built a gadget with his Meccano set, but was dissatisfied. The apparent cause of his dissatisfaction was exactly why Paradine was relieved when he viewed the structure. It was the sort of thing a normal boy would make, vaguely reminiscent of a cubistic ship.

It was a bit too normal to please Scott. He asked Emma more questions, though in private. She thought for a time, and then made more scrawls, with an awkwardly clutched pencil.

"Can you read that stuff?" Jane asked her son one morning.

"Not read it, exactly. I can tell what she means. Not all the time, but mostly."

"Is it writing?"

"N-no. It doesn't mean what it *looks* like."

"Symbolism," Paradine suggested over his coffee.

Jane looked at him, her eyes widening. "Denny—"

He winked and shook his head. Later, when they were alone, he said, "Don't let Holloway upset you. I'm not implying that the kids are corresponding in an unknown tongue. If Emma draws a squiggle and says it's a flower, that's an arbitrary rule—Scott remembers that. Next time she draws the same sort of squiggle, or tries to—well!"

"Sure," Jane said doubtfully. "Have you noticed Scott's been doing a lot of reading lately?"

"I noticed. Nothing unusual, though. No Kant or Spinoza."

"He browses, that's all."

"Well, so did I, at his age," Paradine said, and went off to his morning classes. He lunched with Holloway, which was becoming a daily habit, and spoke of Emma's literary endeavors.

"Was I right about symbolism, Rex?"

The psychologist nodded. "Quite right. Our own language is nothing but arbitrary symbolism now. At least in its application. Look here." On his napkin he drew a very narrow ellipse. "What's that?"

"You mean what does it represent?"

"Yes. What does it suggest to you? It could be a crude representation of—what?"

"Plenty of things," Paradine said. "Rim of a glass. A fried egg. A loaf of French bread. A cigar."

Holloway added a little triangle to his drawing, apex joined to one end of the ellipse. He looked up at Paradine.

"A fish," the latter said instantly.

"Our familiar symbol for a fish. Even without fins, eyes or mouth, it's recognizable, because we've been conditioned to identify this particular shape with our mental picture of a fish. The basis of a rebus. A symbol, to us, means a lot more than what we actually see on paper. What's in your mind when you look at this sketch?"

"Why—a fish."

"Keep going. What do you visualize? Everything!"

"Scales," Paradine said slowly, looking into space. "Water. Foam. A fish's eye. The fins. The colors."

"So the symbol represents a lot more than just that abstract idea *fish*. Note the connotation's that of a noun, not a verb. It's harder to express actions by symbolism, you know. Anyway—reverse the process. Suppose you want to make a symbol for some concrete noun, say *bird*. Draw it."

Paradine drew two connected arcs, concavities down.

"The lowest common denominator," Holloway nodded. "The natural tendency is to simplify. Especially when a child is seeing something for the first time and has few standards of comparison. He tries to identify the new thing with what's already familiar to him. Ever notice how a child draws the ocean?" He didn't wait for an answer; he went on.

"A series of jagged points. Like the oscillating line on a seismograph. When I first saw the Pacific, I was about three. I remember it pretty clearly. It looked—tilted. A flat plain, slanted at an angle. The waves were regular triangles, apex upward. Now I didn't *see* them stylized that way, but later, remembering, I had to find some familiar standard of comparison. Which is the only way of getting any conception of an entirely new thing. The average child tries to draw these regular triangles, but his co-ordination's poor. He gets a seismograph pattern."

"All of which means what?"

"A child sees the ocean. He stylizes it. He draws a certain definite pattern, symbolic, to him, of the sea. Emma's scrawls may be symbols, too. I don't mean that the world looks different to her—brighter, perhaps, and sharper, more vivid and with a slackening of perception above her eye level. What I do mean is that her thought processes are different, that she translates what she sees into abnormal symbols."

"You still believe—"

"Yes, I do. Her mind has been conditioned unusually. It may be that she breaks down what she sees into simple, obvious patterns—and realizes a significance to those patterns that we can't understand. Like the abacus. She saw a pattern in that, though to us it was completely random."

Paradine abruptly decided to taper off these luncheon engagements with Holloway. The man was an alarmist. His theories were growing more fantastic than ever, and he dragged in anything, applicable or not, that would support them.

Rather sardonically he said, "Do you mean Emma's communicating with Scott in an unknown language?"

"In symbols for which she hasn't any words. I'm sure Scott understands a great deal of those—scrawls. To him, an isosceles triangle may represent any factor, though probably a concrete noun. Would a man who knew nothing of chemistry understand what H_2O meant? Would he realize that the symbol could evoke a picture of the ocean?"

Paradine didn't answer. Instead, he mentioned to Holloway Scott's curious remark that the landscape, from the hill, had looked all wrong. A moment later, he was inclined to regret his impulse, for the psychologist was off again.

"Scott's thought patterns are building up to a sum that doesn't equal this world. Perhaps he's subconsciously expecting to see the world where those toys came from."

Paradine stopped listening. Enough was enough. The kids were getting along all right, and the only remaining disturbing factor was Holloway himself. That night, however, Scott evinced an interest, later significant, in eels.

There was nothing apparently harmful in natural history. Paradine explained about eels.

"But where do they lay their eggs? Or do they?"

"That's still a mystery. Their spawning grounds are unknown. Maybe the Sargasso Sea, or the deeps, where the pressure can help them force the young out of their bodies."

"Funny," Scott said, thinking deeply.

"Salmon do the same thing, more or less. They go up rivers to spawn." Paradine went into detail. Scott was fascinated.

"But that's *right*, Dad. They're born in the river, and when they learn how to swim, they go down to the sea. And they come back to lay their eggs, huh?"

"Right."

"Only they wouldn't *come* back," Scott pondered. "They'd just send their eggs—"

"It'd take a very long ovipositor," Paradine said, and vouchsafed some well-chosen remarks upon oviparity.

His son wasn't entirely satisfied. Flowers, he contended, sent their seeds long distances.

"They don't guide them. Not many find fertile soil."

"Flowers haven't got brains, though. Dad, why do people live *here?*"

"Glendale?"

"No—*here*. This whole place. It isn't all there is, I bet."

"Do you mean the other planets?"

Scott was hesitant. "This is only—part of the big place. It's like the river where the salmon go. Why don't people go on down to the ocean when they grow up?"

Paradine realized that Scott was speaking figuratively. He felt a brief chill. The—ocean?

The young of the species are not conditioned to live in the more complete world of their parents. Having developed sufficiently, they enter that world. Later they breed. The fertilized eggs are buried in the sand, far up the river, where later they hatch.

And they learn. Instinct alone is fatally slow. Especially in the case of a specialized genus, unable to cope even with this world, unable to feed or drink or survive, unless someone has foresightedly provided for those needs.

The young, fed and tended, would survive. There would be incubators and robots. They would survive, but they would not know how to swim downstream, to the vaster world of the ocean.

So they must be taught. They must be trained and conditioned in many ways.

Painlessly, subtly, unobtrusively. Children love toys that do things, and if those toys teach at the same time . . .

In the latter half of the nineteenth century an Englishman sat on a grassy bank near a stream. A very small girl lay near him, staring up at the sky. She had discarded a curious toy with which she had been playing, and now was murmuring a wordless little song, to which the man listened with half an ear.

"What was that, my dear?" he asked at last.

"Just something I made up, Uncle Charles."

"Sing it again." He pulled out a notebook.

The girl obeyed.

"Does it mean anything?"

She nodded. "Oh, yes. Like the stories I tell you, you know."

"They're wonderful stories, dear."

"And you'll put them in a book someday?"

"Yes, but I must change them quite a lot, or no one would understand. But I don't think I'll change your little song."

"You mustn't. If you did, it wouldn't mean anything."

"I won't change that stanza, anyway," he promised. "Just what does it mean?"

"It's the way out, I think," the girl said doubtfully. "I'm not sure yet. My magic toys told me."

"I wish I knew what London shop sold these marvelous toys!"

"Mama bought them for me. She's dead. Papa doesn't care."

She lied. She had found the toys in a box one day, as she played by the Thames. And they were indeed wonderful.

Mimsy Were The Borogoves

Her little song—Uncle Charles thought it didn't mean anything. (He wasn't her real uncle, she parenthesized. But he was nice.) The song meant a great deal. It was the way. Presently she would do what it said, and then . . .

But she was already too old. She never found the way.

Paradine had dropped Holloway. Jane had taken a dislike to him, naturally enough, since what she wanted most of all was to have her fears calmed. Since Scott and Emma acted normally now, Jane felt satisfied. It was partly wishful thinking, to which Paradine could not entirely subscribe.

Scott kept bringing gadgets to Emma for her approval. Usually she'd shake her head. Sometimes she would look doubtful. Very occasionally she would signify agreement. Then there would be an hour of laborious, crazy scribbling on scraps of note paper, and Scott, after studying the notations, would arrange and rearrange his rocks, bits of machinery, candle ends and assorted junk. Each day the maid cleaned them away, and each day Scott began again.

He condescended to explain a little to his puzzled father, who could see no rhyme or reason in the game.

"But why this pebble right here?"

"It's hard and round, Dad. It *belongs* there."

"So is this one hard and round."

"Well, that's got vaseline on it. When you get that far, you can't *see* just a hard, round thing."

"What comes next? This candle?"

Scott looked disgusted. "That's toward the end. The iron ring's next."

It was, Paradine thought, like a scout trail through the woods, markers in a labyrinth. But here again was the random factor. Logic halted—familiar logic—at Scott's motives in arranging the junk as he did.

Paradine went out. Over his shoulder he saw Scott pull a crumpled piece of paper and a pencil from his pocket and head for Emma, who was squatted in a corner thinking things over.

Well . . .

Jane was lunching with Uncle Harry, and, on this hot Sunday afternoon, there was little to do but read the papers. Paradine settled himself in the coolest place he could find, with a Collins, and lost himself in the comic strips.

An hour later a clatter of feet upstairs roused him from his doze. Scott's voice was crying exultantly, "This is it, Slug! Come on!"

Paradine stood up quickly, frowning. As he went into the hall the telephone began to ring. Jane had promised to call . . .

His hand was on the receiver when Emma's faint voice squealed with excitement Paradine grimaced. What the devil was going on upstairs?

Scott shrieked, "Look out! This way!"

Paradine, his mouth working, his nerves ridiculously tense, forgot the phone and raced up the stairs. The door of Scott's room was open.

The children were vanishing.

They went in fragments, like thick smoke in a wind, or like movement in a distorting mirror. Hand in hand they went, in a direction Paradine could not understand, and as he blinked there on the threshold, they were gone.

"Emma!" he said, dry-throated. *"Scotty!"*

On the carpet lay a pattern of markers, pebbles, an iron ring—junk. A random pattern. A crumpled sheet of paper blew toward Paradine.

He picked it up automatically.

"Kids. Where are you? Don't hide—*Emma! SCOTTY!"*

Downstairs the telephone stopped. Paradine looked at the paper he held.

It was a leaf torn from a book. There were interlineations and marginal notes, in Emma's meaningless scrawl. A stanza of verse had been so underlined and scribbled over that it was almost illegible, but Paradine was thoroughly familiar with *Through the Looking Glass*. His memory gave him the words—

> *'Twas brillig, and the slithy toves*
>   *Did gyre and gimble in the wabe;*
> *All mimsy were the borogoves,*
>   *And the mome raths outgrabe.*

Idiotically he thought: Humpty Dumpty explained it. A wabe is the plot of grass around a sundial. A sundial. Time. It has something to do with time. A long time ago Scotty asked me what a wabe was. Symbolism.

'Twas brillig . . .

A perfect mathematical formula, giving all the conditions, in symbolism the children had finally understood. The junk on the floor. The toves had to be made slithy—vaseline?—and they had to be placed in a certain relationship, so that they'd gyre and gimble.

Lunacy!

But it had not been lunacy to Emma and Scott. They thought differently. They used *x* logic. Those notes Emma had made on the page—she'd translated Carroll's words into symbols both she and Scott could understand.

The random factor had made sense to the children. They had fulfilled the conditions of the time-span equation. *And the mome raths outgrabe . . .*

Paradine made a rather ghastly little sound, deep in his throat. He looked at the crazy pattern on the carpet. If he could follow it, as the kids had done— But he couldn't. The random factor defeated him. He was conditioned to Euclid.

Even if he went insane, he still couldn't do it. It would be the wrong kind of lunacy.

His mind had stopped working now. But in a moment the stasis of incredulous horror would pass—Paradine crumpled the page in his fingers. "Emma! Scotty!" he called in a dead voice, as though he could expect no response.

Sunlight slanted through the open windows, brightening the golden pelt of Mr. Bear. Downstairs the ringing of the telephone began again. ∎

MEWHU'S JET

Theodore Sturgeon

"WE INTERRUPT THIS PROGRAM TO ANNOUNCE—"

"Jack, don't jump like that! And you've dropped ashes all over your—"

"Aw, Iris, honey, let me listen to—"

"—*at first identified as a comet, the object is pursuing an erratic course through the stratosphere, occasionally dipping as low as*—"

"You make me nervous, Jack. You're an absolute slave to the radio. I wish you paid that much attention to me."

"Darling, I'll argue the point, or pay attention to you, or anything in the wide world you like when I've heard this announcement; but please, *please let me listen!*"

"—*dents of the East Coast are warned to watch for the approach of this ob*—"

"Iris, don't—"

Click!

"Well, of all the selfish, inconsiderate, discourteous—"

"That will do, Jack Garry. It's my radio as much as yours, and I have a right to turn it off when I want to."

"Might I ask why you find it necessary to turn it off at this moment?"

"Because I know the announcement will be repeated any number of times if it's important, and you'll shush me every time. Because I'm not interested in that kind of thing and don't see why I should have it rammed down my throat. Because the only thing you ever want to listen to is something which couldn't possibly affect us. But mostly because you yelled at me!"

"I did *not* yell at you!"

"You *did!* And you're yelling now!"

"*Mom!* Daddy!"

"Oh, Molly, darling, we woke you up!"

"Poor bratlet. Hey, what about your slippers?"

"It isn't cold tonight, Daddy. What was that on the radio?"

"Something buzzing around in the sky, darling. I didn't hear it all."

"A space ship, I betcha."

"You see? You and your so-called science fiction!"

At which point, something like a giant's fist clouted off the two-room top story of the seaside cottage and scattered it down the beach. The lights winked out, and outside the whole waterfront lit up with a brief, shattering blue glare.

"Jacky darling, are you hurt?"

"Mom, he's bleedin'!"

"Jack, honey, say something. *Please* say something."

"Urrrgh," said Jack Garry obediently, sitting up with a soft clatter of pieces of falling lath and plaster. He put his hands gently on the sides of his head and whistled, "Something hit the house."

His red-headed wife laughed half-hysterically. "Not really, darling." She put her arms around him, whisked some dust out of his hair, and began stroking his neck. "I'm . . . frightened, Jack."

"You're frightened!" He looked around shakily in the dim moonlight that filtered in. Radiance from an unfamiliar place caught his bleary gaze, and he clutched Iris's arm. "Upstairs . . . it's gone!" he said hoarsely, struggling to his feet. "Molly's room . . . Molly—"

"I'm here, Daddy. Hey, you're squeezin'!"

"Happy little family," said Iris, her voice trembling. "Vacationing in a quiet little cottage by the sea, so Daddy can write technical articles while Mummy regains her good disposition—without a phone, without movies within miles, and living in a place where the roof flies away. Jack—what hit us?"

"One of those things you refuse to be interested in, that couldn't possibly affect us. Remember?"

"The thing the radio was talking about?"

"I wouldn't be surprised. We'd better get out of here. This place may fall in on us, or burn, or something."

"An' we'll all be kilt," crooned Molly.

"Shut up, Molly. Iris, I'm going to poke around. Better go on out and pick us a place to pitch the tent—if I can find the tent."

"Tent?" Iris gasped.

"Boy oh boy," said Molly.

"Jack Garry, I'm not going to go to bed in a tent. Do you realize that this place will be swarming with people in no time flat?"

"O.K., O.K. Only get out from under what's left of the house. Go for a swim. Take a walk. Or g'wan to bed in Molly's room."

"I'm not going out there by myself."

Jack sighed. "I shouldn've asked you to stay in here," he muttered. "If you're not the contrariest woman ever to— Be quiet, Molly."

"I didn't say anything."

Meeew-w-w!

"Aren't you doing that caterwauling?"

"No, Daddy, truly."

Iris said, "I'd say a cat was caught in the wreckage except that cats are smart and no cat would ever come near this place."

Wuh-wuh-wuh-meeee-ew-w-w!

"What a dismal sound!"

"Jack, that isn't a cat."

Mmmmmew. Mmm—m-m-m.

"Whatever it is," Jack said, "it can't be big enough to be afraid of and make a funny little noise like that." He squeezed Iris's arm and, stepping carefully over the rubble, began peering in and around it. Molly scrambled beside him. He was about to caution her against making so much noise, and then thought better of it. What difference would a little racket make?

The noise was not repeated, and five minutes' searching elicited nothing. Garry went back to his wife, who was fumbling around the shambles of a living room, pointlessly setting chairs and coffee tables back on their legs.

"I didn't find anyth—"

"*Yipe!*"

"Molly! What is it?"

Molly was just outside, in the shrubbery. "Daddy, you better come quick!"

Spurred by the urgency of her tone, he went crashing outside. He found Molly standing rigid, trying to cram both her fists in her mouth at the same time. And at her feet was a man with silver-gray skin and a broken arm, who mewed at him.

"*—Guard and Navy Department have withdrawn their warnings. The pilot of a Pan-American transport has reported that the object disappeared into the zenith. It was last seen eighteen miles east of Normandy Beach, New Jersey. Reports from the vicinity describe it as traveling very slowly, with a hissing noise. Although it reached within a few feet of the ground several times, no damage has been reported, Inves—*"

"Think of that," said Iris, switching off the little three-way portable. "No damage."

"Yeah. And if no one saw the thing hit, no one will be out here to investigate. So you can retire to your downy couch in the tent without fear of being interviewed."

"Go to sleep? Are you mad? Sleep in that flimsy tent with that mewing monster lying there?"

"Oh, heck, Mom, he's sick! He wouldn't hurt anybody."

They sat around a cheerful fire, fed by roof shingles. Jack had set up the tent without much trouble. The silver-gray man was stretched out in the shadows, sleeping lightly and emitting an occasional moan.

Jack smiled at Iris. "Y'know, I love your silly chatter, darling. The way you turned to and set his arm was a pleasure to watch. You didn't think of him as a monster while you were tending to him."

"Didn't I, though? Maybe monster was the wrong word to use. Jack, he has only one bone in his forearm!"

"He has what? Oh, nonsense, honey! 'Tain't scientific. He'd have to have a ball-and-socket joint in his wrist."

Theodore Sturgeon

"He *has* a ball-and-socket joint in his wrist."

"This I have to see," Jack muttered. He picked up a flash lantern and went over to the long prone figure.

Silver eyes blinked up at the light. There was something queer about them. He turned the beam closer. The pupils were not black in that light, but dark green. They all but closed—from the sides, like a cat's. Jack's breath wheezed out. He ran the light over the man's body. It was clad in a bright-blue roomy bathrobe effect, with a yellow sash. The sash had a buckle which apparently consisted of two pieces of yellow metal; there seemed to be nothing to keep them together. They just stayed. When the man had fainted, just as they found him, it had taken almost all Jack's strength to pull them apart.

"Iris."

She got up and came over to him. "Let the poor devil sleep."

"Iris, what color was his robe?"

"Red, with a . . . but it's *blue!*"

"Is now. Iris, what on earth have we got here?"

"I don't know. I don't know. Some poor thing that escaped from an institution for—for—"

"For what?"

"How should I know?" she snapped. "There must be some place where they send creatures that get born like that."

"Creatures don't get born like that, he isn't deformed. He's just different."

"I see what you mean. I don't know why I see what you mean, but I'll tell you something." She stopped, and was quiet for so long that he turned to her, surprised. She said slowly, "I ought to be afraid of him, because he's strange, and ugly, but—I'm not."

"Me too."

"Molly, go back to bed."

"He's a leprechaun."

"Maybe you're right. Go on to bed, chicken, and in the morning you can ask him where he keeps his crock of gold."

"Gee." She went off a little way and stood on one foot, drawing a small circle in the sand with the other. "Daddy?"

"Yes, Molly-m'love."

"Can I sleep in the tent tomorrow, too?"

"If you're good."

"Daddy obviously means," said Iris acidly, "that if you're *not* good he'll have a roof on the house by tomorrow night."

"I'll be good." She disappeared into the tent.

The gray man mewed.

"Well, old guy, what is it?"

The man reached over and fumbled at his splinted arm.

"It hurts him," said Iris. She knelt beside him and, taking the wrist of his good arm, lifted it away from the splint, where he was clawing. The man did not resist, but lay and looked at her with pain-filled, slitted eyes.

"He has six fingers," Jack said. "See?" He knelt beside his wife and gently took the man's wrist. He whistled. "It *is* a ball-and-socket."

"Give him some aspirin."

"That's a good . . . wait." Jack stood pulling his lip in puzzlement. "Do you think we should?"

"Why not?"

"We don't know where he comes from. We know nothing of his body chemistry, or what any of our medicines might do to him."

"He . . . what do you mean, where he comes from?"

"Iris, will you open up your mind just a little? In the face of evidence like this, are you going to even attempt to cling to the idea that this man comes from anywhere on this earth?" Jack said with annoyance. "You know your anatomy. Don't tell me you ever saw a human freak with skin and bones like that! That belt buckle, that material in his clothes . . . come on, now. Drop your prejudices and give your brains a chance."

"You're suggesting things that simply don't *happen!*"

"That's what the man in the street said—in Hiroshima. That's what the old-time aeronaut said from the basket of his balloon when they told him about heavier-than-air craft. That's what—"

"All right, all right, Jack. I know the rest of the speech. If you want dialectics instead of what's left of a night's sleep, I might point out that the things you have mentioned have all concerned human endeavors. Show me any new plastic, a new metal, a new kind of engine, and though I may not begin to understand it, I can accept it because it is of human origin. But this, this man, or whatever he is—"

"I know," said Jack, more gently. "It's frightening because it's strange, and away down underneath we feel that anything strange is necessarily dangerous. That's why we wear our best manners for strangers and not for our friends. But I still don't think we should give this character any aspirin."

"He seems to breathe the same air we do. He perspires, he talks . . . I think he talks."

"You have a point. Well, if it'll ease his pain at all, it may be worth trying. Give him just one."

Iris went to the pump with a collapsible cup from her first-aid kit, and filled it. Kneeling by the silver-skinned man, she propped up his head, gently put the aspirin between his lips, and brought the cup to his mouth. He sucked the water in greedily, and then went completely limp.

"Oh-oh. I was afraid of that."

Iris put her hand over the man's heart. *"Jack!"*

"Is he . . . what is it, Iris?"

"Not dead, if that's what you mean. Will you feel this?"

Jack put his hand beside Iris's. The heart was beating with massive, slow blows, about eight to the minute. Under it, out of phase completely with the main beat, was another, an extremely fast, sharp beat, which felt as if it were going about three hundred.

"He's having some sort of palpitation," Jack said.

"And in two hearts at once!"

Suddenly the man raised his head and uttered a series of ululating shrieks and howls. His eyes opened wide, and across them fluttered a translucent nictating membrane. He lay perfectly still with his mouth open, shrieking and gargling. Then with a lightning movement he snatched Jack's hand to his mouth. A pointed tongue, light-orange and four inches longer than it had any right to be, flicked out and licked Jack's hand. Then the strange eyes closed, the shrieks died to a whimper and faded out, and the man relaxed.

"Sleeping now," said Iris. "Oh, I hope we haven't done anything to him!"

"We've done something. I just hope it isn't serious. Anyhow, his arm isn't bothering him any. That's all we were worried about in the first place."

Iris put a cushion under the man's oddly planed head and touched the beach mattress he was lying on. "He has a beautiful mustache," she said. "Like silver. He looks very old and wise."

"So does an owl. Let's go to bed."

Jack woke early, from a dream in which he had bailed out of a flying motorcycle with an umbrella that turned into a candy cane as he fell. He landed in the middle of some sharp-toothed crags which gave like sponge rubber. He was immediately surrounded by mermaids who looked like Iris and who had hands shaped like spur gears. But nothing frightened him. He awoke smiling, inordinately happy.

Iris was still asleep. Outside somewhere he heard the tinkle of Molly's laugh. He sat up and looked at Molly's camp cot. It was empty. Moving quietly, so as not to disturb his wife, he slid his feet into moccasins and went out.

Molly was on her knees beside their strange visitor, who was squatting on his haunches and—

They were playing patty-cake.

"Molly!"

"Yes, Daddy."

"What are you trying to do? Don't you realize that that man has a broken arm?"

"Oh, gosh, I'm sorry. Do you s'pose I hurt him?"

"I don't know. It's very possible," said Jack Garry testily. He went to the alien, took his good hand.

The man looked up at him and smiled. His smile was peculiarly engaging. All of his teeth were pointed, and they were very widely spaced. "Eeee-yu mow madibu Mewhu," he said.

"That's his name," Molly said excitedly. She leaned forward and tugged at the man's sleeve. "Mewhu. Hey, Mewhu!" And she pointed at her chest.

"Mooly," said Mewhu. "Mooly—Gerry."

"See, Daddy?" Molly said ecstatically. "See?" She pointed at her father. "Daddy. Dah—dee."

"Deedy," said Mewhu.

"No, silly. Daddy."

"Dewdy."

"*Dah*-dy!"

Jack, quite entranced, pointed at himself and said, "Jack."

"Jeek."

"Good enough. Molly, the man can't say 'ah.' He can say 'oo' or 'ee' but not 'ah.' That's good enough."

Jack examined the splints. Iris had done a very competent job. When she realized that instead of the radius-ulna development of a true human, Mewhu had only one bone in his forearm, she had set the arm and laid on two splints instead of one. Jack grinned. Intellectually, Iris would not accept Mewhu's existence even as a possibility; but as a nurse, she not only accepted his body structure but skillfully compensated for its differences.

"I guess he wants to be polite," said Jack to his repentant daughter, "and if you want to play patty-cake he'll go along with you, even if it hurts. Don't take advantage of him, chicken."

"I won't, Daddy."

Jack started up the fire and had a stick crane built and hot water bubbling by the time Iris emerged. "Takes a cataclysm to get you to start breakfast," she grumbled through a pleased smile. "When were you a Boy Scout?"

"Matter of fact," said Garry, "I was once. Will modom now take over?"

"Modom will. How's the patient?"

"Thriving. He and Molly had a patty-cake tournament this morning. His clothes, by the way, are red again."

"Jack, where does he come from?"

"I haven't asked him yet. When I learn to caterwaul, or he learns to talk, perhaps we'll find out. Molly has already elicited the information that his name's Mewhu." Garry grinned. "And he calls me 'Jeek.' "

"Can't pronounce an 'r,' hm?"

"That'll do, woman. Get on with the breakfast."

While Iris busied herself over the fire, Jack went to look at the house. It wasn't as bad as he had thought—a credit to poor construction. Apparently the upper two rooms were a late addition and had just been perched onto the older, comparatively flat-topped lower section. The frame of Molly's bed was bent beyond repair, but the box spring and mattress were intact. The old roof seemed fairly sound, where the removal of the jerry-built little top story had exposed it. The living room would be big enough for him and Iris, and Molly's bed could be set up in the study. There were tools and lumber in the garage, the weather was warm and clear, and Jack Garry was very much attracted by the prospect of hard work for which he would not get paid, as long as it wasn't writing. By the time Iris called him for breakfast, he had most of the debris cleared from the roof and a plan of action mapped out. All he would have to do would be to cover the hole where the stairway landing had been and go over the roof for potential leaks. A good rain, he reflected, would search those out for him quickly enough.

"What about Mewhu?" Iris asked as she handed him an aromatic plate of eggs and bacon. "If we feed him any of this, do you think he'll throw another fit?"

Jack looked at their visitor, who sat on the other side of the fire, very close to Molly, gazing big-eyed at their breakfasts.

"I don't know. We could give him a little, I suppose."

Mewhu inhaled his sample and wailed for more. He ate a second helping, and when Iris refused to fry more eggs, he gobbled toast and jam. Each new thing he tasted he would nibble at, then he would blink twice and bolt it down. The only exception was the coffee. One taste was sufficient. He put it down on the ground and very carefully, very delicately overturned it.

"Can you talk to him?" Iris asked suddenly.

"He can talk to me," declared Molly.

"I've heard him," Jack said.

"Oh, no. I don't mean *that*," Molly denied vehemently. "I can't make any sense out of that stuff."

"What do you mean, then?"

"I . . . I dunno, Mommy. He just—talks to me, that's all."

Jack and Iris looked at each other. "Oh," said Iris. Jack shook his head, looking at his daughter carefully, as if he had not really seen her before. He could think of nothing to say, and rose.

"Think the house can be patched up?"

"Oh, sure." He laughed. "You never did like the color of the upstairs rooms, anyway."

"I don't know what's got into me," Iris said thoughtfully. "I'd have kicked like a mule at any part of this. I'd have packed up and gone home if, say, just a wall was gone upstairs, or if there were just a hole in the roof, or if this . . . this android phenomenon arrived suddenly. But when it all happens at once—I can take it all."

"Question of perspective. Show me a nagging woman and I'll show you one who hasn't enough to worry about."

"You'll get out of my sight or you'll have this frying pan bounced off your skull," said Iris steadily. Jack got.

Molly and Mewhu trailed after him as he returned to the house—and stood side by side goggling at him as he mounted the ladder.

"Whatsha doing, Daddy?"

"Marking off the edges of this hole where the stairway hits the place where the roof isn't, so I can clean up the edges with a saw."

"Oh."

Jack roughed out the area with a piece of charcoal, lopped off the more manageable rough edges with a hatchet, cast about for his saw. It was still in the garage. He climbed down, got it, climbed up again, and began to saw. Twenty minutes of this, and sweat was streaming down his face. He knocked off, climbed down, doused his head at the pump, lit a cigarette, climbed back up on the roof.

"Why don't you jump off and back?"

The roofing job was looking larger and the day seemed warmer than it had. Jack's enthusiasm was in inverse proportion to these factors. "Don't be funny, Molly."

"Yes, but Mewhu wants to know."

"Oh, he does. Ask him to try it."

He went back to work. A few minutes later, when he paused for a breath, Mewhu and Molly were nowhere to be seen. Probably over by the tent, in Iris's hair, he thought, and went on sawing.

"Daddy!"

Daddy's unaccustomed arm and shoulder were, by this time, yelling for help. The dry softwood alternately cheesed the saw out of line and bound it. He answered impatiently, "Well, what?"

"Mewhu says to come. He wants to show you something."

"Show me what? I haven't time to play now, Molly. I'll attend to Mewhu when we get a roof over our heads again."

"But it's for you."

"What is it?"

"The thing in the tree."

"Oh, all right." Prompted more by laziness than by curiosity, Jack climbed back down the ladder. Molly was waiting. Mewhu was not in sight.

"Where is he?"

"By the tree," she said with exaggerated patience, taking his hand. "Come on. It's not far."

She led him around the house and across the bumpy track that was euphemistically known as a road. There was a tree down on the other side. He looked from it to the house, saw that in line with the felled tree and his damaged roof were more broken trees, where something had come down out of the sky, skimmed the tops of the trees,

     Theodore Sturgeon

angling closer to the ground until it wiped the top off his house, and had then risen up and up—to where?

They went deeper into the woods for ten minutes, skirting an occasional branch or fallen tree top, until they came to Mewhu, who was leaning against a young maple. He smiled, pointed up into a tree, pointed to his arm, to the ground. Jack looked at him in puzzlement.

"He fell out of the tree and broke his arm," said Molly.

"How do you know?"

"Well, he just did, Daddy."

"Nice to know. Now can I get back to work?"

"He wants you to get the thing in the tree."

Jack looked upward. Hung on a fork two thirds of the way up the tree was a gleaming object, a stick about five feet long with a streamlined shape on each end, rather like the wingtip tanks of a P-80. "What on earth is that?"

"I dunno. I can't— He tol' me, but I dunno. Anyway, it's for you, so you don't . . . so you don't . . ." She looked at Mewhu for a moment. The alien's silver mustache seemed to swell a little. "—So you don't have to climb the ladder so much."

"Molly, how did you know that?"

"He *told* me, that's all. Gosh, Daddy, don't be mad. I don't know how, honest; he just did, that's all."

"I don't get it," muttered Jack. "Anyhow, what's this about that thing in the tree? I'm supposed to break my arm too?"

"It isn't dark."

"What do you mean by that?"

Molly shrugged. "Ask him."

"Oh, I think I catch that. He fell out of the tree because it was dark. He thinks I can get up there and get the whatzit without hurting myself because I can see what I am doing. He also flatters me. Or is it flattery? How close to the apes does he think we are?"

"What are you talking about, Daddy?"

"Never mind. Why am I supposed to get that thing, anyway?"

"Uh—so's you can jump off the roof."

"That is just silly. However, I do want a look at that thing. Since his ship is gone, that object up there seems to be the only artifact he brought with him except his clothes."

"What's an artifact?"

"Second cousin to an artichoke. Here goes nothin'," and he swung up into the tree. He had not climbed a tree for years, and as he carefully chose his way, it occurred to him that there were probably more efficient ways of gaining altitude.

The tree began to shiver and sway with his weight. He looked down once and decided instantly not to do it again. He looked up and was gratified to see how close he was to the object he was after. He pulled himself up another three feet and was horrified at how far away it was, for the branches were very small up here. He squirmed upward, reached, and his fingers just brushed against the shank of the thing. It had two rings fastened to it, he noticed, each about a foot from the center, large enough to get an arm through. It was one of these which was hung up on a branch. He chinned himself, then, with his unpracticed muscles cracking, took one hand off and reached.

The one-hand chinning didn't come off so well. His arm began to sag. The ring broke off its branch as his weight came on it. He was immediately surrounded by the enthusiastic cracking of breaking shrubbery. He folded his tongue over and got his teeth on it. Since he had a grip on Mewhu's artifact, he held on—even when it came free. He began to fall, tensing himself for the bone-breaking jolt he would get at the bottom.

He fell quite fast at first, and then the stick he was holding began to bear him up. He thought it must have caught on a branch, by some miracle—but it hadn't! He was drifting down like a thistle seed, hanging from the rod, which in some impossible fashion was supporting itself in midair. There was a shrill, faint whooshing sound from the two streamlined fixtures at the ends of the rod. He looked down, blinked sweat out of his eyes, and looked again. Mewhu was grinning a broad and happy grin; Molly was slack-jawed with astonishment.

The closer he came to the ground the slower he went. When, after what seemed an eternity, he felt the blessed pressure of earth under his feet, he had to stand and *pull* the rod down. It yielded slowly, like an eddy-current brake. Dry leaves danced and whirled under the end pieces.

"Gee, Daddy, that was wonderful!"

He swallowed twice to wet down his dry esophagus, and pulled his eyes back in. "Yeah. Fun," he said weakly.

Mewhu came and took the rod out of his hand, and dropped it. It stayed perfectly horizontal, and sank slowly down to the ground, where it lay. Mewhu pointed at it, at the tree, and grinned.

"Just like a parachute. Oh, *gee,* Daddy!"

"You keep away from it," said Jack, familiar with youthful intonation. "Heaven knows what it is. It might go off, or something."

He looked fearfully at the object. It lay quietly, the hissing of the end pieces stilled. Mewhu bent suddenly and picked it up, held it over his head with one hand. Then he calmly lifted his feet and hung from it. It lowered him gently, butt first, until he sat on the ground, in a welter of dead leaves; as soon as he picked it up, the streamlined end pieces had begun to blast again.

"That's the silliest thing I ever saw. Here—let me see it." It was floating about waist-high. He leaned over one of the ends. It had a fine round grille over it. He put out a hand. Mewhu reached out and caught his wrist, shaking his head. Apparently

Theodore Sturgeon

it was dangerous to go too near those ends. Garry suddenly saw why. They were tiny, powerful jet motors of some kind. If the jet was powerful enough to support a man's weight, the intake must be drawing like mad—probably enough to snap a hole through a man's hand like a giant ticket-puncher.

But what controlled it? How was the jet strength adjusted to the weight borne by the device, and to the altitude? He remembered without pleasure that when he had fallen with it from the treetop, he had dropped quite fast, and that he went slower and slower as he approached the ground. And yet when Mewhu had held it over his head, it had borne his weight instantly and lowered him very slowly. And besides, how was it so stable? Why didn't it turn upside down and blast itself and passenger down to earth?

He looked at Mewhu with some increase of awe. Obviously he came from a place where the science was really advanced. He wondered if he would ever be able to get any technical information from his visitor—and if he would be able to understand it. Of course, Molly seemed to be able to—

"He wants you to take it back and try it on the roof," said Molly.

"How can that refugee from a Kuttner opus help me?"

Immediately Mewhu took the rod, lifted it, ducked under it, and slipped his arms through the two rings, so that it crossed his back like a water-bucket yoke. Peering around, he turned to face a clearing in the trees, and before their startled eyes he leaped thirty feet in the air, drifted away in a great arc, and came gently to rest twenty yards away.

Molly jumped up and down and clapped her hands, speechless with delight. The only words Garry could find were a reiterated, "Ah, no!"

Mewhu stood where he was, smiling his engaging smile, waiting for them. They walked toward him, and when they were close he leaped again and soared out toward the road.

"What do you do with a thing like this?" breathed Jack. "Who do you go to, and what do you say to him?"

"Let's just keep him for a pet, Daddy."

Jack took her hand, and they followed the bounding, soaring silver man. A pet! A member of some alien race, from some unthinkable civilization—and obviously highly trained, too, for no ordinary individual would be the first to make such a trip. What was his story? Was he an advance guard? Or was he the sole survivor of his people? How far had he come? From Mars? Venus?

They caught up with him at the house. He was standing by the ladder. His strange rod was lying quiet on the ground. He was fascinatedly operating Molly's yo-yo. When he saw them, he threw down the yo-yo, picked up his device, and, slipping it across his shoulders, sprang high in the air and drifted down to the roof. "Eee-yu!" he said, with emphasis, and jumped off backward. So stable was the rod that as he sank through the air his long body swung to and fro.

"Very nice," said Jack. "Also spectacular. And I have to go back to work." He went to the ladder.

Mewhu bounded over to him and caught his arm, whimpering and whistling in his peculiar speech. He took the rod and extended it toward Jack.

"He wants you to use it," said Molly.

"No, thanks," said Jack, a trace of his tree-climbing vertigo returning to him. "I'd just as soon use the ladder." And he put his hand out to it.

Mewhu, hopping with frustration, reached past him and toppled the ladder. It levered over a box as it fell and struck Jack painfully on the shin.

"I guess you better use the flyin' belt, Daddy."

Jack looked at Mewhu. The silver man was looking as pleasant as he could with that kind of a face; on the other hand, it might just possibly be wise to humor him a little. Being safely on the ground to begin with, Jack felt that it might not matter if the fantastic thing wouldn't work for him. And if it failed him over the roof—well, the house wasn't *very* tall.

He shrugged his arms through the two rings. Mewhu pointed to the roof, to Jack, made a jumping motion. Jack took a deep breath, aimed carefully, and hoping the gadget wouldn't work, jumped.

He shot up close to the house—too close. The eave caught him a resounding thwack on precisely the spot where the ladder had just hit him. The impact barely checked him. He went sailing up over the roof, hovered for a breathless second, and then began to come down. For a moment he thought his flailing legs would find purchase on the far edge of the roof. He just missed it. All he managed to do was to crack the same shin, in the same place, mightily on the other eave. Trailing clouds of profanity, he landed standing—in Iris's wash basket. Iris, just turning from the clothesline, confronted him.

"Jack! What on earth are you . . . get out of that! You're standing right on my wash with your dirty . . . *oh!*"

"Oh-oh!" said Jack, and stepped backward out of the wash basket. His foot went into Molly's express wagon, which Iris used to carry the heavy basket. To get his balance, he leaped—and immediately rose high in the air. This time his luck was better. He soared completely over the kitchen wing of the house and came to earth near Molly and Mewhu.

"Daddy, you were just like a bird! Me next, huh, Daddy?"

"I'm going to be just like a corpse if your mother's expression means what I think it does. Don't you touch that!" He shucked off the "flyin'-belt" and dived into the house just as Iris rounded the corner. He heard Molly's delighted "He went *that* way" as he plowed through the shambles of the living room and out the front door. As the kitchen door slammed he was rounding the house. He charged up to Mewhu, snatched the gadget from him, slipped it on, and jumped. This time his judgment was faultless. He cleared the house easily although he came very near landing astride the clothesline.

Theodore Sturgeon

When Iris, panting and furious, stormed out of the house, he was busily hanging sheets.

"Just what," said Iris, her voice cracking at the seams, "do you think you're doing?"

"Just giving you a hand with the laundry, m'love," said Jack.

"What is that . . . that object on your back?"

"Another evidence of the ubiquity of the devices of science fiction," said Jack blandly. "This is a multilateral, three-dimensional mass adjuster, or pogo-chute. With it I can fly like a gull, evading the cares of the world and the advances of beautiful redheads, at such times as their passions are distasteful to me."

"Sometime in the very near future, you gangling hatrack, I am going to pull the tongue out of your juke box of a head and tie a bowknot in it." Then she laughed.

He heaved a sigh of relief, went and kissed her. "Darling, I am sorry. I was scared silly, dangling from this thing. I didn't see your clothes basket, and if I had I don't know how I'd have steered clear."

"What is it, Jack? How does it work?"

"I dunno. Jets on the ends. They blast hard when there's a lot of weight pushing them toward the earth. They blast harder near the earth than up high. When the weight on them slacks off a bit, they throttle down. What makes them do it, what they use for power—I just wouldn't know. As far as I can see, they suck in air at the top and blow it out through the jets. And, oh yes—they point directly downward no matter which way the rod is turned."

"Where did you get it?"

"Off a tree. It's Mewhu's. Apparently he used it for a parachute. On the way down, a tree branch speared through one of these rings and he slipped out of it and fell and broke his arm."

"What are we going to do with him, Jack?"

"I've been worrying about that myself. We can't sell him to a sideshow." He paused thoughtfully. "There's no doubt that he has a lot that would be of value to humanity. Why, this thing alone would change the face of the earth! Listen—I weigh a hundred and seventy. I *fell* on this thing suddenly, when I lost my grip on a tree, and it bore my weight immediately. Mewhu weighs more than I do, judging from his build. It took his weight when he lifted his feet off the ground while he was holding it over his head. If it can do that, it or a larger version should be able, not only to drive, but to support an aircraft. If for some reason that isn't possible, the power of those little jets certainly could turn a turbine."

"Will it wash clothes?" Iris was glum.

"That's exactly what I mean. Light, portable, and more power than it has any right to have—of course it'll wash clothes. And drive generators, and cars, and . . . Iris, what do you do when you have something as big as this?"

"Call a newspaper, I guess."

"And have a hundred thousand people peeking and prying all over the place, and Congressional investigations, and what all? Uh-uh!"

"Why not ask Harry Zinsser?"

"Harry? I thought you didn't like him."

"I never said that. It's just that you and he go off in the corner and chatter about mulpitude amputation and debilities and reactance and things like that, and I have to sit, knit—and spit when I want someone's attention. Harry's all right."

"Gosh, honey, you've got it. Harry'll know what to do. I'll go right away."

"You'll do nothing of the kind. With that hole in the roof? I thought you said you could have it patched up for the night at least. By the time you get back here it'll be dark."

The prospect of sawing out the ragged hole in the roof was suddenly the least appealing thing in the world. He sighed and went off, mumbling something about the greatest single advance in history awaiting the whim of a woman. He forgot that he was wearing Mewhu's armpit altitudinizer. Only his first two paces were on the ground, and Iris hooted with laughter at his clumsy walking on air. When he reached the ground he set his jaw and leaped lightly up to the roof. "Catch me now, you and your piano legs," he taunted cheerfully, ducked the lancelike clothes prop she hurled at him, and went back to work.

As he sawed, he was conscious of a hubbub down below.

"Dah-dee!" "Mr-r-roo ellue—"

He sighed and put down the saw. "What is it?"

"Mewhu wants his flyin' belt!"

Jack looked at the roof, at the lower shed, and decided that his old bones could stand it if he had to get down without a ladder. He took the jet-tipped rod and dropped it. It stayed perfectly horizontal, falling no slower and no faster than it had when he had ridden it down. Mewhu caught it, deftly slipped his splinted arm through it—it was astonishing how careful he was of the arm, and yet how little it inconvenienced him—then the other arm, and sprang up to join Jack on the roof.

"What do you say, fella?"

"Woopen yew weep."

"I know how you feel." He knew the silver man wanted to tell him something, but he couldn't help him out. He grinned and picked up the saw. Mewhu took it out of his hand and tossed it off the roof, being careful to miss Molly, who was dancing back to get a point of vantage.

"What's the big idea?"

"Dellihew hidden," said Mewhu. "Pento deh numinew heh," and he pointed at the flying belt and at the hole in the roof.

"You mean I'd rather fly off in that thing than work? Brother, you got it. But I'm afraid I have to—"

Mewhu circled his arm, pointing all around the hole in the roof, and pointed again to the pogo-chute, indicating one of the jet motors.

"I don't get it," said Jack.

Mewhu apparently understood, and an expression of amazement crossed his mobile face. Kneeling, he placed his good hand around one of the little jet motors, pressed two tiny studs, and the casing popped open. Inside was a compact, sealed, and simple-looking device, the core of the motor itself, apparently. There seemed to be no other fastening. Mewhu lifted it out and handed it to Jack. It was about the size and shape of an electric razor. There was a button on the side. Mewhu pointed at it, pressed the back, and then moved Jack's hand so that the device was pointed away from them both. Jack, expecting anything, from nothing at all to the "blinding bolt of searing, raw energy" so dear to the science-fiction world, pressed the button.

The gadget hissed, and snuggled back into his palm in an easy recoil.

"That's fine," said Jack, "but what do I do with it?"

Mewhu pointed at Jack's cut, then at the device.

"Oh," said Jack. He bent close, aimed the thing at the end of the saw cut, and pressed the button. Again the hiss and the slight, steady recoil, and a fine line appeared in the wood. It was a cut, about half as thick as the saw cut, clean and even and, as long as he kept his hand steady, very straight. A fine cloud of pulverized wood rose out of the hole in the roof, carried on a swirl of air.

Jack experimented, holding the jet close to the wood and away from it. He found that it cut finer the closer he got to it. As he drew it away from the wood, the slot got wider and the device cut slower until at about eighteen inches it would not cut at all. Delighted, Jack quickly cut and trimmed the hole. Mewhu watched, grinning. Jack grinned back, knowing how he would feel if he introduced a saw to some primitive who was trying to work wood with a machete.

When he was finished, he handed the jet back to the silver man and slapped his shoulder. "Thanks a million, Mewhu."

"Jeek," said Mewhu, and reached for Jack's neck. One of his thumbs lay on Jack's collarbone, the other on his back, over the scapula. Mewhu squeezed twice, firmly.

"That the way you shake hands back home?" smiled Jack. He thought it likely. Any civilized race was likely to have a manual greeting. The handshake had evolved from a raised palm, indicating that the saluter was unarmed. It was quite possible that this was an extension, in a slightly different direction, of the same sign. It would indeed be an indication of friendliness to have two individuals present their throats to each other.

With three deft motions, Mewhu slipped the tiny jet back into its casing and, holding the rod with one hand, stepped off the roof, letting himself be lowered in that amazing thistledown fashion to the ground. Once there, he tossed the rod back. Jack was startled to see it hurtle upward like any earthly object. He grabbed it and missed. It reached the top of its arc, and as soon as it started down again the jets cut in, and it sank easily to him. He put it on and floated down to join Mewhu.

The silver man followed Jack to the garage, where he kept a few pieces of milled lumber. He selected some one-inch pine boards and dragged them out into the middle of the floor, to measure them and mark them off to the size he wanted to knock together a simple trap-door covering for the useless stair well, a process which Mewhu watched with great interest.

Jack took up the flying belt and tried to open the streamlined shell to remove the cutter. It absolutely defied him. He pressed, twisted, wrenched, and pulled. All it did was to hiss gently when he moved it toward the floor.

"Eek, Jeek," said Mewhu. He took the jet from Jack and pressed it. Jack watched closely, then he grinned and took the cutter.

He swiftly cut the lumber up with it, sneering gaily at the ripsaw which hung on the wall. Then he put the whole trap together with a Z-brace, trimmed off the few rough corners, and stood back to admire it. He realized instantly that it was too heavy to carry by himself, let alone lift it to the roof. If Mewhu had two good hands, now—
He scratched his head.

"Carry it on the flyin' belt, Daddy."

"Molly! What made you think of that?"

"Mewhu tol' . . . I mean, I sort of—"

"Let's get this straight once and for all. How does Mewhu talk to you?"

"I dunno, Daddy. It's sort of like I remembered something he said, but not the . . . the words he said. I jus' . . . jus' . . . " she faltered, and then said vehemently, "I don't *know,* Daddy. Truly I don't."

"What'd he say this time?"

She looked at Mewhu. Again Jack noticed the peculiar swelling of Mewhu's silver mustache. She said, "Put the door you jus' made on the flyin' belt and lift it. The flyin' belt'll make it fall slow, and you can push it along while . . . it's . . . fallin'."

Jack looked at the door, at the jet device, and got the idea. When he had slipped the jet rod under the door, Mewhu gave him a lift. Up it came; and then Mewhu, steadying it, towed it well outside the garage before it finally sank to the ground. Another lift, another easy tow, and they covered thirty more feet. In this manner they covered the distance to the house, with Molly skipping and laughing behind, pleading for a ride and praising the grinning Mewhu.

At the house, Jack said, "Well, Einstein Junior, how do we get it up on the roof?"

Mewhu picked up Molly's yo-yo and began to operate it deftly. Doing so, he walked around the corner of the house.

"Hey!"

"He don't know, Daddy. You'll have to figger it out."

"You mean he could dream up that slick trick for carrying it out here and now his brains give out?"

"I guess so, Daddy."

Jack Garry looked after the retreating form of the silver man and shook his head. He was already prepared to expect better than human reasoning from Mewhu, even if it was a little different. He couldn't quite phase this with Mewhu's shrugging off a problem in basic logic. Certainly a man with his capabilities would not have reasoned out such an ingenious method of bringing the door out here without realizing that that was only half the problem. He wondered if the solution was so obvious to Mewhu that he couldn't be bothered explaining it.

Shrugging, Jack went back to the garage and got a small block and tackle. He had to put up a big screw hook on the eave, and another on the new trap door; and once he had laboriously hauled the door up until the tackle was two-locked, it was a little more than arduous to work it over the ege and drag it into position. Mewhu had apparently quite lost interest. It was two hours later, just as he put the last screw in the tower bolt on the trap door and was calling the job finished, that he heard Mewhu begin to shriek again. He dropped his tools, shrugged into the jet stick, and sailed off the roof.

"Iris! Iris! What's the matter?"

"I don't know, Jack. He's . . . "

Jacl pounded around to the front of the house. Mewhu was lying on the ground in the midst of some violent, tearing convulsion. He lay on his back, arching it high, digging his heels into the turf; and his head was bent back at an impossible angle, so that his weight was on his heels and his forehead. His good arm pounded the ground though the splinted one lay limp. His lips writhed and he uttered an edgy, gasping series of ululations quite horrible to listen to. He seemed to be able to scream as loudly when inhaling as when exhaling.

Molly stood beside him, watching him hypnotically. She was smiling. Jack knelt beside the writhing form and tried to steady it. "Molly, stop grinning at the poor fellow."

"But—he's happy, Daddy."

"He's what?"

"Can't you see, silly? He feels good, that's all. He's laughing!"

"Iris, what's the matter with him? Do you know?"

"He took some aspirin again, that's all I can tell you."

"He ate four," said Milly. "He loves 'em."

"What can we do, Jack?"

"I don't know, honey," said Jack worriedly. "Better just let him work it out. Any emetic or sedative we give him might be harmful."

The attack slackened and ceased suddenly, and Mewhu went quite limp. Again, with his hand over the man's chest, Jack felt the strange double pulsing.

"Out cold," he said.

Molly said in a strange, quiet voice, "No, Daddy. He's lookin' at dreams."

"Dreams?"

"A place with a or'nge sky," said Molly. He looked up sharply. Her eyes were closed. "Lots of Mewhus. Hundreds un' hundreds—big ones. As big as Mr. Thorndyke." (Thorndyke was an editor whom they knew in the city. He was six feet seven.) "Round houses, an' big airplanes with . . . sticks fer wings."

"Molly, you're talking nonsense," her mother said worriedly. Jack shushed her. "Go on, baby."

"A place, a room. It's a . . . Mewhu is there and a bunch more. They're in . . . in lines. Rows. There's a big one with a yella hat. He keeps them in rows. Here's Mewhu. He's outa the line. He's jumpin' out th' window with a flyin' belt." There was a long silence. Mewhu moaned.

"Well?"

"Nothin', Daddy . . . wait! It's . . . all . . . fuzzy. Now there's a thing, a kinda summarine. Only on the ground, not in the water. The door's open. Mewhu is . . . is inside. Knobs, and clocks. Pull on the knobs. Push a— Oh, *Oh!* It hurts!" She put her fists to her temples.

"Molly!"

Molly opened her eyes and said quite calmly, "Oh, I'm all right, Mommy. It was a thing in the dream that hurt, but it didn't hurt me. It was all a bunch of fire an' . . . an a sleepy feeling, only bigger. An' it hurt."

"Jack, he'll harm the child!"

"I doubt it," said Jack.

"So do I," said Iris wonderingly, and then, almost inaudibly, "Now, why did I say that?"

"Mewhu's asleep," said Molly suddenly.

"No more dreams?"

"No more dreams. Gee. That was—funny."

"Come and have some lunch," said Iris. Her voice shook a little. They went into the house. Jack looked down at Mewhu, who was smiling peacefully in his sleep. He thought of putting the strange creature to bed, but the day was warm and the grass was thick and soft where he lay. He shook his head and went into the house.

"Sit down and feed," Iris said.

He looked around. "You've done wonders in here," he said. The litter of lath and plaster was gone, and Iris's triumphant antimacassars blossomed from the upholstery. She curtsied. "Thank you, m'lord."

They sat around the card table and began to do damage to tongue sandwiches. "Jack."

"Mm-m?"

"What was that—telepathy?"

"Think so. Something like that. Oh, wait'll I tell Zinsser! He'll never believe it."

"Are you going down to the airfield this afternoon?"

Theodore Sturgeon

"You bet. Maybe I'll take Mewhu with me."

"That would be a little rough on the populace, wouldn't it? Mewhu isn't the kind of fellow you can pass off as your cousin Julius."

"Heck, he'd be all right. He could sit in the back seat with Molly while I talked Zinsser into coming out to have a look at him."

"Why not get Zinsser out here?"

"You know that's silly. When we see him in town he's got time off. Out here he's tied to that airport almost every minute."

"Jack, do you think Molly's quite safe with that creature?"

"Of course. Are you worried?"

"I . . . I am, Jack. But not about Mewhu. About me. I'm worried because I think I should worry more, if you see what I mean."

Jack leaned over and kissed her. "The good old maternal instinct at work," he chuckled. "Mewhu's new and strange and might be dangerous. At the same time Mewhu's hurt, and he's inoffensive, so something in you wants to mother him, too."

"There you really have something," Iris said thoughtfully. "He's as big and ugly as you are, and unquestionably more intelligent. Yet I don't mother you."

Jack grinned. "You're not kiddin'." He gulped his coffee and stood up. "Eat it up, Molly, and go wash your hands and face. I'm going to have a look at Mewhu."

"You're going into the airport, then?" asked Iris.

"If Mewhu's up to it. There's too much I want to know, too much I haven't the brains to figure out. I don't think I'll get all the answers from Zinsser, by any means; but between us we'll figure out what to do about this thing. Iris, it's *big!*"

Full of wild speculation, he stepped out on the lawn. Mewhu was sitting up, happily contemplating a caterpillar.

"Mewhu."

"Dew?"

"How'd you like to take a ride?"

"Hubilly grees. Jeek?"

"I guess you don't get the idea. C'mon," said Jack, motioning toward the garage. Mewhu very, very carefully set the caterpillar down on a blade of grass and rose to follow; and just then the most unearthly crash issued form the garage. For a frozen moment no one moved, and then Molly's voice set up a hair-raising reiterated screech. Jack was pounding toward the garage before he knew he had moved.

"Molly! What is it?"

At the sound of his voice the child shut up as if she were switch-operated.

"Molly!"

"Here I am, Daddy," she said in an extremely small voice. She was standing by the car, her entire being concentrated in her protruding, faintly quivering lower lip. The car was nose-foremost through the back wall of the garage.

"Daddy, I didn't mean to do it; I just wanted to help you get the car out. Are you going to spank me? Please, Daddy, I didn't—"

"*Quiet!*"

She was quiet immediately. "Molly, what on earth possessed you to do a thing like that? You know you're not supposed to touch the starter!"

"I was pretending, Daddy, like it was a summarine that could fly, the way Mewhu did."

Jack threaded his way through this extraordinary shambles of syntax. "Come here," he said sternly. She came, her paces half-size, her feet dragging, her hands behind her where her imagination told her they would do the most good. "I ought to whack you, you know."

"Yeah," she answered tremulously, "I guess you oughta. Not more'n a couple of times, huh, Daddy?"

Jack bit the insides of his cheeks for control, but couldn't make it. He grinned. *You little minx,* he thought. "Tell you what," he said gruffly, looking at the car. The garage was fortunately flimsy, and the few new dents on hood and fenders would blend well with the old ones. "You've got three good whacks coming to you. I'm going to add those on to your next spanking."

"Yes, Daddy," said Molly, her eyes big and chastened. She climbed into the back seat and sat, very straight and small, away back out of sight. Jack cleared away what wreckage he could, and then climbed in, started the old puddle-vaulter, and carefully backed out of the damaged shed.

Mewhu was standing well clear, watching the groaning automobile with startled silver eyes. "Come on in," said Jack, beckoning. Mewhu backed off.

"Mewhu!" cried Molly, putting her head out the rear door. Mewhu said, "Yowk," and came instantly. Molly opened the door and he climbed in, and she shouted with laughter when he crouched down on the floor, and pulled at him until he got up on the seat. Jack drove around the house, stopped, picked up Mewhu's jet rod, blew a kiss through the window to Iris and they were off.

Forty minutes later they wheeled up to the airport after an ecstatic ride during which Molly had kept up a running fire of descriptive commentary on the wonders of a terrestrial countryside. Mewhu had goggled and ogled in a most satisfactory fashion, listening spellbound to the child—sometimes Jack would have sworn that the silver man understood everything she said—and uttering shrieks, exclamatory mewings, and interrogative peeps.

"Now," said Jack, when he had parked at the field boundary, "you two stay in the car for a while. I'm going to speak to Mr. Zinsser and see if he'll come out and meet Mewhu. Molly, do you think you can make Mewhu understand that he's to stay in the car, and out of sight? You see, if other people see him, they'll want to ask a lot of silly questions, and we don't want to embarrass him, do we?"

"No, Daddy. I'll tell him. Mewhu," she said, turning to the silver man. She held his eyes with hers. His mustache swelled, rippled. "You'll be good, won't you, and stay out of sight?"

"Jeek," said Mewhu. "Jeek mereedy."

"He says you're the boss."

Jack laughed, climbing out. "He does, eh?" Did the child really know, or was it mostly a game? "Be good, then. See you soon, Mewhu." Carrying the jet rod, he walked into the building.

Zinsser, as usual, was busy. The field was not large, but it did a great deal of private-plane business, and as traffic manager Zinsser had his hands full. He wrapped one of his pudgy, flexible hands around the phone he was using, "Hi, Garry! What's new out of this world?" he grated cheerfully. "Siddown. With you in a minute." He bumbled cheerfully into the telephone, grinning at Jack as he talked. Jack made himself as comfortable as patience permitted and waited until Zinsser hung up.

"Well, now," said Zinsser, and the phone rang again.

Jack closed his open mouth in annoyance. Zinsser hung up and another bell rang. He picked up a field telephone from its hook on the side of his desk. "Zinsser. Yes—"

"Now that's enough," said Jack to himself. He rose, went to the door, and closed it softly, so that he was alone with the manager. He took the jet rod and, to Zinsser's vast astonishment, stood on his desk, raised the rod high over his head, and stepped off. A hurricane screamed out of the jets. Jack, hanging by his hands from the rod as it lowered him gently through the air, looked over his shoulder. Zinsser's face looked like a red moon in a snow flurry, surrounded as it was by every interoffice memo for the past two weeks.

Anyway, the first thing he did when he could draw a breath was to hang up the phone.

"Thought that would do it," said Jack, grinning.

"You . . . you . . . what *is* that thing?"

"It's a dialectical polarizer," said Jack, alighting. "That is, it makes conversations possible with airport managers who won't get off the phone."

Zinsser was out of his chair and around the desk, remarkably light on his feet for a man his size. "Let me see that."

Jack handed it over and began to talk.

"Look, Mewhu! Here comes a plane!"

Together they watched the Cub slide in for a landing, and squeaked at the little puffs of dust that were thrown up by the tires and flicked away by the slipstream.

"And there goes another one. It's gonna take off!" The little blue low-wing coupé taxied across the field, braked one wheel, swung in its own length, and roared down toward them, lifting to howl away into the sky far over their heads.

"Eeeeeeyow," droned Molly, imitating the sound of the motor as it passed overhead.

"S-s-s-s-sweeeeee!" hissed Mewhu, exactly duplicating the whine of control surfaces in the prop blast.

Molly clapped her hands and shrieked with delight. Another plane began to circle the field. They watched it avidly.

"Come on out and have a look at him," said Jack.

Zinsser looked at his watch. "I can't. All kidding aside, I got to stick by the phone for another half hour at the very least. Will he be all right out there? There's hardly anyone around."

"I think so. Molly's with him, and as I told you, they get along beautifully together. That's one of the things I want to have investigated—that telepathy angle." He laughed suddenly. "That Molly . . . know what she did this afternoon?" He told Zinsser about Molly's driving the car through the wrong end of the garage.

"The little hellion," chuckled Zinsser. "They'll all do it, bless 'em. My brother's kid went to work on the front lawn with his mother's vacuum cleaner the other day." He laughed. "To get back to what's-his-name—Mewhu—and this gadget of his. Jack, we've got to hang on to it. Do you realize that he and his clothes and this thing are the only clues we have as to what he is and where he came from?"

"I sure do. But listen, he's very intelligent. I'm sure he'll be able to tell us plenty."

"You can bet he's intelligent," said Zinsser. "He's probably above average on his planet. They wouldn't send just anyone on a trip like that. Jack, what a pity we don't have his ship!"

"Maybe it'll be back. What's your guess as to where he comes from?"

"Mars, maybe."

"Now, you know better than that. We know Mars has an atmosphere, but it's mighty tenuous. An organism the size of Mewhu would have to have enormous lungs to keep him going. No; Mewhu's used to an atmosphere pretty much like ours."

"That would rule Venus out."

"He wears clothes quite comfortably here. His planet must have not only pretty much the same atmosphere, but the same climate. He seems to be able to take most of our foods, though he's revolted by some of them—and aspirin sends him high as a kite. He gets what looks like a laughing drunk when he takes it."

"You don't say. Let's see, it wouldn't be Jupiter, because he isn't built to take a gravity like that. And the outer planets are too cold, and Mercury is too hot." Zinsser leaned back in his chair and absently mopped his bald head. "Jack, this guy doesn't even come from this solar system!"

"Gosh. I guess you're right. Harry, what do you make of this jet gadget?"

"From the way you say it cuts wood . . . can I see that, by the way?" Zinsser asked.

Theodore Sturgeon

"Sure." Garry went to work on the jet. He found the right studs to press simultaneously. The casing opened smoothly. He lifted out the active core of the device, and, handling it gingerly, sliced a small corner off Zinsser's desk top.

"That is the strangest thing I have ever seen," said Zinsser. "May I see it?"

He took it and turned it over in his hands. "There doesn't seem to be any fuel for it," he said musingly.

"I think it uses air," said Jack.

"But what pushes the air?"

"Air," said Jack. "No, I'm not kidding. I think that in some way it disintegrates part of the air, and uses the energy released to activate a small jet. If you had a shell around this jet, with an intake at one end and a blast tube at the other, it would operate like a high-vacuum pump, dragging more air through."

"Or like an athodyd," said Zinsser. Garry's blood went cold as the manager sighted down into the jet orifice. "For heaven's sake don't push that button."

"I won't. Say—you're right. The tube's concentric. Now, how on earth could a disruption unit be as small and light as that?"

Jack Garry said, "I've been chewing on that all day. I have one answer. Can you take something that sounds really fantastic, so long as it's logical?"

"You know me," grinned Zinsser, waving at a long shelf of back-number science-fiction magazines. "Go ahead."

"Well," said Jack carefully. "You know what binding energy is. The stuff that holds the nucleus of an atom together. If I understand my smattering of nuclear theory properly, it seems possible to me that a sphere of binding energy could be produced that would be stable."

"A sphere? With what inside it?"

"Binding energy—or maybe just nothing . . . space. Anyhow, if you surround that sphere with another, this one a force-field which is capable of penetrating the inner one, or of allowing matter to penetrate it, it seems to me that anything entering that balance of forces would be disrupted. An explosive pressure would be bottled up inside the inner sphere. Now if you bring your penetrating field in contact with the binding-energy sphere, the pressures inside will come blasting out. Incase the whole rig in a device which controls the amount of matter going in one side of the sphere and the amount of orifice allowed for the escape of energy, and incase that further in an outside shell which will give you a stream of air induced violently through it—like the vacuum pump you mentioned—and you have this," and he rapped on the little jet motor.

"Most ingenious," said Zinsser, wagging his head. "Even if you're wrong, it's an ingenious theory. What you're saying, you know, is that all we have to do to duplicate this device is to discover the nature of binding energy and then find a way to make it stay stably in spherical form. After which we figure out the nature of a field which can penetrate binding energy and allow any matter to do likewise—one way." He spread his hands. "That's all. Just learn to actually use the stuff that the longhair boys haven't thought of theorizing about yet, and we're all set."

"Shucks," said Garry. "Mewhu will give us all the dope."

"I hope so, Jack. This can revolutionize the entire industrial world."

"You're understanding," grinned Jack.

The phone rang. Zinsser looked at his watch again. "There's my call." He sat down, answered the phone, and while he went on at great length to some high-powered character at the other end of the line, about bills of lading and charter service and interstate commerce restrictions, Jack lounged against the cut-off corner of the desk and dreamed. Mewhu—a superior member of the superior race, come to Earth to lead barbaric humanity out of its struggling, wasteful ways. He wondered what Mewhu was like at home among his strange people. Young, but very mature, he decided, and gifted in many ways; the pick of the crop, fit to be ambassador to a new and dynamic civilization like Earth's. And what about the ship? Having dropped Mewhu, had it and its pilot returned to the mysterious corner of the universe from which they had come? Or was it circling about somewhere in space, anxiously awaiting word from the adventurous ambassador?

Zinsser cradled his instrument and stood up with a sigh. "A credit to my will power," he said. "The greatest thing that's ever happened to me, and I stuck by the day's work in spite of it. I feel like a kid on Christmas Eve. Let's go have a look at him."

"Wheeeeyouwow!" screamed Mewhu as another rising plane passed over their heads. Molly bounced joyfully up and down on the cushions, for Mewhu was an excellent mimic.

The silver man slipped over the back of the driver's seat in a lithe movement, to see a little better around the corner of a nearby hangar. One of the Cubs had been wheeled into it, and was standing not far away, its prop ticking over.

Molly leaned her elbows on the edge of the seat and stretched her little neck so she could see, too. Mewhu brushed against her head and her hat fell off. He bent to pick it up and bumped his own head on the dashboard, and the glove compartment flew open. His strange pupils narrowed, and the nictating membranes flickered over his eyes as he reached inside. The next thing Molly knew, he was out of the car and running over the parking area, leaping high in the air, mouthing strange noises, and stopping every few jumps to roll and beat with his good hand on the ground.

Horrified, Molly Garry left the car and ran after him. "Mewhu!" she cried. "Mewhu, come *back!*"

He cavorted toward her, his arms outspread. "W-r-r-row-w!" he shouted, rushing past her. Lowering one arm a little and raising the other like an airplane banking, he ran in a wide arc, leaped the little tarmac retaining wall, and bounded out onto the hangar area.

Theodore Sturgeon

Molly, panting and sobbing, stopped and stamped her foot. "Mewhu!" she croaked helplessly. "Daddy said—"

Two mechanics standing near the idling Cub looked around at a sound like a civet-cat imitating an Onondaga war whoop. What they saw was a long-legged, silver-gray apparition, with a silver-white mustache and slotted eyes, dressed in a scarlet robe that turned to indigo. Without a sound, moving as one man, they cut and ran. And Mewhu, with one last terrible shriek of joy, leaped to the plane and disappeared inside.

Molly put her hands to her mouth and her eyes bugged. "Oh, Mewhu," she breathed. "Now, you've done it." She heard pounding feet, turned. Her father was racing toward her, with Mr. Zinsser waddling behind. "Molly! Where's Mewhu?"

Wordlessly she pointed at the Cub, and as if it were a signal the little ship throttled up and began to crawl away from the hangar.

"Hey! Wait! Wait!" screamed Jack Garry uselessly, sprinting after the plane. He leaped the wall but misjudged it because of his speed. His toe hooked it and he sprawled slitheringly, jarringly on the tarmac. Zinsser and Molly ran to him and helped him up. Jack's nose was bleeding. He whipped out a handkerchief and looked out at the dwindling plane. "Mewhu!"

The little plane waddled across the field, bellowed suddenly with power. The tail came up, and it scooted away from them—cross-wind, across the runway. Jack turned to speak to Zinsser and saw the fat man's face absolutely stricken. He followed Zinsser's eyes and there was the other plane, the big six-place cabin job, coming in.

He had never felt so helpless in all his life. Those planes were going to collide. There was nothing anyone could do about it. He watched them, unblinking, almost detachedly. They were hurtling but they seemed to creep; the moment lasted forever. Then, with a twenty-foot altitude, Mewhu cut his gun and dropped a wing. The Cub slowed, leaned into the wind, and *side-slipped* so close under the cabin ship that another coat of paint on either craft would have meant disaster.

Jack didn't know how long he had been holding that breath, but it was agony when he let it out.

"Anyway, he can fly," breathed Zinsser.

"Of course he can fly," snapped Jack. "A prehistoric thing like an airplane would be child's play for him."

"Oh, Daddy, I'm scared."

"I'm not," said Jack hollowly.

"Me, too," said Zinsser with an unconvincing laugh. "The plane's insured."

The Cub arrowed upward. At a hundred feet it went into a skidding turn, harrowing to watch, suddenly winged over, and came shouting down at them. Mewhu buzzed them so close that Zinsser went flat on his face. Jack and Molly simply stood there, wall-eyed. An enormous cloud of dust obscured everything for ninety interminable seconds. When they next saw the plane it was wobbling crazily at a hundred and fifty.

Suddenly Molly screamed piercingly and put her hands over her face.

"Molly! Kiddo, what is it?"

She flung her arms around his neck and sobbed so violently that he knew it was hurting her throat. "Stop it!" he yelled; and then, very gently, he asked, "What's the matter, darling?"

"He's scared. Mewhu's terrible, terrible scared," she said brokenly.

Jack looked up at the plane. It yawed, fell away on one wing.

Zinsser shouted, his voice cracking. "Gun her! Gun her! Throttle up, you idiot!"

Mewhu cut the gun.

Dead stick, the plane winged over and plunged to the ground. The impact was crushing.

Molly said quite calmly, "All Mewhu's pictures have gone out now," and slumped unconscious to the ground.

They got him to the hospital. It was messy, all of it, picking him up, carrying him to the ambulance—

Jack wished fervently that Molly had not seen; but she had sat up and cried as they carried him past. He thought worriedly as he and Zinsser crossed and recrossed in their pacing of the waiting-room that he would have his hands full with the child when this thing was all over.

The resident physician came in, wiping his hands. He was a small man with a nose like a walnut meat. "Who brought that plane-crash case in here—you?"

"Both of us," said Zinsser.

"What—who is he?"

"A friend of mine. Is he . . . will he live?"

"How should I know?" snapped the doctor impatiently. "I have never in my experience—" He exhaled through his nostrils. "The man has two circulatory systems. Two *closed* circulatory systems, and a heart for each. All his arterial blood looks veinous—it's purple. How'd he happen to get hurt?"

"He ate half a box of aspirin out of my car," said Jack. "Aspirin makes him drunk. He swiped a plane and piled it up."

"Aspirin makes him—" The doctor looked at each of them in turn. "I won't ask if you're kidding me. Just to see that . . . that thing in there is enough to kid any doctor. How long has that splint been on his arm?"

Zinsser looked at Jack and Jack said, "About eighteen hours."

"Eighteen *hours?*" The doctor shook his head. "It's so well knitted that I'd say eighteen days." Before Jack could say anything he added. "He needs a transfusion."

"But you can't! I mean, his blood—"

"I know. Took a sample to type it. I have two technicians trying to blend chemicals into plasma so we can approximate it. Both of 'em called me a liar. But he's got to have the transfusion. I'll let you know." He strode out of the room.

"There goes one bewildered medico."

"He's OK," said Zinsser. "I know him well. Can you blame him?"

Theodore Sturgeon

"For feeling that way? Gosh no. Harry, I don't know what I'll do if Mewhu checks out."

"That fond of him?"

"Oh, it isn't only that. But to come so close to meeting a new culture, and then have it slip from our fingers like this, it's too much."

"That jet—Jack, without Mewhu to explain it, I don't think any scientist will be able to build another. It would be like . . . like giving a Damascus sword-smith some tungsten and asking him to draw it into filaments. There the jet would be, hissing when you shove it toward the ground, sneering at you."

"And that telepathy—what J. B. Rhine wouldn't give to be able to study it!"

"Yeah, and what about his origin?" Zinsser asked excitedly. "He isn't from this system. It means that he used an interstellar drive of some kind, or even that space-time warp the boys write about."

"He's got to live," said Jack. "He's got to, or there ain't no justice. There are too many things we've got to know, Harry! Look—he's here. That must mean that some more of his people will come some day."

"Yeah. Why haven't they come before now?"

"Maybe they have. Charles Fort—"

"Aw, look," said Zinsser, "don't let's get this thing out of hand."

The doctor came back. "I think he'll make it."

"Really?"

"Not really. Nothing real about that character. But from all indications, he'll be O.K. Responded very strongly. What does he eat?"

"Pretty much the same as we do, I think."

"You think. You don't seem to know much about him."

"I don't. He only just got here. No—don't ask me where from," said Jack. "You'll have to ask him."

The doctor scratched his head. "He's out of this world. I can tell you that. Obviously adult, but every fracture but one is a green-stick break; kind of thing you see on a three-year-old. Transparent membranes over his— What are you laughing at?" he asked suddenly.

Jack had started easily, with a chuckle, but it got out of control. He roared.

Zinsser said, "Jack! Cut it out. This is a hosp—"

Jack shoved his hand away. "I got to," he said helplessly and went off on another peal.

"You've got to what?"

"Laugh," said Jack, gasping. He sobered, he more than sobered. "It has to be funny, Harry. I won't let it be anything else."

"What the devil do you—"

"Look, Harry. We assumed a lot about Mewhu, his culture, his technology, his origin. We'll never know anything about it!"

"Why? You mean he won't tell us?"

"He won't tell us. I'm wrong. He'll tell us plenty. But it won't do any good. Here's what I mean. Because he's our size, because he obviously arrived in a space ship, because he brought a gadget or two that's obviously the product of a highly advanced civilization, we believe that *he* produced the civilization, that he's a superior individual in his own place."

"Well, he must be."

"He must be? Harry, did Molly invent the automobile?"

"No, but—"

"But she drove one through the back of the garage."

Light began to dawn on Zinsser's moon face. "You mean—"

"It all fits! Remember when Mewhu figured out how to carry that heavy trap door of mine on the jet stick, and then left the problem half-finished? Remember his fascination with Molly's yo-yo? What about that peculiar rapport he has with Molly? Doesn't that begin to look reasonable? Look at Iris's reaction to him—almost maternal, though she didn't know why."

"The poor little fellow," breathed Zinsser. "I wonder if he thought he was home when he landed?"

"Poor little fellow—sure," said Jack, and began to laugh again. "Can Molly tell you how an internal combustion engine works? Can she explain laminar flow on an airfoil?" He shook his head. "You wait and see. Mewhu will be able to tell us the equivalent of Molly's 'I rode in the car with Daddy and we went sixty miles an hour.' "

"But how did he get here?"

"How did Molly get through the back of my garage?"

The doctor shrugged his shoulders helplessly. "His biological reactions do look like those of a child—and if if he is a child, then his rate of tissue restoration will be high, and I'll guarantee he'll live."

Zinsser groaned. "Much good will it do us—and him, poor kid. With a kid's faith in any intelligent adult, he's probably been sure we'd get him home somehow. Well, we haven't got what it takes, and won't have for a long, long time. We don't even know enough to start duplicating that jet of his—and that was just a little kid's toy on his world." ∎

THE WITCHES OF KARRES

James H. Schmitz

I.

It was around the Hub of the evening on the planet of Porlumma that Captain Pausert, commercial traveler from the Republic of Nikkeldepain, met the first of the witches of Karres.

It was just plain fate, so far as he could see.

He was feeling pretty good as he left a high-priced bar on a cobbly street near the spaceport, with the intention of returning straight to his ship. There hadn't been an argument, exactly. But someone grinned broadly, as usual, when the captain pronounced the name of his native system; and the captain had pointed out then, with considerable wit, how much more ridiculous it was to call a planet Porlumma, for instance, than to call it Nikkeldepain.

He proceeded to collect a gradually increasing number of pained stares by a detailed comparison of the varied, interesting and occasionally brilliant role Nikkeldepain had played in history with Porlumma's obviously dull and dumpy status as a sixth-rate Empire outpost.

In conclusion, he admitted frankly that he wouldn't care to be found dead on Porlumma.

Somebody muttered loudly in Imperial Universum that in that case it might be better if he didn't hang around Porlumma too long. But the captain only smiled politely, paid for his two drinks and left.

There was no point in getting into a rhubarb on one of these border planets. Their citizens still had an innocent notion that they ought to act like frontiersmen—but then the Law always showed up at once.

He felt pretty good. Up to the last four months of his young life, he had never looked on himself as being particularly patriotic. But compared to most of the Empire's worlds, Nikkeldepain was downright attractive in its stuffy ways. Besides, he was returning there solvent—would they ever be surprised!

And awaiting him, fondly and eagerly, was Illyla, the Miss Onswud, fair daughter of the mighty Councilor Onswud, and the captain's secretly affianced for almost a year. She alone had believed in him!

The captain smiled and checked at a dark cross-street to get his bearings on the spaceport beacon. Less than half a mile away—He set off again. In about six hours, he'd be beyond the Empire's space borders and headed straight for Illyla.

Yes, she alone had believed! After the prompt collapse of the captain's first commercial venture—a miffel-fur farm, largely on capital borrowed from Councilor Onswud—the future had looked very black. It had even included a probable ten-year stretch of penal servitude for "willful and negligent abuse of intrusted monies." The laws of Nikkeldepain were rough on debtors.

"But you've always been looking for someone to take out the old *Venture* and get her back into trade!" Illyla reminded her father tearfully.

"Hm-m-m, yes! But it's in the blood, my dear! His great-uncle Threbus went the same way! It would be far better to let the law take its course," Councilor Onswud said, glaring at Pausert who remained sulkily silent. He had *tried* to explain that the mysterious epidemic which suddenly wiped out most of the stock of miffels wasn't his fault. In fact, he more than suspected the tricky hand of young Councilor Rapport who had been wagging futilely around Illyla for the last couple of years!

"The *Venture*, now—!" Councilor Onswud mused, stroking his long, craggy chin. "Pausert can handle a ship, at least," he admitted.

That was how it happened. Were they ever going to be surprised! For even the captain realized that Councilor Onswud was unloading all the dead fish that had gathered the dust of his warehouses for the past fifty years on him and the *Venture*, in a last, faint hope of getting *some* return on those half-forgotten investments. A value of eighty-two thousand maels was placed on the cargo; but if he'd brought even three-quarters of it back in cash, all would have been well.

Instead—well, it started with that lucky bet on a legal point with an Imperial Official at the Imperial capitol itself. Then came a six-hour race fairly won against a small, fast private yacht—the old *Venture 7333* had been a pirate-chaser in the last century and could still produce twice as much speed as her looks suggested. From there on, the captain was socially accepted as a sporting man and was in on a long string of jovial parties and meets.

Jovial and profitable—the wealthier Imperials just couldn't resist a gamble and the penalty he always insisted on was that they had to buy!

He got rid of the stuff right and left! Inside of twelve weeks, nothing remained of the original cargo except two score bundles of expensively-built but useless tinklewood fishing poles and one dozen gross bales of useful but unattractive all-weather cloaks. Even on a bet, nobody would take them! But the captain had a strong hunch those items had been hopefully added to the cargo from his own stocks by Councilor Rapport; so his failure to sell them didn't break his heart.

He was a neat twenty percent net ahead, at that point—

And finally came this last-minute rush delivery of medical supplies to Porlumma on the return route. That haul alone would have repaid the miffel-farm losses three times over!

The captain grinned broadly into the darkness. Yes, they'd be surprised—but just where was he now?

He checked again in the narrow street, searching for the portbeacon in the sky. There it was—off to the left and a little behind him. He'd got turned around somehow!

He set off carefully down an excessively dark little alley. It was one of those towns where everybody locked their front doors at night and retired to lit-up, inclosed courtyards at the backs of the houses. There were voices and the rattling of dishes nearby, and occasional whoops of laughter and singing all around him; but it was all beyond high walls which let little or no light into the alley.

It ended abruptly in a cross-alley and another wall. After a moment's debate, the captain turned to his left again. Light spilled out on his new route, a few hundred yards ahead, where a courtyard was opened on the alley. From it, as he approached, came the sound of doors being violently slammed, and then a sudden, loud mingling of voices.

"Yeeee-eep!" shrilled a high, childish voice. It could have been mortal agony, terror, or even hysterical laughter. The captain broke into an apprehensive trot.

"Yes, I see you up there!" a man shouted excitedly in Universum. "I caught you now—you get down from those boxes! I'll skin you alive! Fifty-two customers sick of the stomach ache—YOW!"

The last exclamation was accompanied by a sound as of a small, loosely-built wooden house collapsing, and was followed by a succession of squeals and an angry bellowing, in which the only distinguishable words were: " . . . threw the boxes on me!" Then more sounds of splintering wood. "Hey!" yelled the captain indignantly from the corner of the alley.

All action ceased. The narrow courtyard, brightly illuminated under its single overhead bulb, was half covered with a tumbled litter of what appeared to be empty wooden boxes. Standing with his foot temporarily caught in one of them was a very large, fat man dressed all in white and waving a stick. Momentarily cornered between the wall and two of the boxes, over one of which she was trying to climb, was a smallish, fair-haired girl dressed in a smock of some kind, which was also white. She might be about fourteen, the captain thought—a helpless kid, anyway.

"What *you* want?" grunted the fat man, pointing the stick with some dignity at the captain.

"Lay off the kid!" rumbled the captain, edging into the courtyard.

"Mind your own business!" shouted the fat man, waving his stick like a club. "I'll take care of her! She—"

"I never did!" squealed the girl. She burst into tears.

"Try it, Fat and Ugly!" the captain warned. "I'll ram the stick down your throat!"

He was very close now. With a sound of grunting exasperation, the fat man pulled his foot free of the box, wheeled suddenly and brought the end of the stick down on the top of the captain's cap. The captain hit him furiously in the middle of the stomach.

There was a short flurry of activity, somewhat hampered by shattering boxes everywhere. Then the captain stood up, scowling and breathing hard. The fat man remained sitting on the ground, gasping about " . . . the law!"

Somewhat to his surprise, the captain discovered the girl standing just behind him. She caught his eye and smiled.

"My name's Maleen," she offered. She pointed at the fat man. "Is he hurt bad?"

"Huh—no!" painted the captain. "But maybe we'd better—"

It was too late! A loud, self-assured voice became audible now at the opening to the alley:

"Here, here, here, here, here!" it said in a reproachful, situation-under-control tone that always seemed the same to the captain, on whatever world and in which ever language he heard it.

"What's all this about!" it inquired rhetorically.

"You'll have to come along!" it replied.

Police Court on Porlumma appeared to be a business conducted on a very efficient, round-the-clock basis. They were the next case up.

Nikkeldepain was an odd name, wasn't it, the judge smiled. He then listened attentively to the various charges, countercharges, and denials.

Bruth the Baker was charged with having struck a citizen of a foreign government on the head with a potentially lethal instrument—produced in evidence. Said citizen had admittedly attempted to interfere as Bruth was attempting to punish his slave Maleen—also produced in evidence—whom he suspected of having added something to a batch of cakes she was working on that afternoon, resulting in illness and complaints from fifty-two of Bruth's customers.

Said foreign citizen had also used insulting language—the captain admitted under pressure to "Fat and Ugly."

Some provocation could be conceded for the action taken by Bruth, but not enough. Bruth paled.

Captain Pausert, of the Republic of Nikkeldepain—everybody but the prisoners smiled this time—was charged (a) with said attempted interference, (b) with said insult, (c) with having frequently and severely struck Bruth the Baker in the course of the subsequent dispute.

The blow on the head was conceded to have provided a provocation for charge (c)—but not enough.

Nobody seemed to be charging the slave Maleen with anything. The judge only looked at her curiously, and shook his head.

James H. Schmitz

"As the Court considers this regrettable incident," he remarked, "it looks like two years for you, Bruth; and about three for you, captain. Too bad!"

The captain had an awful sinking feeling. He had seen something and heard a lot of Imperial court methods in the fringe systems. He could probably get out of this three-year rap; but it would be expensive.

He realized that the judge was studying him reflectively.

"The Court wishes to acknowledge," the judge continued, "that the captain's chargeable actions were due largely to a natural feeling of human sympathy for the predicament of the slave Maleen. The Court, therefore, would suggest a settlement as follows—subsequent to which all charges could be dropped:

"That Bruth the Baker resell Maleen of Karres—with whose services he appears to be dissatisfied—for a reasonable sum to Captain Pausert of the Republic of Nikkeldepain."

Bruth the Baker heaved a gusty sigh of relief. But the captain hesitated. The buying of human slaves by private citizens was a very serious offense in Nikkeldepain! Still, he didn't have to make a record of it. If they weren't going to soak him too much—

At just the right moment, Maleen of Karres introduced a barely audible, forlorn, sniffling sound.

"How much are you asking for the kid?" the captain inquired, looking without friendliness at his recent antagonist. A day was coming when he would think less severely of Bruth; but it hadn't come yet.

Bruth scowled back but replied with a certain eagerness: "A hundred and fifty m—" A policeman standing behind him poked him sharply in the side. Bruth shut up.

"Seven hundred maels," the judge said smoothly. "There'll be Court charges, and a fee for recording the transaction—" He appeared to make a swift calculation. "Fifteen hundred and forty-two maels—" He turned to a clerk: "You've looked him up?"

The clerk nodded. "He's right!"

"And we'll take your check," the judge concluded. He gave the captain a friendly smile. "Next case."

The captain felt a little bewildered.

There was something peculiar about this! He was getting out of it much too cheaply. Since the Empire had quit its wars of expansion, young slaves in good health were a high-priced article. Furthermore, he was practically positive that Bruth the Baker had been willing to sell for a tenth of what the captain actually had to pay!

Well, he wouldn't complain. Rapidly, he signed, sealed and thumbprinted various papers shoved at him by a helpful clerk; and made out a check.

"I guess," he told Maleen of Karres, "we'd better get along to the ship."

And now what was he going to do with the kid, he pondered, padding along the unlighted streets with his slave trotting quietly behind him. If he showed up with a pretty girl-slave in Nikkeldepain, even a small one, various good friends there would toss him into ten years or so of penal servitude—immediately after Illyla had personally collected his scalp. They were a moral lot.

Karres—?

"How far off is Karres, Maleen?" he asked into the dark.

"It takes about two weeks," Maleen said tearfully.

Two weeks! The captain's heart sank again.

"What are you blubbering about?" he inquired uncomfortably.

Maleen choked, sniffed, and began sobbing openly.

"I have two little sisters!" she cried.

"Well, well," the captain said encouragingly. "That's nice—you'll be seeing them again soon. I'm taking you home, you know!"

Great Patham—now he'd said it! But after all—

But this piece of good news seemed to be having the wrong effect on his slave: Her sobbing grew much more violent.

"No, I won't," she wailed. "They're here!"

"Huh?" said the captain. He stopped short. "Where?"

"And the people they're with are mean to them, too!" wept Maleen.

The captain's heart dropped clean through his boots. Standing there in the dark, he helplessly watched it coming:

"You could buy them awfully cheap!" she said.

II.

In times of stress, the young life of Karres appeared to take to the heights. It might be a mountainous place.

The Leewit sat on the top shelf of the back wall of the crockery and antiques store, strategically flanked by two expensive-looking vases. She was a doll-sized edition of Maleen; but her eyes were cold and gray instead of blue and tearful. About five or six, the captain vaguely estimated. He wasn't very good at estimating them around that age.

"Good evening," he said, as he came in through the door. The Crockery and Antiques Shop had been easy to find. Like Bruth the Baker's, it was the one spot in the neighborhood that was all lit up.

"Good evening, sir!" said what was presumably the store owner, without looking around. He sat with his back to the door, in a chair approximately at the center of the store and facing the Leewit at a distance of about twenty feet.

" . . . and there you can stay without food or drink till the Holy Man comes in the morning!" he continued immediately, in the taut voice of a man who has gone through hysteria and is sane again. The captain realized he was addressing the Leewit.

"Your other Holy Man didn't stay very long!" the diminutive creature piped, also ignoring the captain. Apparently, she had not yet discovered Maleen behind him.

"This is a stronger denomination—much stronger!" the store owner replied, in a shaking voice but with a sort of relish. *"He'll* exorcise you, all right, little demon—you'll whistle no buttons off him! Your time is up! Go on and whistle all you want! Bust every vase in the place—"

The Leewit blinked her gray eyes thoughtfully at him.

"Might!" she said.

"But if you try to climb down from there," the store owner went on, on a rising note, "I'll chop you into bits—into little, little bits!"

He raised his arm as he spoke and weakly brandished what the captain recognized with a start of horror as a highly ornamented but probably still useful antique battle-ax.

"Ha!" said the Leewit.

"Beg your pardon, sir!" the captain siad, clearing his throat.

"Good evening, sir!" the store owner repeated, without looking around. "What can I do for you?"

"I came to inquire," the captain said hesitantly, "about that child."

The store owner shifted about in his chair and squinted at the captain with red-rimmed eyes.

"You're not a Holy Man!" he said.

"Hello, Maleen!" the Leewit said suddenly. "That him?"

"We've come to buy you," Maleen said. "Shut up!"

"Good!" said the Leewit.

"Buy it? Are you mocking me, sir?" the store owner inquired.

"Shut up, Moonell!" A thin, dark, determined-looking woman had appeared in the doorway that led through the back wall of the store. She moved out a step under the shelves; and the Leewit leaned down from the top shelf and hissed. The woman moved hurriedly back into the doorway.

"Maybe he means it," she said in a more subdued voice.

"I can't sell to a citizen of the Empire," the store owner said defeatedly.

"I'm not a citizen," the captain said shortly. This time, he wasn't going to name it.

"No, he's from Nikkel—" Maleen began.

"Shut up, Maleen!" the captain said helplessly in turn.

"I never heard of Nikkel," the store owner muttered doubtfully.

"Maleen!" the woman called shrilly. "That's the name of one of the others—Bruth the Baker got her. He means it, all right! He's buying them—"

"A hundred and fifty maels!" the captain said craftily, remembering Bruth the Baker. "In cash!"

The store owner looked dazed.

"Not enough, Moonell!" the woman called. "Look at all it's broken! Five hundred maels!"

There was a sound then, so thin the captain could hardly hear it. It pierced at his eardrums like two jabs of a delicate needle. To right and left of him, two highly glazed little jugs went *"Clink-clink!,"* showed a sudden veining of cracks, and collapsed.

A brief silence settled on the store. And now that he looked around more closely, the captain could spot here and there other little piles of shattered crockery—and places where similar ruins apparently had been swept up, leaving only traces of colored dust.

The store owner laid the ax down carefully beside his chair, stood up, swaying a little, and came toward the captain.

"You offered me a hundred and fifty maels!" he said rapidly as he approached. "I accept it here, now, see—before witnesses!" He grabbed the captain's right hand in both of his and pumped it up and down vigorously. "Sold!" he yelled.

Then he wheeled around in a leap and pointed a shaking hand at the Leewit.

"And NOW," he howled, "break something! Break anything! You're his! I'll sue him for every mael he ever made and ever will!"

"Oh, do come help me down, Maleen!" the Leewit pleaded prettily.

For a change, the store of Wansing, the jeweler, was dimly lit and very quiet. It was a sleek, fashionable place in a fashionable shopping block near the spaceport. The front door was unlocked, and Wansing was in.

The three of them entered quietly, and the door sighed quietly shut behind them. Beyond a great crystal display-counter, Wansing was moving about among a number of opened shelves, talking softly to himself. Under the crystal of the counter, and in close-packed rows on the satin-covered shelves, reposed a many-colored gleaming and glittering and shining. Wansing was no piker.

"Good evening, sir!" the captain said across the counter.

"It's morning!" the Leewit remarked from the other side of Maleen.

"Maleen!" said the captain.

"We're keeping out of this," Maleen said to the Leewit.

"All right," said the Leewit.

Wansing had come around jerkily at the captain's greeting, but had made no other move. Like all the slave owners the captain had met on Porlumma so far, Wansing seemed unhappy. Otherwise, he was a large, dark, sleek-looking man with jewels in his ears and a smell of expensive oils and perfumes about him.

"This place is under constant visual guard, of course!" he told the captain gently. "Nothing could possibly happen to me here. Why am I so frightened?"

"Not of me, I'm sure!" the captain said with an uncomfortable attempt at geniality. "I'm glad your store's still open," he went on briskly. "I'm here on business—"

"Oh, yes, it's still open, of course," Wansing said. He gave the captain a slow

James H. Schmitz

smile and turned back to his shelves. "I'm making inventory, that's why! I've been making inventory since early yesterday morning. I've counted them all seven times—"

"You're very thorough," the captain said.

"Very, very thorough!" Wansing nodded to the shelves. "The last time I found I had made a million maels. But twice before that, I had lost approximately the same amount. I shall have to count them again, I suppose!" He closed a shelf softly. "I'm sure I counted those before. But they move about constantly. Constantly! It's horrible."

"You've got a slave here called Goth," the captain said, driving to the point.

"Yes, I have!" Wansing said, nodding. "And I'm sure she understands by now I meant no harm! I do, at any rate. It was perhaps a little—but I'm sure she understands now, or will soon!"

"Where is she?" the captain inquired, a trifle uneasily.

"In her room perhaps," Wansing suggested. "It's not so bad when she's there in her room with the door closed. But often she sits in the dark and looks at you as you go past—" He opened another drawer, and closed it quietly again. "Yes, they do move!" he whispered, as if confirming an earlier suspicion. "Constantly—"

"Look, Wansing," the captain said in a loud, firm voice. "I'm not a citizen of the Empire. I want to buy this Goth! I'll pay you a hundred and fifty maels, cash."

Wansing turned around completely again and looked at the captain. "Oh, you do?" he said. "You're not a citizen?" He walked a few steps to the side of the counter, sat down at a small desk and turned a light on over it. Then he put his face in his hands for a moment.

"I'm a wealthy man," he muttered. "An influential man! The name of Wansing counts for a great deal on Porlumma. When the Empire suggests you buy, you buy, of course—but it need not have been I who bought her! I thought she would be useful in the business—and then, even I could not sell her again with the Empire. She had been here for a week!"

He looked up at the captain and smiled. "One hundred and fifty maels!" he said. "Sold! There are records to be made out—" He reached into a drawer and took out some printed forms. He began to write rapidly. The captain produced identifications.

Maleen said suddenly: "Goth?"

"Right here," a voice murmured. Wansing's hand jerked sharply, but he did not look up. He kept on writing.

Something small and lean and bonelessly supple, dressed in a dark jacket and leggings, came across the thick carpets of Wansing's store and stood behind the captain. This one might be about nine or ten.

"I'll take your check, captain!" Wansing said politely. "You must be an honest man. Besides, I want to frame it."

"And now," the captain heard himself say in the remote voice of one who moves through a strange dream, "I suppose we could go to the ship."

The sky was gray and cloudy; and the streets were lightening. Goth, he noticed, didn't resemble her sisters. She had brown hair cut short a few inches below her ears, and brown eyes with long, black lashes. Her nose was short and her chin was pointed. She made him think of some thin, carnivorous creature, like a weasel.

She looked up at him briefly, grinned, and said: "Thanks!"

"What was wrong with *him?*" chirped the Leewit, walking backwards for a last view of Wansing's store.

"Tough crook," muttered Goth. The Leewit giggled.

"You promoted this just dandy, Maleen!" she stated next.

"Shut up," said Maleen.

"All right," said the Leewit. She glanced up at the captain's face. "You been fighting!" she said virtuously. "Did you win?"

"Of course, the captain won!" said Maleen.

"Good for you!" said the Leewit.

"What about the take-off?" Goth asked the captain. She seemed a little worried.

"Nothing to it!" the captain said stoutly, hardly bothering to wonder how she'd guessed the take-off was the one operation on which he and the old *Venture* consistently failed to co-operate.

"No," said Goth, "I meant when?"

"Right now," said the captain. "They've already cleared us. We'll get the sign any second."

"Good," said Goth. She walked off slowly down the hall toward the back of the ship.

The take-off was pretty bad, but the *Venture* made it again. Half an hour later, with Porlumma dwindling safely behind them, the captain switched to automatic and climbed out of his chair. After considerable experimentation, he got the electric butler adjusted to four breakfasts, hot, with coffee. It was accomplished with a great deal of advice and attempted assistance from the Leewit, rather less from Maleen, and no comments from Goth.

"Everything will be coming along in a few minutes now!" he announced. After wards, it struck him there had been a quality of grisly prophecy about the statement.

"If you'd listened to me," said the Leewit, "we'd have been done eating a quarter of an hour ago!" She was perspiring but triumphant—she had been right all along.

"Say, Maleen," she said suddenly, "you promoting again?"

Premoting? The captain looked at Maleen. She seemed pale and troubled.

"Spacesick?" he suggested. "I've got some pills—"

"No, she's premoting," the Leewit said scowling. "What's up, Maleen?"

"Shut up," said Goth.

"All right," said the Leewit. She was silent a moment, and then began to wriggle. "Maybe we'd better—"

"Shut up," said Maleen.

"It's all ready," said Goth.

"What's all ready?" asked the captain.

"All right," said the Leewit. She looked at the captain. "Nothing," she said.

He looked at them then, and they looked at him—one set each of gray eyes, and brown, and blue. They were all sitting around the control room floor in a circle, the fifth side of which was occupied by the electric butler.

What peculiar little waifs, the captain thought. He hadn't perhaps really realized until now just how very peculiar. They were still staring at him.

"Well, well!" he said heartily. "So Maleen 'premotes' and gives people stomach aches."

Maleen smiled dimly and smoothed back her yellow hair.

"They just thought they were getting them," she murmured.

"Mass history," explained the Leewit, offhandedly.

"Hysteria," said Goth. "The Imperials get their hair up about us every so often."

"I noticed that," the captain nodded. "And little Leewit here—she whistles and busts things."

"It's *the* Leewit," the Leewit said, frowning.

"Oh, I see," said the captain. "Like *the* captain, eh?"

"That's right," said the Leewit. She smiled.

"And what does little Goth do?" the captain addressed the third witch.

Little Goth appeared pained. Maleen answered for her.

"Goth teleports mostly," she said.

"Oh, she does?" said the captain. "I've heard about that trick, too," he added lamely.

"Just small stuff really!" Goth said abruptly. She reached into the top of her jacket and pulled out a cloth-wrapped bundle the size of the captain's two fists. The four ends of the cloth were knotted together. Goth undid the knot. "Like this," she said and poured out the contents on the rug between them. There was a sound like a big bagful of marbles being spilled.

"Great Patham!" the captain swore, staring down at what was a cool quarter-million in jewel stones, or he was still a miffel-farmer.

"Good gosh," said the Leewit, bouncing to her feet. "Maleen, we better get at it right away!"

The two blondes darted from the room. The captain hardly noticed their going. He was staring at Goth.

"Child," he said, "don't you realize they hang you without trial on places like Porlumma, if you're caught with stolen goods?"

"We're not on Porlumma," said Goth. She looked slightly annoyed. "They're for you. You spent money on us, didn't you?"

"Not that kind of money," said the captain. "If Wansing noticed—they're Wansing's, I suppose?"

"Sure!" said Goth. "Pulled them in just before take-off!"

"If he reported, there'll be police ships on our tail any—"

"Goth!" Maleen shrilled.

Goth's head came around and she rolled up on her feet in one motion. "Coming," she shouted. "Excuse me," she murmured to the captain. Then she, too, was out of the room.

But again, the captain scarcely noticed her departure. He had rushed to the control desk with a sudden awful certainty and switched on all screens.

There they were! Two sleek, black ships coming up fast from behind, and already almost in gun-range! They weren't regular police boats, the captain recognized, but auxiliary craft of the Empire's frontier fleets. He rammed the *Venture*'s drives full on. Immediately, red-and-black fire blossoms began to sprout in space behind him—then a finger of flame stabbed briefly past, not a hundred yards to the right of the ship.

But the communicator stayed dead. Porlumma preferred risking the sacrifice of Wansing's jewels to giving them a chance to surrender! To do the captain justice, his horror was due much more to the fate awaiting his three misguided charges than to the fact that he was going to share it.

He was putting the *Venture* through a wildly erratic and, he hoped, aim-destroying series of sideways hops and forward lunges with one hand, and trying to unlimber the turrets of the nova guns with the other, when suddenly—!

No, he decided at once, there was no use trying to understand it—There were just no more Empire ships around. The screens all blurred and darkened simultaneously; and, for a short while, a darkness went flowing and coiling lazily past the *Venture*. Light jumped out of it at him once, in a cold, ugly glare, and receded again in a twisting, unnatural fashion. The *Venture*'s drives seemed dead.

Then, just as suddenly, the old ship jerked, shivered, roared aggrievedly, and was hurling herself along on her own power again!

But Porlumma's sun was no longer in evidence. Stars gleamed and shifted distantly against the blackness of deep space all about. The patterns seemed familiar, but he wasn't a good enough navigator to be sure.

The captain stood up stiffly, feeling a heavy cloud. And at that moment, with a wild, hilarious clacking like a metallic hen, the electric butler delivered four breakfasts, hot, one after the other, right onto the center of the control room floor.

The first voice said distinctly: "Shall we just leave it on?"

A second voice, considerably more muffled, replied: "Yes, let's! You never know when you need it—"

The third voice, tucked somewhere in between them, said simply: *"Whew!"*

Peering about the dark room in bewilderment, the captain realized suddenly that the voices had come from the speaker of an intership communicator, leading to what had once been the *Venture*'s captain's cabin.

He listened; but only a dim murmuring came from it now, and then nothing at all. He started towards the hall, then returned and softly switched off the communicator. He went quietly down the hall until he came to the captain's cabin. Its door was closed.

He listened a moment, and opened it suddenly.

There was a trio of squeals:

"Oh, don't! You spoiled it!"

The captain stood motionless. Just one glimpse had been given him of what seemed to be a bundle of twisted black wires arranged loosely like the frame of a truncated cone on—or was it just above?—a table in the center of the cabin. Where the tip of the cone should have been burned a round, swirling, orange fire. About it, their faces reflecting its glow, stood the three witches.

Then the fire vanished; the wires collapsed. There was only ordinary light in the room. They were looking up at him variously—Maleen with smiling regret, the Leewit in frank annoyance, Goth with no expression at all.

"What out of Great Patham's Seventh Hell was that?" inquired the captain, his hair bristling slowly.

The Leewit looked at Goth; Goth looked at Maleen. Maleen said doubtfully: "We can just tell you its name—"

"That was the Sheewash Drive," said Goth.

"The what-drive?" asked the captain.

"Sheewash," repeated Maleen.

"The one you have to do it with yourself," the Leewit said helpfully.

"Shut up," said Maleen.

There was a long pause. The captain looked down at the handful of thin, black, twelve-inch wires scattered about the table top. He touched one of them. It was dead-cold.

"I see," he said. "I guess we're all going to have a long talk." Another pause. "Where are we now?"

"About three light-years down the way you were going," said Goth. "We only worked it thirty seconds."

"Twenty-eight!" corrected Maleen, with the authority of her years. "The Leewit was getting tired."

"I see," said Captain Pausert carefully. "Well, let's go have some breakfast."

III.

They ate with a silent voraciousness, dainty Maleen, the exquisite Leewit, supple Goth, all alike. The captain, long finished, watched them with amazement and—now at last—with something like awe.

"It's the Sheewash Drive," explained Maleen finally, catching his expression.

"Takes it out of you!" said Goth.

The Leewit grunted affirmatively and stuffed on.

"Can't do too much of it," said Maleen. "Or too often. It kills you sure!"

"What," said the captain, "*is* the Sheewash Drive?"

They became reticent. People did it on Karres, said Maleen, when they had to go somewhere else fast. Everybody knew how there.

"But of course," she added, "we're pretty young to do it right!"

"We did it pretty good!" the Leewit contradicted positively. She seemed to be finished at last.

"But how?" said the captain.

Reticence thickened almost visibly. If you couldn't do it, said Maleen, you couldn't understand it either.

He gave it up, for the time being.

"I guess I'll have to take you home next," he said; and they agreed.

Karres, it developed, was in the Iverdahl System. He couldn't find any planet of that designation listed in his maps of the area, but that meant nothing. The maps were old and often inaccurate, and local names changed a lot.

Barring the use of weird and deadly miracle-drives, that detour was going to cost him almost a month in time—and a good chunk of his profits in power used up. The jewels Goth had illegally teleported must, of course, be returned to their owner, he explained. He'd intended to look severely at the culprit at that point; but she'd meant well, after all! They were extremely peculiar children, but still children—they couldn't really understand.

He would stop off en route to Karres at an Empire planet with banking facilities to take care of that matter, the captain added. A planet far enough off so the police wouldn't be likely to take any particular interest in the *Venture*.

A dead silence greeted this schedule. It appeared that the representative of Karres did not think much of his logic.

"Well," Maleen sighed at last, "we'll see you get your money back some other way then!"

The junior witches nodded coldly.

"How did you three happen to get into this fix?" the captain inquired, with the intention of changing the subject.

They'd left Karres together on a jaunt of their own, they explained. No, they hadn't run away—he got the impression that such trips were standard procedure for juveniles in that place. They were on another planet, a civilized one but beyond the borders and law of Empire, when the town they were in was raided by a small fleet of slavers. They were taken along with most of the local youngsters.

"It's a wonder," he said reflectively, "you didn't take over the ship."

"Oh, brother!" exclaimed the Leewit.

"Not that ship!" said Goth.

"That was an Imperial Slaver!" Maleen informed him. "You behave yourself every second on those crates."

Just the same, the captain thought as he settled himself to rest in the control room on a couch he had set up there, it was no longer surprising that the Empire wanted no young slaves from Karres to be transported into the interior! Oddest sort of children— But he ought to be able to get his expenses paid by their relatives. Something very profitable might even be made of this deal—

Have to watch the record-entries though! Nikkeldepain's laws were explicit about the penalties invoked by anything resembling the purchase and sale of slaves.

He'd thoughtfully left the intership communicator adjusted so he could listen in on their conversation in the captain's cabin. However, there had been nothing for some time beyond frequent bursts of childish giggling. Then came a succession of piercing shrieks from the Leewit. It appeared she was being forcibly washed behind the ears by Maleen and obliged to brush her teeth, in preparation for bedtime.

It had been agreed that he was not to enter the cabin, because—for reasons not given—they couldn't keep the Sheewash Drive on in his presence; and they wanted to have it ready, in case of an emergency. Piracy was rife beyond the Imperial borders, and the *Venture* would keep beyond the border for a good part of the trip, to avoid the more pressing danger of police pursuit instigated by Porlumma. The captain had explained the potentialities of the nova guns the *Venture* boasted, or tried to. Possibly, they hadn't understood. At any rate, they seemed unimpressed.

The Sheewash Drive! Boy, he thought in sudden excitement, if he could just get the principles of that. Maybe he would!

He raised his head suddenly. The Leewit's voice had lifted clearly over the communicator:

" . . . not such a bad old dope!" the childish treble remarked.

The captain blinked indignantly.

"He's not so old," Maleen's soft voice returned. "And he's certainly no dope!"

He smiled. Good kid, Maleen.

"Yeah, yeah!" squeaked the Leewit offensively. "Maleen's sweet onthuulp!"

A vague commotion continued for a while, indicating, he hoped, that someone he could mention was being smothered under a pillow.

He drifted off to sleep before it was settled.

If you didn't happen to be thinking of what they'd done, they seemed more or less like normal children. Right from the start, they displayed a flattering interest in the captain and his background; and he told them all all about everything and everybody in Nikkeldepain. Finally, he even showed them his treasured pocket-sized picture of

Illyla—the one with which he'd held many cozy conversations during the earlier part of his trip.

Almost at once, though, he realized that was a mistake. They studied it intently in silence, their heads crowded close together.

"Oh, brother!" the Leewit whispered then, with entirely the wrong kind of inflection.

"Just what did you mean by that?" the captain inquired coldly.

"Sweet!" murmured Goth. But it was the way she closed her eyes briefly, as though gripped by a light spasm of nausea.

"Shut up, Goth!" Maleen said sharply. "I think she's very swee . . . I mean, she looks very nice!" she told the captain.

The captain was disgruntled. Silently, he retrieved the maligned Illyla and returned her to his breast pocket. Silently, he went off and left them standing there.

But afterwards, in private, he took it out again and studied it worriedly. His Illyla! He shifted the picture back and forth under the light. It wasn't really a very good picture of her, he decided. It had been bungled! From certain angles, one might even say that Illyla did look the least bit insipid.

What was he thinking, he thought, shocked.

He unlimbered the nova gun turrets next and got in a little firing practice. They had been sealed when he took over the *Venture* and weren't supposed to be used, except in absolute emergencies. They were somewhat uncertain weapons, though very effective, and Nikkeldepain had turned to safer forms of armament many decades ago. But on the third day out from Nikkeldepain, the captain made a brief notation in his log:

"Attacked by two pirate craft. Unsealed nova guns. Destroyed one attacker; survivor fled—"

He was rather pleased by that crisp, hard-bitten description of desperate space-adventure, and enjoyed rereading it occasionally. It wasn't true, though. He had put in an interesting four hours at the time pursuing and annihilating large, craggy chunks of substance of a meteorite-cloud he found the *Venture* plowing through. Those nova guns were fascinating stuff! You'd sight the turrets on something; and so long as it didn't move after that, it was all right. If it did move, it got it—unless you relented and deflected the turrets first. They were just the thing for arresting a pirate in midspace.

The *Venture* dipped back into the Empire's borders four days later and headed for the capitol of the local province. Police ships challenged them twice on the way in; and the captain found considerable comfort in the awareness that his passengers foregathered silently in their cabin on these occasions. They didn't tell him they were set to use the Sheewash Drive—somehow it had never been mentioned since that first day; but he knew the queer orange fire was circling over its skimpy framework of twisted wires there and ready to act.

James H. Schmitz

However, the space police waved him on, satisfied with routine identification. Apparently, the *Venture* had not become generally known as a criminal ship, to date.

Maleen accompanied him to the banking institution that was to return Wansing's property to Porlumma. Her sisters, at the captain's definite request, remained on the ship.

The transaction itself went off without a visible hitch. The jewels would reach their destination in Porlumma within a month. But he had to take out a staggering sum in insurance—"Piracy, thieves!" smiled the clerk. "Even summary capital punishment won't keep the rats down." And, of course, he had to register name, ship, home planet, and so on. But since they already had all that information in Porlumma, he gave it without hesitation.

On the way back to the spaceport, he sent off a sealed message by radio-relay to the bereaved jeweler, informing him of the action taken, and regretting the misunderstanding.

He felt a little better after that, though the insurance payment had been a severe blow! If he didn't manage to work out a decent profit on Karres somehow, the losses on the miffel farm would hardly be covered now.

Then he noticed that Maleen was getting uneasy.

"We'd better hurry!" was all she would say, however. Her face grew pale.

The captain understood. She was having another premonition! The hitch to this premoting business was, apparently, that when something was brewing you were informed of the bare fact but had to guess at most of the details. They grabbed an aircab and raced back to the spaceport.

They had just been cleared there when he spotted a small group of uniformed men coming along the dock on the double. They stopped short and then scattered, as the *Venture* lurched drunkenly sideways into the air. Everyone else in sight was scattering, too.

That was a very bad take-off—one of the captain's worst! Once afloat, however, he ran the ship promptly into the nightside of the planet and turned her nose towards the border. The old pirate-chaser had plenty of speed when you gave her the reins; and throughout the entire next sleep-period, he let her use it all.

The Sheewash Drive was not required that time.

Next day, he had a lengthy private talk with Goth on the Golden Rule and the Law, with particular reference to individual property rights. If Councilor Onswud had been monitoring the sentiments expressed by the captain, he could not have failed to rumble surprised approval. The delinquent herself listened impassively; but the captain fancied she showed distinct signs of being rather impressed by his earnestness.

It was two days after that—well beyond the borders again—when they were obliged to make an unscheduled stop at a mining moon. For the captain discovered he had already miscalculated the extent to which the prolonged run on overdrive after leaving the capitol was going to deplete the *Venture*'s reserves. They would have to juice up—

A large, extremely handsome Sirian freighter lay beside them at the Moon station. It was half a battlecraft really, since it dealt regularly beyond the borders. They had to wait while it was being serviced; and it took a long time. The Sirians turned out to be as unpleasant as their ship was good-looking—a snooty, conceited, hairy lot who talked only their own dialect and pretended to be unfamiliar with Imperial Universum.

The captain found himself getting irked by their bad manners—particularly when he discovered they were laughing over his argument with the service superintendent about the cost of repowering the *Venture*.

"You're out in deep space, captain!" said the superintendent. "And you haven't juice enough left even to travel back to the Border. You can't expect Imperial prices here!"

"It's not what you charged *them!*" The captain angrily jerked his thumb at the Sirian.

"Regular customers!" the superintendent shrugged. "You start coming by here every three months like they do, and we can make an arrangement with you, too."

It was outrageous—it actually put the *Venture* back in the red! But there was no help for it.

Nor did it improve the captain's temper when he muffed the takeoff once more—and then had to watch the Sirian floating into space, as sedately as a swan, a little behind him!

An hour later, as he sat glumly before the controls, debating the chance of recouping his losses before returning to Nikkeldepain, Maleen and the Leewit hurriedly entered the room. They did something to a port screen.

"They sure are!" the Leewit exclaimed. She seemed childishly pleased.

"Are what?" the captain inquired absently.

"Following us," said Maleen. She did not sound pleased. "It's that Sirian ship, Captain Pausert—"

The captain stared bewilderedly at the screen. There *was* a ship in focus there. It was quite obviously the Sirian and, just as obviously, it was following them.

"What do they want?" he wondered. "They're stinkers but they're not pirates. Even if they were, they wouldn't spend an hour running after a crate like the *Venture!*"

Maleen said nothing. The Leewit observed, "Oh, brother! Got their bow-turrets out now—better get those nova guns ready!"

"But it's all nonsense!" the captain said, flushing angrily. He turned suddenly toward the communicators. "What's that Empire general beam-length?"

".0044," said Maleen.

A roaring, abusive voice flooded the control room immediately. The one word

James H. Schmitz

understandable to the captain was *"Venture."* It was repeated frequently, sometimes as if it were a question.

"Sirian!" said the captain. "Can you understand them?" he asked Maleen.

She shook her head. "The Leewit can—"

The Leewit nodded, her gray eyes glistening.

"What are they saying?"

"They says you're for stopping," the Leewit translated rapidly, but apparently retaining much of the original sentence-structure. "They says you're for skinning alive . . . ha! They says you're for stopping right now and for only hanging. They says—"

Maleen scuttled from the control room. The Leewit banged the communicator with one small fist.

"Beak-Wock!" she shrieked. It sounded like that, anyway. The loud voice paused a moment.

"Beak-Wock?" it returned in an aggrieved, demanding roar.

"Beak-Wock!" the Leewit affirmed with apparent delight. She rattled off a string of similar-sounding syllables. She paused.

A howl of inarticulate wrath responded.

The captain, in a whirl of outraged emotions, was yelling at the Leewit to shut up, at the Sirian to go to Great Patham's Second Hell—the worst—and wrestling with the nova gun adjustors at the same time. He'd had about enough! He'd—

SSS-whoosh!

It was the Sheewash Drive.

"And where are we now?" the captain inquired, in a voice of unnatural calm.

"Same place, just about," said the Leewit. "Ship's still on the screen. Way back though—take them an hour again to catch up." She seemed disappointed; then brightened. "You got lots of time to get the guns ready!"

The captain didn't answer. He was marching down the hall toward the rear of the *Venture*. He passed the captain's cabin and noted the door was shut. He went on without pausing. He was mad clean through—he knew what had happened!

After all he'd told her, Goth had teleported again.

It was all there, in the storage. Items of half a pound in weight seemed to be as much as she could handle. But amazing quantities of stuff had met that one requirement—bottles filled with what might be perfume or liquor or dope, expensive-looking garments and cloths in a shining variety of colors, small boxes, odds, ends and, of course, jewelry!

He spent half an hour getting it loaded into a steel space crate. He wheeled the crate into the rear lock, sealed the inside lock and pulled the switch that activated the automatic launching device.

The Witches of Karres

The outside lock clicked shut. He talked back to the control room. The Leewit was still in charge, fiddling with the communicators.

"I could try a whistle over them," she suggested, glancing up. She added: "But they'd bust somewheres, sure."

"Get them on again!" the captain said.

"Yes, sir," said the Leewit, surprised.

The roaring voice came back faintly.

"SHUT UP!" the captain shouted in Imperial Universum.

The voice shut up.

"Tell them they can pick up their stuff—it's been dumped out in a crate!" the captain told the Leewit. "Tell them I'm proceeding on my course. Tell them if they follow me one light-minute beyond that crate, I'll come back for them, shoot their front end off, shoot their rear end off, and ram 'em in the middle."

"Yes, SIR!" the Leewit sparkled. They proceeded on their course.

Nobody followed.

"Now I want to speak to Goth," the captain announced. He was still at a high boil. "Privately," he added. "Back in the storage—"

Goth followed him expressionlessly into the storage. He closed the door to the hall. He'd broken off a two-foot length from the tip of one of Councilor Rapport's over-priced tinklewood fishing poles. It made a fair switch.

But Goth looked terribly small just now! He cleared his throat. He wished for a moment he were back on Nikkeldepain.

"I warned you," he said.

Goth didn't move. Between one second and the next, however, she seemed to grow remarkably. Her brown eyes focused on the captain's Adam's apple; her lip lifted at one side. A slightly hungry look came into her face.

"Wouldn't try that!" she murmured.

Mad again, the captain reached out quickly and got a handful of leathery cloth. There was a blur of motion, and what felt like a small explosion against his left kneecap. He grunted with anguished surprise and fell back on a bale of Councilor Rapport's all-weather cloaks. But he had retained his grip—Goth fell half on top of him, and that was still a favorable position. Then her head snaked around, her neck seemed to extend itself; and her teeth snapped his wrist.

Weasels don't let go—

"Didn't think he'd have the nerve!" Goth's voice came over the communicator. There was a note of grudging admiration in it. It seemed that she was inspecting her bruises.

All tangled up in the job of bandaging his freely bleeding wrist, the captain hoped she'd find a good plenty to count. His knee felt the size of a sofa pillow and throbbed like a piston engine.

James H. Schmitz

"The captain is a brave man," Maleen was saying reproachfully. "You should have known better—"

"He's not very *smart*, though!" the Leewit remarked suggestively.

There was a short silence.

"Is he? Goth? Eh?" the Leewit urged.

"Perhaps not very," said Goth.

"You two lay off him!" Maleen ordered. "Unless," she added meaningly, "you want to *swim* back to Karres—on the Egger Route!"

"Not me," the Leewit said briefly.

"You could still do it, I guess," said Goth. She seemed to be reflecting. "All right—we'll lay off him. It was a fair fight, anyway."

IV.

They raised Karres the sixteenth day after leaving Porlumma. There had been no more incidents; but then, neither had there been any more stops or other contacts with the defenseless Empire. Maleen had cooked up a poultice which did wonders for his knee. With the end of the trip in sight, all tensions had relaxed; and Maleen, at least, seemed to grow hourly more regretful at the prospect of parting.

After a brief study, Karres could be distinguished easily enough by the fact that it moved counterclockwise to all the other planets of the Iverdahl System.

Well, it would, the captain thought.

They came soaring into its atmosphere on the dayside without arousing any visible interest. No communicator signals reached them; and no other ships showed up to look them over. Karres, in fact, had all the appearance of a completely uninhabited world. There were a larger number of seas, too big to be called lakes and too small to be oceans, scattered over its surface. There was one enormously towering ridge of mountains that ran from pole to pole, and any number of lesser chains. There were two good-sized ice caps; and the southern section of the planet was speckled with intermittent stretches of snow. Almost all of it seemed to be dense forest.

It was a handsome place, in a wild, somber way.

They went gliding over it, from noon through morning and into the dawn fringe—the captain at the controls, Goth and the Leewit flanking him at the screens, and Maleen behind him to do the directing. After a few initial squeals, the Leewit became oddly silent. Suddenly the captain realized she was blubbering.

Somehow, it startled him to discover that her homecoming had affected the Leewit to that extent. He felt Goth reach out behind him and put her hand on the Leewit's shoulder. The smallest witch sniffled happily.

" 'S beautiful!" she growled.

He felt a resurgence of the wondering, protective friendliness they had aroused in him at first. They must have been having a rough time of it, at that. He sighed; it seemed a pity they hadn't got along a little better!

"Where's everyone hiding?" he inquired, to break up the mood. So far, there hadn't been a sign of human habitation.

"There aren't many people on Karres," Maleen said from behind his shoulder. "But we're going to The Town—you'll meet about half of them there!"

"What's that place down there?" the captain asked with sudden interest. Something like an enormous lime-white bowl seemed to have been set flush into the floor of the wide valley up which they were moving.

"That's the Theater where . . . *ouch!*" the Leewit said. She fell silent then but turned to give Maleen a resentful look.

"Something strangers shouldn't be told about, eh?" the captain said tolerantly. Goth glanced at him from the side.

"We've got rules," she said.

He let the ship down a little as they passed over "the Theater where—" It was a sort of large, circular arena, with numerous steep tiers of seats running up around it. But all was bare and deserted now.

On Maleen's direction, they took the next valley fork to the right and dropped lower still. He had his first look at Karres' animal life then. A flock of large, creamy-white birds, remarkably Terrestrial in appearance, flapped by just below them, apparently unconcerned about the ship. The forest underneath had opened out into a long stretch of lush meadow land, with small creeks winding down into its center. Here a herd of several hundred head of beasts was grazing—beasts of mastodonic size and build, with hairless, shiny black hides. The mouths of their long, heavy heads were twisted up into sardonic, crocodilian grins as they blinked up at the passing *Venture*.

"Black Bollems," said Goth, apparently enjoying the captain's expression. "Lots of them around; they're tame. But the gray mountain ones are good hunting."

"Good eating, too!" the Leewit said. She licked her lips daintily. "Breakfast—!" she sighed, her thought diverted to a familiar track. "And we ought to be just in time!"

"There's the field!" Maleen cried, pointing. "Set her down there, captain!"

The "field" was simply a flat meadow of close-trimmed grass running smack against the mountainside to their left. One small vehicle, bright blue in color, was parked on it; and it was bordered on two sides by very tall, blue-black trees.

That was all.

The captain shook his head. Then he set her down.

The town of Karres was a surprise to him in a good many ways. For one thing, there was much more of it than you would have thought possible after flying over the area. It stretched for miles through the forest, up the flanks of the mountain and across the valley—little clusters of houses or individual ones, each group screened from all the rest and from the sky overhead by the trees.

They liked color on Karres; but then they hid it away! The houses were bright as flowers, red and white, apple-green, golden-brown—all spick and span, scrubbed and polished and aired with that brisk, green forest-smell. At various times of the day, there was also the smell of remarkably good things to eat. There were brooks and pools and a great number of shaded vegetable gardens to the town. There were risky-looking treetop playgrounds, and treetop platforms and galleries which seemed to have no particular purpose. On the ground was mainly an enormously confusing maze of paths—narrow trails of sandy soil snaking about among great brown tree roots and chunks of gray mountain rock, and half covered with fallen needle leaves. The first six times the captain set out unaccompanied, he'd lost his way hopelessly within minutes, and had to be guided back out of the forest.

But the most hidden of all were the people! About four thousand of them were supposed to live in the town, with as many more scattered about the planet. But you never got to see more than three or four at any one time—except when now and then a pack of children, who seemed to the captain to be uniformly of the Leewit's size, would burst suddenly out of the undergrowth across a path before you, and vanish again.

As for the others, you did hear someone singing occasionally; or there might be a whole muted concert going on all about, on a large variety of wooden musical instruments which they seemed to enjoy tootling with, gently.

But it wasn't a real town at all, the captain thought. They didn't live like people, these Witches of Karres—it was more like a flock of strange forest birds that happened to be nesting in the same general area. Another thing: they appeared to be busy enough—but what was their business?

He discovered he was reluctant to ask Toll too many questions about it. Toll was the mother of his three witches; but only Goth really resembled her. It was difficult to picture Goth becoming smoothly matured and pleasantly rounded; but that was Toll. She had the same murmuring voice, the same air of sideways observation and secret reflection. And she answered all the captain's questions with apparent frankness; but he never seemed to get much real information out of what she said.

It was odd, too! Because he was spending several hours a day in her company, or in one of the next rooms at any rate, while she went about her housework. Toll's daughters had taken him home when they landed; and he was installed in the room that belonged to their father—busy just now, the captain gathered, with some sort of research of a geological nature elsewhere on Karres. The arrangement worried him a little at first, particularly since Toll and he were mostly alone in the house. Maleen was going to some kind of school; she left early in the morning and came back late in the afternoon; and Goth and Leewit were just plain running wild! They usually got in long after the captain had gone to bed and were off again before he turned out for breakfast.

It hardly seemed like the right way to raise them! One afternoon, he found the Leewit curled up and asleep in the chair he usually occupied on the porch before the house. She slept there for four solid hours, while the captain sat nearby and leafed gradually through a thick book with illuminated pictures called "Histories of Ancient Yarthe." Now and then, he sipped at a cool, green, faintly intoxicating drink Toll had placed quietly beside him some while before, or sucked an aromatic smoke from the enormous pipe with a floor rest, which he understood was a favorite of Toll's husband.

Then the Leewit woke up suddenly, uncoiled, gave him a look between a scowl and a friendly grin, slipped off the porch and vanished among the trees.

He couldn't quite figure that look! It might have meant nothing at all in particular, but—

The captain laid down his book then and worried a little more. It was true, of course, that nobody seemed in the least concerned about his presence. All of Karres appeared to know about him, and he'd met quite a number of people by now in a casual way. But nobody came around to interview him or so much as dropped in for a visit. However, Toll's husband presumably would be returning presently, and—

How long had he been here, anyway?

Great Patham, the captain thought, shocked. He'd lost count of the days!

Or was it weeks?

He went in to find Toll.

"It's been a wonderful visit," he said, "but I'll have to be leaving, I guess. Tomorrow morning, early—"

Toll put some fancy sewing she was working on back in a glass basket, laid her thin, strong witch's hands in her lap, and smiled up at him.

"We thought you'd be thinking that," she said, "and so we— You know, captain, it was quite difficult to find a way to reward you for bringing back the children?"

"It was?" said the captain, suddenly realizing he'd also clean forgotten he was broke! And now the wrath of Onswud lay close ahead.

"Gold and jewel stones would have been just right, of course!" she said, "but unfortunately, while there's no doubt a lot of it on Karres somewhere, we never got around to looking for it. And we haven't money—none that you could use, that is!"

"No, I don't suppose you do," the captain agreed sadly.

"However," said Toll, "we've all been talking about it in the town, and so we've loaded a lot of things aboard your ship that we think you can sell at a fine profit!"

"Well now," the captain said gratefully, "that's fine of—"

"There are furs," said Toll, "the very finest furs we could fix up—two thousand of them!"

"Oh!" said the captain, bravely keeping his smile. "Well, that's wonderful!"

"And essences of perfume!" said Toll. "Everyone brought one bottle of their own, so that's eight thousand three hundred and twenty-three bottles of perfume essences—all different!"

"Perfume!" said the captain. "Fine, fine—but you really shouldn't—"

"And the rest of it," Toll concluded happily, "is the green Lepti liquor you like so much, and the Wintenberry jellies!" She frowned. "I forgot just how many jugs and jars," she admitted, "but there were a lot. It's all loaded now. And do you think you'll be able to sell all that?" she smiled.

"I certainly can!" the captain said stoutly. "It's wonderful stuff, and there's nothing like it in the Empire."

Which was very true. They wouldn't have considered miffel-furs for lining on Karres. But if he'd been alone he would have felt like he wanted to burst into tears.

The witches could not have picked more completely unsalable items if they'd tried! Furs, cosmetics, food and liquor—he'd be shot on sight if he got caught trying to run that kind of merchandise into the Empire. For the same reason that they couldn't use it on Nikkeldepain—they were that scared of contamination by goods that came from uncleared worlds!

He breakfasted alone next morning. Toll had left a note beside his plate, which explained in a large, not too legible script that she had to run off and fetch the Leewit; and that if he was gone before she got back she was wishing him good-by and good luck.

He smeared two more buns with Wintenberry jelly, drank a large mug of cone-seed coffee, finished every scrap of the omelet of swan hawk eggs and then, in a state of pleasant repletion, toyed around with his slice of roasted Bollem liver. Boy, what food! He must have put on fifteen pounds since he landed on Karres.

He wondered how Toll kept that sleek figure.

Regretfully, he pushed himself away from the table, pocketed her note for a souvenir, and went out on the porch. There a tear-stained Maleen hurled herself into his arms.

"Oh, captain!" she sobbed. "You're leaving—"

"Now, now!" the captain murmured, touched and surprised by the lovely child's grief. He patted her shoulders soothingly. "I'll be back," he said rashly.

"Oh, yes, do come back!" cried Maleen. She hesitated and added: "I become marriageable two years from now, Karres time—"

"Well, well," said the captain, dazed. "Well, now—"

He set off down the path a few minutes later, with a strange melody tinkling in his head. Around the first curve, it changed abruptly to a shrill keening which seemed to originate from a spot some two hundred feet before him. Around the next curve, he entered a small, rocky clearing full of pale, misty, early-morning sunlight and what looked like a slow-motion fountain of gleaming rainbow globes. These turned out to be clusters of large, vari-hued soap bubbles which floated up steadily from a wooden tub full of hot water, soap and the Leewit. Toll was bent over the tub; and the Leewit was objecting to a morning bath, with only that minimum of interruptions required to keep her lungs pumped full of a fresh supply of air.

As the captain paused beside the little family group, her red, wrathful face came up over the rim of the tub and looked at him.

"Well, Ugly," she squealed, in a renewed outburst of rage, "who you staring at?" Then a sudden determination came into her eyes. She pursed her lips.

Toll up-ended her promptly and smacked the Leewit's bottom.

"She was going to make some sort of a whistle at you," she explained hurriedly. "Perhaps you'd better get out of range while I can keep her head under. And good luck, captain!"

Karres seemed even more deserted than usual this morning. Of course, it was quite early. Great banks of fog lay here and there among the huge dark trees and the small bright houses. A breeze sighed sadly far overhead. Faint, mournful bird-cries came from still higher up—it could have been swan hawks reproaching him for the omelet.

Somewhere in the distance, somebody tootled on a wood-instrument, very gently.

He had gone halfway up the path to the landing field, when something buzzed past him like an enormous wasp and went *CLUNK!* into the bole of a tree just before him.

It was a long, thin, wicked-looking arrow. On its shaft was a white card; and on the card was printed in red letters:

STOP, MAN OF NIKKELDEPAIN!

The captain stopped and looked around slowly and cautiously. There was no one in sight. What did it mean?

He had a sudden feeling as if all of Karres were rising up silently in one stupendous, cool, foggy trap about him. His skin began to crawl. What was going to happen?

"Ha-ha!" said Goth, suddenly visible on a rock twelve feet to his left and eight feet above him. "You did stop!"

The captain let his breath out slowly.

"What else did you think I'd do?" he inquired. He felt a little faint.

She slid down from the rock like a lizard and stood before him. "Wanted to say good-by!" she told him.

Thin and brown, in jacket, breeches, boots, and cap of gray-green rock-lichen color, Goth looked very much in her element. The brown eyes looked up at him steadily; the mouth smiled faintly; but there was no real expression on her face at all. There was a quiverful of those enormous arrows slung over her shoulder, and some arrow-shooting gadget—not a bow—in her left hand.

She followed his glance.

"Bollem hunting up the mountain," she explained. "The wild ones. They're better meat—"

The captain reflected a moment. That's right, he recalled; they kept the tame Bollem

James H. Schmitz

herds mostly for milk, butter, and cheese. He'd learned a lot of important things about Karres, all right!

"Well," he said, "good-by, Goth!"

They shook hands gravely. Goth was the real Witch of Karres, he decided—more so than her sisters, more so even than Toll. But he hadn't actually learned a single thing about any of them.

Peculiar people!

He walked on, rather glumly.

"Captain!" Goth called after him. He turned.

"Better watch those take-offs," Goth called, "or you'll kill yourself yet!"

The captain cussed softly all the way up to the *Venture*.

And the take-off was terrible! A few swan hawks were watching but, he hoped, no one else.

V.

There wasn't the remotest possibility, of course, of resuming direct trade in the Empire with the cargo they'd loaded for him. But the more he thought about it now, the less likely it seemed that Councilor Onswud was going to let a genuine fortune slip through his hands on a mere technicality of embargoes. Nikkeldepain knew all the tricks of interstellar merchandising; and the councilor himself was undoubtedly the slickest unskinned miffel in the Republic.

More hopefully, the captain began to wonder whether some sort of trade might not be made to develop eventually between Karres and Nikkeldepain. Now and then, he also thought of Maleen growing marriageable two years hence, Karres time. A handful of witch-notes went tinkling through his head whenever that idle reflection occurred.

The calendric chronometer informed him he'd spent three weeks there. He couldn't remember how their year compared with the standard one.

He found he was getting remarkably restless on this homeward run; and it struck him for the first time that space travel could also be nothing much more than a large hollow period of boredom. He made a few attempts to resume his sessions of small-talk with Illyla, via her picture; but the picture remained aloof.

The ship seemed unnaturally quiet now—that was the trouble! The captain's cabin, particularly, and the hall leading past it had become as dismal as a tomb.

But at long last, Nikkeldepain II swam up on the screen ahead. The captain put the *Venture 7333* on orbit, and broadcast the ship's identification number. Half an hour later, Landing Control called him. He repeated the identification number, and added the ship's name, his name, owner's name, place of origin and nature of cargo.

The cargo had to be described in detail.

"Assume Landing Orbit 21, 203 on your instruments," Landing Control instructed him. "A customs ship will come out to inspect."

He went on the assigned orbit and gazed moodily from the vision ports at the flat continents and oceans of Nikkeldepain II as they drifted by below. A sense of equally flat depression overcame him unexpectedly. He shook it off and remembered Illyla.

Three hours later, a ship ran up next to him; and he shut off the orbital drive. The communicator began buzzing. He switched it on.

"Vision, please!" said an official-sounding voice. The captain frowned, located the vision-stud of the communicator screen and pushed it down. Four faces appeared in vague outline on the screen, looking at him.

"Illyla!" the captain said.

"At least," young Councilor Rapport said unpleasantly, "he's brought back the ship, Father Onswud!"

"Illyla!" said the captain.

Councilor Onswud said nothing. Neither did Illyla. They both seemed to be staring at him, but the screen wasn't good enough to permit the study of expression in detail.

The fourth face, an unfamiliar one above a uniform collar, was the one with the official-sounding voice.

"You are instructed to open the forward lock, Captain Pausert," it said, "for an official investigation."

It wasn't till he was releasing the outer lock to the control room that the captain realized it wasn't Customs who had sent a boat out to him, but the police of the Republic.

However, he hesitated for only a moment. Then the outer lock gaped wide.

He tried to explain. They wouldn't listen. They had come on board in contamination-proof repulsor suits, all four of them; and they discussed the captain as if he weren't there. Illyla looked pale and angry and beautiful, and avoided looking at him.

However, he didn't want to speak to her before the other anyway.

They strolled back to the storage and gave the Karres cargo a casual glance.

"Damaged his lifeboat, too!" Councilor Rapport remarked.

They brushed past him down the narrow hallway and went back to the control room. The policeman asked to see the log and commercial records. The captain produced them.

The three men studied them briefly. Illyla gazed stonily out at Nikkeldepain II.

"Not too carefully kept!" the policeman pointed out.

"Surprising he bothered to keep them at all!" said Councilor Rapport.

"But it's all clear enough!" said Councilor Onswud.

They straightened up then and faced him in a line. Councilor Onswud folded his arms and projected his craggy chin. Councilor Rapport stood at ease, smiling faintly. The policeman became officially rigid.

Illyla remained off to one side, looking at the three.

"Captain Pausert," the policeman said, "the following charges—substantiated in part by this preliminary investigation—are made against you—"

James H. Schmitz

"Charges?" said the captain.

"Silence, please!" rumbled Councilor Onswud.

"First: material theft of a quarter-million value of maels of jewels and jeweled items from a citizen of the Imperial Planet of Porlumma—"

"They were returned!" the captain protested.

"Restitution, particularly when inspired by fear of retribution, does not affect the validity of the original charge," Councilor Rapport quoted, gazing at the ceiling.

"Second," continued the policeman. "Purchase of human slaves, permitted under Imperial law but prohibited by penalty of ten years to lifetime penal servitude by the laws of the Republic of Nikkeldepain—"

"I was just taking them back where they belonged!" said the captain.

"We shall get to that point presently," the policeman replied. "Third, material theft of sundry items in the value of one hundred and eighty thousand maels from a ship of the Imperial Planet of Lepper, accompanied by threats of violence to the ship's personnel—"

"I might add in explanation of the significance of this particular charge," added Councilor Rapport, looking at the floor, "that the Regency of Sirius, containing Lepper, is allied to the Republic of Nikkeldepain by commercial and military treaties of considerable value. The Regency has taken the trouble to point out that such hostile conduct by a citizen of the Republic against citizens of the Regency is likely to have an adverse effect on the duration of the treaties. The charge thereby becomes compounded by the additional charge of a treasonable act against the Republic—"

He glanced at the captain. "I believe we can forestall the accused's plea that these pilfered goods also were restored. They were, in the face of superior force!"

"Fourth," the policeman went on patiently, "depraved and licentious conduct while acting as commercial agent, to the detriment of your employer's business and reputation—"

"WHAT?" choked the captain.

"—involving three of the notorious Witches of the Prohibited Planet of Karres—"

"Just like his great-uncle Threbus!" nodded Councilor Onswud gloomily. "It's in the blood, I always say!"

"—and a justifiable suspicion of a prolonged stay on said Prohibited Planet of Karres—"

"I never heard of that place before this trip!" shouted the captain.

"Why don't you read your Instructions and Regulations then?" shouted Councilor Rapport. "It's all there!"

"Silence, please!" shouted Councilor Onswud.

"Fifth," said the policeman quietly, "general willful and negligent actions resulting in material damage and loss to your employer to the value of eighty-two thousand maels."

"I've still got fifty-five thousand. And the stuff in the storage," the captain said, also quietly, "is worth half a million, at least!"

"Contraband and hence legally valueless!" the policeman said. Councilor Onswud cleared his throat.

"It will be impounded, of course," he said. "Should a method of resale present itself, the profits, if any, will be applied to the cancellation of your just debts. To some extent, that might reduce your sentence." He paused. "There is another matter—"

"The sixth charge," the policeman said, "is the development *and* public demonstration of a new type of space drive, which should have been brought promptly and secretly to the attention of the Republic of Nikkeldepain!"

They all stared at him—alertly and quite greedily.

So *that* was it—the Sheewash Drive!

"Your sentence may be greatly reduced, Pausert," Councilor Onswud said wheedlingly, "if you decide to be reasonable now. What have you discovered?"

"Look out, Father!" Illyla said sharply.

"Pausert," Councilor Onswud inquired in a fading voice, "what is that in your hand?"

"A Blythe gun," the captain said, boiling.

There was a frozen stillness for an instant. Then the policeman's right hand made a convulsive movement.

"Uh-uh!" said the captain warningly.

Councilor Rapport started a slow step backwards.

"Stay where you are!" said the captain.

"Pausert!" Councilor Onswud and Illyla cried out together.

"Shut up!" said the captain.

There was another stillness.

"If you'd looked," the captain said, in an almost normal voice, "you'd have seen I've got the nova gun turrets out. They're fixed on that boat of yours. The boat's lying still and keeping its little yap shut. You do the same—"

He pointed a finger at the policeman. "You got a repulsor suit on," he said. "Open the inner port lock and go squirt yourself back to your boat!"

The inner port lock groaned open. Warm air left the ship in a long, lazy wave, scattering the sheets of the *Venture*'s log and commercial records over the floor. The thin, cold upper atmosphere of Nikkeldepain II came eddying in.

"You next, Onswud!" the captain said.

And a moment later: "Rapport, you just turn around—"

Young Councilor Rapport went through the port at a higher velocity than could be attributed reasonably to his repulsor units. The captain winced and rubbed his foot. But it had been worth it.

"Pausert," said Illyla in justifiable apprehension, "you are stark, staring mad!"

"Not at all, my dear," the captain said cheerfully. "You and I are now going to take off and embark on a life of crime together."

"But, Pausert—"

"You'll get used to it," the captain assured her, "just like I did. It's got Nikkeldepain beat every which way."

"Pausert," Illyla said, whitefaced, "we told them to bring up revolt ships!"

"We'll blow them out through the stratosphere," the captain said belligerently, reaching for the port-control switch. He added, "But they won't shoot anyway while I've got you on board!"

Illyla shook her head. "You just don't understand," she said desperately. "You can't make me stay!"

"Why not?" asked the captain.

"Pausert," said Illyla, "I am Madame Councilor Rapport."

"Oh!" said the captain. There was a silence. He added, crestfallen: "Since when?"

"Five months ago, yesterday," said Illyla.

"Great Patham!" cried the captain, with some indignation. "I'd hardly got off Nikkeldepain then! We were engaged!"

"Secretly . . . and I guess," said Illyla, with a return of spirit, "that I had a right to change my mind!"

There was another silence.

"Guess you had, at that," the captain agreed. "All right—the port's still open, and your husband's waiting in the boat. Beat it!"

He was alone. He let the ports slam shut and banged down the oxygen release switch. The air had become a little thin.

He cussed.

The communicator began rattling for attention. He turned it on.

"Pausert!" Councilor Onswud was calling in a friendly but shaking voice. "May we not depart, Pausert? Your nova guns are still fixed on this boat!"

"Oh, that—" said the captain. He deflected the turrets a trifle. "They won't go off now. Scram!"

The police boat vanished.

There was other company coming, though. Far below him but climbing steadily, a trio of revolt ships darted past on the screen, swung around and came back for the next turn of their spiral. They'd have to get a good deal closer before they started shooting; but they'd try to stay under him so as not to knock any stray chunks out of Nikkeldepain.

He sat a moment, reflecting. The revolt ships went by once more. The captain punched in the *Venture*'s secondary drives, turned her nose towards the planet and let her go. There were some scattered white puffs around as he cut through the revolt ships' plane of flight. Then he was below them, and the *Venture* groaned as he took her out of the dive.

The revolt ships were already scattering and nosing over for a countermaneuver. He picked the nearest one and swung the nova guns toward it.

"—and ram them in the middle!" he muttered between his teeth.

SSS-whoosh!

It was the Sheewash Drive—but, like a nightmare now, it kept on and on!

VI.

"Maleen!" the captain bawled, pounding at the locked door of the captain's cabin. "Maleen—shut it off! Cut it off! You'll kill yourself. Maleen!"

The *Venture* quivered suddenly throughout her length, then shuddered more violently, jumped and coughed; and commenced sailing along on her secondary drives again. He wondered how many light-years from everything they were by now. It didn't matter!

"Maleen!" he yelled. "Are you all right?"

There was a faint *thump-thump* inside the cabin, and silence. He lost almost a minute finding the right cutting tool in the storage. A few seconds later, a section of door panel sagged inwards; he caught it by one edge and came tumbling into the cabin with it.

He had the briefest glimpse of a ball of orange-colored fire swirling uncertainly over a cone of oddly bent wires. Then the fire vanished, and the wires collapsed with a loose rattling to the table top.

The crumpled small shape lay behind the table, which was why he didn't discover it at once. He sagged to the floor beside it, all the strength running out of his knees.

Brown eyes opened and blinked at him blearily.

"Sure takes it out of you!" Goth grunted. "Am I hungry!"

"I'll whale the holy, howling tar out of you again," the captain roared, "if you ever—"

"Quit your bawling!" snarled Goth. "I got to eat."

She ate for fifteen minutes straight, before she sank back in her chair, and sighed.

"Have some more Wintenberry jelly," the captain offered anxiously. She looked pretty pale.

Goth shook her head. "Couldn't—and that's about the first thing you've said since you fell through the door, howling for Maleen. Ha-ha! Maleen's *got* a boyfriend!"

"Button your lip, child," the captain said. "I was thinking." He added, after a moment: "Has she really?"

"Picked him out last year," Goth nodded. "Nice boy from town—they get married as soon as she's marriageable. She just told you to come back because she was upset about you. Maleen had a premonition you were headed for awful trouble!"

"She was quite right, little chum," the captain said nastily.

"What were you thinking about?" Goth inquired.

"I was thinking," said the captain, "that as soon as we're sure you're going to be all right, I'm taking you straight back to Karres!"

"I'll be all right now," Goth said. "Except, likely, for a stomach ache. But you can't take me back to Karres."

"Who will stop me, may I ask?" the captain asked.

"Karres is gone," Goth said.

"Gone?" the captain repeated blankly, with a sensation of not quite definable horror bubbling up in him.

"Not blown up or anything," Goth reassured him. "They just moved it! The Imperialists got their hair up about us again. But this time, they were sending a fleet with the big bombs and stuff, so everybody was called home. But they had to wait then till they found out where we were—me and Maleen and the Leewit. Then you brought us in; and they had to wait again, and decide about you. But right after you'd left . . . *we'd* left, I mean . . . they moved it."

"Where?"

"Great Patham!" Goth shrugged. "How'd I know? There's lots of places!"

There probably were, the captain admitted silently. A scene came suddenly before his eyes—that lime-white, arenalike bowl in the valley, with the steep tiers of seats around it, just before they'd reached the town of Karres—"the Theater where—"

But now there was unnatural night-darkness all over and about that world; and the eight thousand-some Witches of Karres sat in circles around the Theater, their heads bent towards one point in the center, where orange fire washed hugely about the peak of a cone of curiously twisted girders.

And a world went racing off at the speeds of the Sheewash Drive! There'd be lots of places, all right. What peculiar people!

"Anyway," he sighed. "if I've got to start raising you—don't say 'Great Patham' any more. That's a cuss word!"

"I learned it from you!" Goth pointed out.

"So you did, I guess," the captain acknowledged. "I won't say it either. Aren't they going to be worried about you?"

"Not very much," said Goth. "We don't get hurt often—especially when we're young. That's when we can do all that stuff like teleporting, and whistling, like the Leewit. We lose it mostly when we get older—they're working on that now so we won't. About all Maleen can do right now is premote!"

"She premotes just dandy, though," the captain said. "The Sheewash Drive—they can all do that, can't they?"

"Uh-huh!" Goth nodded. "But that's learned stuff. That's one of the things they already studied out." She added, a trace uncomfortably: "I can't tell you about that till you're one yourself."

"Till I'm what myself?" the captain asked, becoming puzzled again.

"A witch, like us," said Goth. "We got our rules. And that won't be for four years, Karres time."

"It won't, eh?" said the captain. "What happens then?"

"That's when I'm marriageable age," said Goth, frowning at the jar of Wintenberry jelly. She pulled it toward her and inspected it carefully. "I got it all fixed," she told the jelly firmly, "as soon as they started saying they ought to pick out a wife for you on Karres, so you could stay. I said it was me, right away; and everyone else said finally that was all right then—even Maleen, because she had this boyfriend."

"You mean," said the captain, stunned, "this was all planned out on Karres?"

"Sure," said Goth. She pushed the jelly back where it had been standing, and glanced up at him again. "For three weeks, that's about all everyone talked about in the town! It set a precedent—"

She paused doubtfully.

"That would explain it," the captain admitted.

"Uh-huh," Goth nodded relieved, settling back in her chair. "But it was my father who told us how to do it so you'd break up with the people on Nikkeldepain. He said it was in the blood."

"What was in the blood?" the captain said patiently.

"That you'd break up with them. That's Threbus, my father," Goth informed him. "You met him a couple of times in the town. Big man with a blond beard—Maleen and the Leewit take after him."

"You wouldn't mean my great-uncle Threbus?" the captain inquired. He was in a state of strange calm by now.

"That's right," said Goth. "He liked you a lot."

"It's a small Galaxy," said the captain philosophically. "So that's where Threbus wound up! I'd like to meet him again some day."

"We'll start after Karres four years from now, when you learn about those things," Goth said. "We'll catch up with them all right. That's still thirteen hundred and seventy-two Old Sidereal days," she added, "but there's a lot to do in between. You want to pay the money you owe back to those people, don't you? I got some ideas—"

"None of those teleporting tricks now!" the captain warned.

"Kid stuff!" Goth said scornfully. "I'm growing up. This'll be fair swapping. But we'll get rich."

"I wouldn't be surprised," the captain admitted. He thought a moment. "Seeing we've turned out to be distant relatives, I suppose it is all right, too, if I adopt you meanwhile—"

"Sure," said Goth. She stood up.

"Where you going?" the captain asked.

"Bed," said Goth. "I'm tired." She stopped at the hall door. "About all I can tell

James H. Schmitz

you about us till then," she said, "you can read in those Regulations, like the one man said—the one you kicked off the ship. There's a lot about us in there. Lots of lies, too, though!"

"And when did you find out about the communicator between here and the captain's cabin?" the captain inquired.

Goth grinned. "A while back," she admitted. "The others never noticed!"

"All right," the captain said. "Good night, witch—if you get a stomach ache, yell and I'll bring the medicine."

"Good night," Goth yawned. "I will, I think."

"And wash behind your ears!" the captain added, trying to remember the bedtime instructions he'd overheard Maleen giving the junior witches.

"All right," said Goth sleepily. The hall door closed behind her—but half a minute later, it was briskly opened again. The captain looked up startled from the voluminous stack of "General Instructions and Space Regulations of the Republic of Nikkeldepain" he'd just discovered in one of the drawers of the control desk. Goth stood in the doorway, scowling and wide-awake.

"And you wash behind yours!" she said.

"Huh?" said the captain. He reflected a moment. "All right," he said. "We both will, then."

"Right," said Goth, satisfied.

The door closed once more.

The captain began to run his finger down the lengthy index of K's—or could it be under W? ∎

MIKAL'S SONGBIRD
Orson Scott Card

The doorknob turned. That would be dinner.

Ansset rolled over on the hard bed, his muscles aching. As always, he tried to ignore the burning feeling of guilt in the pit of his stomach.

But it was not Husk with food on a tray. This time it was the man called Master, though Ansset believed that was not his name. Master was always angry and fearsomely strong, one of the few men who could make Ansset feel and act like the eleven-year-old child his body said he was.

"Get up, Songbird."

Ansset slowly stood. They kept him naked in his prison, and only his pride kept him from turning away from the harsh eyes that looked him up and down. Ansset's cheeks burned with shame that took the place of the guilt he had wakened to.

"It's a good-bye feast we're having for you, Chirp, and ye're going to twitter for us."

Ansset shook his head.

"If ye can sing for the bastard Mikal, ye can sing for honest freemen."

Ansset's eyes blazed. "Watch how you speak of him, you barbarian traitor! He's your emperor!"

Master advanced a step, raising his hand angrily. "My orders was not to mark you, Chirp, but I can give you pain that doesn't leave a scar if ye don't mind how you talk to a freeman. Now ye'll sing."

Ansset, afraid of the man's brutality as only someone who has never known physical punishment can be afraid, nodded—but still hung back. "Can you please give me my clothing?"

"It ain't cold where we're going," Master retorted.

"I've never sung like this," Ansset said, embarrassed. "I've never performed without clothing."

Master leered. "What is it then that you *do* without clothing? Mikal's catamite has naw secrets we can't see."

Ansset didn't understand the word, but he understood the leer, and he followed Master out the door and down a dark corridor with his heart even more darkly filled with shame. He wondered why they were having a "good-bye feast" for him. Was he to be set free? (Had someone paid some unknown ransom for him?) Or was he to be killed?

The floor rocked gently as they walked down the wooden corridor. Ansset had long since decided he was imprisoned on a ship. The amount of real wood used in it would have seemed gaudy and pretentious in a rich man's home. Here it seemed only shabby.

Far above he could hear the distant cry of a bird, and a steady singing sound that he imagined to be wind whipping through ropes and cables. He had sung the melody himself sometimes, and often harmonized.

And then Master opened the door and with a mocking bow indicated that Ansset should enter first. The boy stopped in the doorframe. Gathered around a long table were twenty or so men, some of whom he had seen before, all of them dressed in the strange costumes of Earth barbarians. Ansset couldn't help remembering Mikal's raucous laughter whenever they came to court, pretendng to be heirs of great civilizations that to minds accustomed to thinking on a galactic scale were petty and insignificant indeed. And yet as he stood looking at their rough faces and unsmiling eyes, he felt that it was he, with the soft skin of the imperial court, that was petty and insignificant, a mere naked child, while these men held the strength of worlds in their rough, gnarled hands.

They looked at him with the same curious, knowing, lustful look that Master had given him. Ansset relaxed his stomach and firmed his back and ribs to conquer emotion, as he had been taught in the Songhouse before he turned three. He stepped into the room.

"Up on the table!" roared Master behind him, and hands lifted him onto the wood smeared with spilled wine and rough with crumbs and fragments of food. "Now sing, ye little bastarrd."

The eyes looked his naked body over, and Ansset almost cried. But he was a Songbird, and many called him the best who had ever lived. Hadn't Mikal brought him from one end of the galaxy to his new Capital on old Earth? And when he sang, no matter who the audience, he would sing well.

And so he closed his eyes and shaped the ribs around his lungs, and let a low tone pass through his throat. At first he sang without words, soft and low, knowing the sound would be hard to hear. "Louder," someone said, but he ignored the instructions. Gradually the jokes and laughter died down as the men strained to hear.

The melody was a wandering one, passing through tones and quartertones easily, gracefully, still low in pitch, but rising and falling rhythmically. Unconsciously Ansset moved his hands in strange gestures to accompany his song. He was never aware of those gestures, except that once he had read in a newsheet, "To hear Mikal's Songbird is heavenly, but to watch his hands dance as he sings is nirvana." That was a prudent thing to write about Mikal's favorite—when the writer lived in Capital. Nevertheless, no one had even privately disputed the comment.

And now Ansset began to sing words. They were words of his own captivity, and the melody became high, in the soft upper notes that opened his throat and tightened the muscles at the back of his head and tensed the muscles along the front of his thighs. The notes pierced, and as he slid up and down through haunting thirdtones (a technique that few Songbirds could master) his words spoke of dark, shameful evenings in a dirty cell, a longing for the kind looks of Father Mikal (not by name, never by name in front of these barbarians), of dreams of the broad lawns that stretched from the palace to the Susquehanna River, and of lost, forgotten days that ended in wakeful evenings in a tiny cell of splintered wood.

And he sang of his guilt.

At last he became tired, and the song drifted off into a whispered dorian scale that ended on the wrong note, on a dissonant note that faded into silence that sounded like part of the song.

Finally Ansset opened his eyes. All the men who were not weeping were watching him. None seemed willing to break the mood, until a youngish man down the table said in the thick accent, "Ah, but thet was better than hame and Mitherma." His comment was greeted by sighs and chuckles of agreement, and the looks that met Ansset's eyes were no longer leering and lustful, but rather soft and kind. Ansset had never thought to see such looks in those rough faces.

"Will ye have some wine, boy?" asked Master's voice behind him, and Husk poured. Ansset sipped the wine, and dipped a finger in it to cast a drop into the air in the graceful gesture of court. "Thank you," he said, handing back the metal cup with the same grace he would have used with a goblet at court. He lowered his head, though it hurt him to use that gesture of respect to such men, and asked, "May I leave now?"

"Do you have to? Can't you sing again?" the men around the table murmured, as if they had forgotten he was their prisoner. And Ansset refused as if he were free to choose. "I can't do it twice. I can never do it twice."

They lifted him off the table, then, and Master's strong arms carried him back to his room. Ansset lay on the bed after the door locked shut, trembling. The last time he had sung was for Mikal, and the song had been light and happy. Then Mikal had smiled the soft smile that only touched his old face when he was alone with his Songbird, had touched the back of Ansset's hand, and Ansset had kissed the old hand and gone out to walk along the river. It was then that they had taken him—rough hands from behind, the sharp slap of the needle, and then waking in the cell where now he lay looking at the walls.

He always woke in the evening, aching from some unknown effort of the day, and wracked by guilt. He strained to remember, but always in the effort drifted off to sleep, only to wake again the next evening suffering from the lost day behind him. But tonight he did not try to puzzle out what lay behind the blocks in his mind. Instead he drifted off to sleep thinking of the songs in Mikal's kind gray eyes, humming of the firm hands that ruled an empire a galaxy wide and could still stroke the forehead of a sweet-singing child and weep at a sorrowful song. Ah, sang Ansset in his mind, ah, the weeping of Mikal's sorrowful hands.

Orson Scott Card

Ansset woke walking down a street.

"Out of the way, ya chark!" shouted a harsh accent behind him, and Ansset dodged to the left as an eletrecart zipped past his right arm. "Sausages," shouted a sign on the trunk behind the driver.

Then Ansset was seized by a terrible vertigo as he realized that he was not in the cell of his captivity, that he was fully dressed (in native Earth costume, but clothing for all that), was alive, was free. The quick joy that realization brought was immediately soured by a rush of the old guilt, and the conflicting emotions and the suddenness of his liberation were too much for him, and for a moment too long he forgot to breathe, and the darkening ground slid sideways, tipped up, hit him—

"Hey, boy, are you all right?"

"Did the chark slam you, boy?"

"Ya got the license number? Ya got the number?"

"Four-eight-seven something, who can tell."

"He's comin' around and to."

Ansset opened his eyes. "Where is this place?" he asked softly.

Why, this is Northet, they said.

"How far is the palace?" Ansset asked, vaguely remembering that Northet was a town not far to the north and east of Capital.

"The palace? What palace?"

"Mikal's palace—I must go to Mikal—" Ansset tried to get up, but his head spun and he staggered. Hands held him up.

"The kit's kinky, that's what."

"Mikal's palace."

"It's only eighteen kilometer, boy, ya plan to fly?"

The joke brought a burst of laughter, but Ansset impatiently regained control of his body and stood. Whatever drug had kept him unconscious was now nearly worked out of his system. "Find me a policeman," Ansset said. "Mikal will want to see me immediately."

Some still laughed, a man's voice said, "We'll be sure to tell him you're here when he comes to my house for supper!" but some others looked carefully at Ansset, realizing he spoke without American accent, and that his bearing was not that of a streetchild, despite his clothing. "Who are you, boy?"

"I'm Ansset. Mikal's Songbird."

Then there was silence, and half the crowd rushed off to find the policeman, and the other half stayed to look at him and realize how beautiful his eyes were, to touch him with their own eyes and hold the moment to tell about it to children and grandchildren. Ansset, Mikal's Songbird, more valuable than all the treasure Mikal owned.

"I touched him myself, helping him up, I held him up."

"You would've fallen, but for me, Sir," said a large strong man bowing ridiculously low.

Mikal's Songbird   **103**

"Can I shake your hand, Sir?"

Ansset smiled at them, not in amusement but in gratitude for their respect for him. "Thank you. You've all helped me. Thank you."

The policeman came, and after apologizing for the dirtiness of his armored eletrecart he lifted Ansset onto the seat and took him to the headquarters, where a flyer from the palace was already settling down on the pad. The Chamberlain leaped from the flyer, along with half a dozen servants, who gingerly touched Ansset and helped him to the flyer. The door slid shut, and Ansset closed his eyes to hide the tears as he felt the ground rush away as the palace came to meet him.

But for two days they kept him away from Mikal. "Quarantine," they said at first, until Ansset stamped his foot and said, "Nonsense," and refused to answer any more of the hundreds of questions they kept firing at him from dawn to dark and long after dark. The Chamberlain came.

"What's this I hear about you not wanting to answer questions, my boy?" asked the Chamberlain with the false joviality that Ansset had long since learned to recognize as a mask for anger or fear.

"I'm not your boy," Ansset retorted, determined to frighten some cooperation out of the Chamberlain. Now and then it had worked in the past. "I'm Mikal's and he wants to see me. Why am I being kept like a prisoner?"

"Quaran—"

"Chamberlain, I'm healthier than I've ever been before, and these questions don't have a thing to do with my health."

"All right," the Chamberlain said, fluttering his hands with impatience and nervousness. Ansset had once sung to Mikal of the Chamberlain's hands, and Mikal had laughed for hours at some of the words. "I'll explain. But don't get angry at me, because it's Mikal's orders."

"That I be kept away from him?"

"Until you answer the questions! You've been in court long enough, Songbird, and you're surely bright enough to know that Mikal has enemies in this world."

"I know that. Are you one of them?" Ansset was deliberately goading the Chamberlain, using his voice like a whip in all the ways that made the Chamberlain angry and fretful and so forgetful.

"Hold your tongue, boy!" the Chamberlain said. Ansset inwardly smiled. Victory. "You're also bright enough to know that you weren't kidnapped five months ago by any friends of the emperor's. We have to know *everything* about your captivity."

"I've told you everything a hundred times over."

"You haven't told us how you spent your days."

Again Ansset felt a stab of emotion. "I don't remember my days."

"And that's why you can't see Mikal!" the Chamberlain snapped. "Do you think we don't know what happened? We've used the probes and the tasters and no matter how skillfully we question, we can't get past the blocks. Either the person who worked on your mind laid the blocks very skillfully, or you yourself are holding them locked, and either way we can't get in."

"I can't help it," Ansset said, realizing now what the questioning meant. "How can you think I mean any danger to Father Mikal?"

The Chamberlain smiled beatifically, in the pose he reserved for polite triumph. "Behind the block, someone may have very carefully planted a command for you to—"

"I'm not an assassin!" Ansset shouted.

"How would you know," the Chamberlain snarled back. "It's my duty to protect the person of the emperor. Do you know now many assassination attempts we stop? Dozens, every week. The poison, the treason, the weapons, the traps, that's what half the people who work here *do*, is watch everyone who comes in and watch each other too. Most of the assassination attempts are stopped immediately. Some get closer. Yours may be the closest of all."

"Mikal must want to see me!"

"Of course he does, Ansset! And that's exactly why you can't—because whoever worked on your mind must know that you're the only person that Mikal would allow near him after something like this—Ansset! Ansset, you little fool! Call the Captain of the Guard. Ansset, slow down!"

But the Chamberlain was slowing down with age, and he steadily lost ground to Ansset as the boy darted down the corridors of the palace. Ansset knew all the quickest ways, since exploring the palace was one of the most pleasant of his pastimes, and in five years in Mikal's service no one knew the labyrinth better than Ansset.

He was stopped routinely at the doors to the Great Hall, and he quickly made his way through the detectors. (Poison? No. Metal? No. Energy? No. Identification? Clear) and he was just about to step through the vast doors when the Captain of the Guard arrived.

"Stop the boy."

Ansset was stopped.

"Come back here, Songbird," the Captain barked. but Ansset could see, at the far end of the huge platinum room, the small chair and the whitehaired man who sat on it. Surely Mikal could see him! Surely he'd call!

"Bring the boy back here before he embarrasses everyone by calling out." Ansset was dragged back. "If you must know, Ansset, Mikal gave me orders to bring you within the hour, even before you made your ridiculous escape from the Chamberlain. But you'll be searched first. My way."

Ansset was taken off into one of the search rooms. He was stripped and his clothing was replaced with fresh clothes (that didn't fit! Ansset thought angrily), and then the searchers' fingers probed, painfully and deep, every aperture of his body that might hold a weapon. ("No weapon, and your prostate gland's all right, too," one of them joked. Ansset didn't laugh.) Then the needles, probing far under the skin to sample for hidden poisons. A layer of skin was bloodlessly peeled off his palms and the soles of his feet, to be sampled for poisons or flexible plastic needles. The pain was irritating. The delay was excruciating.

But Ansset bore what had to be borne. He only showed anger or impatience when he thought that doing so might gain some good effect. No one, not even Mikal's Songbird, survived long at court unless he remained in control of his temper, however he had to hide it.

At last Ansset was pronounced clean.

"Wait," the Captain of the Guard said. "I don't trust you yet."

Ansset gave him a long, cold look. But the Captain of the Guard—like the Chamberlain—was one of the few people at court who knew Mikal well enough to know they had nothing to fear from Ansset unless they really treated him unjustly, for Mikal never did favors, not even for the boy, who was the only human being Mikal had ever shown a personal need for. And they knew Ansset well enough to know that he would never ask Mikal to punish someone unfairly, either.

The Captain took a nylon cord and bound Ansset's hands together behind him, first at the wrists, and then just below the elbows. The constriction was painful.

"You're hurting me," Ansset said.

"I may be saving my emperor's life," the Captain answered blandly. And then Ansset passed through the huge doors to the Great Hall, his arms bound, surrounded by guards with lasers drawn, preceded by the Captain of the Guard.

Ansset still walked proudly, but he felt a heavy fury toward the guards, toward the courtiers and supplicants and guards and officials lining the walls of the unfurnished room, and especially toward the Captain. Only toward Mikal did he feel no anger.

They let him stop.

Mikal raised his hand in the ritual of recognition. Ansset knew that Mikal laughed at the rituals when they were alone together—but in front of the court, the ritual had to be followed strictly.

Ansset dropped to his knees on the cold and shining platinum floor.

"My Lord," he said in clear, bell-like tones that he knew would reverberate from the metal ceiling, "I am Ansset, and I have come to ask for my life." In the old days, Mikal had once explained, that ritual had real meaning, and many a rebel lord or soldier had died on the spot. Even now, the pro forma surrender of life was taken seriously, as Mikal maintained constant vigilance over his empire.

"Why should I spare you?" Mikal asked, his voice old but firm. Ansset thought he heard a quaver of eagerness in the voice. More likely a quaver of age, he told himself. Mikal would never allow himself to reveal emotion in front of the court.

"You should not," Ansset said. This was leaving the ritual, and going down the dark road that met danger head-on. Mikal must have been told of the Chamberlain's fears. Therefore, if Ansset made any attempt to hide the danger, his life would be forfeited by law.

"Why not?" Mikal said, impassively.

"Because, my Lord Mikal Imperator, I was kidnapped and held for five months, and during those months things were done to me that are now locked behind blocks in my mind. I may, unwittingly, be an assassin. I must not be allowed to live."

"Nevertheless," Mikal answered, "I grant you your life."

Ansset, his muscles strong enough even after his captivity to allow him to bow despite his bound arms, touched his lips to the floor.

"Why are you bound?"

"For your safety, my Lord."

"Unbind him," said Mikal. The Captain of the Guard untied the nylon cord.

His arms free, Ansset stood. He went beyond form, and he turned his voice into a song, with an edge to his voice that snapped every head in the hall toward him. "My Lord, Father Mikal," he sang, "there is a place in my mind where even I cannot go. In that place my captors may have taught me to want to kill you." The words were a warning, but the song said safety, the song said love, and Mikal arose from his throne. He understood what Ansset was asking and he would grant it.

"I would rather, my Son Ansset, I would rather meet death in your hands than any other's. Your life is more valuable to me than my own." Then Mikal turned and went back into the door that led to his private chambers. Ansset and the Captain of the Guard followed, and as they left the whispers rose to a roar. Mikal had gone much farther than Ansset had even hoped. The entire Capital—and in a few weeks, the entire empire—would hear how Mikal had called his Songbird *Son Ansset*, and the words, "Your life is more valuable to me than my own," would become the stuff of legends.

Ansset sighed a song as he entered the familiar rooms where Father Mikal lived.

Mikal turned abruptly and glared at the Captain of the Guard. "What did you mean by that little trick, you bastard?"

"I tied his hands as a precaution. I was within my duties as a warden of the gate."

"I know you were within your duties, but you might use some common decency. What harm can an eleven-year-old boy do when you've probably skinned him alive searching for weapons and you have a hundred lasers trained on him at every moment!"

"I wanted to be sure."

"Well, you're too damned thorough. Get out. And don't let me ever catch you being any less thorough, even when it makes me angry. Get out!" The Captain of the Guard left, Mikal's roar following him. As soon as the door closed, Mikal started to laugh. "What an ass! What a colossal donkey!" Then he threw himself to the floor with all the vigor of a young man, though Ansset knew his age to be one hundred and twenty-three, which was old, in a civilization where death normally came at a hundred and fifteen. Under him the floor that had been rigid when his weight pressed down on the two small spaces touched by his feet now softened, gave gently to fit the contours of his body. Ansset also went to the floor, and lay there laughing.

"Are you glad to be home, Ansset?" Mikal asked tenderly.

"Now I am. Until this moment I wasn't home."

"Ansset, my Son, you never can speak without singing." Mikal laughed softly.

Ansset took the sound of the laugh and turned it into a song. It was a soft song, and it was short, but at the end of it Mikal was lying on his back looking at the ceiling, tears streaming down from his eyes.

"I didn't mean the song to be sad, Father Mikal."

"How was I to know that now, in my dotage, I'd do the foolish thing I avoided all my life? Oh, I've loved like I've done every other passionate thing, but when they took you I discovered, my Son, that I need you." Mikal rolled over and looked at the beautiful face of the boy who lay looking at him adoringly. "Don't worship me, boy, I'm an old bastard who'd kill his mother if one of my enemies hadn't already done it."

"You'd never harm me."

"I harm everything I love," Mikal said bitterly. Then he let his face show concern. "We were afraid for you. Since you were gone there was an outbreak of insane crime. People were kidnapped for no reason on the street, some in broad daylight, and a few days later their bodies would be found, broken and torn by someone or something. No ransom notes. Nothing. We thought you had been taken like that, and that somewhere we'd find your body. Are you whole? Are you well?"

"I'm stronger than I've ever been before." Ansset laughed. "I tested my strength against the hook of my hammock, and I'm afraid I ripped it out of the wall."

Mikal reached out and touched Ansset's hand. "I'm afraid," Mikal said, and Ansset listened, humming softly, as Mikal talked. The emperor never spoke in names and dates and facts and plans, for then if Ansset were taken by an enemy the enemy would know too much. He spoke to the Songbird in emotions instead, and Ansset sang solace to him. Other Songbirds had pretty voices, others could impress the crowds, and, indeed, Mikal used Ansset for just that purpose on certain state occasions. But of all Songbirds, only Ansset could sing his soul; and he loved Mikal from his soul.

Late in the night Mikal shouted in fury about his empire: "Did I build it to fall? Did I burn over a dozen worlds and rape a hundred others just to have the whole thing fall in chaos when I die?" He leaned down and whispered to Ansset, their eyes a few inches apart, "They call me Mikal the Terrible, but I built it so it would stand like an umbrella over the galaxy. They have it now: peace and prosperity and as much freedom as their little minds can cope with. But when I die they'll throw it all away." Mikal whirled and shouted at the walls of his soundproofed chamber, "In the name of nationalities and religions and races and family inheritances the fools will rip the umbrella down and then wonder why, all of a sudden, it's raining."

Ansset sang to him of hope.

"There's no hope. I have fifty sons, three of them legitimate, all of them fools who try to flatter me. They couldn't keep the empire for a week, not all of them, not any

Orson Scott Card

of them. There's not a man I've met in all my life who could control what I've built in my lifetime. When I die, it all dies with me." And Mikal sank to the floor wearily.

For once Ansset did not sing. Instead he jumped to his feet, the floor turning firm under him. He raised an arm above his head, and said, "For you, Father Mikal, I'll grow up to be strong! Your empire shall not fall!" He spoke with such grandeur in his childish speaking voice that both he and Mikal had to laugh.

"It's true, though," Mikal said, tousling the child's hair. "For you I'd do it, I'd give you the empire, except they'd kill you. And even if I lived long enough to train you to be a ruler of men, I wouldn't do it. The man who will be my heir must be cruel and vicious and sly and wise, completely selfish and ambitious, contemptuous of all other people, brilliant in battle, able to outguess and outmaneuver every enemy, and strong enough inside himself to live utterly alone all his life." Mikal smiled. "Even *I* don't fit my list of qualifications, because now I'm not utterly alone."

And then, as Mikal drifted off to sleep, Ansset sang to him of his captivity, the songs and words of his time of loneliness in captivity, and as the men on the ship had wept, so Mikal wept, only more. Then they both slept.

A few days later Mikal, Ansset, the Chamberlain, and the Captain of the Guard met in Mikal's small receiving room, where a solid block of clear glass as perfect as a lens stretched as a meters-long table from one end of the room to the other. They gathered at one end. The Chamberlain was adamant.

"Ansset is a danger to you, my Lord."

The Captain of the Guard was equally adamant. "We found the conspirators and killed them all."

The Chamberlain rolled his eyes heavenward in disgust.

The Captain of the Guard became angry, though he kept the fact hidden behind heavy-lidded eyes. "It all fit—the accent that Ansset told us they had, the wooden ship, calling each other freemen, their emotionalism—they could have been no one else but the Freemen of Eire. Just another nationalist group, but they have a lot of sympathizers here in America—damn these 'nations,' where but on old Earth would people subdivide their planet and think the subdivisions meant anything."

"So you went in and wiped them all out," the Chamberlain sneered, "and not one of them had any knowledge of the plot."

"Anyone who could block out the Songbird's mind as well as he did can hide a conspiracy like that!" the Captain of the Guard snapped back.

"Our enemy is subtle," the Chamberlain said. "He kept everything else from Ansset's knowledge—so why did he let him have all these clues that steered us to Eire? I think we were given bait and you bit. Well, I haven't bitten yet, and I'm still looking."

"In the meantime," Mikal said, "try to avoid harassing Ansset too much."

"I don't mind," Ansset hurriedly said, though he minded very much: the constant searches, the frequent interrogations, the hypnotherapy, the guards who followed him constantly to keep him from meeting with anyone.

"I mind," Mikal said. "It's good for you to keep watch, because we still don't know what they've done to Ansset's mind. But in the meantime, let Ansset's life be worth living." Mikal glared pointedly at the Captain of the Guard, who got up and left. Then Mikal turned to the Chamberlain and said, "I don't like how easily the Captain was fooled by such an obvious ploy. Keep up your investigation. And tell me anything your spies within the Captain's forces might have to say."

The Chamberlain tried for a moment to protest that he had no such spies—but Mikal laughed until the Chamberlain gave up and promised to complete a report.

"My days are numbered," Mikal said to Ansset. "Sing to me of numbered days." And so Ansset sang him a playful song about a man who decided to live for two hundred years and so counted his age backward, by the number of years he had left. "And he died when he was only eighty-three," Ansset sang, and Mikal laughed and tossed another log on the fire. Only an emperor or a peasant in the protected forests of Siberia could afford to burn wood.

Then one day Ansset, as he wandered through the palace, noticed a different direction and a quickened pace to the hustling and bustling of servants down the halls. He went to the Chamberlain.

"Try to keep quiet about it," the Chamberlain said. "You're coming with us, anyway."

And within an hour Ansset rode beside Mikal in an armored car as a convoy swept out of Capital. The roads were kept clear, and in an hour and fifteen minutes the armored car stopped. Ansset bounded out of the hatchway. He was startled to see that the entire convoy was missing, and only the single armored car remained. He immediately suspected treachery, and looked down at Mikal in fright.

"Don't worry," Mikal said. "We sent the convoy on."

They got out of the car and with a dozen picked guards (not from the palace guard, Ansset noticed) they made their way through a sparse wood, along a stream, and finally to the banks of a huge river.

"The Delaware," whispered the Chamberlain to Ansset, who had already guessed as much.

"Keep your esoterica to yourself," Mikal said, sounding irritable, which meant he was enjoying himself immensely. He hadn't been a part of any kind of planetside military operation in forty years, ever since he became an emperor and had to control fleets and planets instead of a few ships and a thousand men. There was a spring to his step that belied his century and a quarter.

Finally the Chamberlain stopped. "That's the house, and that's the boat."

A flatboat was moored on the river by a shambling wooden house that looked like it had been built during the American colonial revival over a hundred years before.

They crept up on the house, but it was empty, and when they rushed the flatboat

Orson Scott Card

the only man on board aimed a laser at his own face and blasted it to a cinder. Not before Ansset had recognized him, though.

"That was Husk," Ansset said, feeling sick as he looked at the ruined corpse. Inexplicably, he felt a nagging guilt. "He's the man who fed me."

Then Mikal and the Chamberlain followed Ansset through the boat. "It's not the same," Ansset said.

"Of course not," said the Chamberlain. "The paint is fresh. And there's a smell of new wood. They've been remodeling. But is there anything familiar?"

There was. Ansset found a tiny room that could have been his cell, though now it was painted bright yellow and a new window let sunlight flood into the room. Mikal examined the window frame. "New," the emperor pronounced. And by trying to imagine the interior of the flatboat as it might have been unpainted, Ansset was able to find the large room where he had sung his last evening in captivity. There was no table. But the room seemed the same size, and Ansset agreed that this could very well have been the place he was held.

Down in the ship they heard the laughter of children and a passing eletrecart that clattered along the bumpy old, asphalt road. The Chamberlain laughed. "Sorry I took you the long way. It's really quite a populated area. I just wanted to be sure they didn't have time to be warned."

Mikal curled his lip. "If it's a populated area we should have arrived in a bus. A group of armed men walking along a river are much more conspicuous."

"I'm not a tactician, " said the Chamberlain.

"Tactician enough," said Mikal. "We'll go back to the palace now. Do you have anyone you can trust to make the arrest? I don't want him harmed."

But it didn't do any good to give orders to that effect. When the Captain of the Guard was arrested, he raged and stormed and then a half-hour later, before there was time to examine him with the probe and taster, one of the guards slipped him some poison and he drifted off into death. The Chamberlain rashly had the offending guard impaled with nails until he bled to death.

Ansset was confused as he watched Mikal rage at the Chamberlain. It was obviously a sham, or half a sham, and Ansset was certain that the Chamberlain knew it. "Only a fool would have killed that soldier! How did the poison get into the palace past the detectors? How did the soldier get it to the Captain? None of the questions will ever be answered now!"

The Chamberlain made the mandatory ritual resignation. "My Lord Imperator, I was a fool. I deserve to die. I resign my position and ask for you to have me killed."

Following the ritual, but obviously annoyed by having it thrust at him before he was through raging, Mikal lifted his hand and said, "Damn right you're a fool." Then, in proper form, he said, "I grant you your life because of your infinitely valuable services to me in apprehending the traitor in the first place." Mikal cocked his head to one side. "So, Chamberlain, who do you think I should make the next Captain of the Guard?"

Ansset almost laughed out loud. It was an impossible question to answer. The safest answer (and the Chamberlain liked to do safe things) would be to say he had never given the matter any thought at all, and wouldn't presume to advise the emperor on such a vital matter. But even so, the moment would be tense for the Chamberlain.

And Ansset was shocked to hear the Chamberlain answer, "Riktors Ashen, of course, my Lord."

The "of course" was insolent. The naming of the man was ridiculous. At first Ansset looked at Mikal to see fury there. But instead Mikal was smiling. "Why of course," he said blandly. "Riktors Ashen is the obvious choice. Tell him in my name that he's appointed."

Even the Chamberlain, who had mastered the art of blandness at will, looked surprised for a moment. Again Ansset almost laughed. He saw Mikal's victory: the Chamberlain had probably named the one man in the palace guard that the Chamberlain had no control over, assuming that Mikal would never pick the man the Chamberlain recommended. And so Mikal had picked him: Riktors Ashen, the victor of the battle of Mantrynn, a planet that had revolted only three years before. He was known to be incorruptible, brilliant, and reliable. Well, now he'd have a chance to prove his reputation, Ansset thought.

Then he was startled out of his reverie by Mikal's voice. "Do you know what his last words were to me?"

By the instant understanding that needed no referents for Mikal's pronouns, Ansset knew he was talking about the now-dead Captain of the Guard.

"He said, 'Tell Mikal that my death frees more plotters than it kills.' And then he said that he loved me. Imagine, that cagey old bastard saying he loved me. I remember him twenty years ago when he killed his closest friend in a squabble over a promotion. The bloodiest men get most sentimental in their old age, I suppose."

Ansset asked a question—it seemed a safe time. "My Lord, why was the Captain arrested?"

"Hmmm?" Mikal looked surprised. "Oh, I suppose no one told you, then. He visited that house regularly throughout your captivity. He said he visited a woman there. But the neighbors all testified under the probe that a woman never lived there. And the Captain was a master at establishing mental blocks."

"Then the conspiracy is broken!" Ansset said, joyfully assuming that the guards would stop harassing him and the questions would finally end.

"The conspiracy is barely dented. Someone was able to get poison to the Captain. Therefore plotters still exist within the palace. And therefore Riktors Ashen will be instructed to keep a close watch on you."

Ansset tried to keep the smile on his face. He failed.

"I know, I know," Mikal said wearily. "But it's still locked in your mind."

It was unlocked the next day. The court was gathered in the Great Hall, and Ansset resigned himself to a morning of wandering through the halls—or else standing near Mikal as he received the boring procession of dignitaries paying their respects to the emperor (and then going home to report how soon they thought Mikal the Terrible would die, and who might succeed him, and what the chances were for grabbing a piece of the empire). Because the palace bored him and he wanted to be near Mikal, and because the Chamberlain smiled at him and asked, "Are you coming to court?" Ansset decided to attend.

The order of dignitaries had been carefully worked out to honor loyal friends and humiliate upstarts whose dignity needed deflating. A minor official from a distant star cluster was officially honored, the first business of the day, and then the rituals began: princes and presidents and satraps and governors, depending on what title survived the conquest a decade or a score or fourscore years ago, all proceeding forward with their retinue, bowing (how low they bowed showed how afraid they were of Mikal, or how much they wanted to flatter him), uttering a few words, asking for private audience, being put off or being invited, in an endless array.

Ansset was startled to see a group of Black Kinshasans attired in their bizarre old Earth costumes. Kinshasa insisted it was an independent nation, a pathetic nose-thumbing claim when empires of planets had been swallowed up by Mikal Conqueror. Why were they being allowed to wear their native regalia and have an audience? Ansset raised an eyebrow at the Chamberlain, who also stood near the throne.

"It was Mikal's idea," the Chamberlain said voicelessly. "He's letting them come and present a petition right before the president of Stuss. Those toads from Stuss'll be madder than hell."

At that moment Mikal raised his hand for some wine. Obviously he was as bored as anyone else.

The Chamberlain poured the wine, tasted it, as was the routine, and then took a step toward Mikal's throne. Then he stopped, and beckoned to Ansset, who was already moving back to Mikal's side. Surprised at the summons, Ansset came over.

"Why don't *you* take the wine to Mikal, Sweet Songbird?" the Chamberlain said. The surprise fell away from Ansset's eyes, and he took the wine and headed purposefully back to Mikal's throne.

At that moment, however, pandemonium broke loose. The Kinshasan envoys reached into their elaborate curly-haired headdresses and withdrew wooden knives—which could pass every test given by machines at the doors of the palace. They rushed toward the throne. The guards fired quickly, their lasers dropping five of the Kinshasans, but all had aimed at the foremost assassins, and three continued unharmed. They rushed toward the throne, arms extended so the knives were already aimed directly at Mikal's heart.

Mikal, old and unarmed, rose to meet them. A guard managed to shift his aim and get off a shot, but it was wild, and the others were hurriedly recharging their lasers—which only took a moment, but that was a moment too long.

Mikal looked death in the eye and did not seem disappointed.

But at that moment Ansset threw the wine goblet at one of the attackers and then leaped out in front of the emperor. He jumped easily into the air, and kicked the jaw of the first of the attackers. The angle of the kick was perfect, the force sharp and incredibly hard, and the Kinshasan's head flew fifty feet away into the crowd, as his body slid forward until the wooden knife touched Mikal's foot. Ansset came down from the jump in time to bring his hand upward into the abdomen of another attacker so sharply that his arm was buried to the elbow in bowels, and his fingers crushed the man's heart.

The other attacker paused just a moment, thrown from his relentless charge by the sudden onslaught from the child who stood so harmlessly by the emperor's throne. That pause was long enough for recharged lasers to be aimed, to flash, and the last Kinshasan assassin fell, dropping ashes as he collapsed, flaming slightly.

The whole thing, from the appearance of the wooden knives to the fall of the last attacker, had taken five seconds.

Ansset stood still in the middle of the hall, gore on his arm, blood splashed all over his body. He looked at the gory hand, at the body he had pulled it out of. A rush of long-blocked memories came back, and he remembered other such bodies, other heads kicked from torsos, other men who had died as Ansset learned the skill of killing with his hands. The guilt that had troubled him before swept through him with new force now that he knew the why of it.

The searches had all been in vain. Ansset himself was the weapon that was to have been used against Father Mikal.

The smell of blood and broken intestines combined with the emotions sweeping his body, and he doubled over, shuddering as he vomited.

The guards gingerly approached him, unsure what they should do.

But the Chamberlain was sure. Ansset heard the voice, trembling with fear at how close the assassination had come, and how easily a different assassination could have come, saying, "Keep him under guard. Wash him. Never let him be out of a laser's aim for a moment. Then bring him to Mikal's chambers in an hour."

The guards looked toward Mikal, who nodded.

Ansset was still white and weak when he came into Mikal's chambers. The guards still had lasers trained on him. The Chamberlain and the new Captain of the Guard, Riktors Ashen, stood between Mikal and the boy.

"Songbird," Riktors said, "it seems that someone taught you new songs."

Ansset lowered his head.

"You must have studied under a master."

"I n-never," Ansset stuttered. He had never stuttered in his life.

"Don't torture the boy, Captain," Mikal said.

The Chamberlain launched into his pro forma resignation. "I should have examined the boy's muscle structure and realized what new skills he had been given. I submit my resignation. I beg you to take my life."

The Chamberlain must be even more worried than usual, Ansset thought with that part of his mind that was still capable of thinking. The old man had prostrated himself in front of the emperor.

"Shut up and get up," Mikal said rudely. The Chamberlain arose with his face gray. Mikal had not followed the ritual. The Chamberlain's life was still on the line.

"We will now be certain," Mikal said to Riktors. "Show him the pictures."

Ansset stood watching as Riktors took a packet off a table and began removing newsheet clippings from it. Ansset looked at the first one and was merely sickened a little. The second one he recognized, and he gasped. With the third one he wept and threw the pictures away from him.

"Those are the pictures," Mikal said, "of the people who were kidnapped and murdered during your captivity."

"I k-killed them," Ansset said, dimly aware that there was no trace of song in his voice, just the frightened stammering of an eleven-year-old boy caught up in something too monstrous for him to comprehend. "They had me practice on them."

"*Who* had you practice!" Riktors demanded.

"They! The voices—from the box." Ansset struggled to hold onto memories that had been hidden from him by the block. He also longed to let the block in his mind slide back into place, forget again, shut it out.

"What box?" Riktors would not let up.

"The box. A wooden box. Maybe a receiver, maybe a recording, I don't know."

"Did you know the voice?"

"Voices. Never the same. Not even for the same sentence, the voices changed for every word."

Ansset kept seeing the faces of the bound men he was told to maim and then kill. He remembered that though he cried out against it, he was still forced to do it.

"How did they force you to do it!"

Was Riktors reading his mind? "I don't know. I don't know. There were words, and then I had to."

"What words?"

"I don't know! I never knew!" And Ansset was crying again.

Mikal spoke softly. "Who taught you how to kill that way?"

"A man. I never knew his name. On the last day, he was tied where the others had been. The voices made me kill him." Ansset struggled with the words, the struggle made harder by the realization that this time, when he had killed his teacher, he had not had to be forced. He had killed because he hated the man. "I murdered him."

"Nonsense," the Chamberlain said. "You were a tool."

"I said to shut up," Mikal said curtly. "Can you remember anything else, my Son?"

"I killed the crew of the ship, too. All except Husk. The voices told me to. And then there were footsteps, above me, on the deck."

"Did you see who it was?"

Ansset forced himself to remember. "No. He told me to lie down. He must have known the—code, whatever it is, I didn't want to obey him, but I did."

"And?"

"Footsteps, and a needle in my arm, and I woke up on the street."

Everyone was silent then, for a few moments, all of them thinking quickly. The Chamberlain broke first. "My Lord, the great threat to you and the strength of the Songbird's love for you must have impelled him despite the mental block—"

"Chamberlain," Mikal said, "your life is over if you speak again before I address you. Captain. I want to know how those Kinshasans got past your guard?"

"They were dignitaries. By your order, my Lord, no dignitaries are given the body search. Their wooden knives passed all the detectors. I'm surprised this hadn't been tried before."

Ansset noticed that Riktors spoke confidently, not coweringly as another Captain might have done after assassins got through his guard. And, better in control of himself, Ansset listened for the melodies of Riktors's voice. They were strong. They were dissonant. Ansset wondered if he would be able to detect Riktors in a lie. To a strong, selfish man all things that he chose to say became truth, and the songs of his voice said nothing.

"Riktors, you will prepare orders for the utter destruction of Kinshasa."

Riktors saluted.

"Before Kinshasa is destroyed—and that means destroyed, not a blade of grass, Riktors—before Kinshasa is destroyed, I want to know what connection there is between the assassination attempt this morning and the manipulation of my Songbird."

Riktors saluted again. Mikal spoke to the Chamberlain. "Chamberlain, what would you recommend I do with my Songbird?"

As usual, the Chamberlain took the safe way. "My Lord, it is not a matter to which I have given thought. The disposition of your Songbird is not a matter on which I feel it proper to advise you."

"Very carefully said, my dear Chamberlain." Ansset tried to be calm as he listened to them discuss how he should be disposed of. Mikal raised his hand in the gesture that, by ritual, spared the Chamberlain's life. Ansset would have laughed at the Chamberlain's struggle not to show his relief, but this was not a time for laughter, because Ansset knew his relief would not come so easily.

"My Lord," Ansset said, "I beg you to put me to death."

"Dammit, Ansset, I'm sick of the rituals," Mikal said.

Orson Scott Card

"This is no ritual," Ansset said, his voice tired and husky from misuse. "And this is no song, Father Mikal. I'm a danger to you."

"I know it." Mikal looked back and forth between Riktors and the Chamberlain.

"Chamberlain, have Ansset's possessions put together and readied for shipment to Alwiss. The prefect there is Timmis Hortmang, prepare a letter of explanation and a letter of mark. Ansset will arrive there wealthier than anyone else in the prefecture. Those are my orders. See to it." He turned his head downward and to the right. Both Riktors and the Chamberlain moved to leave. Ansset—and therefore the guards who had lasers trained on him—did not.

"Father Mikal," Ansset said softly, and he realized that the words had been a song. But Mikal made no answer. He only got up from the chair and left the chamber.

Ansset had several hours before nightfall, and he spent them wandering through the palace and the palace grounds. The guards dogged his steps. At first he let the tears flow. Then, as the horror of the morning hid again behind the only partly broken block in his mind, he remembered what the Songmaster had taught him, again and again, "When you want to weep, let the tears come through your throat. Let pain come from the pressure in your thighs. Let sorrow rise and resonate through your head."

Walking by the Susquehanna on the cold lawns of autumn afternoon shade, Ansset sang his grief. He sang softly, but the guards heard his song, and could not help but weep for him, too.

He stopped at a place where the water looked cold and clear, and began to strip off his tunic, preparing to swim. A guard reached out and stopped him. Ansset noticed the laser pointed at his foot. "I can't let you do that. Mikal gave orders you were not to be allowed to take your own life."

"I only want to swim," Ansset answered, his voice low with persuasion.

"I would be killed if any harm came to you," the guard said.

"I give you my oath that I will only swim, and not try to break free."

The guard considered. The other guards seemed content to leave the decision up to him. Ansset hummed a sweet melody that he knew oozed confidence. The guard gave in.

Ansset stripped and dove into the water. It was icy cold, and stung him. He swam in broad strokes upstream, knowing that to the guards on the bank he would already seem like only a speck on the surface of the river. Then he dove and swam under the water, holding his breath as only a singer or a pearl diver could, and swam across the current toward the near shore, where the guards were waiting. He could hear, though muffled by the water, the cries of the guards. He surfaced, laughing.

Two of the guards had already thrown off their boots and were up to their waists in water, preparing to try to catch Ansset's body as it swept by. But Ansset kept laughing at them, and they turned at him angrily.

"Why did you worry?" Ansset said. "I gave my word."

Then the guards relaxed, and Ansset swam for an hour under the afternoon sun. The motion of the water, and constant exertion to keep place against the current took his mind off his troubles, to some extent. Only one guard watched him now, while the others played polys, casting fourteen-sided dice in a mad gambling game that soon engrossed them.

Ansset swam underwater from time to time, listening to the different sound the guards' quarreling and laughing made when water covered his ears. The sun was nearly down now, and Ansset dove underwater again to swim to shore on one breath. He was halfway to shore when he heard the sharp call of a bird overhead, muffled as it was by the river.

Ansset made a sudden connection in his mind, and came up immediately, coughing and sputtering. He dogpaddled in to shore, shook himself, and put on his tunic, wet as he was.

"We've got to get back to the palace," he said, filling his voice with urgency, putting the pitch high to penetrate the guards' sluggishness after an hour of gaming. The guards quickly followed him, overtook him.

"Where are you going?" one of them asked.

"To see Mikal."

"We're not to do that—we were ordered! You can't go to Mikal."

But Ansset walked on, fairly sure that until he actually got close to the emperor, the guards would not try to restrain him. Even if they had not been present for the demonstration of Ansset's skill in the Great Hall that morning, the story would surely have reached their ears that Mikal's Songbird could kill two men in two seconds.

He had heard the call of a bird as he swam underwater. He remembered that on his last night of captivity in the ship, he had heard the cry of another bird high above him. But never, never had he heard another sound from outside.

And yet where the flatboat was the city noise had come loudly, could be heard clearly below decks. Therefore even if the boat were his prison, it had not been moored by that house. And if that were so, the evidence against the former Captain of the Guard was a fraud. And Ansset knew now who in the court had taken Ansset to use as an assassin.

They were met in a corridor by a messenger. "There you are. The Lord Mikal commands the presence of the Songbird, as quickly as possible. Here," he said, handing the orders to the guard who made decisions, who took out his verifier and passed it over the seal on the orders. A sharp buzz testified that the orders were genuine.

"All right then, Songbird," said the guard. "We'll go there after all." Ansset started to run. The guards kept up easily, following him through the labyrinth. To them it was almost a game, and one of them said, between breaths, "I never knew this way led where we're going!" to which one of the other guards replied, "And you'll never find it again, either."

Orson Scott Card

And then they were in Mikal's chambers. Ansset's hair was still wet, and his tunic still clung to his small body where it had not yet had time to dry from the river water.

Mikal was smiling. "Ansset, my Son, it's fine now." Mikal waved an arm, dismissing the guards. "We were so foolish to think we needed to send you away," he said. "The Captain was the only one in the plot close enough to give the signal. Now that he'd dead, no one knows it! You're safe now—and so am I!"

Mikal's speech was jovial, delighted, but Ansset, who knew the songs of his voice as well as he knew his own, read in the words a warning, a lie, a declaration of danger. Ansset did not run to him. He waited.

"In fact," Mikal said, "you're my best possible bodyguard. You look small and weak, you're always by my side, and you can kill faster than a guard with a laser." Mikal laughed. Ansset was not fooled. There was no mirth in the laugh.

But the Chamberlain and Captain Riktors Ashen were fooled, and they laughed along with Mikal. Ansset forced himself to laugh, too. He listened to the sounds the others were making. Riktors sounded sincere enough, but the Chamberlain—

"It's a cause for celebration. Here's wine," said the Chamberlain. "I brought us wine. Ansset, why don't you pour it?"

Ansset shuddered with memories. "I?" he asked, surprised, and then not surprised at all. The Chamberlain held out the full bottle and the empty goblet. "For the Lord Mikal," the Chamberlain said.

Ansset shouted and dashed the bottle to the floor. "Make him keep silent!"

The suddenness of Ansset's violent action brought Riktors's laser out of his belt and into his hand.

"Don't let the Chamberlain speak!"

"Why not?" asked Mikal innocently, but Ansset knew there was no innocence behind the words. For some reason Mikal was pretending not to understand.

The Chamberlain believed it, believed he had a moment. He said quickly, almost urgently, "Why did you do that? I have another bottle. *Sweet Songbird, let Mikal drink deeply!*"

The words hammered into Ansset's brain, and by reflex he whirled and faced Mikal. He knew what was happening, knew and screamed against it in his mind. But his hands came up against his will, his legs bent, he compressed to spring, all so quickly that he couldn't stop himself. He knew that in less than a second his hand would be buried in Mikal's face, Mikal's beloved face, Mikal's smiling face—

Mikal was smiling at him, kindly and without fear. Ansset stopped in midspring, forced himself to turn aside, despite the tearing in his brain. He could be forced to kill, but he couldn't be forced to kill that face. He shoved his hand into the floor, bursting the tense surface, releasing the gel to flow out across the room.

Ansset hardly noticed the pain in his arm where the impact had broken the skin and the gel was agonizing the wound. All he felt was the pain in his mind as he still struggled against the compulsion he had only just barely deflected, that still drove him to try to kill Mikal, that still he fought against, fought down, tried to block.

His body heaved upward, his hand flew threw the air, and shattered the back of the chair where Mikal still sat. Blood spurted and splashed, and Ansset was relieved to see that it was his own blood, and not Mikal's.

In the distance he heard Mikal's voice saying, "Don't shoot him." And, as suddenly as it had come, the compulsion ceased. His mind spun as he heard the Chamberlain's words fading away: *"Songbird, what have you done!"*

Those were the words that had set him free.

Exhausted and bleeding, Ansset lay on the floor, his right arm covered with blood. The pain reached him now, and he groaned, though his groan was as much a song of ecstasy as of pain. Somehow Ansset had withstood it long enough, and he had not killed Father Mikal.

Finally he rolled over and sat up, nursing his arm. The bleeding had settled to a slow trickle.

Mikal was still sitting in the chair, despite its shattered back where Ansset's hand had struck. The Chamberlain stood where he had stood ten seconds before, at the beginning of Ansset's ordeal, the goblet looking ridiculous in his hand. Riktors's laser was aimed at the Chamberlain.

"Call the guards, Captain," Mikal said.

"I already have," Riktors said. The button on his belt was glowing. Guards came quickly into the room. "Take the Chamberlain to a cell," he ordered them. "If any harm comes to him, all of you will die and your families, too. Do you understand?" The guards understood.

Ansset held his arm. Mikal and Riktors Ashen waited while a doctor treated it. The pain subsided.

The doctor left.

Riktors spoke first. "Of course you knew it was the Chamberlain, my Lord." Mikal smiled faintly.

"That was why you let him persuade you to call Ansset back here." Mikal's smile grew broader.

"But, my Lord, only you could have known that the Songbird would be strong enough to resist a compulsion that was five months in the making."

Mikal laughed. And this time Ansset heard mirth in the laughter.

"Riktors Ashen. Will they call you Riktors the Usurper? Or Riktors the Great?"

It took the Captain of the Guard a moment to realize what had been said. Only a moment. But before his hand could reach his laser, which was back in his belt, Mikal's hand held a laser that was pointed at Riktor's heart.

"Ansset, my Son, will you take the Captain's laser from him?"

Ansset got up and took the Captain's laser from him. He could hear the song of

Orson Scott Card

triumph in Mikal's voice. But Ansset's head was still spinning, and he didn't understand why lasers had been drawn between the emperor and his incorruptible Captain.

"Only one mistake, Riktors. Otherwise brilliantly done. And I really don't see how you could have avoided the mistake, either."

"You mean Ansset's strength?"

"Not even I counted on that. I was prepared to kill him, if I needed to," Mikal said, and Ansset, listening, knew it was true. He wondered why that knowledge didn't hurt him. He had always known that, eventually, not even he would be indispensable to Mikal, if somehow his death served some vital purpose.

"Then I made no mistakes," Riktors said. "How did you know?"

"Because my Chamberlain, unless he were under some sort of compulsion, would never have had the courage to suggest your name as the Captain's successor. And without that, you wouldn't have been in a position to take over after you exposed the Chamberlain as the engineer of my assassination, would you? It was good. The guard would have followed you loyally. No taint of assassination would have touched you. Of course, the entire empire would have rebelled immediately. But you're a good tactician and a better strategist, and your men would have followed you well. I'd have given you one chance in four of making it—and that's better odds than any other man in the empire."

"I gave myself even odds," Riktors said, but Ansset heard the fear singing through the back of his brave words. Well, why not? Death was certain now, and Ansset knew of no one, except perhaps an old man like Mikal, who could look at death, especially death that also meant failure, without some fear.

But Mikal did not push the button on the laser.

"Kill me now and finish it," Riktors Ashen said.

Mikal tossed the laser away. "With this? It has no charge. The Chamberlain installed a charge detector at every door in my chambers over fifteen years ago. He would have known if I was armed."

Immediately Riktors took a step forward, the beginning of a rush toward the emperor Just as quickly Ansset was on his feet, despite the bandaged arm ready to kill with the other hand, with his feet, with his head. Riktors stopped cold.

"Ah," Mikal said, "no one knows like you do what my bodyguard can accomplish in so short a time."

And Ansset realized that if Mikal's laser was not loaded, he couldn't have stopped Ansset if Ansset had not had strength enough to stop himself. Mikal *had* trusted him.

And Mikal spoke again. "Riktors, your mistakes were very slight. I hope you have learned from them. So that when an assassin as bright as you are tries to take *your* life, you know all the enemies you have and all the allies you can call on and exactly what you can expect from each."

Ansset's hands trembled. "Let me kill him now," he said.

Mikal sighed. "Don't kill for pleasure, my Son. If you ever kill for pleasure you'll come to hate yourself. Besides, weren't you listening? I'm going to adopt Riktors Ashen as my heir."

"I don't believe you," Riktors said. But Ansset heard hope in his voice.

"I'll call in my sons—they stay around court, hoping to be closest to the palace when I die," Mikal said. "I'll make them sign an oath to respect you as my heir. Of course they'll all sign it, and of course you'll have them all killed the moment you take the throne. And, let's see, that moment will be three weeks from tomorrow, that should give us time. I'll abdicate in your favor, sign all the papers, it'll make the headlines on the newssheets for days. I can just see all the potential rebels tearing their hair with rage. It's a pleasant picture to retire on."

Ansset didn't understand. "Why?" he asked. "He tried to kill you."

Mikal only laughed. It was Riktors who answered. "He thinks I can hold his empire together. But I want to know the price."

Mikal leaned forward on his chair. "A small price. A house for myself and my Songbird until I die. And then he is to be free for the rest of his life, with an income that doesn't make him dependent on anybody's favors. Simple enough?"

"I agree."

"How prudent." And Mikal laughed again.

The vows were made, the abdication and coronation took a great deal of pomp and the Capital's caterers became wealthy. All the contenders were slaughtered, and Riktors spent a year going from system to system to quell (brutally) all the rebellions.

After the first few planets were burned over, the other rebellions mostly quelled themselves.

It was only the day after the newssheets announced the quelling of the most threatening rebellion that the soldiers appeared at the door of the little house in Brazil where Mikal and Ansset lived.

"How can he!" Ansset cried out in anguish when he saw the soldiers at the door. "He gave his word."

"Open the door for them, Son," Mikal said.

"They're here to kill you!"

"A year was all that I hoped for. I've had that year. Did you really expect Riktors to keep his word? There isn't room in the galaxy for two heads that know the feel of the imperial crown."

"I can kill most of them before they could come near. If you hide, perhaps—"

"Don't kill anyone, Ansset. That's not your song. The dance of your hands is nothing without the dance of your voice, Songbird."

The soldiers began to beat on the door, which, because it was steel, did not give way easily. "They'll blow it open in a moment," Mikal said. "Promise me you won't kill anyone. No matter who. Please. Don't avenge me."

"I will."

"Don't avenge me. Promise. On your life. On your love for me."

Ansset promised. The door blew open. The soldiers killed Mikal with a flash of lasers that turned his body to ashes. They kept firing until nothing but ashes was left. Then they gathered them up. Ansset watched, keeping his promise but wishing with all his heart that somewhere in his mind there was a wall he could hide behind. Unfortunately, he was too sane.

They took the ashes of the emperor and twelve-year-old Ansset to Capital. The ashes were placed in a huge urn, and displayed with state honors. Ansset they brought to the funeral feast under heavy guard, for fear of what his hands might do.

After the meal, at which everyone pretended to be somber, Riktors called Ansset to him. The guards followed, but Riktors waved them away. The crown rested on his hair.

"I know I'm safe from you," Riktors said.

"You're a lying bastard," Ansset said, "and if I hadn't given my word I'd tear you end to end."

It might have seemed ludicrous that a twelve-year-old should speak that way to an emperor, but Riktors didn't laugh. "If I weren't a lying bastard, Mikal would never have given the empire to me."

Then Riktors stood. "My friends," he said, and the sycophants gave a cheer. "From now on I am not to be known as Riktors Ashen, but as Riktors Mikal. The name Mikal shall pass to all my successors on the throne, in honor of the man who built this empire and brought peace to all mankind." Riktors sat amid the applause and cheers, which sounded like some of the people might have been sincere. It was a nice speech, as impromptu speeches went.

Then Riktors commanded Ansset to sing.

"I'd rather die," Ansset said.

"You will, when the time comes," Riktors answered.

Ansset sang then, standing on the table so that everyone could see him, just as he had stood to sing to an audience he hated on his last night of captivity in the ship. His song was wordless, for all the words he might have said were treason. Instead he sang melody, flying unaccompanied from mode to mode, each note torn from his throat in pain, each note bringing pain to the ears that heard it. The song broke up the banquet as the grief they had all pretended to feel now burned within them. Many went home weeping; all felt the great loss of the man whose ashes dusted the bottom of the urn.

Only Riktors stayed at the table after Ansset's song was over.

"Now," Ansset said, "they'll never forget Father Mikal."

"Or Mikal's Songbird," Riktors said. "But I am Mikal now, as much of him as could survive. A name and an empire."

"There's nothing of Father Mikal in you," Ansset said coldly.

"Is there not?" Riktors said softly. "Were you fooled by Mikal's public cruelty?

No, Songbird." And in his voice Ansset heard the hints of pain that lay behind the harsh and haughty emperor.

"Stay and sing for me, Songbird," Riktors said. Pleading played around the edges of his voice.

Ansset reached out his hand and touched the urn of ashes that rested on the table. "I'll never love you," he said, meaning the words to hurt.

"Nor I you," Riktors answered. "But we may, nonetheless, feed each other something that we hunger for. Did Mikal sleep with you?"

"He never wanted to. I never offered."

"Neither will I," Riktors said. "I only want to hear the songs."

There was no voice in Ansset for the word he decided to say. He nodded. Riktors had the grace not to smile. He just nodded in return, and left the table. Before he reached the doors, Ansset spoke: "What will you do with this?"

Riktors looked at where Ansset rested his hand. "The relics are yours. Do what you want." Then Riktors Mikal was gone.

Ansset took the urn of ashes into the chamber where he and Father Mikal had sung so many songs to each other. Ansset stood for a long time before the fire, humming the memories to himself. He gave the songs back to Father Mikal, and then reached out and emptied the urn on the blazing fire.

The ashes put the fire out.

"The transition is complete," Songmaster Onn said to Songmaster Esste as soon as the door was closed.

"I was afraid," Songmaster Esste confided in a low melody that trembled. "Riktors Ashen is not unwise. But Ansset's songs are stronger than wisdom."

They sat together in the cold sunlight that filtered through the windows of the High Room of the Songhouse. "Ah," sang Songmaster Onn, and the melody was of love for Songmaster Esste.

"Don't praise me. The gift and power were Ansset's."

"But the teacher was Esste. In other hands Ansset might have been used as a tool for power, for wealth, for control. In your hands—"

"No, Brother Onn. Ansset himself is too much made of love and loyalty. He makes other men desire what he himself already is. He is a tool that cannot be used for evil."

"Will he ever know?"

"Perhaps; I do not think he yet suspects the power of his gift. It would be better if he never found out how little like the other Songbirds he is. And as for the last block in his mind—we laid that well. He will never know it is there, and so he will never search for the truth about who controlled the transfer of the crown."

Songmaster Onn sang tremulously of the delicate plots woven in the mind of a child of five, plots that could have unwoven at any point. "But the weaver was wise, and the cloth has held."

Orson Scott Card

"Mikal Conqueror," said Songmaster Esste, "learned to love peace more than he loved himself, and so will Riktors Mikal. That is enough. We have done our duty for mankind. Now we must teach other little Songbirds."

"Only the old songs," sighed Songmaster Onn.

"No," answered Songmaster Esste with a smile. "We will teach them to sing of Mikal's Songbird."

"Ansset has already sung that."

They walked slowly out of the High Room as Songmaster Esste whispered, "Then we will harmonize!" Their laughter was music down the stairs. ∎

IN HIDING
Wilmar H. Shiras

Peter Welles, psychiatrist, eyed the boy thoughtfully. Why had Timothy Paul's teacher sent him for examination?

"I don't know, myself, that there's really anything wrong with Tim," Miss Page had told Dr. Welles. "He seems perfectly normal. He's rather quiet as a rule, doesn't volunteer answers in class or anything of that sort. He gets along well enough with other boys and seems reasonably popular, although he has no special friends. His grades are satisfactory—he gets B faithfully in all his work. But when you've been teaching as long as I have, Peter, you get a feeling about certain ones. There is a tension about him—a look in his eyes sometimes—and he is very absentminded."

"What would your guess be?" Welles had asked. Sometimes these hunches were very valuable. Miss Page had taught school for thirty-odd years; she had been Peter's teacher in the past, and he thought highly of her opinion.

"I ought not to say," she answered. "There's nothing to go on—yet. But he might be starting something, and if it could be headed off—"

"Physicians are often called before the symptoms are sufficiently marked for the doctor to be able to see them," said Welles. "A patient, or the mother of a child, or any practiced observer, can often see that something is going to be wrong. But it's hard for the doctor in such cases. Tell me what you think I should look for."

"You won't pay too much attention to me? It's just what occurred to me, Peter; I know I'm not a trained psychiatrist. But it could be delusions of grandeur. Or it could be a withdrawing from the society of others. I always have to speak to him twice to get his attention in class—and he has no real chums."

Welles had agreed to see what he could find, and promised not to be much influenced by what Miss Page herself called "an old woman's notions."

Timothy, when he presented himself for examination, seemed like an ordinary boy. He was perhaps a little small for his age, he had big dark eyes and close-cropped dark curls, thin sensitive fingers and—yes, a decided air of tension. But many boys were nervous on their first visit to the—psychiatrist. Peter often wished that he was able to concentrate on one or two schools, and spend a day a week or so getting acquainted with all the youngsters.

In response to Welles' preliminary questioning, Tim replied in a clear, low voice, politely and without wasting words. He was thirteen years old, and lived with his grandparents. His mother and father had died when he was a baby, and he did not remember them. He said that he was happy at home, and that he liked school "pretty well," that he liked to play with other boys. He named several boys when asked who his friends were.

"What lessons do you like at school?"

Tim hesitated, then said: "English, and arithmetic . . . and history . . . and geography," he finished thoughtfully. Then he looked up, and there was something odd in the glance.

"What do you like to do for fun?"

"Read, and play games."

"What games?"

"Ball games . . . and marbles . . . and things like that. I like to play with other boys," he added, after a barely perceptible pause, "anything they play."

"Do they play at your house?"

"No; we play on the school grounds. My grandmother doesn't like noise."

Was that the reason? When a quiet boy offers explanations, they may not be the right ones.

"What do you like to read?"

But about his reading Timothy was vague. He liked, he said, to read "boys' books," but could not name any.

Welles gave the boy the usual intelligence tests. Tim seemed willing, but his replies were slow in coming. *Perhaps,* Welles thought, *I'm imagining this, but he is too careful—too cautious.* Without taking time to figure exactly, Welles knew what Tim's I.Q. would be—about 120.

"What do you do outside of school?" asked the psychiatrist.

"I play with the other boys. After supper, I study my lessons."

"What did you do yesterday?"

"We played ball on the school playground."

Welles waited a while to see whether Tim would say anything of his own accord. The seconds stretched into minutes.

"Is that all?" said the boy finally. "May I go now?"

"No; there's one more test I'd like to give you today. A game, really. How's your imagination?"

"I don't know."

"Cracks on the ceiling—like those over there—do they look like anything to you? Faces, animals, or anything?"

Tim looked.

"Sometimes. And clouds, too. Bob saw a cloud last week that was like a hippo." Again the last sentence sounded like something tacked on at the last moment, a careful addition made for a reason.

Welles got out the Rorschach cards. But at the sight of them, his patient's tension increased, his wariness became unmistakably evident. The first time they went through the cards, the boy could scarcely be persuaded to say anything but, "I don't know."

"You can do better than this," said Welles. "We're going through them again. If you don't see anything in these pictures, I'll have to mark you a failure," he explained. "That won't do. You did all right on the other things. And maybe next time we'll do a game you'll like better."

"I don't feel like playing this game now. Can't we do it again next time?"

"May as well get it done now. It's not only a game, you know, Tim; it's a test. Try harder, and be a good sport."

So Tim, this time, told what he saw in the ink blots. They went through the cards slowly, and the test showed Tim's fear, and that there was something he was hiding; it showed his caution, a lack of trust, and an unnaturally high emotional self-control.

Miss Page had been right; the boy needed help.

"Now," said Welles cheerfully, "that's all over. We'll just run through them again quickly and I'll tell you what other people have seen in them."

A flash of genuine interest appeared on the boy's face for a moment.

Welles went through the cards slowly, seeing that Tim was attentive to every word. When he first said, "And some see what you saw here," the boy's relief was evident. Tim began to relax, and even to volunteer some remarks. When they had finished he ventured to ask a question.

"Dr. Welles, could you tell me the name of this test?"

"It's sometimes called the Rorschach test, after the man who worked it out."

"Would you mind spelling that?"

Welles spelled it, and added: "Sometimes it's called the inkblot test."

Tim gave a start of surprise, and then relaxed again with a visible effort.

"What's the matter? You jumped."

"Nothing."

"Oh, come on! Let's have it," and Welles waited.

"Only that I thought about the ink-pool in the Kipling stories," said Tim, after a minute's reflection. "This is different."

"Yes, very different," laughed Welles. "I've never tried that. Would you like to?"

"Oh, no, sir," cried Tim earnestly.

"You're a little jumpy today," said Welles. "We've time for some more talk, if you are not too tired."

"No, I'm not very tired," said the boy warily.

Welles went to a drawer and chose a hypodermic needle. It wasn't usual, but perhaps—"I'll just give you a little shot to relax your nerves, shall I? Then we'd get on better."

When he turned around, the stark terror on the child's face stopped Welles in his tracks.

"Oh, no! Don't! Please, please, please, don't!"

Welles replaced the needle and shut the drawer before he said a word.

"I won't," he said, quietly. "I didn't know you didn't like shots. I won't give you any, Tim."

The boy, fighting for self-control, gulped and said nothing.

"It's all right," said Welles, lighting a cigarette and pretending to watch the smoke rise. Anything rather than appear to be watching the badly shaken small boy shivering in the chair opposite him. "Sorry. You didn't tell me about the things you don't like, the things you're afraid of."

The words hung in the silence.

"Yes," said Timothy slowly. "I'm afraid of shots. I hate needles. It's just one of those things." He tried to smile.

"We'll do without them, then. You've passed all the tests, Tim, and I'd like to walk home with you and tell your grandmother about it. Is that all right with you?"

"Yes, sir."

"We'll stop for something to eat," Welles went on, opening the door for his patient. "Ice cream, or a hot dog."

They went out together.

Timothy Paul's grandparents, Mr. and Mrs. Herbert Davis, lived in a large old-fashioned house that spelled money and position. The grounds were large, fenced, and bordered with shrubbery. Inside the house there was little that was new, everything was well-kept. Timothy led the psychiatrist to Mr. Davis's library, and then went in search of his grandmother.

When Welles saw Mrs. Davis, he thought he had some of the explanation. Some grandmothers are easy-going, jolly, comparatively young. This grandmother was, as it soon become apparent, quite different.

"Yes, Timothy is a pretty good boy," she said, smiling on her grandson. "We have always been strict with him, Dr. Welles, but I believe it pays. Even when he was a mere baby, we tried to teach him right ways. For example, when he was barely three I read him some little stories. And a few days later he was trying to tell us, if you will believe it, that he could read! Perhaps he was too young to know the nature of a lie, but I felt it my duty to make him understand. When he insisted, I spanked him. The child had a remarkable memory, and perhaps he thought that was all there was to reading. Well! I don't mean to brag of my brutality," said Mrs. Davis, with a charming smile. "I assure you, Dr. Welles, it was a painful experience for me. We've had very little occasion for punishments. Timothy is a good boy."

Welles murmured that he was sure of it.

"Timothy, you may deliver your papers now," said Mrs. Davis. "I am sure Dr. Welles will excuse you." And she settled herself for a good long talk about her grandson.

Timothy, it seemed, was the apple of her eye. He was a quiet boy, an obedient boy, and a bright boy.

"We have our rules, of course. I have never allowed Timothy to forget that children should be seen and not heard, as the good old-fashioned saying is. When he first learned to turn somersaults, when he was three or four years old, he kept coming to me and saying, 'Grandmother, see me!' I simply had to be firm with him. 'Timothy,' I said, 'let us have no more of this! It is simply showing off. If it amuses you to turn somersaults, well and good. But it doesn't amuse me to watch you endlessly doing it. Play if you like, but do not demand admiration.' "

"Did you never play with him?"

"Certainly I played with him. And it was a pleasure to me also. We—Mr. Davis and I—taught him a great many games, and many kinds of handicraft. We read stories to him and taught him rhymes and songs. I took a special course in kindergarten craft, to amuse the child—and I must admit that it amused me also!" added Tim's grandmother, smiling reminiscently. "We made houses of toothpicks, with balls of clay at the corners. His grandfather took him for walks and drives. We no longer have a car, since my husband's sight has begun to fail him slightly, so now the garage is Timothy's workshop. We had windows cut in it, and a door, and nailed the large doors shut."

It soon became clear that Tim's life was not all strictures by any means. He had a workshop of his own, and upstairs beside his bedroom was his own library and study. "He keeps his books and treasures there," said his grandmother, "his own little radio, and his schoolbooks, and his typewriter. When he was only seven years old, he asked us for a typewriter. But he is a careful child, Dr. Welles, not at all destructive, and I had read that in many schools they make use of typewriters in teaching young children to read and write and to spell. The words look the same as in printed books, you see; and less muscular effort is involved. So his grandfather got him a very nice noiseless typewriter, and he loved it dearly. I often hear it purring away as I pass through the hall. Timothy keeps his own rooms in good order, and his shop also. It is his own wish. You know how boys are—they do not wish others to meddle with their belongings. 'Very well, Timothy,' I told him, 'if a glance shows me that you can do it yourself properly, nobody will go into your rooms; but they must be kept neat.' And he has done so for several years. A very neat boy, Timothy."

"Timothy didn't mention his paper route," remarked Welles. "He said only that he plays with other boys after school."

"Oh, but he does," said Mrs. Davis. "He plays until five o'clock, and then he delivers his papers. If he is late, his grandfather walks down and calls him. The school is not very far from here, and Mr. Davis frequently walks down and watches the boys at their play. The paper route is Timothy's way of earning money to feed his cats. Do you care for cats, Dr. Welles?"

"Yes, I like cats very much," said the psychiatrist. "Many boys like dogs better."

"Timothy had a dog when he was a baby—a collie." Her eyes grew moist. "We all loved Ruff dearly. But I am no longer young, and the care and training of a dog is difficult. Timothy is at school or at the Boy Scout camp or something of the sort a great part of the time, and I thought it best that he should not have another dog. But you wanted to know about our cats, Dr. Welles. I raise Siamese cats."

"Interesting pets," said Welles cordially. "My aunt raised them at one time."

"Timothy is very fond of them. But three years ago he asked me if he could have a pair of black Persians. At first I thought not; but we like to please the child, and he promised to build their cages himself. He had taken a course in carpentry at vacation school. So he was allowed to have a pair of beautiful black Persians. But the very first litter turned out to be short-haired, and Timothy confessed that he had mated his queen to my Siamese tom, to see what would happen. Worse yet, he had mated his tom to one of my Siamese queens. I really was tempted to punish him. But, after all, I could see that he was curious as to the outcome of such crossbreeding. Of course I said the kittens must be destroyed. The second litter was exactly like the first—all black, with short hair. But you know what children are. Timothy begged me to let them live, and they were his first kittens. Three in one litter, two in the other. He might keep them, I said, if he would take full care of them and be responsible for all the expense. He mowed lawns and ran errands and made little footstools and bookcases to sell, and did all sorts of things, and probably used his allowance, too. But he kept the kittens and has a whole row of cages in the yard beside his workshop."

"And their offspring?" inquired Welles, who could not see what all this had to do with the main question, but was willing to listen to anything that might lead to information.

"Some of the kittens appear to be pure Persian, and others pure Siamese. These he insisted on keeping, although, as I have explained to him, it would be dishonest to sell them, since they are not pure-bred. A good many of the kittens are black short-haired and these we destroy. But enough of cats, Dr. Welles. And I am afraid I am talking too much about my grandson."

"I can understand that you are very proud of him," said Welles.

"I must confess that we are. And he is a bright boy. When he and his grandfather talk together, and with me also, he asks very intelligent questions. We do not encourage him to voice his opinions—I detest the smart-Alec type of small boy—and yet I believe they would be quite good opinions for a child of his age."

"Has his health always been good?" asked Welles.

"On the whole, very good. I have taught him the value of exercise, play, wholesome food and suitable rest. He has had a few of the usual childish ailments, not seriously. And he never has colds. But, of course, he takes his cold shots twice a year when we do."

"Does he mind the shots?" asked Welles, as casually as he could.

"Not at all. I always say that he, though so young, sets an example I find hard to follow. I still flinch, and really rather dread the ordeal."

Welles looked toward the door at a sudden, slight sound.

Timothy stood there, and he had heard. Again, fear was stamped on his face and terror looked out of his eyes.

"Timothy," said his grandmother, "don't stare."

"Sorry, sir," the boy managed to say.

"Are your papers all delivered? I did not realize we had been talking for an hour, Dr. Welles. Would you like to see Timothy's cats?" Mrs. Davis inquired graciously. "Timothy, take Dr. Welles to see your pets. We have had quite a talk about them."

Welles got Tim out of the room as fast as he could. The boy led the way around the house and into the side yard where the former garage stood.

There the man stopped.

"Tim," he said, "you don't have to show me the cats if you don't want to."

"Oh, that's all right."

"Is that part of what you are hiding? If it is, I don't want to see it until you are ready to show me."

Tim looked up at him then.

"Thanks," he said. "I don't mind about the cats. Not if you like cats really."

"I really do. But, Tim, this I would like to know: You're not afraid of the needle. Could you tell me why you were afraid . . . why you said you were afraid . . . of my shot? The one I promised not to give you after all?"

Their eyes met.

"You won't tell?" asked Tim.

"I won't tell."

"Because it was pentothal. Wasn't it?"

Welles gave himself a slight pinch. Yes, he was awake. Yes, this was a little boy asking him about pentothal. A boy who—yes, certainly, a boy who knew about it.

"Yes, it was," said Welles. "A very small dose. You know what it is?"

"Yes, sir. I . . . I read about it somewhere. In the papers."

"Never mind that. You have a secret—something you want to hide. That's what you are afraid about, isn't it?"

The boy nodded dumbly.

"If it's anything wrong, or that might be wrong, perhaps I could help you. You'll want to know me better, first. You'll want to be sure you can trust me. But I'll be glad to help, any time you say the word, Tim. Or I might stumble on to things the way I did just now. One thing though—I never tell secrets."

"Never?"

"Never. Doctors and priests don't betray secrets. Doctors seldom, priests never. I guess I am more like a priest, because of the kind of doctoring I do."

Wilmar H. Shiras

He looked down at the boy's bowed head.

"Helping fellows who are scared sick," said the psychiatrist very gently. "Helping fellows in trouble, getting things straight again, fixing things up, unsnarling tangles. When I can, that's what I do. And I don't tell anything to anybody. It's just between that one fellow and me."

But, he added to himself, *I'll have to find out. I'll have to find out what ails this child. Miss Page is right—he needs me.*

They went to see the cats.

There were the Siamese in their cages, and the Persians in their cages, and there, in several small cages, the short-haired black cats and their hybrid offspring. "We take them into the house, or let them into this big cage, for exercise," explained Tim. "I take mine into my shop sometimes. These are all mine. Grandmother keeps hers on the sun porch."

"You'd never know these were not all pure-bred," observed Welles. "Which did you say were the full Persians? Any of their kittens here?"

"No; I sold them."

"I'd like to buy one. But these look just the same—it wouldn't make any difference to me. I want a pet, and wouldn't use it for breeding stock. Would you sell me one of these?"

"Timothy shook his head.

"I'm sorry. I never sell any but the pure-breds."

It was then that Welles began to see what problem he faced. Very dimly he saw it, with joy, relief, hope and wild enthusiasm.

"Why not?" urged Welles. "I can wait for a pure-bred, if you'd rather, but why not one of these? They look just the same. Perhaps they'd be more interesting."

Tim looked at Welles for a long, long minute.

"I'll show you," he said. "Promise to wait here? No, I'll let you come into the workroom. Wait a minute, please."

The boy drew a key from under his blouse, where it had hung suspended from a chain, and unlocked the door of his shop. He went inside, closed the door, and Welles could hear him moving about for a few moments. Then he came to the door and beckoned.

"Don't tell Grandmother," said Tim. "I haven't told her yet. If it lives, I'll tell her next week."

In the corner of the shop under a table there was a box, and in the box there was a Siamese cat. When she saw a stranger she tried to hide her kittens; but Tim lifted her gently, and then Welles saw. Two of the kittens looked like little white rats with stringy tails and smudgy paws, ears and nose. But the third—yes, it was going to be a different sight. It was going to be a beautiful cat if it lived. It had long, silky white hair like the finest Persian, and the Siamese markings were showing up plainly.

Welles caught his breath.

"Congratulations, old man! Haven't you told anyone yet?"

"She's not ready to show. She's not a week old."

"But you're going to show her?"

"Oh, yes, Grandmother will be thrilled. She'll love her. Maybe there'll be more."

"You knew this would happen. You made it happen. You planned it all from the start," accused Welles.

"Yes," admitted the boy.

"How did you know?"

The boy turned away.

"I read it somewhere," said Tim.

The cat jumped back into the box and began to nurse her babies. Welles felt as if he could endure no more. Without a glance at anything else in the room—and everything else was hidden under tarpaulins and newspapers—he went to the door.

"Thanks for showing me, Tim," he said. "And when you have any to sell, remember me. I'll wait. I want one like that."

The boy followed him out and locked the door carefully.

"But Tim," said the psychiatrist, "that's not what you were afraid I'd find out. I wouldn't need a drug to get you tell me this, would I?"

Tim replied carefully, "I didn't want to tell this until I was ready. Grandmother really ought to know first. But you made me tell you."

"Tim," said Peter Welles earnestly, "I'll see you again. Whatever you are afraid of, don't be afraid of me. I often guess secrets. I'm on the way to guessing yours already. But nobody else need ever know."

He walked rapidly home, whistling to himself from time to time. Perhaps he, Peter Welles, was the luckiest man in the world.

He had scarcely begun to talk to Timothy on the boy's next appearance at the office, when the phone in the hall rang. On his return, when he opened the door he saw a book in Tim's hands. The boy made a move as if to hide it, and thought better of it.

Welles took the book and looked at it.

"Want to know more about Rorschach, eh?" he asked.

"I saw it on the shelf. I—"

"Oh, that's all right," said Welles, who had purposely left the book near the chair Tim would occupy. "But what's the matter with the library?"

"They've got some books about it, but they're on the closed shelves. I couldn't get them." Tim spoke without thinking first, and then caught his breath.

But Welles replied calmly: "I'll get it out for you. I'll have it next time you come. Take this one along today when you go. Tim, I mean it—you can trust me."

"I can't tell you anything," said the boy. "You've found out some things. I wish . . . oh, I don't know what I wish! But I'd rather be let alone. I don't need help. Maybe I never will. If I do, can't I come to you then?"

Wilmar H. Shiras

Welles pulled out his chair and sat down slowly.

"Perhaps that would be the best way, Tim. But why wait for the ax to fall? I might be able to help you ward it off—what you're afraid of. You can kid people along about the cats; tell them you were fooling around to see what would happen. But you can't fool all of the people all of the time, they tell me. Maybe with me to help, you could. Or with me to back you up, the blowup would be easier. Easier on your grandparents, too."

"I haven't done anything wrong!"

"I'm beginning to be sure of that. But things you try to keep hidden may come to light. The kitten—you could hide it, but you don't want to. You've got to risk something to show it."

"I'll tell them I read it somewhere."

"That wasn't true, then. I thought not. You figured it out."

There was silence.

Then Timothy Paul said: "Yes, I figured it out. But that's my secret."

"It's safe with me."

But the boy did not trust him yet. Welles soon learned that he had been tested. Tim took the book home, and returned it, took the library books which Welles got for him, and in due course returned them also. But he talked little and was still wary. Welles could talk all he liked, but he got little or nothing out of Tim. Tim had told all he was going to tell. He would talk about nothing except what any boy would talk about.

After two months of this, during which Welles saw Tim officially once a week and unofficially several times—showing up at the school playground to watch games, or meeting Tim on the paper route and treating him to a soda after it was finished—Welles had learned very little more. He tried again. He had probed no more during the two months, respected the boy's silence, trying to give him time to get to know and trust him.

But one day he asked: "What are you going to do when you grow up, Tim? Breed cats?"

Tim laughed a denial.

"I don't know what, yet. Sometimes I think one thing, sometimes another."

This was a typical boy answer. Welles disregarded it.

"What would you like to do best of all?" he asked.

Tim leaned forward eagerly. "What you do!" he cried.

"You've been reading up on it, I suppose," said Welles, as casually as he could. "Then you know, perhaps, that before anyone can do what I do, he must go through it himself, like a patient. He must also study medicine and be a full-fledged doctor, of course. You can't do that yet. But you can have the works now, like a patient."

"Why? For the experience?"

"Yes. And for the cure. You'll have to face that fear and lick it. You'll have to straighten out a lot of other things, or at least face them."

"My fear will be gone when I'm grown up," said Timothy. "I think it will. I hope it will."

"Can you be sure?"

"No," admitted the boy. "I don't know exactly why I'm afraid. I just know I *must* hide things. Is that bad, too?"

"Dangerous, perhaps."

Timothy thought a while in silence. Welles smoked three cigarettes and yearned to pace the floor, but dared not move.

"What would it be like?" asked Tim finally.

"You'd tell me about yourself. What you remember. Your childhood—the way your grandmother runs on when she talks about you."

"She sent me out of the room. I'm not supposed to think I'm bright," said Tim, with one of his rare grins.

"And you're not supposed to know how well she reared you?"

"She did fine," said Tim. "She taught me all the wisest things I ever knew."

"Such as what?"

"Such as shutting up. Not telling all you know. Not showing off."

"I see what you mean," said Welles. "Have you heard the story of St. Thomas Aquinas?"

"No."

"When he was a student in Paris, he never spoke out in class, and the others thought him stupid. One of them kindly offered to help him, and went over all the work very patiently to make him understand it. And then one day they came to a place where the other student got all mixed up and had to admit he didn't understand. Then Thomas suggested a solution and it was the right one. He knew more than any of the others all the time; but they called him the Dumb Ox."

Tim nodded gravely.

"And when he grew up?" asked the boy.

"He was the greatest thinker of all time," said Welles. "A fourteenth-century super-brain. He did more original work than any other ten great men; and died young."

After that, it was easier.

"How do I begin?" asked Timothy.

"You'd better begin at the beginning. Tell me all you can remember about your early childhood, before you went to school."

Tim gave this his consideration.

"I'll have to go forward and backward a lot," he said. "I couldn't put it all in order."

"That's all right. Just tell me today all you can remember about that time of your

Wilmar H. Shiras

life. By next week you'll have remembered more. As we go on to later periods of your life, you may remember things that belonged to an earlier time; tell them then. We'll make some sort of order out of it."

Welles listened to the boy's revelations with growing excitement. He found it difficult to keep outwardly calm.

"When did you begin to read?" Welles asked.

"I don't know when it was. My grandmother read me some stories, and somehow I got the idea about the words. But when I tried to tell her I could read, she spanked me. She kept saying I couldn't, and I kept saying I could, until she spanked me. For a while I had a dreadful time, because I didn't know any word she hadn't read to me—I guess I sat beside her and watched, or else I remembered and then went over it by myself right after. I must have learned as soon as I got the idea that each group of letters on the page was a word."

"The word-unit method," Welles commented. "Most self-taught readers learned like that."

"Yes. I have read about it since. And Macaulay could read when he was three, but only upside-down, because of standing opposite when his father read the Bible to the family."

"There are many cases of children who learned to read as you did, and surprised their parents. Well? How did you get on?"

"One day I noticed that two words looked almost alike and sounded almost alike. They were 'can' and 'man.' I remember staring at them and then it was like something beautiful boiling up in me. I began to look carefully at the words, but in a crazy excitement. I was a long while at it, because when I put down the book and tried to stand up I was stiff all over. But I had the idea, and after that it wasn't hard to figure out almost any words. The really hard words are the common ones that you get all the time in easy books. Other words are pronounced the way they are spelled."

"And nobody knew you could read?"

"No. Grandmother told me not to say I could, so I didn't. She read to me often, and that helped. We had a great many books, of course. I liked those with pictures. Once or twice they caught me with a book that had no pictures, and then they'd take it away and say, 'I'll find a book for a little boy."

"Do you remember what books you liked then?"

"Books about animals, I remember. And geographies. It's funny about animals—"

Once you got Timothy started, thought Welles, it wasn't hard to get him to go on talking.

"One day I was at the zoo," said Tim, "and by the cages alone. Grandmother was resting on a bench and she let me walk along by myself. People were talking about the animals, and I began to tell them all I knew. It must have been funny in a way, because I had read a lot of words I couldn't pronounce correctly, words I had never heard spoken. They listened and asked me questions, and I thought I was just like grandfather, teaching them the way he sometimes taught me. And then they called another man to come, and said, 'Listen to this kid; he's a scream!'' and I saw they were all laughing at me.''

Timothy's face was redder than usual, but he tried to smile as he added, "I can see now how it must have sounded funny. And unexpected, too; that's a big point in humor. But my little feelings were so dreadfully hurt that I ran back to my grandmother crying, and she couldn't find out why. But it served me right for disobeying her. She always told me not to tell people things; she said a child had nothing to teach its elders.''

"Not in that way, perhaps—at that age.''

"But, honestly, some grown people don't know very much,'' said Tim. "When we went on the train last year, a woman came up and sat beside me and started to tell me things a little boy should know about California. I told her I'd lived here all my life, but I guess she didn't even know we are taught things in school, and she tried to tell me things, and almost everything was wrong.''

"Such as what?'' asked Welles, who had also suffered from tourists.

"We . . . she said so many things . . . but I thought this was the funniest: She said all the Missions were so old and interesting, and I said yes, and she said, 'You know, they were all built long before Columbus discovered America,' and I thought she meant it for a joke, so I laughed. She looked very serious and said, 'Yes, those people all come up here from Mexico.' I suppose she thought they were Aztec temples.''

Welles, shaking with laughter, could not but agree that many adults were sadly lacking in the rudiments of knowledge.

"After that zoo experience, and a few others like it, I began to get wise to myself,'' continued Tim. "People who knew things didn't want to hear me repeating them, and people who didn't know, wouldn't be taught by a four-year-old baby. I guess I was four when I began to write.''

"How?''

"Oh, I just thought if I couldn't say anything to anybody at any time, I'd burst. So I began to put it down—in printing, like in books. Then I found out about writing, and we had some old-fashioned schoolbooks that taught how to write. I'm left-handed. When I went to school, I had to use my right hand. But by then I had learned how to pretend that I didn't know things. I watched the others and did as they did. My grandmother told me to do that.''

"I wonder why she said that,'' marveled Welles.

"She knew I wasn't used to other children, she said, and it was the first time she had left me to anyone else's care. So, she told me to do what the others did and what my teacher said,'' explained Tim simply, "and I followed her advice literally. I pretended I didn't know anything, until the others began to know it, too. Lucky I was so shy. But there were things to learn, all right. Do you know, when I was first sent

Wilmar H. Shiras

to school, I was disappointed because the teacher dressed like other women. The only picture of teachers I had noticed were those in an old Mother Goose book, and I thought that all teachers wore hoop skirts. But as soon as I saw her, after the little shock of surprise, I knew it was silly, and I never told.''

The psychiatrist and the boy laughed together.

"We played games. I had to learn to play with children, and not be surprised when they slapped or pushed me. I just couldn't figure out why they'd do that, or what good it did them. But if it was to surprise me, I'd say 'Boo' and surprise them some time later; and if they were mad because I had taken a ball or something they wanted, I'd play with them.''

"Anybody ever try to beat you up?"

"Oh, yes. But I had a book about boxing—with pictures. You can't learn much from pictures, but I got some practice too, and that helped. I didn't want to win, anyway. That's what I like about games of strength or skill—I'm fairly matched, and I don't have to be always watching in case I might show off or try to boss somebody around.''

"You must have tried bossing sometimes."

"In books, they all cluster around the boy who can teach new games and think up new things to play. But I found out that doesn't work. They just want to do the same thing all the time—like hide and seek. It's no fun if the first one to be caught is 'it' next time. The rest just walk in any old way and don't try to hide or even to run, because it doesn't matter whether they are caught. But you can't get the boys to see that, and play right, so the last one caught is 'it'.''

Timothy looked at his watch.

"Time to go," he said. "I've enjoyed talking to you, Dr. Welles. I hope I haven't bored you too much.''

Welles recognized the echo and smiled appreciatively at the small boy.

"You didn't tell me about the writing. Did you start to keep a diary?"

"No. It was a newspaper. One page a day, no more and no less. I still keep it," confided Tim. "But I get more on the page now. I type it.''

"And you write with either hand now?"

"My left hand is my own secret writing. For school and things like that I use my right hand.''

When Timothy had left, Welles congratulated himself. But for the next month he got no more. Tim would not reveal a single significant fact. He talked about ball-playing, he described his grandmother's astonished delight over the beautiful kitten, he told of its growth and the tricks it played. He gravely related such enthralling facts as that he liked to ride on trains, that his favorite wild animal was the lion, and that he greatly desired to see snow falling. But not a word of what Welles wanted to hear. The psychiatrist, knowing that he was again being tested, waited patiently.

Then one afternoon when Welles, fortunately unoccupied with a patient, was smoking a pipe on his front porch, Timothy Paul strode into the yard.

"Yesterday Miss Page asked me if I was seeing you and I said yes. She said she hoped my grandparents didn't find it too expensive, because you had told her I was all right and didn't need to have her worrying about me. And then I said to Grandma, was it expensive for you to talk to me, and she said, 'Oh no, dear; the school pays for that. It was your teacher's idea that you have a few talks with Dr. Welles.' "

"I'm glad you came to me, Tim, and I'm sure you didn't give me away to either of them. Nobody's paying me. The school pays for my services if a child is in a bad way and his parents are poor. It's a new service, since 1956. Many maladjusted children can be helped—much more cheaply to the state than the cost of having them go crazy or become criminals or something. You understand all that. But—sit down, Tim!—I can't charge the state for you, and I can't charge your grandparents. You're adjusted marvelously well in every way, as far as I can see; and when I see the rest, I'll be even more sure of it."

"Well—gosh! I wouldn't have come—" Tim was stammering in confusion. "You ought to be paid. I take up so much of your time. Maybe I'd better not come any more."

"I think you'd better. Don't you?"

"Why are you doing it for nothing, Dr. Welles?"

"I think you know why."

The boy sat down in the glider and pushed himself meditatively back and forth. The glider squeaked.

"You're interested. You're curious," he said.

"That's not all, Tim."

Squeak-squeak. Squeak-squeak.

"I know," said Timothy. "I believe it. Look, is it all right if I call you Peter? Since we're friends."

At their next meeting, Timothy went into details about his newspaper. He had kept all the copies, from the first smudged, awkwardly printed pencil issues to the very latest neatly typed ones. But he would not show Welles any of them.

"I just put down every day the things I most wanted to say, the news or information or opinion I had to swallow unsaid. So it's a wild medley. The earlier copies are awfully funny. Sometimes I guess what they were all about, what made me write them. Sometimes I remember. I put down the books I read too, and mark them like school grades, on two points—how I liked the book, and whether it was good. And whether I had read it before, too."

"How many books do you read? What's your reading speed?"

It proved that Timothy's reading speed on new books of adult level varied from eight hundred to nine hundred fifty words a minute. The average murder mystery—he

Wilmar H. Shiras

loved them—took him a little less than an hour. A year's homework in history, Tim performed easily by reading his textbook through three or four times during the year. He apologized for that, but explained that he had to know what was in the book so as not to reveal in examinations too much that he had learned from other sources. Evenings, when his grandparents believed him to be doing homework, he spent his time reading other books, or writing his newspaper, "or something." As Welles had already guessed, Tim had read everything in his grandfather's library, everything of interest in the public library that was not on the closed shelves, and everything he could order from the state library.

"What do the librarians say?"

"They think the books are for my grandfather. I tell them that, if they ask what a little boy wants with such a big book. Peter, telling so many lies is what gets me down. I have to do it, don't I?"

"As far as I can see, you do," agreed Welles. "But here's material for a while in my library. There'll have to be a closed shelf here, too, though, Tim."

"Could you tell me why? I know about the library books. Some of them might scare people, and some are—"

"Some of my books might scare you too, Tim. I'll tell you a little about abnormal psychology if you like, one of these days, and then I think you'll see that until you're actually trained to deal with such cases, you'd be better off not knowing too much about them."

"I don't want to be morbid," agreed Tim. "All right. I'll read only what you give me. And from now on I'll tell you things. There was more than the newspaper, you know."

"I thought as much. Do you want to go on with your tale?"

"It started when I first wrote a letter to a newspaper—of course, under a pen name. They printed it. For a while I had a high old time of it—a letter almost every day, using all sorts of pen names. Then I branched out to magazines, letters to the editor again. And stories—I tried stories."

He looked a little doubtfully at Welles, who said only: "How old were you when you sold the first story?"

"Eight," said Timothy. "And when the check came, with my name on it, 'T. Paul,' I didn't know what in the world to do."

"That's a thought. What did you do?"

"There was a sign in the window of the bank. I always read signs, and that one came back to my mind. 'Banking By Mail.' You can see I was pretty desperate. So I got the name of a bank across the Bay and I wrote them—on my typewriter—and said I wanted to start an account, and here was a check to start it with. Oh, I was scared stiff, and had to keep saying to myself that, after all, nobody could do much to me. It was my own money. But you don't know what it's like to be only a small boy! They sent the check back to me and I died ten deaths when I saw it. But the letter explained. I hadn't endorsed it. They sent me a blank to fill out about myself. I didn't know how many lies I dared to tell. But it was my money and I had to get it. If I could get it into the bank, then some day I could get it out. I gave my business as 'author' and I gave my age as twenty-four. I thought that was awfully old.''

"I'd like to see the story. Do you have a copy of the magazine around?''

"Yes,'' said Tim. "But nobody noticed it—I mean, 'T. Paul' could be anybody. And when I saw magazines for writers on the newsstands and bought them, I got on to the way to use a pen name on the story and my own name and address up in the corner. Before that I used a pen name and sometimes never got the things back or heard about them. Sometimes I did, though.''

"What then?''

"Oh, then I'd endorse the check payable to me and sign the pen name, and then sign my own name under it. Was I scared to do that! But it was my money.''

"Only stories?''

"Articles, too. And things. That's enough of that for today. Only—I just wanted to say—a while ago, T. Paul told the bank he wanted to switch some of the money over to a checking account. To buy books by mail, and such. So, I could pay you, Dr. Welles—'' with sudden formality.

"No, Tim,'' said Peter Welles firmly. "The pleasure is all mine. What I want is to see the story that was published when you were eight. And some of the other things that made T. Paul rich enough to keep a consulting psychiatrist on the payroll. And, for the love of Pete, will you tell me how all this goes on without your grandparents' knowing a thing about it?''

"Grandmother thinks I send in box tops and fill out coupons,'' said Tim. "She doesn't bring in the mail. She says her little boy gets such a big bang out of that little chore. Anyway that's what she said when I was eight. I played mailman. And there were box tops—I showed them to her, until she said, about the third time, that really she wasn't greatly interested in such matters. By now she has the habit of waiting for me to bring in the mail.''

Peter Welles thought that was quite a day of revelation. He spent a quiet evening at home, holding his head and groaning, trying to take it all in.

And that I.Q.—120, nonsense! The boy had been holding out on him. Tim's reading had obviously included enough about I.Q. tests, enough puzzles and oddments in magazines and such, to enable him to stall successfully. What could he do if he would co-operate?

Welles made up his mind to find out.

He didn't find out. Timothy Paul went swiftly through the whole range of Superior Adult tests without a failure of any sort. There were no tests yet devised that could measure his intelligence. While he was still writing his age with one figure, Timothy Paul had faced alone, and solved alone, problems that would have baffled the average

Wilmar H. Shiras

adult. He had adjusted to the hardest task of all—that of appearing to be a fairly normal, B-average small boy.

And it must be that there was more to find out about him. What did he write? And what did he do besides read and write, learn carpentry and breed cats and magnificently fool his whole world?

When Peter Welles had read some of Tim's writings he was surprised to find that the stories the boy had written were vividly human, the product of close observation of human nature. The articles, on the other hand, were closely reasoned and showed thorough study and research. Apparently Tim read every word of several newspapers and a score or more of periodicals.

"Oh, sure," said Tim, when questioned. "I read everything. I go back once in a while and review old ones, too."

"If you can write like this," demanded Welles, indicating a magazine in which a staid and scholarly article had appeared, "and this"—this was a man-to-man political article giving the arguments for and against a change in the whole Congressional system—"then why do you always talk to me in the language of an ordinary stupid schoolboy?"

"Because I'm only a boy," replied Timothy. "What would happen if I went around talking like that?"

"You might risk it with me. You've showed me these things."

"I'd never dare to risk talking like that. I might forget and do it again before others. Besides, I can't pronounce half the words."

"What!"

"I never look up a pronunciation," explained Timothy. "In case I do slip and use a word beyond the average, I can anyway hope I didn't say it right."

Welles shouted with laughter, but was sober again as he realized the implications back of that thoughtfulness.

"You're just like an explorer living among savages," said the psychiatrist. "You have studied the savages carefully and tried to imitate them so they won't know there are differences."

"Something like that," acknowledged Tim.

"That's why your stories are so human," said Welles. "That one about the awful girl—"

They both chuckled.

"Yes, that was my first story," said Tim. "I was almost eight, and there was a boy in my class who had a brother, and the boy next door was the other one, the one who was picked on."

"How much of the story was true?"

"The first part. I used to see, when I went over there, how that girl picked on Bill's brother's friend, Steve. She wanted to play with Steve all the time herself and whenever he had boys over, she'd do something awful. And Steve's folks were like

I said—they wouldn't let Steve do anything to a girl. When she threw all the watermelon rinds over the fence into his yard, he just had to pick them all up and say nothing back; and she'd laugh at him over the fence. She got him blamed for things he never did, and when he had work to do in the yard she'd hang out of her window and scream at him and make fun. I thought first, what made her act like that, and then I made up a way for him to get even with her, and wrote it out the way it might have happened."

"Didn't you pass the idea on to Steve and let him try it?"

"Gosh, no! I was only a little boy. Kids seven don't give ideas to kids ten. That's the first thing I had to learn—to be always the one that kept quiet, especially if there was any older boy or girl around, even only a year or two older. I had to learn to look blank and let my mouth hang open and say, 'I don't get it,' to almost everything."

"And Miss Page thought it was odd that you had no close friends of your own age," said Welles. "You must be the loneliest boy that ever walked this earth, Tim. You've lived in hiding like a criminal. But tell me, what are you afraid of?"

"I'm afraid of being found out, of course. The only way I can live in this world is in disguise—until I'm grown up, at any rate. At first it was just my grandparents' scolding me and telling me not to show off, and the way people laughed if I tried to talk to them. Then I saw how people hate anyone who is better or brighter or luckier. Some people sort of trade off; if you're bad at one thing you're good at another, but they'll forgive you for being good at some things, if you're not good at others so they can balance it off. They can beat you at something. You have to strike a balance. A child has no chance at all. No grownup can stand it to have a child know anything he doesn't. Oh, a little thing if it amuses them. But not much of anything. There's an old story about a man who found himself in a country where everyone else was blind. I'm like that—but they shan't put out my eyes. I'll never let them know I can see anything."

"Do you see things that no grown person can see?"

Tim waved his hand towards the magazines.

"Only like that, I meant. I hear people talking in street cars and stores, and while they work, and around. I read about the way they act—in the news. I'm like them, just like them, only I seem about a hundred years older—more matured."

"Do you mean that none of them have much sense?"

"I don't mean that exactly. I mean that so few of them have any, or show it if they do have. They don't even seem to want to. They're good people in their way, but what could they make of me? Even when I was seven, I could understand their motives, but they couldn't understand their own motives. And they're so lazy—they don't seem to want to know or to understand. When I first went to the library for books, the books I learned from were seldom touched by any of the grown people. But they were meant for ordinary grown people. But the grown people didn't want to know things—they only wanted to fool around. I feel about most people the way my

Wilmar H. Shiras

grandmother feels about babies and puppies. Only she doesn't have to pretend to be a puppy all the time," Tim added, with a little bitterness.

"You have a friend now, in me."

"Yes, Peter," said Tim, brightening up. "And I have pen friends, too. People like what I write, because they can't see I'm only a little boy. When I grow up—"

Tim did not finish that sentence. Welles understood, now, some of the fears that Tim had not dared to put into words at all. When he grew up, would he be as far beyond all other grownups as he had, all his life, been above his contemporaries? The adult friends whom he now met on fairly equal terms—would they then, too, seem like babies or puppies?

Peter did not dare to voice the thought, either. Still less did he venture to hint at another thought. Tim, so far, had no great interest in girls; they existed for him as part of the human race, but there would come a time when Tim would be a grown man and would wish to marry. And where among the puppies could he find a mate?

"When you're grown up, we'll still be friends," said Peter. "And who are the others?"

It turned out that Tim had pen friends all over the world. He played chess by correspondence—a game he never dared to play in person, except when he forced himself to move the pieces about idly and let his opponent win at least half the time. He had, also, many friends who had read something he had written, and had written to him about it, thus starting a correspondence-friendship. After the first two or three of these, he had started some on his own account, always with people who lived at a great distance. To most of these he gave a name which, although not false, looked it. That was Paul T. Lawrence. Lawrence was his middle name; and with a comma after the Paul, it was actually his own name, for which T. Paul of the large bank account was his reference.

"Pen friends abroad? Do you know languages?"

Yes, Tim did. He had studied by correspondence, also; many universities gave extension courses in that manner, and lent the student records to play so that he could learn the correct pronunciation. Tim had taken several such courses, and learned other languages from books. He kept all these languages in practice by means of the letters to other lands and the replies which came to him.

"I'd buy a dictionary, and then I'd write to the mayor of some town, or to a foreign newspaper, and ask them to advertise for some pen friends to help me learn the language. We'd exchange souvenirs and things."

Nor was Welles in the least surprised to find that Timothy had also taken other courses by correspondence. He had completed, within three years, more than half the subjects offered by four separate universities, and several other courses, the most recent being Architecture. The boy, not yet fourteen, had completed a full course in that subject, and had he been able to disguise himself as a full-grown man, could have gone out at once and built almost anything you'd like to name, for he also knew much of the trades involved.

"It always said how long an average student took, and I'd take that long," said Tim, "so, of course, I had to be working several schools at the same time."

"And carpentry at the playground summer school?"

"Oh, yes. But there I couldn't do too much, because people could see me. But I learned how, and it made a good cover-up, so I could make cages for the cats, and all that sort of thing. And many boys are good with their hands. I like to work with my hands. I built my own radio, too—it gets all the foreign stations, and that helps me with my languages."

"How did you figure it out about the cats?" said Welles.

"Oh, there had to be recessives, that's all. The Siamese coloring was a recessive, and it had to be mated with another recessive. Black was one possibility, and white was another, but I started with black because I liked it better. I might try white too, but I have so much else on my mind—"

He broke off suddenly and would say no more.

Their next meeting was by prearrangement at Tim's workship. Welles met the boy after school and they walked to Tim's home together; there the boy unlocked his door and snapped on the lights.

Welles looked around with interest. There was a bench, a tool chest. Cabinets, padlocked. A radio, clearly not store-purchased. A file cabinet, locked. Something on a table, covered with a cloth. A box in the corner—no, two boxes in two corners. In each of them was a mother cat with kittens. Both mothers were black Persians.

"This one must be all black Persian," Tim explained. "Her third litter and never a Siamese marking. But this one carries both recessives in her. Last time she had a Siamese shorthaired kitten. This morning—I had to go to school. Let's see."

They bent over the box where the new-born kittens lay. One kitten was like the mother. The other two were Siamese-Persian; a male and a female.

"You've done it again, Tim!" shouted Welles. "Congratulations!"

They shook hands in jubilation.

"I'll write in the record," said the boy blissfully.

In a nickel book marked "Compositions" Tim's left hand added the entries. He had used the correct symbols—F_1, F_2, F_3; Ss, Bl.

"The dominants in capitals," he explained, "B for black and S for short hair; the recessives in small letters—s for Siamese, l for long hair. Wonderful to write ll or ss again, Peter! Twice more. And the other kitten is carrying the Siamese marking as a recessive."

He closed the book in triumph.

"Now," and he marched to the covered thing on the table, "my latest big secret."

Tim lifted the cloth carefully and displayed a beautifully built doll house. No, a

Wilmar H. Shiras

model house—Welles corrected himself swiftly. A beautiful model, and—yes, built to scale.

"The roof comes off. See, it has a big storage room and a room for a play room or a maid or something. Then I lift off the attic—"

"Good heavens!" cried Peter Welles. "Any little girl would give her soul for this!"

"I used fancy wrapping papers for the wallpapers. I wove the rugs on a little hand loom," gloated Timothy. "The furniture's just like real, isn't it? Some I bought; that's plastic. Some I made of construction paper and things. The curtains were the hardest; but I couldn't ask Grandmother to sew them—"

"Why not?" the amazed doctor managed to ask.

"She might recognize this afterwards," said Tim, and he lifted off the upstairs floor.

"Recognize it? You haven't showed it to her? Then when would she see it?"

"She might not," admitted Tim. "But I don't like to take some risks."

"That's a very livable floor plan you've used," said Welles, bending closer to examine the house in detail.

"Yes, I thought so. It's awful how many house plans leave no clear wall space for books or pictures. Some of them have doors placed so you have to detour around the dining room table every time you go from the living room to the kitchen, or so that a whole corner of a room is good for nothing, with doors at all angles. Now, I designed this house to—"

"You designed it, Tim!"

"Why, sure. Oh, I see—you thought I built it from blueprints I'd bought. My first model home, I did, but the architecture courses gave me so many ideas that I wanted to see how they would look. Now, the cellar and game room—"

Welles came to himself an hour later and gasped when he looked at his watch.

"It's too late. My patient has gone home again by this time. I may as well stay—how about the paper route?"

"I gave that up. Grandmother offered to feed the cats as soon as I gave her the kitten. And I wanted the time for this. Here are the pictures of the house."

The color prints were very good.

"I'm sending them and an article to the magazines," said Tim. "This time I'm T. L. Paul. Sometimes I used to pretend all the different people I am were talking together—but now I talk to you instead, Peter."

"Will it bother the cats if I smoke? Thanks. Nothing I'm likely to set on fire, I hope? Put the house together and let me sit here and look at it. I want to look in through the windows. Put its lights on. There."

The young architect beamed, and snapped on the little lights.

"Nobody can see in here. I got Venetian blinds; and when I work in here, I even shut them sometimes."

"If I'm to know all about you, I'll have to go through the alphabet from A to Z," said Peter Welles. "This is Architecture. What else in the A's?"

"Astronomy. I showed you those articles. My calculations proved correct. Astrophysics—I got A in the course, but haven't done anything original so far. Art, no. I can't paint or draw very well, except mechanical drawing. I've done all the Merit Badge work in scouting, all through the alphabet."

"Darned if I can see you as a Boy Scout," protested Welles.

"I'm a very good Scout. I have almost as many badges as any other boy my age in the troop. And at camp I do as well as most city boys."

"Do you do a good turn every day?"

"Yes," said Timothy. "Started that when I first read about Scouting—I was a Scout at heart before I was old enough to be a Cub. You know, Peter, when you're very young, you take all that seriously about the good deed every day, and the good habits and ideals and all that. And then you get older and it begins to seem funny and childish and posed and artificial, and you smile in a superior way and make jokes. But there is a third step, too, when you take it all seriously again. People who make fun of the Scout Law are doing the boys a lot of harm; but those who believe in things like that don't know how to say so, without sounding priggish and platitudinous. I'm going to do an article on it before long."

"Is the Scout Law your religion—if I may put it that way?"

"No," said Timothy. "But 'a Scout is Reverent.' Once I tried to study the churches and find out what was the truth. I wrote letters to pastors of all denominations—all those in the phone book and the newspaper—when I was on a vacation in the East, I got the names, and then wrote after I got back. I couldn't write to people here in the city. I said I wanted to know which church was true, and expected them to write to me and tell me about theirs, and argue with me, you know. I could read library books, and all they had to do was recommend some, I told them, and then correspond with me a little about them."

"Did they?"

"Some of them answered," said Tim, "but nearly all of them told me to go to somebody near me. Several said they were very busy men. Some gave me the name of a few books, but none of them told me to write again, and . . . and I was only a little boy. Nine years old, so I couldn't talk to anybody. When I thought it over, I knew that I couldn't very well join any church so young, unless it was my grandparents' church. I keep on going there—it is a good church and it teaches a great deal of truth, I am sure. I'm reading all I can find, so when I am old enough I'll know what I must do. How old would you say I should be, Peter?"

"College age," replied Welles. "You are going to college? By then, any of the pastors would talk to you—except those that are too busy!"

"It's a moral problem, really. Have I the right to wait? But I have to wait. It's like

Wilmar H. Shiras

telling lies—I have to tell some lies, but I hate to. If I have a moral obligation to join the church as soon as I find it, well, what then? I can't until I'm eighteen or twenty?"

"If you can't, you can't. I should think that settles it. You are legally a minor, under the control of your grandparents, and while you might claim the right to go where your conscience leads you, it would be impossible to justify and explain your choice without giving yourself away entirely—just as you are obliged to go to school until you are at least eighteen, even though you know more than most Ph.D.'s. It's all part of the game, and He who made you must understand that."

"I'll never tell you any lies," said Tim. "I was getting so desperately lonely—my pen pals didn't know anything about me really. I told them only what was right for them to know. Little kids are satisfied to be with other people, but when you get a little older you have to make friends, really."

"Yes, that's a part of growing up. You have to reach out to others and share thoughts with them. You've kept to yourself too long as it is."

"It wasn't that I wanted to. But without a real friend, it was only pretense, and I never could let my playmates know anything about me. I studied them and wrote stories about them and it was all of them, but it was only a tiny part of me."

"I'm proud to be your friend, Tim. Every man needs a friend. I'm proud that you trust me."

Tim patted the cat a moment in silence and then looked up with a grin.

"How would you like to hear my favorite joke?" he asked

"Very much," said the psychiatrist, bracing himself for almost any major shock.

"It's records. I recorded this from a radio program."

Welles listened. He knew little of music, but the symphony which he heard pleased him. The announcer praised it highly in little speeches before and after each movement. Timothy giggled.

"Like it?"

"Very much. I don't see the joke."

"I wrote it."

"Tim, you're beyond me! But I still don't get the joke."

"The joke is that I did it by mathematics. I calculated what ought to sound like joy, grief, hope, triumph, and all the rest, and—it was just after I had studied harmony; you know how mathematical that is."

Speechless, Welles nodded.

"I worked out the rhythms from different metabolisms—the way you function when under the influences of these emotions; the way your metabolic rate varies, your heartbeats and respiration and things. I sent it to the director of that orchestra, and he didn't get the idea that it was a joke—of course I didn't explain—he produced the music. I get nice royalties from it, too."

"You'll be the death of me yet," said Welles in deep sincerity. "Don't tell me anything more today; I couldn't take it. I'm going home. Maybe by tomorrow I'll see the joke and come back to laugh. Tim, did you ever fail at anything?''

"There are two cabinets full of articles and stories that didn't sell. Some of them I feel bad about. There was the chess story. You know, in 'Through the Looking Glass,' it wasn't a very good game, and you couldn't see the relation of the moves to the story very well.''

"I never could see it at all.''

"I thought it would be fun to take a championship game and write a fantasy about it, as if it were a war between two little old countries, with knights and foot-soldiers, and fortified walls in charge of captains, and the bishops couldn't fight like warriors, and, of course, the queens were women—people don't kill them, not in hand-to-hand fighting and . . . well, you see? I wanted to make up the attacks and captures, and keep the people alive, a fairytale war you see, and make the strategy of the game and the strategy of the war coincide, and have everything fit. It took me ever so long to work it out and write it. To understand the game as a chess game and then to translate it into human actions and motives, and put speeches to it to fit different kinds of people. I'll show it to you. I loved it. But nobody would print it. Chess players don't like fantasy, and nobody else likes chess. You have to have a very special kind of mind to like both. But it was a disappointment. I hoped it would be published, because the few people who like that sort of thing would like it *very* much.''

"I'm sure I'll like it.''

"Well, if you do like that sort of thing, it's what you've been waiting all your life in vain for. Nobody else has done it.'' Tim stopped, and blushed as red as a beet. "I see what Grandmother means. Once you get started bragging, there's no end to it. I'm sorry, Peter.''

"Give me the story. I don't mind, Tim—brag all you like to me; I understand. You might blow up if you never expressed any of your legitimate pride and pleasure in such achievements. What I don't understand is how you have kept it all under for so long.''

"I had to,'' said Tim.

The story was all its young author had claimed. Welles chuckled as he read it, that evening. He read it again, and checked all the moves and the strategy of them. It was really a fine piece of work. Then he thought of the symphony, and this time he was able to laugh. He sat up until after midnight, thinking about the boy. Then he took a sleeping pill and went to bed.

The next day he went to see Tim's grandmother. Mrs. Davis received him graciously.

"Your grandson is a very interesting boy,'' said Peter Welles carefully. "I'm asking a favor of you. I am making a study of various boys and girls in this district, their abilities and backgrounds and environment and character traits and things like that. No names will ever be mentioned, of course, but a statistical report will be kept, for

Wilmar H. Shiras

ten years or longer, and some case histories might later be published. Could Timothy be included?''

"Timothy is such a good, normal little boy, I fail to see what would be the purpose of including him in such a survey.''

"That is just the point. We are not interested in maladjusted persons in this study. We eliminate all psychotic boys and girls. We are interested in boys and girls who succeed in facing their youthful problems and making satisfactory adjustments to life. If we could study a selected group of such children, and follow their progress for the next ten years at least—and then publish a summary of the findings, with no names used—''

"In that case, I see no objection," said Mrs. Davis.

"If you'd tell me, then, something about Timothy's parents—their history?''

Mrs. Davis settled herself for a good long talk.

"Timothy's mother, my only daughter, Emily," she began, "was a lovely girl. So talented. She played the violin charmingly. Timothy is like her, in the face, but has his father's dark hair and eyes. Edwin had very fine eyes.''

"Edwin was Timothy's father?''

"Yes. The young people met while Emily was at college in the East. Edwin was studying atomics there.''

"Your daughter was studying music?''

"No; Emily was taking the regular liberal arts course. I can tell you little about Edwin's work, but after their marriage he returned to it and . . . you understand, it is painful for me to recall this, but their deaths were such a blow to me. They were young.''

Welles held his pencil ready to write.

"Timothy has never been told. After all, he must grow up in this world, and how dreadfully the world has changed in the past thirty years, Dr. Welles! But you would not remember the days before 1945. You have heard, no doubt, of the terrible explosion in the atomic plant, when they were trying to make a new type of bomb? At the time, none of the workers seemed to be injured. They believed the protection was adequate. But two years later they were all dead or dying.''

Mrs. Davis shook her head, sadly. Welles held his breath, bent his head, scribbled.

"Tim was born just fourteen months after the explosion, fourteen months to the day. Everyone still thought that no harm had been done. But the radiation had some effect which was very slow—I do not understand such things—Edwin died, and then Emily came home to us with the boy. In a few months she, too, was gone.

"Oh, but we do not sorrow as those who have no hope. It is hard to have lost her, Dr. Welles, but Mr. Davis and I have reached the time of life when we can look forward to seeing her again. Our hope is to live until Timothy is old enough to fend for himself. We were so anxious about him; but you see he is perfectly normal. The specialists made all sorts of tests. But nothing is wrong with Timothy.''

The psychiatrist stayed a little longer, took a few more notes, and made his escape as soon as he could. Going straight to the school, he had a few words with Miss Page and then took Tim to his office, where he told him what he had learned.

"You mean—I'm a mutation?"

"A mutant. Yes, very likely you are. I don't know. But I had to tell you at once."

"Must be a dominant, too," said Tim, "coming out this way in the first generation. You mean—there may be more? I'm not the only one?" he added in great excitement. "Oh, Peter, even if I grow up past you I won't have to be lonely?"

There. He had said it.

"It could be, Tim. There's nothing else in your family that could account for you."

"But I have never found anyone at all like me. I would have known. Another boy or girl my age—like me—I would have known."

"You came West with your mother. Where did the others go, if they existed? The parents must have scattered everywhere, back to their homes all over the country, all over the world. We can trace them, though. And, Tim, haven't you thought it's just a little bit strange that with all your pen names and various contacts, people don't insist more on meeting you? Everything gets done by mail. It's almost as if the editors are used to people who hide. It's almost as if people are used to architects and astronomers and composers whom nobody ever sees, who are only names in care of other names at post office boxes. There's a chance—just a chance, mind you—that there are others. If there are, we'll find them."

"I'll work out a code they will understand," said Tim, his face screwed up in concentration. "In articles—I'll do it—several magazines and in letters I can enclose copies—some of my pen friends may be the ones—"

"I'll hunt up the records—they must be on file somewhere—psychologists and psychiatrists know all kinds of tricks—we can make some excuse to trace them all—the birth records—"

Both of them were talking at once, but all the while Peter Welles was thinking sadly, perhaps he had lost Tim now. If they did find those others, those to whom Tim rightfully belonged, where would poor Peter be? Outside, among the puppies—

Timothy Paul looked up and saw Peter Welles's eyes on him. He smiled.

"You were my first friend, Peter, and you shall be forever," said Tim. "No matter what, no matter who."

"But we must look for the others," said Peter.

"I'll never forget who helped me," said Tim.

An ordinary boy of thirteen may say such a thing sincerely, and a week later have forgotten all about it. But Peter Welles was content. Tim would never forget. Tim would be his friend always. Even when Timothy Paul and those like him should unite in a maturity undreamed of, to control the world if they chose, Peter Welles would be Tim's friend—not a puppy, but a beloved friend—as a loyal dog, loved by a good master, is never cast out. ∎

Wilmar H. Shiras

WEYR SEARCH

Anne McCaffrey

When is a legend legend? Why is a myth a myth? How old and disused must a fact be for it to be relegated to the category: Fairy tale? And why do certain facts remain incontrovertible, while others lose their validity to assume a shabby, unstable character?

Rukbat, in the Sagittarian sector, was a golden G-type star. It had five planets, plus one stray it had attracted and held in recent millennia. Its third planet was enveloped by air man could breathe, boasted water he could drink, and possessed a gravity which permitted man to walk confidently erect. Men discovered it, and promptly colonized it, as they did every habitable planet they came to and then—whether callously or through collapse of empire, the colonists never discovered, and eventually forgot to ask—left the colonies to fend for themselves.

When men first settled on Rukbat's third world, and named it Pern, they had taken little notice of the stranger-planet, swinging around its primary in a wildly erratic elliptical orbit. Within a few generations they had forgotten its existence. The desperate path the wanderer pursued brought it close to is stepsister every two hundred [Terran] years at perihelion.

When the aspects were harmonious and the conjunction with its sister-planet close enough, as it often was, the indigenous life of the wanderer sought to bridge the space gap to the more temperate and hospitable planet.

It was during the frantic struggle to combat this menace dropping through Pern's skies like silver threads, that Pern's contact with the mother-planet weakened and broke. Recollections of Earth receded further from Pernese history with each successive generation until memory of their origins degenerated past legend or myth, into oblivion.

To forestall the incursions of the dreaded Threads, the Pernese, with the ingenuity of their forgotten Yankee forebears and between first onslaught and return, developed a highly specialized variety of a life form indigenous to their adopted planet—the winged, tailed, and firebreathing dragons, named for the Earth legend they resembled. Such humans as had a high empathy rating and some innate telepathic ability were trained to make use of and preserve this unusual animal, whose ability to teleport was of immense value in the fierce struggle to keep Pern bare of Threads.

The dragons and their dragonmen, a breed apart, and the shortly renewed menace they battled, created a whole new group of legends and myths.

As the menace was conquered the populace in the Holds of Pern settled into a more comfortable way of life. Most of the dragon Weyrs eventually were abandoned, and the descendants of heroes fell into disfavor, as the legends fell into disrepute.

This, then, is a tale of legends disbelieved and their restoration. Yet—how goes a legend? When is myth?

Drummer, beat, and piper, blow,
Harper, strike, and soldier, go.
Free the flame and sear the grasses
Till the dawning Red Star passes.

Lessa woke, cold. Cold with more than the chill of the everlastingly clammy stone walls. Cold with the prescience of a danger greater than when, ten full Turns ago, she had run, whimpering, to hide in the watch-wher's odorous lair.

Rigid with concentration, Lessa lay in the straw of the redolent cheese room, sleeping quarters shared with the other kitchen drudges. There was an urgency in the ominous portent unlike any other forewarning. She touched the awareness of the watch-wher, slithering on its rounds in the courtyard. It circled at the choke-limit of its chain. It was restless, but oblivious to anything unusual in the pre-dawn darkness.

The danger was definitely not within the walls of Hold Ruath. Nor approaching the paved perimeter without the Hold where relentless grass had forced new growth through the ancient mortar, green witness to the deterioration of the once stone-clean Hold. The danger was not advancing up the now little-used causeway from the valley, nor lurking in the craftsmen's stony holdings at the foot of the Hold's cliff. It did not scent the wind that blew from Tillek's cold shores. But still it twanged sharply through her senses, vibrating every nerve in Lessa's slender frame. Fully roused, she sought to identify it before the prescient mood dissolved. She cast outward, toward the Pass, farther than she had ever pressed. Whatever threatened was not in Ruatha . . . yet. Nor did it have a familiar flavor. It was not, then, Fax.

Lessa had been cautiously pleased that Fax had not shown himself at Hold Ruath in three full Turns. The apathy of the craftsmen, the decaying farmholds, even the green-etched stones of the Hold infuriated Fax, self-styled Lord of the High Reaches, to the point where he preferred to forget the reason why he had subjugated the once proud and profitable Hold.

Lessa picked her way among the sleeping drudges, huddled together for warmth, and glided up the worn steps to the kitchen-proper. She slipped across the cavernous kitchen to the stable-yard door. The cobbles of the yard were icy through the thin soles of her sandals and she shivered as the pre-dawn air penetrated her patched garment.

The watch-wher slithered across the yard to greet her, pleading, as it always did, for release. Glancing fondly down at the awesome head, she promised it a good rub presently. It crouched, groaning, at the end of its chain as she continued to the grooved steps that led to the rampart over the Hold's massive gate. Atop the tower, Lessa stared towards the east where the stony breasts of the Pass rose in black relief against the gathering day.

Indecisively she swung to her left, for the sense of danger issued from that direction as well. She glanced upward, her eyes drawn to the red star which had recently begun to dominate the dawn sky. As she stared, the star radiated a final ruby pulsation before its magnificence was lost in the brightness of Pern's rising sun.

For the first time in many Turns, Lessa gave thought to matters beyond Pern, beyond her dedication to vengeance on the murderer Fax for the annihilation of her family. Let him but come within Ruath Hold now and he would never leave.

But the brilliant ruby sparkle of the Red Star recalled the Disaster Ballads—grim narratives of the heroism of the dragonriders as they braved the dangers of *between* to breathe fiery death on the silver Threads that dropped through Pern's skies. Not one Thread must fall to the rich soil, to burrow deep and multiply, leaching the earth of minerals and fertility. Straining her eyes as if vision would bridge the gap between peril and person, she stared intently eastward. The watch-wher's thin, whistled question reached her just as the prescience waned.

Dawnlight illumined the tumbled landscape, the unplowed fields in the valley below. Dawnlight fell on twisted orchards, where the sparse herds of milchbeasts hunted stray blades of spring grass. Grass in Ruatha grew where it should not, died where it should flourish. An odd brooding smile curved Lessa's lips. Fax realized no profit from his conquest of Ruatha . . . nor would he, while she, Lessa, lived. And he had not the slightest suspicion of the source of this undoing.

Or had he? Lessa wondered, her mind still reverberating from the savage prescience of danger. East lay Fax's ancestral and only legitimate Hold. Northeast lay little but bare and stony mountains and Benden, the remaining Weyr, which protected Pern.

Lessa stretched, arching her back, inhaling the sweet, untainted wind of morning.

A cock crowed in the stableyard. Lessa whirled, her face alert, eyes darting around the outer Hold lest she be observed in such an uncharacteristic pose. She unbound her hair, letting it fall about her face concealingly. Her body drooped into the sloppy posture she affected. Quickly she thudded down the the stairs, crossing to the watch-wher. It lurred piteously, its great eyes blinking against the growing daylight. Oblivious to the stench of its rank breath, she hugged the scaly head to her, scratching its ears and eye ridges. The watch-wher was ecstatic with pleasure, its long body trembling, its clipped wings rustling. It alone knew who she was or cared. And it was the only creature in all Pern she trusted since the day she had blindly sought refuge in its dark stinking lair to escape Fax's thirsty swords that had drunk so deeply of Ruathan blood.

Slowly she rose, cautioning it to remember to be as vicious to her as to all, should anyone be near. It promised to obey her, swaying back and forth to emphasize its reluctance.

The first rays of the sun glanced over the Hold's outer wall. Crying out, the watchwher darted into its dark nest. Lessa crept back to the kitchen and into the cheese room.

> From the Weyr and from the Bowl
> Bronze and brown and blue and green
> Rise the dragonmen of Pern,
> Aloft, on wing, seen, then unseen.

F'lar on bronze Mnementh's great neck appeared first in the skies above the chief Hold of Fax, so-called Lord of the High Reaches. Behind him, in proper wedge formation, the wingmen came into sight. F'lar checked the formation automatically; as precise as at the moment of entry to *between*.

As Mnementh curved in an arc that would bring them to the perimeter of the Hold, consonant with the friendly nature of this visitation, F'lar surveyed with mounting aversion the disrepair of the ridge defenses. The firestone pits were empty and the rock-cut gutters radiating from the pits were greentinged with a mossy growth.

Was there even one lord in Pern who maintained his Hold rocky in observance of the ancient Laws? F'lar's lips tightened to a thinner line. When this Search was over and the Impression made, there would have to be a solemn, punitive Council held at the Weyr. And by the golden shell of the queen, he, F'lar, meant to be its moderator. He would replace lethargy with industry. He would scour the green and dangerous scum from the heights of Pern, the grass blades from its stoneworks. No verdant skirt would be condoned in any farmhold. And the tithings which had been so miserly, so grudgingly presented would, under pain of firestoning, flow with decent generosity into the Dragonweyr.

Mnementh rumbled approvingly as he vaned his pinions to land lightly on the grass-etched flagstones of Fax's Hold. The bronze dragon furled his great wings, and F'lar heard the warning claxon in the Hold's Great Tower. Mnementh dropped to his knees as F'lar indicated he wished to dismount. The bronze rider stood by Mnementh's huge wedge-shaped head, politely awaiting the arrival of the Hold lord. F'lar idly gazed down the valley, hazy with warm spring sunlight. He ignored the furtive heads that peered at the dragonman from the parapet slits and the cliff windows.

F'lar did not turn as a rush of air announced the arrival of the rest of the wing. He knew, however, when F'nor, the brown rider, his halfbrother, took the customary position on his left, a dragon-length to the rear. F'lar caught a glimpse of F'nor's boot-heel twisting to death the grass crowding up between the stones.

An order, muffled to an intense whisper, issued from within the great court, beyond the open gates. Almost immediately a group of men marched into sight, led by a heavyset man of medium height.

Mnementh arched his neck, angling his head so that his chin rested on the ground.

Mnementh's many-faceted eyes, on a level with F'lar's head, fastened with disconcerting interest on the approaching party. The dragons could never understand why they generated such abject fear in common folk. At only one point in his lifespan would a dragon attack a human and that could be excused on the grounds of simple ignorance. F'lar could not explain to the dragon the politics behind the necessity of inspiring awe in the holders, lord and craftsman alike. He could only observe that the fear and apprehension showing in the faces of the advancing squad which troubled Mnementh was oddly pleasing to him, F'lar.

"Welcome, Bronze Rider, to the Hold of Fax, Lord of the High Reaches. He is at your service," and the man made an adequately respectful salute.

The use of the third person pronoun could be construed, by the meticulous, to be a veiled insult. This fit in with the information F'lar had on Fax, so he ignored it. His information was also correct in describing Fax as a greedy man. It showed in the restless eyes which flicked at every detail of F'lar's clothing, at the slight frown when the intricately etched swordhilt was noticed.

F'lar noticed, in his own turn, the several rich rings which flashed on Fax's left hand. The overlord's right hand remained slightly cocked after the habit of the professional swordsman. His tunic, of rich fabric, was stained and none too fresh. The man's feet, in heavy wher-hide boots, were solidly planted, weight balanced forward on his toes. A man to be treated cautiously, F'lar decided, as one should the conqueror of five neighboring Holds. Such greedy audacity was in itself a revelation. Fax had married into a sixth . . . and had legally inherited, however unusual the circumstances, the seventh. He was a lecherous man by reputation.

Within these seven Holds, F'lar anticipated a profitable Search. Let R'gul go southerly to pursue Search among the indolent, if lovely, women there. The Weyr needed a strong woman this time; Jora had been worse than useless with Nemorth. Adversity, uncertainty: those were the conditions that bred the qualities F'lar wanted in a weyrwoman.

"We ride in Search," F'lar drawled softly, "and request the hospitality of your Hold, Lord Fax."

Fax's eyes widened imperceptibly at mention of Search.

"I had heard Jora was dead," Fax replied, dropping the third person abruptly as if F'lar had passed some sort of test by ignoring it. "So Nemorth has a new queen, hm-m-m?" he continued, his eyes darting across the rank of the ring, noting the disciplined stance of the riders, the healthy color of the dragons.

F'lar did not dignify the obvious with an answer.

"And, my Lord—?" Fax hesitated, expectantly inclining his head slightly toward the dragonman.

For a pulse beat, F'lar wondered if the man were deliberately provoking him with such subtle insults. The name of bronze riders should be as well known throughout

Pern as the name of the Dragonqueen and her Weyrwoman. F'lar kept his face composed, his eyes on Fax's.

Leisurely, with the proper touch of arrogance, F'nor stepped forward, stopping slightly behind Mnementh's head, one hand negligently touching the jaw hinge of the huge beast.

"The Bronze Rider of Mnementh, Lord F'lar, will require quarters for himself. I, F'nor, brown rider, prefer to be lodged with the wingmen. We are, in number, twelve."

F'lar liked that touch of F'nor's, totting up the wing strength, as if Fax were incapable of counting. F'nor had phrased it so adroitly as to make it impossible for Fax to protest the insult.

"Lord F'lar," Fax said through teeth fixed in a smile, "the High Reaches are honored with your Search."

"It will be to the credit of the High Reaches," F'lar replied smoothly, "if one of its own supplies the Weyr."

"To our everlasting credit," Fax replied as suavely. "In the old days, many notable weyrwomen came from my Holds."

"Your Holds?" asked F'lar, politely smiling as he emphasized the plural. "Ah, yes, you are now overlord of Ruatha, are you not? There have been many from that Hold."

A strange tense look crossed Fax's face. "Nothing good comes from Ruath Hold." Then he stepped aside, gesturing F'lar to enter the Hold.

Fax's troop leader barked a hasty order and the men formed two lines, their metal-edged boots flicking sparks from the stones.

At unspoken orders, all the dragons rose with a great churning of air and dust. F'lar strode nonchalantly past the welcoming files. The men were rolling their eyes in alarm as the beasts glided above to the inner courts. Someone on the high tower uttered a frightened yelp as Mnementh took his position on that vantage point. His great wings drove phosophoric-scented air across the inner court as he maneuvered his great frame onto the inadequate landing space.

Outwardly oblivious to the consternation, fear, and awe the dragons inspired, F'lar was secretly amused and rather pleased by the effect. Lords of the Holds needed this reminder that they must deal with dragons, not just with riders, who were men, mortal and murderable. The ancient respect for dragonmen as well as dragonkind must be reinstilled in modern breasts.

"The Hold has just risen from table, Lord F'lar, if . . . " Fax suggested. His voice trailed off at F'lar's smiling refusal.

"Convey my duty to your lady, Lord Fax," F'lar rejoined, noticing with inward satisfaction the tightening of Fax's jaw muscles at the ceremonial request.

"You would prefer to see your quarters first?" Fax countered.

F'lar flicked an imaginary speck from his soft wher-hide sleeve and shook his head. Was the man buying time to sequester his ladies as the old-time lords had?

"Duty first," he said with a rueful shrug.

"Of course," Fax all but snapped and strode smartly ahead, his heels pounding out the anger he could not express otherwise. F'lar decided he had guessed correctly.

F'lar and F'nor followed at a slower pace through the double-doored entry with its massive metal panels, into the great hall, carved into the cliffside.

"They eat not badly," F'nor remarked casually to F'lar, appraising the remnants still on the table.

"Better than the Weyr, it would seem," F'lar replied dryly.

"Young roasts and tender," F'nor said in a bitter undertone, "while the stringy, barren beasts are delivered up to us."

"The change is overdue," F'lar murmured, then raised his voice to conversational level. "A well-favored hall," he was saying amiably as they reached Fax. Their reluctant host stood in the portal to the inner Hold, which, like all such Holds, burrowed deep into stone, traditional refuge of all in time of peril.

Deliberately, F'lar turned back to the banner-hung Hall. "Tell me, Lord Fax, do you adhere to the old practices and mount a dawn guard?"

Fax frowned, trying to grasp F'lar's meaning.

"There is always a guard at the Tower."

"An easterly guard?"

Fax's eyes jerked towards F'lar, then to F'nor.

"There are always guards," he answered sharply, "on all the approaches."

"Oh, just the approaches," and F'lar nodded wisely to F'nor.

"Where else?" demanded Fax, concerned, glancing from one dragonman to the other.

"I must ask that of your harper. You do keep a trained harper in your Hold?"

"Of course. I have several trained harpers," and Fax jerked his shoulders straighter. F'lar affected not to understand.

"Lord Fax is the overlord of six other Holds," F'nor reminded his wingleader.

"Of course," F'lar assented, with exactly the same inflection Fax had used a moment before.

The mimicry did not go unnoticed by Fax, but as he was unable to construe deliberate insult out of an innocent affirmative, he stalked into the glow-lit corridors. The dragonmen followed.

The women's quarters in Fax's Hold been moved from the traditional innermost corridors to those at cliff-face. Sunlight poured down from three double-shuttered, deep-casement windows in the outside wall. F'lar noted that the bronze hinges were well oiled, and the sills regulation spear-length. Fax had not, at least, diminished the protective wall.

The chamber was richly hung with appropriately gentle scenes of women occupied in all manner of feminine tasks. Doors gave off the main chamber on both sides into smaller sleeping alcoves and from these, at Fax's bidding, his women hesitantly emerged. Fax sternly gestured to a blue-gowned woman, her hair white-streaked, her face lined with disappointments and bitterness, her body swollen with pregnancy. She advanced awkwardly, stopping several feet from her lord. From her attitude, F'lar deduced that she came no closer to Fax than was absolutely necessary.

"The Lady of Crom, mother of my heirs," Fax said without pride or cordiality.

"My Lady—" F'lar hesitated, waiting for her name to be supplied.

She glanced warily at her lord. "Gemma," Fax snapped curtly.

F'lar bowed deeply. "My Lady Gemma, the Weyr is on Search and requests the Hold's hospitality."

"My Lord F'lar," the Lady Gemma replied in a low voice, "you are most welcome."

F'lar did not miss the slight slur on the adverb nor the fact that Gemma had no trouble naming him. His smile was warmer than courtesy demanded, warm with gratitude and sympathy. Looking at the number of women in these quarters, F'lar thought there might be one or two Lady Gemma could bid farewell without regret.

Fax preferred his women plump and small. There wasn't a saucy one in the lot. If there once had been, the spirit had been beaten out of her. Fax, no doubt, was stud, not lover. Some of the covey had not all winter long made much use of water, judging by the amount of sweet oil gone rancid in their hair. Of them all, if these were all, the Lady Gemma was the only willful one; and she, too old.

The amenities over, Fax ushered his unwelcome guests outside, and led the way to the quarters he had assigned the bronze rider.

"A pleasant room," F'lar acknowledged, stripping off gloves and wher-hide tunic, throwing them carelessly to the table. "I shall see to my men and the beasts. They have been fed recently," he commented, pointing up Fax's omission in inquiring. "I request liberty to wander through the crafthold."

Fax sourly granted what was a dragonman's traditional privilege.

"I shall not further disrupt your routine, Lord Fax, for you must have many demands on you, with seven Holds to supervise." F'lar inclined his body slightly to the overlord, turning away as a gesture of dismissal. He could imagine the infuriated expression on Fax's face from the stamping retreat.

F'nor and the men had settled themselves in a hastily vacated barrackroom. The dragons were perched comfortably on the rocky ridges above the Hold. Each rider kept his dragon in light, but alert, charge. There were to be no incidents on a Search. As a group, the dragonmen rose at F'lar's entrance.

"No tricks, no troubles, but look around closely," he said laconically. "Return by sundown with the names of any likely prospects." He caught F'nor's grin, remembering how Fax had slurred over some names. "Descriptions are in order and craft affiliation."

The men nodded, their eyes glinting with understanding. They were flatteringly confident of a successful Search even as F'lar's doubts grew now that he had seen Fax's women. By all logic, the pick of the High Reaches should be in Fax's chief Hold—but they were not. Still, there were many large craftholds, not to mention the six other High Holds to visit. All the same . . .

In unspoken accord F'lar and F'nor left the barracks. The men would follow, unobtrusively, in pairs or singly, to reconnoiter the crafthold and the nearer farmholds. The men were as overtly eager to be abroad as F'lar was privately. There had been a time when dragonmen were frequent and favored guests in all the great Holds throughout Pern, from southern Fort to high north Igen. This pleasant custom, too, had died along with other observances, evidence of the low regard in which the Weyr was presently held. F'lar vowed to correct this.

He forced himself to trace in memory the insidious changes. The Records, which each Weyrwoman kept, were proof of the gradual, but perceptible, decline, traceable through the past two hundred full Turns. Knowing the facts did not alleviate the condition. And F'lar was of that scant handful in the Weyr itself who did credit Records and Ballad alike. The situation might shortly reverse itself radically if the old tales were to be believed.

There was a reason, an explanation, a purpose, F'lar felt, for every one of the Weyr laws from First Impression to the Firestones: from the grass-free heights to ridge-running gutters. For elements as minor as controlling the appetite of a dragon to limiting the inhabitants of the Weyr. Although why the other five Weyrs had been abandoned, F'lar did not know. Idly he wondered if there were records, dusty and crumbling, lodged in the disused Weyrs. He must contrive to check when next his wings flew patrol. Certainly there was no explanation in Benden Weyr.

"There is industry but no enthusiasm," F'nor was saying, drawing F'lar's attention back to their tour of the crafthold.

They had descended the guttered ramp from the Hold into the crafthold proper, the broad roadway lined with cottages up to the imposing stone crafthalls. Silently F'lar noted moss-clogged gutters on the roofs, the vines clasping the walls. It was painful for one of his calling to witness the flagrant disregard of simple safety precautions. Growing things were forbidden near the habitations of mankind.

"News travels fast," F'nor chuckled, nodding at a hurrying craftsman, in the smock of a baker, who gave them a mumbled good day. "Not a female in sight."

His observation was accurate. Women should be abroad at this hour, bringing in supplies from the storehouses, washing in the river on such a bright warm day, or going out to the farmholds to help with planting. Not a gowned figure in sight.

"We used to be preferred mates," F'nor remarked caustically.

"We'll visit the Clothmen's Hall first. If my memory serves me right . . ."

"As it always does . . . " F'nor interjected wryly. He took no advantage of their blood relationship but he was more at ease with the bronze rider than most of the dragonmen, the other bronze riders included. F'lar was reserved in a closeknit society of easy equality. He flew a tightly disciplined wing but men maneuvered to serve under him. His wing always excelled in the Games. None ever floundered in *between* to disappear forever and no beast in his wing sickened, leaving a man in dragonless exile from the Weyr, a part of him numb forever.

"L'tol came this way and settled in one of the High Reaches," F'lar continued.

"L'tol?"

"Yes, a green rider from S'lel's wing. You remember."

An ill-timed swerve during the Spring Games had brought L'tol and his beast into the full blast of a phosphene emission from S'lel's bronze Tuenth. L'tol had been thrown from his beast's neck as the dragon tried to evade the blast. Another wingmate had swooped to catch the rider but the green dragon, his left wing crisped, his body scorched, had died of shock and phosphene poisoning.

"L'tol would aid our Search," F'nor agreed as the two dragonmen walked up to the bronze doors of the Clothmen's Hall. They paused on the threshold, adjusting their eyes to the dimmer light within. Glows punctuated the wall recesses and hung in clusters above the larger looms where the finer tapestries and fabrics were woven by master craftsmen. The pervading mood was one of quiet, purposeful industry.

Before their eyes had adapted, however, a figure glided to them, with a polite, if curt, request for them to follow him.

They were led to the right of the entrance, to a small office, curtained from the main hall. Their guide turned to them, his face visible in the wallglows. There was that air about him that marked him indefinably as a dragonman. But his face was lined deeply, one side seamed with old burnmarks. His eyes, sick with a hungry yearning, dominated his face. He blinked constantly.

"I am now Lytol," he said in a harsh voice.

F'lar nodded acknowledgment.

"You would be F'lar," Lytol said, "and you, F'nor. You've both the look of your sire."

F'lar nodded again.

Lytol swallowed convulsively, the muscles in his face twitching as the presence of dragonmen revived his awareness of exile. He essayed a smile.

"Dragons in the sky! The news spread faster than Threads."

"Nemorth has a new queen."

"Jora dead?" Lytol asked concernedly, his face cleared of its nervous movement for a second.

F'lar nodded.

Lytol grimaced bitterly. "R'gul again, huh." He stared off in the middle distance, his eyelids quiet but the muscles along his jaw took up the constant movement.

"You've the High Reaches? All of them?" Lytol asked, turning back to the drag-onman, a slight emphasis on "all."

F'lar gave an affirmative nod again.

"You've seen the women." Lytol's disgust showed through the words. It was a statement, not a question, for he hurried on. "Well, there are no better in all the High Reaches," and his tone expressed utmost disdain.

"Fax likes his women comfortably fleshed and docile," Lytol rattled on. "Even the Lady Gemma has learned. It'd be different if he didn't need her family's support. Oh, it would be different indeed. So he keeps her pregnant, hoping to kill her in childbed one day. And he will. He will."

Lytol drew himself up, squaring his shoulders, turning full to the two dragonmen. His expression was vindictive, his voice low and tense.

"Kill that tyrant, for the sake and safety of Pern. Of the Weyr. Of the queen. He only bides his time. He spreads discontent among the other lords. He"—Lytol's laughter had an hysterical edge to it now—"he fancies himself as good as dragonmen."

"There are no candidates then in this Hold?" F'lar said, his voice sharp enough to cut through the man's preoccupation with his curious theory.

Lytol stared at the bronze rider. "Did I not say it?"

"What of Ruath Hold?"

Lytol stopped shaking his head and looked sharply at F'lar, his lips curling in a cunning smile. He laughed mirthlessly.

"You think to find a Torene, or a Moreta, hidden at Ruath Hold in these times? Well, all of that Blood are dead. Fax's blade was thirsty that day. He knew the truth ⌐f those harpers' tales, that Ruathan lords gave full measure of hospitality to dragonmen and the Ruathan were a breed apart. There were, you know," Lytol's voice dropped to a confiding whisper, "exiled Weyrmen like myself in that Line."

F'lar nodded gravely, unable to contradict the man's pitiful attempt at self-esteem.

"No," and Lytol chuckled softly. "Fax gets nothing from that Hold but trouble. And the women Fax used to take . . ." his laugh turned nasty in tone. "It is rumored he was impotent for months afterwards."

"Any families in the holdings with Weyr blood?"

Lytol frowned, glanced surprised at F'lar. He rubbed the scarred side of his face thoughtfully.

"There were," he admitted slowly. "There were. But I doubt if any live on." He thought a moment longer, then shook his head emphatically.

F'lar shrugged.

"I wish I had better news for you," Lytol murmured.

"No matter," F'lar reassured him, one hand poised to part the hanging in the doorway.

Lytol came up to him swiftly, his voice urgent.

"Heed what I say, Fax is ambitious. Force R'gul, or whoever is Weyrleader next, to keep watch on the High Reaches."

Lytol jabbed a finger in the direction of the Hold. "He scoffs openly at tales of the Threads. He taunts the harpers for the stupid nonsense of the old ballads and has banned from their repertoire all dragonlore. The new generation will grow up totally ignorant of duty, tradition, and precaution."

F'lar was not surprised to hear that on top of Lytol's other disclosures. Yet the Red Star pulsed in the sky and the time was drawing near when they would hysterically reavow the old allegiances in fear for their very lives.

"Have you been abroad in the early morning of late?" asked F'nor, grinning maliciously.

"I have," Lytol breathed out in a hushed, choked whisper. "I have . . ." A groan was wrenched from his guts and he whirled away from the dragonmen, his head bowed between hunched shoulders. "Go," he said, gritting his teeth. And, as they hesitated, he pleaded, *"Go!"*

F'lar walked quickly from the room, followed by F'nor. The bronze rider crossed the quiet dim Hall with long strides and exploded into the startling sunlight. His momentum took him into the center of the square. There he stopped so abruptly that F'nor, hard on his heels, nearly collided with him.

"We will spend exactly the same time within the other Halls," he announced in a tight voice, his face averted from F'nor's eyes. F'lar's throat was constricted. It was difficult, suddenly, for him to speak. He swallowed hard, several times.

"To be dragonless . . ." murmured F'nor, pityingly. The encounter with Lytol had roiled his depths in a mournful way to which he was unaccustomed. That F'lar appeared equally shaken went far to dispel F'nor's private opinion that his half-brother was incapable of emotion.

"There is no other way once First Impression has been made. You know that," F'lar roused himself to say curtly. He strode off to the Hall bearing the Leathermen's device.

> The Hold is barred
> The Hall is bare.
>   And men vanish.
> The soil is barren,
> The rock is bald.
>   All hope banish.

Lessa was shoveling ashes from the hearth when the agitated messenger staggered into the Great Hall. She made herself as inconspicuous as possible so the Warder would not dismiss her. She had contrived to be sent to the Great Hall that morning, knowing that the Warder intended to brutalize the Head Clothman for the shoddy quality of the goods readied for shipment to Fax.

"Fax is coming! With dragonmen!" the man gasped out as he plunged into the dim Great Hall.

The Warder, who had been about to lash the Head Clothman, turned, stunned, from his victim. The courier, a farmholder from the edge of Ruatha, stumbled up to the Warder, so excited with his message that he grabbed the Warder's arm.

"How dare you leave your Hold?" and the Warder aimed his lash at the astonished holder. The force of the first blow knocked the man from his feet. Yelping, he scrambled out of reach of a second lashing. "Dragonmen indeed! Fax? Ha! He shuns Ruatha. There!" The Warder punctuated each denial with another blow, kicking the helpless wretch for good measure, before he turned breathless to glare at the clothman and the two underwarders. "How did he get in here with such a threadbare lie?" The Warder stalked to the great door. It was flung open just as he reached out for the iron handle. The ashen-faced guard officer rushed in, nearly toppling the Warder.

"Dragonmen! Dragons! All over Ruatha!" the man gibbered, arms flailing wildly. He, too, pulled at the Warder's arm, dragging the stupefied official toward the outer courtyard, to bear out the truth of his statement.

Lessa scooped up the last pile of ashes. Picking up her equipment, she slipped out of the Great Hall. There was a very pleased smile on her face under the screen of matted hair.

A dragonman at Ruatha! She must somehow contrive to get Fax so humiliated, or so infuriated, that he would renounce his claim to the Hold, in the presence of a dragonman. Then she could claim her birthright.

But she would have to be extraordinarily wary. Dragonriders were men apart. Anger did not cloud their intelligence. Greed did not sully their judgment. Fear did not dull their reactions. Let the dense-witted believe human sacrifice, unnatural lusts, insane revel. She was not so gullible. And those stories went against her grain. Dragonmen were still human and there was Weyr blood in *her* veins. It was the same color as that of anyone else; enough of hers had been spilled to prove that.

She halted for a moment, catching a sudden shallow breath. Was this the danger she had sensed four days ago at dawn? The final encounter in her struggle to regain the Hold? No—there had been more to that portent than revenge.

The ash bucket banged against her shins as she shuffled down the low-ceilinged corridor to the stable door. Fax would find a cold welcome. She had laid no new fire on the hearth. Her laugh echoed back unpleasantly from the damp walls. She rested her bucket and propped her broom and shovel as she wrestled with the heavy bronze door that gave into the new stables.

They had been built outside the cliff of Ruatha by Fax's first Warder, a subtler man than all eight of his successors. He had achieved more than all the others and Lessa had honestly regretted the necessity of his death. But he would have made her revenge impossible. He would have caught her out before she had learned how to camouflage herself and her little interferences. What had his name been? She could not recall. Well, she regretted his death.

The second man had been properly greedy, and it had been easy to set up a pattern of misunderstanding between Warder and craftsmen. That one had been determined to squeeze all profit from Ruathan goods so that some of it would drop into his pocket before Fax suspected a shortage. The craftsmen who had begun to accept the skillful diplomacy of the first Warder bitterly resented the second's grasping, high-handed ways. They resented the passing of the Old Line and, even more so, the way of its passing. They were unforgiving of the insult to Ruatha, its now secondary position in the High Reaches; and they resented the individual indignities that holders, craftsmen and farmers alike, suffered under the second Warder. It took little manipulation to arrange for matters at Ruatha to go from bad to worse.

The second was replaced and his successor fared no better. He was caught diverting goods, the best of the goods at that. Fax had had him executed. His bony head still hung in the main firepit above the great Tower.

The present incumbent had not been able to maintain the Hold in even the sorry condition in which he had assumed its management. Seemingly simple matters developed rapidly into disasters. Like the production of cloth . . . Contrary to his boasts to Fax, the quality had not improved, and the quantity had fallen off.

Now Fax was here. And with dragonmen! Why dragonmen? The import of the question froze Lessa, and the heavy door closing behind her barked her heels painfully. Dragonmen used to be frequent visitors at Ruatha, that she knew, and even vaguely remembered. Those memories were like a harper's tale, told of someone else, not something within her own experience. She had limited her fierce attention to Ruatha only. She could not even recall the name of Queen or Weyrwoman from the instructions of her childhood, nor could she recall hearing mention of any queen or weyrwoman by anyone in the Hold these past ten Turns.

Perhaps the dragonmen were finally going to call the lords of the Holds to task for the disgraceful show of greenery about the Holds. Well, Lessa was to blame for much of that in Ruatha, but she defied even a dragonman to confront her with her guilt. Did all Ruatha fall to the Threads it would be better than remaining dependent to Fax! The heresy shocked Lessa even as she thought it.

Wishing she could as easily unburden her conscience of such blasphemy, she ditched the ashes on the stable midden. There was a sudden change in air pressure around her. Then a fleeting shadow caused her to glance up.

From behind the cliff above glided a dragon, its enormous wings spread to their fullest as he caught the morning updraft. Turning effortlessly, he descended. A second, a third, a full wing of dragons followed in soundless flight and patterned descent, graceful and awesome. The claxon rang belatedly from the Tower and from within the kitchen there issued the screams and shrieks of the terrified drudges.

Lessa took cover. She ducked into the kitchen, where she was instantly seized by the assistant cook and thrust with a buffet and a kick toward the sinks. There she was put to scrubbing grease-encrusted serving bowls with cleansing sand.

The yelping canines were already lashed to the spitrun, turning a scrawny herdbeast that had been set to roast. The cook was ladling seasonings on the carcass, swearing at having to offer so poor a meal to so many guests, and some of them high-rank. Winter-dried fruits from the last scanty harvest had been set to soak and two of the oldest drudges were scraping roots.

An apprentice cook was kneading bread; another, carefully spicing a sauce. Looking fixedly at him, she diverted his hand from one spice box to a less appropriate one as he gave a final shake to the concoction. She added too much wood to the wall oven, insuring ruin for the breads. She controlled the canines deftly, slowing one and speeding the other so that the meat would be underdone on one side, burned on the other. That the feast should be a fast, the food presented found inedible, was her whole intention.

Above in the Hold, she had no doubt that certain other measures, undertaken at different times for this exact contingency, were being discovered.

Her fingers bloodied from a beating, one of the Warder's women came shrieking into the kitchen, hopeful of refuge there.

"Insects have eaten the best blankets to shreds! And a canine who had littered on the best linens snarled at me as she gave suck! And the rushes are noxious, the best chambers full of debris driven in by the winter wind. Somebody left the shutters ajar. Just a tiny bit, but it was enough . . ." the woman wailed, clutching her hand to her breast and rocking back and forth.

Lessa bent with great industry to shine the plates.

Watch-wher, watch-wher,
In your lair,
Watch well, watch-wher!
Who goes there?

"The watch-wher is hiding something," F'lar told F'nor as they consulted in the hastily cleaned Great Hall. The room delighted to hold the wintry chill although a generous fire now burned on the hearth.

"It was but gibbering when Canth spoke to it," F'nor remarked. He was leaning against the mantel, turning slightly from side to side to gather some warmth. He watched his wingleader's impatient pacing.

"Mnementh is calming it down," F'lar replied. "He may be able to sort out the nightmare. The creature may be more senile than aware, but . . ."

"I doubt it," F'nor concurred helpfully. He glanced with apprehension up at the webhung ceiling. He was certain he'd found most of the crawlers, but he didn't fancy their sting. Not on top of the discomforts already experienced in this forsaken Hold. If the night stayed mild, he intended curling up with Canth on the heights. "That would be more reasonable than anything Fax or his Warder have suggested."

"Hm-m-m," F'lar muttered, frowning at the brown rider.

"Well, it's unbelievable that Ruatha could have fallen to such disrepair in ten short Turns. Every dragon caught the feeling of power and it's obvious the watch-wher has been tampered with. That takes a good deal of control."

"From someone of the Blood," F'lar reminded him.

F'nor shot his wingleader a quick look, wondering if he could possibly be serious in the light of all information to the contrary.

"I grant you there is power here, F'lar," F'nor conceded. "It could easily be a hidden male of the old Blood. But we need a female. And Fax made it plain, in his inimitable fashion, that he left none of the old Blood alive in the Hold the day he took it. No, no." The brown rider shook his head, as if he could dispel the lack of faith in his wingleader's curious insistence that the Search would end in Ruath with Ruathan blood.

"That watch-wher is hiding something and only someone of the Blood of its Hold can arrange that," F'lar said emphatically. He gestured around the Hall and toward the walls, bare of hangings. "Ruatha has been overcome. But she resists . . . subtly. I say it points to the old Blood, *and* power. Not power alone."

The obstinate expression in F'lar's eyes, the set of his jaw, suggested that F'nor seek another topic.

"The pattern was well-flown today," F'nor suggested tentatively. "Does a dragonman good to ride a flaming beast. Does the beast good, too. Keeps the digestive process in order."

F'lar nodded sober agreement. "Let R'gul temporize as he chooses. It is fitting and proper to ride a firespouting beast and these holders need to be reminded of Weyr power."

"Right now, anything would help our prestige," F'nor commented sourly. "What had Fax to say when he hailed you in the Pass?" F'nor knew his question was almost impertinent but if it were, F'lar would ignore it.

F'lar's slight smile was unpleasant and there was an ominous glint in his amber eyes.

"We talked of rule and resistance."

"Did he not also draw on you?" F'nor asked.

F'lar's smile deepened. "Until he remembered I was dragonmounted."

"He's considered a vicious fighter," F'nor said.

"I am at some disadvantage?" F'lar asked, turning sharply on his brown rider, his face too controlled.

"To my knowledge, no," F'nor reassured his leader quickly. F'lar had tumbled every man in the Weyr, efficiently and easily. "But Fax kills often and without cause."

"And because we dragonmen do not seek blood, we are not to be feared as fighters?" snapped F'lar. "Are you ashamed of your heritage?"

"I? No!" F'nor sucked in his breath. "Nor any of our wing!" he added proudly. "But there is that in the attitude of the men in this progression of Fax's that . . . that makes me wish some excuse to fight."

"As you observed today, Fax seeks some excuse. And," F'lar added thoughtfully, "there is something here in Ruatha that unnerves our noble overlord."

He caught sight of Lady Tela, whom Fax had so courteously assigned him for comfort during the progression, waving to him from the inner Hold portal.

"A case in point. Fax's Lady Tela is some three months gone."

F'nor frowned at that insult to his leader.

"She giggles incessantly and appears so addlepated that one cannot decide whether she babbles out of ignorance or at Fax's suggestion. As she has apparently not bathed all winter, and is not, in any case, my ideal, I have" — F'lar grinned maliciously — "deprived myself of her kind offices."

F'nor hastily cleared his throat and his expression as Lady Tela approached them. He caught the unappealing odor from the scarf or handkerchief she waved constantly. Dragonmen endured a great deal for the Weyr. He moved away, with apparent courtesy, to join the rest of the dragonmen entering the Hall.

F'lar turned with equal courtesy to Lady Tela as she jabbered away about the terrible condition of the rooms which Lady Gemma and the other ladies had been assigned.

"The shutters, both sets, were ajar all winter long and you should have seen the trash on the floors. We finally got two of the drudges to sweep it all into the fireplace. And then that smoked something fearful 'til a man was sent up." Lady Tela giggled. "He found the access blocked by a chimney stone fallen aslant. The rest of the chimney, for a wonder, was in good repair."

She waved her handkerchief. F'lar held his breath as the gesture wafted an unappealing odor in his direction.

He glanced up the Hall toward the inner Hold door and saw Lady Gemma descending, her steps slow and awkward. Some subtle difference about her gait attracted him and he stared at her, trying to identify it.

"Oh, yes, poor Lady Gemma," Lady Tela babbled, sighing deeply. "We are so concerned. Why Lord Fax insisted on her coming, I do not know. She is not near her time and yet . . ." The lighthead's concern sounded sincere.

F'lar's incipient hatred for Fax and his brutality matured abruptly. He left his partner chattering to thin air and courteously extended his arm to Lady Gemma to support her down the steps and to the table. Only the brief tightening of her fingers on his forearm betrayed her gratitude. Her face was very white and drawn, the lines deeply etched around mouth and eyes, showing the effort she was expending.

"Some attempt has been made, I see, to restore order to the Hall," she remarked in a conversational tone.

"Some," F'lar admitted dryly, glancing around the grandly proportioned Hall, its rafter festooned with the webs of many Turns. The inhabitants of those gossamer nests dropped from time to time, with ripe splats, to the floor, onto the table and into the serving platters. Nothing replaced the old banners of the Ruathan Blood, which had been removed from the stark brown stone walls. Fresh rushes did obscure the greasy flagstones. The trestle tables appeared recently sanded and scraped, and the platters gleamed dully in the refreshed glows. Unfortunately, the brighter light was a mistake for it was much too unflattering.

"This was such a graceful Hall," Lady Gemma murmured for F'lar's ears alone.

"You were a friend?" he asked, politely.

"Yes, in my youth," her voice dropped expressively on the last word, evoking for F'lar a happier girlhood. "It was a noble line!"

"Think you *one* might have escaped the sword?"

Lady Gemma flashed him a startled look, then quickly composed her features, lest the exchange be noted. She gave a barely perceptible shake of her head and then shifted her awkward weight to take her place at the table. Graciously she inclined her head towards F'lar, both dismissing and thanking him.

F'lar returned to his own partner and placed her at the table on his left. As the only person of rank who would dine that night at Ruath Hold, Lady Gemma was seated on his right; Fax would be beyond her. The dragonmen and Fax's upper soldiery would sit at the lower tables. No guildmen had been invited to Ruatha. Fax arrived just then with his current lady and two underleaders, the Warder bowing them effusively into the Hall. The man, F'lar noticed, kept a good distance from his overlord—as well a Warder might whose responsibility was in this sorry condition. F'lar flicked a crawler away. Out of the corner of his eye, he saw Lady Gemma wince and shudder.

Fax stamped up to the raised table, his face black with suppressed rage. He pulled back his chair roughly, slamming it into Lady Gemma's before he seated himself. He pulled the chair to the table with a force that threatened to rock the none-too-stable trestle-top from its supporting legs. Scowling, he inspected his goblet and plate, fingering the surface, ready to throw them aside if they displeased him.

"A roast and fresh bread, Lord Fax, and such fruits and roots as are left. Had I but known of your arrival, I could have sent to Crom for . . ."

"Sent to Crom?" roared Fax, slamming the plate he was inspecting onto the table so forcefully the rim bent under his hands. The Warder winced again as if he himself had been maimed.

"The day one of my Holds cannot support itself *or* the visit of its rightful overlord, I shall renounce it."

Anne McCaffrey

Lady Gemma gasped. Simultaneously the dragons roared. F'lar felt the unmistakable surge of power. His eyes instinctively sought F'nor at the lower table. The brown rider—all the dragonmen—had experienced that inexplicable shaft of exultation.

"What's wrong, Dragonman?" snapped Fax.

F'lar, affecting unconcern, stretched his legs under the table and assumed an indolent posture in the heavy chair.

"Wrong?"

"The dragons!"

"Oh, nothing. They often roar . . . at the sunset, at a flock of passing wherries, at mealtimes," and F'lar smiled amiably at the Lord of the High Reaches. Beside him his tablemate gave a squeak.

"Mealtimes? Have they not been fed?"

"Oh, yes. Five days ago."

"Oh. Five . . . days ago? And are they hungry . . . now?" Her voice trailed into a whisper of fear, her eyes grew round.

"In a few days," F'lar assured her. Under cover of his detached amusement, F'lar scanned the Hall. That surge had come from nearby. Either in the Hall or just outside. It must have been from within. It came so soon upon Fax's speech that his words must have triggered it. And the power had had an indefinably feminine touch to it.

One of Fax's women? F'lar found that hard to credit. Mnementh had been close to all of them and none had shown a vestige of power. Much less, with the exception of Lady Gemma, any intelligence.

One of the Hall women? So far he had seen only the sorry drudges and the aging females the Warder had as housekeepers. The Warder's personal woman? He must discover if that man had one. One of the Hold guards' women? F'lar suppressed an intense desire to rise and search.

"You mount a guard?" he asked Fax casually.

"Double at Ruath Hold!" he was told in a tight, hard voice, ground out from somewhere deep in Fax's chest.

"Here?" F'lar all but laughed out loud, gesturing around the sadly appointed chamber.

"Here! Food!" Fax changed the subject with a roar.

Five drudges, two of them women in brown-gray rags such that F'lar hoped they had had nothing to do with the preparation of the meal, staggered in under the emplattered herdbeast. No one with so much as a trace of power would sink to such depths, unless . . .

The aroma that reached him as the platter was placed on the serving table distracted him. It reeked of singed bone and charred meat. The Warder frantically sharpened his tools as if a keen edge could somehow slice acceptable portions from this unlikely carcass.

Lady Gemma caught her breath again, and F'lar saw her hands curl tightly around the armrests. He saw the convulsive movement of her throat as she swallowed. He, too, did not look forward to this repast.

The drudges reappeared with wooden trays of bread. Burnt crusts had been scraped and cut, in some places, from the loaves before serving. As other trays were borne in, F'lar tried to catch sight of the faces of the servitors. Matted hair obscured the face of the one who presented a dish of legumes swimming in greasy liquid. Revolted, F'lar poked through the legumes to find properly cooked portions to offer Lady Gemma. She waved them aside, her face ill-concealing her discomfort.

As F'lar was about to turn and serve Lady Tela, he saw Lady Gemma's hand clutch convulsively at the chair arms. He realized that she was not merely nauseated by the unappetizing food. She was seized with labor contractions.

F'lar glanced in Fax's direction. The overlord was scowling blackly at the attempts of the Warder to find edible portions of meat to serve.

F'lar touched Lady Gemma's arm with light fingers. She turned just enough to look at F'lar from the corner of her eye. She managed a socially correct half-smile.

"I dare not leave just now, Lord F'lar. He is always dangerous at Ruatha. And it may only be false pangs."

F'lar was dubious as he saw another shudder pass through her frame. The woman would have been a fine weyrwoman, he thought ruefully, were she but younger.

The Warder, his hands shaking, presented Fax the sliced meats. There were slivers of overdone flesh and portions of almost edible meats, but not much of either.

One furious wave of Fax's broad fist and the Warder had the plate, meats and juice, square in the face. Despite himself, F'lar sighed, for those undoubtedly constituted the only edible portions of the entire beast.

"You call this food? *You call this food?*" Fax bellowed. His voice boomed back from the bare vault of the ceiling, shaking crawlers from their webs as the sound shattered the fragile strands. "Slop! *Slop!*"

F'lar rapidly brushed crawlers from Lady Gemma, who was helpless in the throes of a very strong contraction.

"It's all we had on such short notice," the Warder squealed, juices streaking down his cheeks. Fax threw the goblet at him and the wine went streaming down the man's chest. The steaming dish of roots followed, and the man yelped as the hot liquid splashed over him.

"My lord, my lord, had I but known!"

"Obviously, Ruatha *cannot* support the visit of its Lord. You must renounce it," F'lar heard himself saying.

His shock at such words issuing from his mouth was as great as that of everyone else in the Hall. Silence fell, broken by the splat of falling crawlers and the drip of root liquid from the Warder's shoulders to the rushes. The grating of Fax's boot-heel was clearly audible as he swung slowly around to face the bronze rider.

As F'lar conquered his own amazement and rapidly tried to predict what to do next to mend matters, he saw F'nor rise slowly to his feet, hand on dagger hilt.

"I did not hear you correctly?" Fax asked, his face blank of all expression, his eyes snapping.

Unable to comprehend how he could have uttered such an arrant challenge, F'lar managed to assume a languid pose.

"You did mention," he drawled, "that if any of your Holds could not support itself and the visit of its rightful overlord, you would renounce it."

Fax stared back at F'lar, his face a study of swiftly suppressed emotions, the glint of triumph dominant. F'lar, his face stiff with the forced expression of indifference, was casting swiftly about in his mind. In the name of the Egg, had he lost all sense of discretion?

Pretending utter unconcern, he stabbed some vegetables onto his knife and began to munch on them. As he did so, he noticed F'nor glancing slowly around the Hall, scrutinizing everyone. Abruptly F'lar realized what had happened. Somehow, in making that statement, he, a dragonman, had responded to a covert use of the power. F'lar, the bronze rider, was being put into a position where he would *have* to fight Fax. Why? For what end? To get Fax to renounce the Hold? Incredible! But there could be only one possible reason for such a turn of events. An exultation as sharp as pain swelled within F'lar. It was all he could do to maintain his pose of bored indifference, all he could do to turn his attention to thwarting Fax, should he press for a duel. A duel would serve no purpose. He, F'lar, had no time to waste on it.

A groan escaped Lady Gemma and broke the eye-locked stance of the two antagonists. Irritated, Fax looked down at her, fist clenched and half-raised to strike her for her temerity in interrupting her lord and master. The contraction that contorted the swollen belly was as obvious as the woman's pain. F'lar dared not look toward her but he wondered if she had deliberately groaned aloud to break the tension.

Incredibly, Fax began to laugh. He threw back his head, showing big, stained teeth, and roared.

"Aye, renounce it, in favor of her issue, if it is male . . . and lives!" he crowed, laughing raucously.

"Heard and witnessed!" F'lar snapped, jumping to his feet and pointing to his riders. They were on their feet in the instant. "Heard and witnessed!" they averred in the traditional manner.

With that movement, everyone began to babble at once in nervous relief. The other women, each reacting in her way to the imminence of birth, called orders to the servants and advice to each other. They converged toward Lady Gemma, hovering undecidedly out of Fax's range, like silly wherries disturbed from their roosts. It was obvious they were torn between their fear of their lord and their desire to reach the laboring woman.

He gathered their intentions as well as their reluctance and, still stridently laughing, knocked back his chair. He stepped over it. strode down to the meatstand and stood hacking off pieces with his knife, stuffing them, juice dripping, into his mouth without ceasing his guffawing.

As F'lar bent toward Lady Gemma to assist her out of her chair, she grabbed his arm urgently. Their eyes met, hers clouded with pain. She pulled him closer.

"He means to kill you, Bronze Rider. He loves to kill," she whispered.

"Dragonmen are not easily killed, but I am grateful to you."

"I do not want you killed," she said, softly, biting at her lip. "We have so few bronze riders."

F'lar stared at her, startled. Did she, Fax's lady, actually believe in the Old Laws?

F'lar beckoned to two of the Warder's men to carry her up into the Hold. He caught Lady Tela by the arm as she fluttered past him.

"What do you need?"

"Oh, oh," she exclaimed, her face twisted with panic; she was distractedly wringing her hands, "water, hot. Clean cloths. And a birthing-woman. Oh, yes, we must have a birthing-woman."

F'lar looked about for one of the Hold women, his glance sliding over the first disreputable figure who had started to mop up the spilled food. He signaled instead for the Warder and peremptorily ordered him to send for the woman. The Warder kicked at the drudge on the floor.

"You . . . you! Whatever your name is, go get her from the crafthold. You must know who she is."

The drudge evaded the parting kick the Warder aimed in her direction with a nimbleness at odds with her appearance of extreme age and decrepitude. She scurried across the Hall and out the kitchen door.

Fax sliced and speared meat, occasionally bursting out with a louder bark of laughter as his inner thoughts amused him. F'lar sauntered down to the carcass and, without waiting for invitation from his host, began to carve neat slices also, beckoning his men over. Fax's soldiers, however, waited until their lord had eaten his fill.

Lord of the Hold, your charge is sure
In thick walls, metal doors and no verdure.

Lessa sped from the Hall to summon the birthing-woman, seething with frustration. So close! So close! How could she come so close and yet fail? Fax should have challenged the dragonman. And the dragonman was strong and young, his face that of a fighter, stern and controlled. He should not have temporized. Was all honor dead in Pern, smothered by green grass?

And why, oh why, had Lady Gemma chosen that precious moment to go into labor? If her groan hadn't distracted Fax, the fight would have begun and not even Fax, for all his vaunted prowess as a vicious fighter, would have prevailed against a dragonman who had her—Lessa's—support! The Hold must be secured to its rightful Blood again. Fax must not leave Ruatha, alive, again!

Above her, on the High Tower, the great bronze dragon gave forth a weird croon, his many-faceted eyes sparkling in the gathering darkness.

Unconsciously she silenced him as she would have done the watch-wher. Ah, that watch-wher. He had not come out of his den at her passing. She knew the dragons had been at him. She could hear him gibbering in panic.

The slant of the road toward the crafthold lent impetus to her flying feet and she had to brace herself to a sliding stop at the birthing-woman's stone threshold. She banged on the closed door and heard the frightened exclamation within.

"A birth. A birth at the Hold," Lessa cried.

"A birth?" came the muffled cry and the latches were thrown up on the door. "At the Hold?"

"Fax's lady and, as you love life, hurry! For if it is male, it will be Ruatha's own lord."

That ought to fetch her, thought Lessa, and in that instant, the door was flung open by the man of the house. Lessa could see the birthing-woman gathering up her things in haste, piling them into her shawl. Lessa hurried the woman out, up the steep road to the Hold, under the Tower gate, grabbing the woman as she tried to run at the sight of a dragon peering down at her. Lessa drew her into the Court and pushed her, resisting, into the Hall.

The woman clutched at the inner door, balking at the sight of the gathering there. Lord Fax, his feet up on the trestle table, was paring his fingernails with his knife blade, still chuckling. The dragonmen in their wher-hide tunics were eating quietly at one table while the soldiers were having their turn at the meat.

The bronze rider noticed their entrance and pointed urgently towards the inner Hold. The birthing-woman seemed frozen to the spot. Lessa tugged futilely at her arm, urging her to cross the Hall. To her surprise, the bronze rider strode to them.

"Go quickly, woman, Lady Gemma is before her time," he said, frowning with concern, gesturing imperatively towards the Hold entrance. He caught her by the shoulder and led her all unwilling, Lessa tugging away at her other arm.

When they reached the stairs, he relinquished his grip, nodding to Lessa to escort her the rest of the way. Just as they reached the massive inner door, Lessa noticed how sharply the dragonman was looking at them—at her hand, on the birthing-woman's arm. Warily, she glanced at her hand and saw it, as if it belonged to a stranger: the long fingers, shapely despite dirt and broken nails; her small hand, delicately boned, gracefully placed despite the urgency of the grip. She blurred it and hurried on.

Honor those the dragons heed,
In thought and favor, word and deed.
Worlds are lost or worlds are saved

By those dangers dragon-braved.

Dragonman, avoid excess;
Greed will bring the Weyr distress;
To the ancient Laws adhere,
Prospers thus the Dragonweyr.

An unintelligible ululation raised the waiting men to their feet, startled from private meditations and the diversion of Bonethrows. Only Fax remained unmoved at the alarm, save that the slight sneer, which had settled on his face hours past, deepened to smug satisfaction.

"Dead-ed-ed," the tidings reverberated down the rocky corridors of the Hold. The weeping lady seemed to erupt out of the passage from the Inner Hold, flying down the steps to sink into an hysterical heap at Fax's feet. "She's dead. Lady Gemma is dead. There was too much blood. It was too soon. She was too old to bear more children."

F'lar couldn't decide whether the woman was apologizing for, or exulting in, the woman's death. She certainly couldn't be criticizing her Lord for placing Lady Gemma in such peril. F'lar, however, was sincerely sorry at Gemma's passing. She had been a brave, fine woman.

And now, what would be Fax's next move? F'lar caught F'nor's identically quizzical glance and shrugged expressively.

"The child lives!" a curiously distorted voice announced, penetrating the rising noise in the Great Hall. The words electrified the atmosphere. Every head slewed round sharply toward the portal to the Inner Hold where the drudge, a totally unexpected messenger, stood poised on the top step.

"It is male!" This announcement rang triumphantly in the still Hall.

Fax jerked himself to his feet, kicking aside the wailer at his feet, scowling ominously at the drudge. "What did you say, woman?"

"The child lives. It is male," the creature repeated, descending the stairs.

Incredulity and rage suffused Fax's face. His body seemed to coil up.

"Ruatha has a new lord!" Staring intently at the overlord, she advanced, her mien purposeful, almost menacing.

The tentative cheers of the Warder's men were drowned by the roaring of the dragons.

Fax erupted into action. He leaped across the intervening space, bellowing. Before Lessa could dodge, his fist crashed down across her face. She fell heavily to the stone floor, where she lay motionless, a bundle of dirty rags.

"Hold, Fax!" F'lar's voice broke the silence as the Lord of the High Reaches flexed his leg to kick her.

Fax whirled, his hand automatically closing on his knife hilt.

Anne McCaffrey

"It was heard and witnessed, Fax," F'lar cautioned him, one hand outstretched in warning, "by dragonmen. Stand by your sworn and witnessed oath!"

"Witnessed? By dragonmen?" cried Fax with a derisive laugh. "Dragonwomen, you mean," he sneered, his eyes blazing with contempt, as he made one sweeping gesture of scorn.

He was momentarily taken aback by the speed with which the bronze rider's knife appeared in his hand.

"Dragonwomen?" F'lar queried, his lips curling back over his teeth, his voice dangerously soft. Glowlight flickered off his circling knife as he advanced on Fax.

"Women! Parasites on Pern. The Weyr power is over. Over!" Fax roared, leaping forward to land in a combat crouch.

The two antagonists were dimly aware of the scurry behind them, of tables pulled roughly aside to give the duelists space. F'lar could spare no glance at the crumpled form of the drudge. Yet he was sure, through and beyond instinct sure, that she was the source of power. He had felt it as she entered the room. The dragons' roaring confirmed it. If that fall had killed her . . . He advanced on Fax, leaping high to avoid the slashing blade as Fax unwound from the crouch with a powerful lunge.

F'lar evaded the attack easily, noticing his opponent's reach, deciding he had a slight advantage there. But not much. Fax had had much more actual hand-to-hand killing experience than had he whose duels had always ended at first blood on the practice floor. F'lar made due note to avoid closing with the burly lord. The man was heavy-chested, dangerous from sheer mass. F'lar must use agility as his weapon, not brute strength.

Fax feinted, testing F'lar for weakness or indiscretion. The two crouched, facing each other across six feet of space, knife hands weaving, their free hands, spread-fingered, ready to grab.

Again Fax pressed the attack. F'lar allowed him to close, just near enough to dodge away with a backhanded swipe. Fabric ripped under the tip of his knife. He heard Fax snarl. The overlord was faster on his feet than his bulk suggested and F'lar had to dodge a second time, feeling Fax's knife score his wherhide jerkin.

Grimly the two circled, each looking for an opening in the other's defense. Fax plowed in, trying to corner the lighter, faster man between raised platform and wall.

F'lar countered, ducking low under Fax's flailing arm, slashing obliquely across Fax's side. The overlord caught at him, yanking savagely, and F'lar was trapped against the other man's side, straining desperately with his left hand to keep the knife arm up. F'lar brought up his knee and ducked away as Fax gasped and buckled from the pain in his groin, but Fax struck in passing. Suddenly fire laced F'lar's left shoulder.

Fax's face was red with anger and he wheezed from pain and shock. But the infuriated lord straightened up and charged. F'lar was forced to sidestep quickly before Fax could close with him. F'lar put the meat table between them, circling warily, flexing his shoulder to assess the extent of the knife's slash. It was painful, but the arm could be used.

Suddenly Fax scooped up some fatty scraps from the meat tray and hurled them at F'lar. The dragonman ducked and Fax came around the table with a rush. F'lar leaped sideways. Fax's flashing blade came within inches of his abdomen, as his own knife sliced down the outside of Fax's arm. Instantly the two pivoted to face each other again, but Fax's left arm hung limply at his side.

F'lar darted in, pressing his luck as the Lord of the High Reaches staggered. But F'lar misjudged the man's condition and suffered a terrific kick in the side as he tried to dodge under the feinting knife. Doubled with pain, F'lar rolled frantically away from his charging adversary. Fax was lurching forward, trying to fall on him, to pin the lighter dragonman down for a final thrust. Somehow F'lar got to his feet, attempting to straighten to meet Fax's stumbling charge. His very position saved him. Fax overreached his mark and staggered off balance. F'lar brought his right hand over with as much strength as he could muster and his blade plunged through Fax's unprotected back until he felt the point stick in the chest plate.

The defeated lord fell flat to the flagstones. The force of his descent dislodged the dagger from his chestbone and an inch of bloody blade re-emerged.

F'lar stared down at the dead man. There was no pleasure in killing, he realized, only relief that he himself was still alive. He wiped his forehead on his sleeve and forced himself erect, his side throbbing with the pain of that last kick and his left shoulder burning. He half-stumbled to the drudge, still sprawled where she had fallen.

He gently turned her over, noting the terrible bruise spreading across her cheek under the dirty skin. He heard F'nor take command of the tumult in the Hall.

The dragonman laid a hand, trembling in spite of an effort to control himself, on the woman's breast to feel for a heartbeat. . . . It was there, slow but strong.

A deep sigh escaped him for either blow or fall could have proved fatal. Fatal, perhaps, for Pern as well.

Relief was colored with disgust. There was no telling under the filth how old this creature might be. He raised her in his arms, her light body no burden even to his battleweary strength. Knowing F'nor would handle any trouble efficiently, F'lar carried the drudge to his own chamber.

Putting the body on the high bed, he stirred up the fire and added more glows to the bedside bracket. His gorge rose at the thought of touching the filthy mat of hair but nonetheless and gently, he pushed it back from the face, turning the head this way and that. The features were small, regular. One arm, clear of rags, was reasonably clean above the elbow but marred by bruises and old scars. The skin was firm and unwrinkled. The hands, when he took them in his, were filthy but well-shaped and delicately boned.

F'lar began to smile. Yes, she had blurred that hand so skillfully that he had actually doubted what he had first seen. And yes, beneath grime and grease, she was young.

Anne McCaffrey

Young enough for the Weyr. And no born drab. There was no taint of common blood here. It was pure, no matter whose the line, and he rather thought she was indeed Ruathan. One who had by some unknown agency escaped the massacre ten Turns ago and bided her time for revenge. Why else force Fax to renounce the Hold?

Delighted and fascinated by this unexpected luck, F'lar reached out to tear the dress from the unconscious body and found himself constrained not to. The girl had roused. Her great, hungry eyes fastened on his, not fearful or expectant; wary.

A subtle change occurred in her face. F'lar watched, his smile deepening, as she shifted her regular features into an illusion of disagreeable ugliness and great age.

"Trying to confuse a dragonman, girl?" he chuckled. He made no further move to touch her but settled against the great carved post of the bed. He crossed his arms sternly on his chest, thought better of it immediately, and eased his sore arm. "Your name, girl, and rank, too."

She drew herself upright slowly against the headboard, her features no longer blurred. They faced each other across the high bed.

"Fax?"

"Dead. Your name!"

A look of exulting triumph flooded her face. She slipped from the bed, standing unexpectedly tall. "Then I reclaim my own. I am of the Ruathan Blood. I claim Ruath," she announced in a ringing voice.

F'lar stared at her a moment, delighted with her proud bearing. Then he threw back his head and laughed.

"This? This crumbling heap?" He could not help but mock the disparity between her manner and her dress. "Oh, no. Besides, Lady, we dragonmen heard and witnessed Fax's oath renouncing the Hold in favor of his heir. Shall I challenge the babe, too, for you? And choke him with his swaddling cloths?"

Her eyes flashed, her lips parted in a terrible smile.

"There is no heir. Gemma died, the babe unborn. I lied."

"Lied?" F'lar demanded, angry.

"Yes," she taunted him with a toss of her chin. "I lied. There was no babe born. I merely wanted to be sure you challenged Fax."

He grabbed her wrist, stung that he had twice fallen to her prodding.

"You provoked a dragonman to fight? To kill? *When he is on Search?*"

"Search? Why should I care about a Search? I've Ruatha as my Hold again. For ten Turns, I have worked and waited, schemed and suffered for that. What could your Search mean to me?"

F'lar wanted to strike that look of haughty contempt from her face. He twisted her arm savagely, bringing her to his feet before he released his grip. She laughed at him, and scuttled to one side. She was on her feet and out the door before he could give chase.

Swearing to himself, he raced down the rocky corridors, knowing she would have to make for the Hall to get out of the Hold. However, when he reached the Hall, there was no sign of her fleeing figure among those still loitering.

"Has that creature come this way?" he called to F'nor who was, by chance, standing by the door to the Court.

"No. Is she the source of power after all?"

"Yes, she is," F'lar answered, galled all the more. "And Ruathan Blood at that!"

"Oh ho! Does she depose the babe, then?" F'nor asked, gesturing toward the birthing-woman, who occupied a seat close to the now-blazing hearth.

F'lar paused, about to return to search the Hold's myriad passages. He stared, momentarily confused, at the brown rider.

"Babe? What babe?"

"The male child Lady Gemma bore," F'nor replied, surprised by F'lar's uncomprehending look.

"It lives?"

"Yes. A strong babe, the woman says, for all that he was premature and taken forcibly from his dead dame's belly."

F'lar threw back his head with a shout of laughter. For all her scheming, she had been outdone by truth.

At that moment, he heard Mnementh roar in unmistakeable elation and the curious warble of other dragons.

"Mnementh has caught her," F'lar cried, grinning with jubilation. He strode down the steps, past the body of the former Lord of the High Reaches and out into the main court.

He saw that the bronze dragon was gone from his Tower perch and called him. An agitation drew his eyes upward. He saw Mnementh spiraling down into the Court, his front paws clasping something. Mnementh informed F'lar that he had seen her climbing from one of the high windows and had simply plucked her from the ledge, knowing the dragonman sought her. The bronze dragon settled awkwardly onto his hind legs, his wings working to keep him balanced. Carefully he set the girl on her feet and formed a precise cage around her with his huge talons. She stood motionless within that circle, her face toward the wedge-shaped head that swayed above her.

The watch-wher, shrieking terror, anger, and hatred, was lunging violently to the end of its chain, trying to come to Lessa's aid. It grabbed at F'lar as he strode to the two.

"You've courage enough, girl," he admitted, resting one hand casually on Mnementh's upper claw. Mnementh was enormously pleased with himself and swiveled his head down for his eye ridges to be scratched.

"You did not lie, you know," F'lar said, unable to resist taunting the girl.

Slowly she turned toward him, her face impassive. She was not afraid of dragons, F'lar realized with approval.

"The babe lives. And it is male."

She could not control her dismay and her shoulders sagged briefly before she pulled herself erect.

"Ruatha is mine," she insisted in a tense low voice.

"Aye, and it would have been, had you approached me directly when the wing arrived here."

Her eyes widened. "What do you mean?"

"A dragonman may champion anyone whose grievance is just. By the time we reached Ruath Hold, I was quite ready to challenge Fax given any reasonable cause, despite the Search." This was not the whole truth but F'lar must teach this girl the folly of trying to control dragonmen. "Had you paid any attention to your harper's songs, you'd know your rights. And," F'lar's voice held a vindictive edge that surprised him, "Lady Gemma might not now lie dead. She suffered far more at that tyrant's hand than you."

Something in her manner told him that she regretted Lady Gemma's death, that it had affected her deeply.

"What good is Ruatha to you now?" he demanded, a broad sweep of his arm taking in the ruined courtyard and the Hold, the entire unproductive valley of Ruatha. "You have indeed accomplished your ends; a profitless conquest and its conqueror's death." F'lar snorted: "All seven Holds will revert to their legitimate Blood, and time they did. One Hold, one lord. Of course, you might have to fight others, infected with Fax's greed. Could you hold Ruatha against attack . . . now . . . in her decline?"

"Ruatha is mine!"

"Ruatha?" F'lar's laugh was derisive. "When you could be Weyrwoman?"

"Weyrwoman?" she breathed, staring at him.

"Yes, little fool. I said I rode in Search . . . it's about time you attended to more than Ruatha. And the object of my Search is . . . you!"

She stared at the finger he pointed at her as if it were dangerous.

"By the First Egg, girl, you've power in you to spare when you can turn a dragonman, all unwitting, to do your bidding. Ah, but never again, for now I am on guard against you."

Mnementh crooned approvingly, the sound a soft rumble in his throat. He arched his neck so that one eye was turned directly on the girl, gleaming in the darkness of the court.

F'lar noticed with detached pride that she neither flinched nor blanched at the proximity of an eye greater than her own head.

"He likes to have his eye ridges scratched," F'lar remarked in a friendly tone, changing tactics.

"I know," she said softly and reached out a hand to do that service.

"Nemorth's queen," F'lar continued, "is close to death. This time we must have a strong Weyrwoman."

"This time—the Red Star?" the girl gasped, turning frightened eyes to F'lar.

"You understand what it means?"

"There is danger . . ." she began in a bare whisper, glancing apprehensively eastward.

F'lar did not question by what miracle she appreciated the imminence of danger. He had every intention of taking her to the Weyr by sheer force if necessary. But something within him wanted very much for her to accept the challenge voluntarily. A rebellious Weyrwoman would be even more dangerous than a stupid one. This girl had too much power and was too used to guile and strategy. It would be a calamity to antagonize her with injudicious handling.

"There is danger for all Pern. Not just Ruatha," he said, allowing a note of entreaty to creep into his voice. "And *you* are needed. Not by Ruatha," a wave of his hand dismissed that consideration as a negligible one compared to the total picture. "We are doomed without a strong Weyrwoman. Without you."

"Gemma kept saying *all* the bronze riders were needed," she murmured in a dazed whisper.

What did she mean by that statement? F'lar frowned. Had she heard a word he had said? He pressed his argument, certain only that he had already struck one responsive chord.

"You've won here. Let the babe," he saw her startled rejection of that idea and ruthlessly qualified it, ". . . Gemma's babe . . . be reared at Ruatha. You have command of all the Holds as Weyrwoman, not ruined Ruatha alone. You've accomplished Fax's death. Leave off vengeance."

She stared at F'lar with wonder, absorbing his words.

"I never thought beyond Fax's death," she admitted slowly. "I never thought what should happen then."

Her confusion was almost childlike and struck F'lar forcibly. He had had no time, or desire, to consider her prodigious accomplishment. Now he realized some measure of her indomitable character. She could not have been much over ten Turns of age herself when Fax had murdered her family. Yet somehow, so young, she had set herself a goal and managed to survive both brutality and detection long enough to secure the usurper's death. What a Weyrwoman she would be! In the tradition of those of Ruathan blood. The light of the paler moon made her look young and vulnerable and almost pretty.

"You can be Weyrwoman," he insisted gently.

"Weyrwoman," she breathed, incredulous, and gazed round the inner court bathed in soft moonlight. He thought she wavered.

"Or perhaps you enjoy rags?" he said, making his voice harsh, mocking. "And matted hair, dirty feet, and cracked hands? Sleeping in straw, eating rinds? You are young . . . that is, I assume you are young," and his voice was frankly skeptical. She glared at him, her lips firmly pressed together. "Is this the be-all and end-all of your ambition? What are you that this little corner of the great world is *all* you want?"

He paused and with utter contempt added, "The blood of Ruatha has thinned, I see. You're afraid!"

"I am Lessa, daughter of the Lord of Ruath," she countered, stung. She drew herself erect. Her eyes flashed. "I am afraid of nothing!"

F'lar contented himself with a slight smile.

Mnementh, however, threw up his head, and stretched out his sinuous neck to its whole length. His full-throated peal rang out down the valley. The bronze communicated his awareness to F'lar that Lessa had accepted the challenge. The other dragons answered back, their warbles shriller than Mnementh's bellow. The watch-wher which had cowered at the end of its chain lifted its voice in a thin, unnerving screech until the Hold emptied of its startled occupants.

"F'nor," the bronze rider called, waving his wingleader to him. "Leave half the flight to guard the Hold. Some nearby lord might think to emulate Fax's example. Send one rider to the High Reaches with the glad news. You go directly to the Cloth Hall and speak to L'to . . . Lytol." F'lar grinned. "I think he would made an exemplary Warder and Lord Surrogate for this Hold in the name of the Weyr and the babe."

The brown rider's face expressed enthusiasm for his mission as he began to comprehend his leader's intentions. With Fax dead and Ruatha under the protection of dragonmen, particularly that same one who had dispatched Fax, the Hold would have wise management.

"She caused Ruatha's deterioration?" he asked.

"And nearly ours with her machinations," F'lar replied, but having found the admirable object of his Search he could now be magnanimous. "Suppress your exultation, brother," he advised quickly as he took note of F'nor's expression. "The new queen must also be Impressed."

"I'll settle arrangements here. Lytol is an excellent choice," F'nor said.

"Who is this Lytol?" demanded Lessa pointedly. She had twisted the mass of filthy hair back from her face. In the moonlight the dirt was less noticeable. F'lar caught F'nor looking at her with an all-too-easily-read expression. He signaled F'nor, with a peremptory gesture, to carry out his orders without delay.

"Lytol is a dragonless man," F'lar told the girl, "no friend to Fax. He will ward the Hold well and it will prosper." He added persuasively with a quelling stare full on her, "Won't it?"

She regarded him somberly, without answering, until he chuckled softly at her discomfiture.

"We'll return to the Weyr," he announced, proffering a hand to guide her to Mnementh's side.

The bronze one had extended his head toward the watch-wher who now lay panting on the ground, its chain limp in the dust.

"Oh," Lessa sighed, and dropped beside the grotesque beast. It raised its head slowly, lurring piteously.

"Mnementh says it is very old and soon will sleep itself to death."

Lessa cradled the bestial head in her arms, scratching it behind the ears.

"Come, Lessa of Pern," F'lar said, impatient to be up and away.

She rose slowly but obediently. "It saved me. It knew me."

"It knows it did well," F'lar assured her, brusquely, wondering at such an uncharacteristic show of sentiment in her.

He took her hand again, to help her to her feet and lead her back to Mnementh. As they turned, he glimpsed the watch-wher, launching itself at a dead run after Lessa. The chain, however, held fast. The beast's neck broke, with a sickeningly audible snap.

Lessa was on her knees in an instant, cradling the repulsive head in her arms.

"Why, you foolish thing, why?" she asked in a stunned whisper as the light in the beast's green-gold eyes dimmed and died out.

Mnementh informed F'lar that the creature had lived this long only to preserve the Ruathan line. At Lessa's imminent departure, it had welcomed death.

A convulsive shudder went through Lessa's slim body. F'lar watched as she undid the heavy buckle that fastened the metal collar about the watch-wher's neck. She threw the tether away with a violent motion. Tenderly she laid the watch-wher on the cobbles. With one last caress to the clipped wings, she rose in a fluid movement and walked resolutely to Mnementh without a single backward glance. She stepped calmly to the dragon's raised leg and seated herself, as F'lar directed, on the great neck.

F'lar glanced around the courtyard at the remainder of his wing, which had reformed there. The Hold folk had retreated back into the safety of the Great Hall. When his wingmen were all astride, he vaulted to Mnementh's neck, behind the girl.

"Hold tightly to my arms," he ordered her as he took hold of the smallest neck ridge and gave the command to fly.

Her fingers closed spasmodically around his forearm as the great bronze dragon took off, the enormous wings working to achieve height from the vertical takeoff. Mnementh preferred to fall into flight from a cliff or tower. Like all dragons, he tended to indolence. F'lar glanced behind him, saw the other dragonmen form the flight line, spread out to cover those still on guard at Ruatha Hold.

When they had reached a sufficient altitude, he told Mnementh to transfer, going *between* to the Weyr.

Only a gasp indicated the girl's astonishment as they hung *between*. Accustomed as he was to the sting of the profound cold, to the awesome utter lack of light and sound, F'lar still found the sensations unnerving. Yet the uncommon transfer spanned no more time than it took to cough thrice.

Mnementh rumbled approval of this candidate's calm reaction as they flicked out of the eerie *between*.

And then they were above the Weyr, Mnementh setting his wings to glide in the bright daylight, half a world away from night-time Ruatha.

As they circled above the great stony trough of the Weyr, F'lar peered at Lessa's face, pleased with the delight mirrored there; she showed no trace of fear as they hung a thousand lengths above the high Benden mountain range. Then, as the seven dragons roared their incoming cry, an incredulous smile lit her face.

The other wingmen dropped into a wide spiral, down, down while Mnementh elected to descend in lazy circles. The dragonmen peeled off smartly and dropped, each to his own tier in the caves of the Weyr. Mnementh finally completed his leisurely approach to their quarters, whistling shrilly to himself as he braked his forward speed with a twist of his wings, dropping lightly at last to the ledge. He crouched as F'lar swung the girl to the rough rock, scored from thousands of clawed landings.

"This leads only to our quarters," he told her as they entered the corridor, vaulted and wide for the easy passage of great bronze dragons.

As they reached the huge natural cavern that had been his since Mnementh achieved maturity, F'lar looked about him with eyes fresh from his first prolonged absence from the Weyr. The huge chamber was unquestionably big, certainly larger than most of the halls he had visited in Fax's procession. Those halls were intended as gathering places for men, not the habitations of dragons. But suddenly he saw his own quarters were nearly as shabby as all Ruatha. Benden was, of a certainty, one of the oldest dragonweyrs, as Ruatha was one of the oldest Holds, but that excused nothing. How many dragons had bedded in that hollow to make solid rock conform to dragon proportions! How many feet had worn the path past the dragon's weyr into the sleeping chamber, to the bathing room beyond where the natural warm spring provided ever-fresh water! But the wall hangings were faded and unraveling and there were grease stains on lintel and floor that should be sanded away.

He noticed the wary expression on Lessa's face as he paused in the sleeping room.

"I must feed Mnementh immediately. So you may bathe first," he said, rummaging in a chest and finding clean clothes for her, discards of other previous occupants of his quarters, but far more presentable than her present covering. He carefully laid back in the chest the white wool robe that was traditional Impression garb. She would wear that later. He tossed several garments at her feet and a bag of sweetsand, gesturing to the hanging that obscured the way to the bath.

He left her, then, the clothes in a heap at her feet, for she made no effort to catch anything.

Mnementh informed him that F'nor was feeding Canth and that he, Mnementh, was hungry too. *She* didn't trust F'lar but she wasn't afraid of himself.

"Why should she be afraid of you?" F'lar asked. "You're cousin to the watch-wher who was her only friend."

Mnementh informed F'lar that he, a fully matured bronze dragon, was no relation to any scrawny, crawling, chained, and wing-clipped watch-wher.

F'lar, pleased at having been able to tease the bronze one, chuckled to himself. With great dignity, Mnementh curved down to the feeding ground.

> By the Golden Egg of Faranth
> By the Weyrwoman, wise and true,
> Breed a flight of bronze and brown wings,
> Breed a flight of green and blue.
> Breed riders, strong and daring,
> Dragon-loving, born as hatched,
> Flight of hundreds soaring skyward,
> Man and dragon fully matched.

Lessa waited until the sound of the dragonman's footsteps proved he had really gone away. She rushed quickly through the big cavern, heard the scrape of claw and the *whoosh* of the mighty wings. She raced down the short passageway, right to the edge of the yawning entrance. There was the bronze dragon circling down to the wider end of the mile-long barren oval that was Benden Weyr. She had heard of the Weyrs, as any Pernese had, but to be in one was quite a different matter.

She peered up, around, down that sheer rock face. There was no way off but by dragon wing. The nearest cave mouths were an unhandy distance above her, to one side, below her on the other. She was neatly secluded here.

Weyrwoman, he had told her. His woman? In his weyr? Was that what he had meant? No, that was not the impression she got from the dragon. It occurred to her, suddenly, that it was odd she had understood the dragon. Were common folk able to? Or was it the dragonman blood in her line? At all events, Mnementh had inferred something greater, some special rank. She remembered vaguely that, when dragonmen went on Search, they looked for certain women. Ah, certain women. She was one, then, of several contenders. Yet the bronze rider had offered her the position as if she and she, alone, qualified. He had his own generous portion of conceit, that one, Lessa decided. Arrogant he was, though not a bully like Fax.

She could see the bronze dragon swoop down to the running herdbeasts, saw the strike, saw the dragon wheel up to settle on a far ledge to feed. Instinctively she drew back from the opening, back into the dark and relative safety of the corridor.

The feeding dragon evoked scores of horrid tales. Tales at which she had scoffed but now . . . Was it true, then, that dragons did eat human flesh? Did . . . Lessa halted that trend of thought. Dragonkind was no less cruel than mankind. The dragon, at least, acted from bestial need rather than bestial greed.

Assured that the dragonman would be occupied a while, she crossed the larger cave into the sleeping room. She scooped up the clothing and the bag of cleansing sand and proceeded to the bathing room.

To be clean! To be completely clean and to be able to stay that way. With distaste, she stripped off the remains of the rags, kicking them to one side. She made a soft mud with the sweetsand and scrubbed her entire body until she drew blood from various half-healed cuts. Then she jumped into the pool, gasping as the warm water made the sweetsand foam in the lacerations.

It was a ritual cleansing of more than surface soil. The luxury of cleanliness was ecstasy.

Finally satisfied she was as clean as one long soaking could make her, she left the pool, reluctantly. Wringing out her hair she tucked it up on her head as she dried herself. She shook out the clothing and held one garment against her experimentally. The fabric, a soft green, felt smooth under her watershrunken fingers, although the nap caught on her roughened hands. She pulled it over her head. It was loose but the darker green overtunic had a sash which she pulled in tight at the waist. The unusual sensation of softness against her bare skin made her wriggle with voluptuous pleasure. The skirt, no longer a ragged hem of tatters, swirled heavily around her ankles. She smiled. She took up a fresh drying cloth and began to work on her hair.

A muted sound came to her ears and she stopped, hands poised, head bent to one side. Straining, she listened. Yes, there were sounds without. The dragonman and his beast must have returned. She grimaced to herself with annoyance at this untimely interruption and rubbed harder at her hair. She ran fingers through the half-dry tangles, the motions arrested as she encountered snarls. Vexed, she rummaged on the shelves until she found, as she had hoped to, a coarse-toothed metal comb.

Dry, her hair had a life of its own suddenly, crackling about her hands and clinging to face and comb and dress. It was difficult to get the silky stuff under control. And her hair was longer than she had thought, for clean and unmatted, it fell to her waist—when it did not cling to her hands.

She paused, listening, and heard no sound at all. Apprehensively, she stepped to the curtain and glanced warily to the sleeping room. It was empty. She listened and caught the perceptible thoughts of the sleepy dragon. Well, she would rather meet the man in the presence of a sleepy dragon than in a sleeping room. She started across the floor and, out of the corner of her eye, caught sight of a strange woman as she passed a polished piece of metal hanging on the wall.

Amazed, she stopped short, staring, incredulous, at the face the metal reflected. Only when she put her hands to her prominent cheekbones in a gesture of involuntary surprise and the reflection imitated the gesture, did she realize she looked at herself.

Why, that girl in the reflector was prettier than Lady Tela, than the clothman's daughter! But so thin. Her hands of their own volition dropped to her neck, to the protruding collarbones, to her breasts which did not entirely accord with the gauntness of the rest of her. The dress was too large for her frame, she noted with an unexpected emergence of conceit born in that instant of delighted appraisal. And her hair . . . it stood out around her head like an aureole. It wouldn't lie contained. She smoothed it down with impatient fingers, automatically bringing locks forward to hang around her face. As she irritably pushed them back, dismissing a need for disguise, the hair drifted up again. A slight sound, the scrape of a boot against stone, caught her back from her bemusement. She waited, momentarily expecting him to appear. She was suddenly timid. With her face bare to the world, her hair behind her ears, her body outlined by a clinging fabric, she was stripped of her accustomed anonymity and was, therefore, in her estimation, vulnerable.

She controlled the desire to run away—the irrational fear. Observing herself in the looking metal, she drew her shoulders back, tilted her head high, chin up; the movement caused her hair to crackle and cling and shift about her head. She was Lessa of Ruatha, of a fine old Blood. She no longer needed artifice to preserve herself; she must stand proudly bare-faced before the world . . . and that dragonman.

Resolutely she crossed the room, pushing aside the hanging on the doorway to the great cavern.

He was there, beside the head of the dragon, scratching its eye ridges, a curiously tender expression on his face. The tableau was at variance with all she had heard of dragonmen.

She had, of course, heard of the strange affinity between rider and dragon but this was the first time she realized that love was part of that bond. Or that this reserved, cold man was capable of such deep emotion.

He turned slowly, as if loathe to leave the bronze beast. He caught sight of her and pivoted completely round, his eyes intense as he took note of her altered appearance. With quick, light steps, he closed the distance between them and ushered her back into the sleeping room, one strong hand holding her by the elbow.

"Mnementh has fed lightly and will need quiet to rest," he said in a low voice. He pulled the heavy hanging into place across the opening.

Then he held her away from him, turning her this way and that, scrutinizing her closely, curious and slightly surprised.

"You wash up . . . pretty, yes, almost pretty," he said, amused condescension in his voice. She pulled roughly away from him, piqued. His low laugh mocked her. "After all, how could one guess what was under the grime of . . . ten full Turns?"

At length he said, "No matter. We must eat and I shall require your services." At her startled exclamation, he turned, grinning maliciously now as his movement revealed the caked blood on his left sleeve. "The least you can do is bathe wounds honorably received fighting your battle."

He pushed aside a portion of the drape that curtained the inner wall. "Food for two!" he roared down a black gap in the sheer stone.

She heard a subterranean echo far below as his voice resounded down what must be a long shaft.

"Nemorth is nearly rigid," he was saying as he took supplies from another drape-hidden shelf, "and the Hatching will soon begin anyhow."

A coldness settled in Lessa's stomach at the mention of a Hatching. The mildest

Anne McCaffrey

tales she had heard about that part of dragonlore were chilling, the worst dismayingly macabre. She took the things he handed her numbly.

"What? Frightened?" the dragonman taunted, pausing as he stripped off his torn and bloodied shirt.

With a shake of her head, Lessa turned her attention to the wide-shouldered, well-muscled back he presented her, the paler skin of his body decorated with random bloody streaks. Fresh blood welled from the point of his shoulder for the removal of his shirt had broken the tender scabs.

"I will need water," she said and saw she had a flat pan among the items he had given her. She went swiftly to the pool for water, wondering how she had come to agree to venture so far from Ruatha. Ruined though it was, it had been hers and was familiar to her from Tower to deep cellar. At the moment the idea had been proposed and insidiously prosecuted by the dragonman, she had felt capable of anything, having achieved, at last, Fax's death. Now, it was all she could do to keep the water from slopping out of the pan that shook unaccountably in her hands.

She forced herself to deal only with the wound. It was a nasty gash, deep where the point had entered and torn downward in a gradually shallower slice. His skin felt smooth under her fingers as she cleansed the wound. In spite of herself, she noticed the masculine odor of him, compounded not unpleasantly of sweat, leather, and an unusual muskiness which must be from close association with dragons.

She stood back when she had finished her ministration. He flexed his arm experimentally in the constricting bandage and the motion set the muscles rippling along side and back.

When he faced her, his eyes were dark and thoughtful.

"Gently done. My thanks." His smile was ironic.

She backed away as he rose but he only went to the chest to take out a clean, white shirt.

A muted rumble sounded, growing quickly louder.

Dragons roaring? Lessa wondered, trying to conquer the ridiculous fear that rose within her. Had the Hatching started? There was no watch-wher's lair to secrete herself in, here.

As if he understood her confusion, the dragonman laughed good-humoredly and, his eyes on hers, drew aside the wall covering just as some noisy mechanism inside the shaft propelled a tray of food into sight.

Ashamed of her unbased fright and furious that he had witnessed it, Lessa sat rebelliously down on the fur-covered wall seat, heartily wishing him a variety of serious and painful injuries which she could dress with inconsiderate hands. She would not waste future opportunities.

He placed the tray on the low table in front of her, throwing down a heap of furs for his own seat. There was meat, bread, a tempting yellow cheese, and even a few pieces of winter fruit. He made no move to eat nor did she, though the thought of a piece of fruit that was ripe, instead of rotten, set her mouth to watering. He glanced up at her, and frowned.

"Even in the Weyr, the lady breaks bread first," he said, and inclined his head politely to her.

Lessa flushed, unused to any courtesy and certainly unused to being first to eat. She broke off a chunk of bread. It was like nothing she remembered having tasted before. For one thing, it was fresh-baked. The flour had been finely sifted, without trace of sand or hull. She took the slice of cheese he proffered her and it, too, had an uncommonly delicious sharpness. Made bold by this indication of her changed status, Lessa reached for the plumpest piece of fruit.

"Now," the dragonman began, his hand touching hers to get her attention.

Guiltily she dropped the fruit, thinking she had erred. She stared at him, wondering at her fault. He retrieved the fruit and placed it back in her hand as he continued to speak. Wide-eyed, disarmed, she nibbled, and gave him her full attention.

"Listen to me. You must not show a moment's fear, whatever happens on the Hatching Ground. And you must not let her overeat." A wry expression crossed his face. "One of our main functions is to keep a dragon from excessive eating."

Lessa lost interest in the taste of the fruit. She placed it carefully back in the bowl and tried to sort out not what he had said, but what his tone of voice implied. She looked at the dragonman's face, seeing him as a person, not a symbol, for the first time.

There was a blackness about him that was not malevolent; it was a brooding sort of patience. Heavy black hair, heavy black brows; his eyes, a brown light enough to seem golden, were all too expressive of cynical emotions, or cold hauteur. His lips were thin but well-shaped and in repose almost gentle. Why must he always pull his mouth to one side in disapproval or in one of those sardonic smiles? At this moment, he was completely unaffected.

He meant what he was saying. He did not want her to be afraid. There was no reason for her, Lessa, *to* fear.

He very much wanted her to succeed. In keeping whom from overeating what? Herd animals? A newly hatched dragon certainly wasn't capable of eating a full beast. That seemed a simple enough task to Lessa . . . Main function? *Our* main function?

The dragonman was looking at her expectantly.

"Our main function?" she repeated, an unspoken request for more information inherent in her inflection.

"More of that later. First things first," he said, impatiently waving off other questions.

"But what happens?" she insisted.

"As I was told so I tell you. No more, no less. Remember these two points. No fear, and no overeating."

"But . . ."

Anne McCaffrey

"You, however, need to eat. Here." He speared a piece of meat on his knife and thrust it at her, frowning until she managed to choke it down. He was about to force more on her but she grabbed up her half-eaten fruit and bit down into the firm sweet sphere instead. She had already eaten more at this one meal than she was accustomed to having all day at the Hold.

"We shall soon eat better at the Weyr," he remarked, regarding the tray with a jaundiced eye.

Lessa was surprised. This was a feast, in her opinion.

"More than you're used to? Yes, I forgot you left Ruatha with bare bones indeed." She stiffened.

"You did well at Ruatha. I mean no criticism," he added, smiling at her reaction. But look at you," and he gestured at her body, that curious expression crossing his face, half-amused, half-contemplative. "I should not have guessed you'd clean up pretty," he remarked. "Nor with such hair." This time his expression was frankly admiring.

Involuntarily she put one hand to her head, the hair crackling over her fingers. But what reply she might have made him, indignant as she was, died aborning. An unearthly keening filled the chamber.

The sounds set up a vibration that ran down the bones behind her ear to her spine. She clapped both hands to her ears. The noise rang through her skull despite her defending hands. As abruptly as it started, it ceased.

Before she knew what he was about, the dragonman had grabbed her by the wrist and pulled her over to the chest.

"Take those off," he ordered, indicating dress and tunic. While she stared at him stupidly, he held up a loose white robe, sleeveless and beltless, a matter of two lengths of fine cloth fastened at shoulder and side seams. "Take it off, or do I assist you?" he asked, with no patience at all.

The wild sound was repeated and its unnerving tone made her fingers fly faster. She had no sooner loosened the garments she wore, letting them slide to her feet, than he had thrown the other over her head. She managed to get her arms in the proper places before he grabbed her wrist again and was speeding with her out of the room, her hair whipping out behind her, alive with static.

As they reached the outer chamber, the bronze dragon was standing in the center of the cavern, his head turned to watch the sleeping-room door. He seemed impatient to Lessa; his great eyes sparkled iridescently. His manner breathed an inner excitement of great proportions and from his throat a high-pitched croon issued, several octaves below the unnerving cry that had roused them all.

With a yank that rocked her head on her neck, the dragonman pulled her along the passage. The dragon padded beside them at such speed that Lessa fully expected they would all catapult off the ledge. Somehow, at the crucial stride, she was a-perch the bronze neck, the dragonman holding her firmly about the waist. In the same fluid movement, they were gliding across the great bowl of the Weyr to the higher wall opposite. The air was full of wings and dragon tails, rent with a chorus of sounds, echoing and re-echoing across the stony valley.

Mnementh set what Lessa was certain would be a collision course with other dragons, straight for a huge round blackness in the cliff face, high up. Magically, the beasts filed in, the greater wingspread of Mnementh just clearing the sides of the entrance.

The passageway reverberated with the thunder of wings. The air compressed around her thickly. Then they broke out into a gigantic cavern.

Why, the entire mountain must be hollow, thought Lessa, incredulous. Around the enormous cavern, dragons perched in serried ranks, blues, greens, browns, and only two great bronze beasts like Mnementh, on ledges meant to accommodate hundreds. Lessa gripped the bronze neck scales before her, instinctively aware of the imminence of a great event.

Mnementh wheeled downward, disregarding the ledge of the bronze ones. Then all Lessa could see was what lay on the sandy floor of the great cavern: dragon eggs. A clutch of ten monstrous, mottled eggs, their shells moving spasmodically as the fledglings within tapped their way out. To one side, on a raised portion of the floor, was a golden egg, larger by half again the size of the mottled ones. Just beyond the golden egg lay the motionless ochre hulk of the old queen.

Just as she realized Mnementh was hovering over the floor in the vicinity of that egg, Lessa felt the dragonman's hands on her, lifting her from Mnementh's neck.

Apprehensively, she grabbed at him. His hands tightened and inexorably swung her down. His eyes, fierce and gray, locked with hers.

"Remember, Lessa!"

Mnementh added an encouragement, one great compound eye turned on her. Then he rose from the floor. Lessa half-raised one hand in entreaty, bereft of all support, even that of the sure inner compulsion which had sustained her in her struggle for revenge on Fax. She saw the bronze dragon settle on the first ledge, at some distance from the other two bronze beasts. The dragonman dismounted and Mnementh curved his sinuous neck until his head was beside his rider. The man reached up absently, it seemed to Lessa, and caressed his mount.

Loud screams and wailings diverted Lessa and she saw more dragons descend to hover just above the cavern floor, each rider depositing a young woman until there were twelve girls, including Lessa. She remained a little apart from them as they clung to each other. She regarded them curiously. The girls were not injured in any way she could see, so why such weeping? She took a deep breath against the coldness within her. Let *them* be afraid. She was Lessa of Ruatha and did not need to be afraid.

Just then, the golden egg moved convulsively. Gasping as one, the girls edged away from it, back against the rocky wall. One, a lovely blonde, her heavy plait of golden

Anne McCaffrey

hair swinging just above the ground, started to step off the raised floor and stopped, shrieking, backing fearfully toward the scant comfort of her peers.

Lessa wheeled to see what cause there might be for the look of horror on the girl's face. She stepped back involuntarily herself.

In the main section of the sandy arena, several of the handful of eggs had already cracked wide open. The fledglings, crowing weakly, were moving toward . . . and Lessa gulped . . . the young boys standing stolidly in a semi-circle. Some of them were no older than she had been when Fax's army had swooped down on Ruath Hold.

The shrieking of the women subsided to muffled gasps. A fledgling reached out with claw and beak to grab a boy.

Lessa forced herself to watch as the young dragon mauled the youth, throwing him roughly aside as if unsatisfied in some way. The boy did not move and Lessa could see blood seeping onto the sand from dragon-inflicted wounds.

A second fledgling lurched against another boy and halted, flapping its damp wings impotently, raising its scrawny neck and croaking a parody of the encouraging croon Mnementh often gave. The boy uncertainly lifted a hand and began to scratch the eye ridge. Incredulous, Lessa watched as the fledgling, its crooning increasingly more mellow, ducked its head, pushing at the boy. The child's face broke into an unbelieving smile of elation.

Tearing her eyes from this astounding sight, Lessa saw that another fledgling was beginning the same performance with another boy. Two more dragons had emerged in the interim. One had knocked a boy down and was walking over him, oblivious to the fact that its claws were raking great gashes. The fledgling who followed its hatch-mate stopped by the wounded child, ducking its head to the boy's face, crooning anxiously. As Lessa watched, the boy managed to struggle to his feet, tears of pain streaming down his cheeks. She could hear him pleading with the dragon not to worry, that he was only scratched a little.

It was over very soon. The young dragons paired off with boys. Green riders dropped down to carry off the unacceptable. Blue riders settled to the floor with their beasts and led the couples out of the cavern, the young dragons squealing, crooning, flapping wet wings as they staggered off, encouraged by their newly acquired weyr-mates.

Lessa turned resolutely back to the rocking golden egg, knowing what to expect and trying to divine what the successful boys had, or had not done, that caused the baby dragons to single them out.

A crack appeared in the golden shell and was greeted by the terrified screams of the girls. Some had fallen into little heaps of white fabric, others embraced tightly in their mutual fear. The crack widened and the wedge head broke through, followed quickly by the neck, gleaming gold. Lessa wondered with unexpected detachment how long it would take the beast to mature, considering its by no means small size at birth. For the head was larger than that of the male dragons and they had been large enough to overwhelm sturdy boys of ten full Turns.

Lessa was aware of a loud hum within the Hall. Glancing up at the audience, she realized it emanated from the watching bronze dragons, for this was the birth of their mate, their queen. The hum increased in volume as the shell shattered into fragments and the golden, glistening body of the new female emerged. It staggered out, dipping its sharp beak into the soft sand, momentarily trapped. Flapping its wet wings, it righted itself, ludicrous in its weak awkwardness. With sudden and unexpected swiftness, it dashed toward the terror-stricken girls.

Before Lessa could blink, it shook the first girl with such violence her head snapped audibly and she fell limply to the sand. Disregarding her, the dragon leaped toward the second girl but misjudged the distance and fell, grabbing out with one claw for support and raking the girl's body from shoulder to thigh. The screaming of the mortally injured girl distracted the dragon and released the others from their horrified trance. They scattered in panicky confusion, racing, running, tripping, stumbling, falling across the sand toward the exit the boys had used.

As the golden beast, crying piteously, lurched down from the raised arena toward the scattered women, Lessa moved. Why hadn't that silly clunk-headed girl stepped aside, Lessa thought, grabbing for the wedge-head, at birth not much larger than her own torso. The dragon's so clumsy and weak she's her own worst enemy.

Lessa swung the head round so that the many-faceted eyes were forced to look at her . . . and found herself lost in that rainbow regard.

A feeling of joy suffused Lessa, a feeling of warmth; tenderness, unalloyed affection and instant respect and admiration flooded mind and heart and soul. Never again would Lessa lack an advocate, a defender, an intimate, aware instantly of the temper of her mind and heart, of her desires. How wonderful was Lessa, the thought intruded into Lessa's reflections, how pretty, how kind, how thoughtful, how brave and clever!

Mechanically, Lessa reached out to scratch the exact spot on the soft eye ridge.

The dragon blinked at her wistfully, extremely sad that she had distressed Lessa. Lessa reassuringly patted the slightly damp, soft neck that curved trustingly toward her. The dragon reeled to one side and one wing fouled on the hind claw. It hurt. Carefully, Lessa lifted the erring foot, freed the wing, folding it back across the dorsal ridge with a pat.

The dragon began to croon in her throat, her eyes following Lessa's every move. She nudged at Lessa and Lessa obediently attended the other eye ridge.

The dragon let it be known she was hungry.

"We'll get you something to eat directly," Lessa assured her briskly and blinked back at the dragon in amazement. How could she be so callous? It was a fact that this little menace had just now seriously injured, if not killed, two women.

She wouldn't have believed her sympathies could swing so alarmingly toward the beast. Yet it was the most natural thing in the world for her to wish to protect this fledgling.

The dragon arched her neck to look Lessa squarely in the eyes. Ramoth repeated wistfully how exceedingly hungry she was, confined so long in that shell without nourishment.

Lessa wondered how she knew the golden dragon's name, and Ramoth replied: Why shouldn't she know her own name since it was hers and no one else's? And then Lessa was lost again in the wonder of those expressive eyes.

Oblivious to the descending bronze dragons, uncaring of the presence of their riders, Lessa stood caressing the head of the most wonderful creature on all Pern, fully prescient of troubles and glories, but most immediately aware that Lessa of Pern was Weyrwoman to Ramoth the Golden, for now and forever. ■

MEETING OF MINDS
Ted Reynolds

During descent orbit, I found myself comparing the sight of Heiwa with that of old Earth. I stomped the thought out quickly. That wasn't me remembering. It was Barbara Simmon, and she'd been dead the better part of a century.

Still, as we (no, I, *I*) screeched down through the atmosphere, the gaudy slapstick landscape did summon up all the standard images of that distant seedrock. Not that I had much mood for surface-gazing. The alien blackship and its maggot crew couldn't be far behind me.

I pretty near had to sit on my hands to keep them from overriding the automatic descent program. The computed descent was probably the fastest way down alive, but it sure seemed to take forever to reach the ground.

I landed in a clearing some kilometers from the newly completed dome of the second Heiwan colony, and was out almost before the clods of dirt sliced up by our landing had ceased to pelt down. Without a word of farewell to the one-man ship which had brought me two abysmally lonely months from Tairé, I loped toward the scarlet arc of dome visible through the local greenery. I was met on the far side of the clearing by the presumable apex of colonial officialdom, in faded dungarees and woven sunshade hat.

"Tim Hume?" he assumed correctly. He was out of breath and sweating even more than I was. Well, he was more ponderous. "Caldoza," he identified briefly, tapping his own chest. "Hurry up."

We jogged up a footpath through the familiar mix of Earth/Tairé/Vyborg trees and shrubs towards the red metal sheath ahead.

"The alien ship, how far behind?" Caldoza wheezed.

"Can't be more than a few hours," I said. "That's *if* they were at their top speed when we passed them coming in."

Caldoza glanced at me over his shoulder. " 'We'? I thought you came alone, Hume."

"I did. You must have misheard me. I said '*I* passed them'."

"Sorry," he said.

Both sides of the path were now lined with simple wooden crosses, crescents, stars; the grave markers of the first colony. Birth dates, scattered across half a century, death dates—all the same day.

"Apologize for this . . . haste," gasped Caldoza, as we pounded through the dome entry, armed guards zipping it closed behind us. Heavy gunnery nosed out peekports on either side. "Expected you'd have at least a day to rest up from your trip. But under the circumstances . . . here . . . in here . . . just hope you can come up with something in time." We plunged into the shingle shack and collapsed onto packing crates in lieu of chairs. He wiped his reddened face, and leaned towards me over the plank which served as a desk. "What do you think, Hume? Can you get us something we can use in the next couple of hours?"

"How the hell should I know?" I complained. "Whoever had to perform a regression under such . . . such stinking unprepared conditions before?"

He nodded. "I sympathize, believe me. But . . . I guess you're as committed as anyone here, now it's come down to it. I don't have to point that out."

I wished he hadn't. I'd been trying not to think about it. I had come to unlock the only unread clue to a defense against the particularly unpleasant aliens who had brutally wiped out the first Heiwan colony, five years before, should they hypothetically strike again, here or elsewhere. That I had arrived just in time to share the same fate with the second colony if I didn't work fast seemed reverse serendipity with a vengeance.

"So where are the kids now?" I asked.

"The boy? He's asleep, already under preparatory sedation. The girl's beyond working with," said Caldoza.

I raised my eyebrows.

Caldoza looked understandably ill at ease. "Dr. Bergoff tried to regress her three days ago," he explained shortly. "It didn't work."

"Oh," I commented, and then, tightly, "Just how badly didn't it work?" My hopes had been on the older child, the four-year-old girl.

"Very badly," said Caldoza. "Complete catatonia."

"*Goddamn* you idiots," leaping up, slamming my fist on the desk, as Caldoza cowered from me. "Don't you ever . . . " It wasn't me, it was Michael Haskins, and I shut him off fast. I didn't need his righteous indignation now . . . or, I added to myself, ever.

I settled back on my crate.

"Sorry," I said. "It's been a dreary trip, but that wasn't fair of me. I assume you had reasons for pushing it without expert help?"

"Sure we did. The intrasystem packetboat spotted the blackship cruising the outer planets last week. For all we knew, it might attack before you arrived. We didn't feel we could wait. After all, we're still defenseless against a weapon we don't understand."

I nodded, distractedly. "You do realize, even if I can made an immediate breakthrough, there still may be nothing in the boy's memories that can help us understand what killed them."

"Of course," agreed Caldoza. "And even if we were to fully understand it, at this late date, we might well find ourselves without the whatever-it-might-be that could defend against it." His thick lips twisted wryly. "I keep thinking of a scenario where we find out that we're all safe if we take four ounces of castor oil each. Or something like that. But . . . " he shrugged broad shoulders phlegmatically, "what else can we do but try—and pray?"

I shrugged in my turn. I sat for a moment, linking my fingers together, first right thumb on top, which felt right, then left on top, which felt oddly askew. "Nothing," I said at last. "That's what I'm here for," then made a fist.

The first supply ship to ground on Heiwa after the massacre had found eighty-three slaughtered colonists of all ages, and three alien corpses. The first category had died almost instantaneously from massive cerebral hemorrhaging; the latter had been ripped apart by small-arms fire.

The aliens had resembled nothing so much as hundred-kilo versions of the maggots that already swarmed in the remains of both themselves and the humans. Disgusting buggers. Even the autopsy reports gave me nightmares. If intelligence of the human variety is to be measured by the ability to turn up on planets far from one's origins, and the ability to destroy other life forms effectively, these aliens appeared to be the first species of human-like intelligence yet encountered.

And that was all we knew.

There was one possible source of additional information, but we had been waiting for it to become available. Every colonist on Heiwa had been murdered; but perhaps their memories lingered on. A girl baby had been born the year after the massacre among the gutsy colonists who were already rebuilding on the graveyard of the first; a boy the year after that; by now there were half a dozen babies.

Regression had recently been demonstrated with adequate scientific rigor on Tairé. The girl, at least, must have been conceived within a few weeks of the massacre; she should have picked up *some* colonist's memories, psyche, life force, whatever you want to call it. The later children—maybe; we had no idea yet if the memories of the dead faded out, wandered off, or hung around forever. Besides, the girl would learn to communicate a year earlier. She was by far our best hope.

But then, starting four months before, came sightings of alien light-swallowing black vessels, in scattered human systems all along this leg of the Arm. Panic grew; each colony feared to be the next victim. We couldn't wait any longer to regress the girl.

And now that best hope was blown, and I had to work with a three-year-old who could barely babble. To say nothing of carrying through in a couple of hours a regression that usually took weeks to perform effectively. My chances weren't good. As for the kid's chances of a viable mental future, I hated to think.

"Didn't you get any information at all from the four-year-old before she . . . phased out?" I asked Caldoza.

"A bit, but nothing useful," he said. "We can correlate with the records of the first colony and identify the memories she's keyed into. She was a Tech. Second Class

Ted Reynolds

George Terrace, twenty-three years old. He was in the communications shack at the time of the attack, never saw an alien, wasn't near the fighting. His memories up to the time of death pretty much verify the voice tape they found five years ago. Here . . . ." He fiddled with a recorder on the desk, and keyed it on. The room filled with a voice, that of a terrified child, sounding a dead man's last thought.

" . . . says an unidentified number of creatures were left in the clearing by the alien shuttle before it lifted. Hsimen tells me to keep monitoring the orbiting blackship to see if they release any more shuttles . . . Someone screams on the radio, 'They killed Mullins, just like that' . . . I don't want to go on, I don't *want* to . . . "

Woman's voice, expressionless: "You must go on."

"I'm on my feet, Hsimen says 'Sit down, George' and screams and grabs his head. It hurts, rifle fire from the radio . . . I don't want to remember, please . . . Oh, God, it hurts, it . . . " and the girlish voice shrieked shrilly, a high pitch that seemed to go on eternally. It cut into sudden silence an instant before Caldoza switched off.

"Sweet merciful God," said Michael or Barbara. I don't think it was me.

"She never came out of that," said Caldoza. "That's what we got anyway. Backs up the voice recording, the blackship, the seeming unprovoked nature of the attack. But no clue to the nature of the weapon, much less possible defenses. Wish we could have been linked to somebody closer to the actual aliens, but that was George Terrace's memory, and it's all we got."

I stood up and walked to the door. The smokey disk of Casseiopeia RF Blue, darkened to magenta by the dome, hung high in the far sky.

"So it's got to be the three-year-old," I said heavily. "He doesn't have a name, I gather."

"He was named Herbie, Herbert, at birth," said Caldoza. "But as soon as we got your Institute's recommendations, we stopped calling him by name. Tried to atrophy any feeling of self-identity on his part as much as possible. What your recommendations called Alternative Three; as little barrier as possible to his identifying with past lifetimes."

And as little ego of his own to get back to as possible, I thought. Alternative Three: maximum success in prenatal memory combined with minimum chance of ego survival. Alternative Two: heavy ego preparation; little chance of psychic harm, but equally little odds of attaining past memories at all. Alternative One: taking the ordinary half-set human mishmash, and seeing what happens . . . like they did with me.

Poor Herbie with no name; he was getting a rawer deal than I had.

"It's got to be done right," Caldoza was saying nervously. "So he won't go off like the girl did. But that's what you're supposed to be good at, isn't it?"

I frowned, more at my thoughts than at his mother-henning. "No one has *ever* regressed a three-year-old before," I said. "Nor a four-year-old—successfully. You better realize I don't work miracles."

"But you're in this too," Caldoza insisted on reminding me. "So I know you'll do your best. Come on, let's wake the boy up."

We went out into the violet glare of Cass. RF Blue, and crossed the packed earth compound to another row of structures.

"Any sign of the blackship yet?" I was wondering.

He tapped his ear. "I'm getting constant reports," he said. "No sighting yet."

"Maybe they're not coming."

"We should be so lucky."

We strode along the line of buildings, typical first-generation colony. Hastily raised from wood hacked from trees planted decades back, in early preparation for eventual habitation. If the spruce and squirrels and goats survive fifty years, humans move in. Rough, dim, uncomfortable, ugly shacks. We call them 'throw-ups.'

The dome was the colonists' only luxury, and it must have cost them their next three generations' eyeteeth. Anyway, it was something the first colony hadn't had. That might make a difference. I doubted it. None of the things the dome was made to stop would have been able to cause such fatalities anyway.

The few grim colonists crossing the compound paid us little attention. Most were armed with frighteningly inadequate weapons. Did they know it was the damned deadly unknown universe they were up against? Of course; this far from man's sphere, this was all they had, all they could afford. Maxims. Flintlocks. Peashooters.

I asked suddenly, "What did the boy's parents have to say about your taking the kid over? We could hardly get away with it on Tairé without a State order and a lot of public stink." The question was so unlike my usual concerns that for a moment I thought Barbara had asked it. But she wasn't there; it had been me.

Caldoza didn't break step. "They understand the situation, even if they don't like it. Either one human life aborted, or what happened to the first colony may happen again . . . and again."

"Lucky he had parents that were so self-sacrificing. Or maybe just not very paternal," Mike Haskins added. Or the habit patterns engendered by sixty years of Mike's memories added. The ghost of Mike cost me a fair number of friends.

Caldoza had stopped and faced me. "We're human," he said tightly. "It's not your business, really, but Sarah, the girl Dr. Bergoff sent into catatonia . . . Dr. Bergoff is her mother. At the moment, the mother is little better off than the child. As for Herbie's parents . . . " He looked at me hard, "I think you'd better drop the subject."

We gulped.

Did I say 'we'? I meant 'I,' of course. I gulped. I.

My own regressions had shaped my character, if only in total reaction to the lives that Michael Haskins and Barbara Simmon had lived. Whatever had happened to that young Timmy Hume, the usual human adolescent mix of selfishness and altruism? He had been picked up for the early regression studies, and they had changed him

Ted Reynolds

forever. I had become one of the first to be scientifically and demonstrably lured back across the threshold of prenatal memories; and the very first to be regressed two successive lives back. I had become capable of recalling, as the popular media liked to call it, my previous existences.

Which was not the truth of it at all, I still insisted to myself. *I* was Timothy Hume, and I had never existed in this universe before my conception on Tairé in 2403 old count. And Michael Haskins, born in 2344 on old Earth, had *died* on Tairé, forever and permanently, in 2403. Nothing but his life's memories lingered on, to be picked up by a newly conceived embryo, and buried at a level so deep that, though every human back through the genetic chain of time had had them, hardly anyone suspected they were there, much less retrievable.

And Barb Simmon had died on old Earth in 2344, at the age of 17, and she was not Michael, and she was definitely not me. So I kept telling myself.

I knew who I was, little Timmy Hume of 604-L Greenreach, Hogarth City, Tairé, now in a grownup body. And I would not want to have been either of those other persons who had bequeathed me their legacies of memory. I refused to admit any shared being with Michael Haskins, who had lived out his term of life in rational hypocrisy, doing nothing of what he could have done because people were just too stupid and society too evil to think of changing. And thinking on his death-bed, "But was this *all?*"

And I certainly admitted no part of Barbara Simmon, who loved everybody and trusted everybody and died of gang rape at seventeen, thinking "but there's some terrible mistake."

So I spent a lot of time trying to insulate the life memories of these two defunct losers from contaminating my own; and a hell of a lot of effort trying *not* to remember their lives, and particularly their deaths. I refused to make use of Barbara's musical skill on the pianolin, or Mike's mild telepathic talents. They weren't mine, so I disowned them. There was pressure on me from the Institute to keep pushing the horizons back; they wanted to make me a living, breathing collection of futile human lives all the way back to Dilmun and Altamira. There was no way. I knew what that would do to me.

Reincarnation isn't what it's cracked up to be.

People these days like to call it "eternal rebirth." The ancient Hindus understood the process better.

They called it "eternal redeath."

I looked down on the sleeping child, and then riffled through the reports once more. I had to admit the preparation Dr. Bergoff had given him had been thorough. This boy not only didn't know who he was, he didn't even know he was *supposed* to be anybody.

For an amateur, working from recommendations sent two hundred light-years, Dr. Bergoff had done creditably. In the absence of a qualified hypnotist in the colony, the boy had at least been given a full course of suggestion under hypnotic drugs. Now all I needed to restore my confidence was the memory of all the regressions I had successfully carried out in my career—and of course, the recommended fifteen days in which to feel out a solid regression.

Caldoza's voice came through the unit in my left ear. "Hume, hate to have to mention it, but the blackship just showed up on our monitors."

I took a deep breath. Well, had I expected different? I thumbed my communication switch.

"How long do you figure we've got?"

"Maybe an hour till they're in orbit," said Caldoza. "Plus however long they stay in orbit, plus however long it takes them to descend, plus however long they stay in their shuttle before they come out . . . " He paused.

"Got you," I said. "Look, just tell me when the damned slugs reach orbit, when they launch a shuttle, when they touch down, when they emerge. And anything unexpected. And speak softly. Otherwise, leave me alone, right?"

"Okay, Hume. Good luck." He clicked off.

I set the strobes working, and the colors began to swirl down and around and up the floor and walls and ceiling of the dim room. Then I touched the shoulder of the sleeping boy. He opened blue-gray eyes without moving another muscle, and looked up at me. No expression.

"I'm Tim Hume," I told him. "Do you mind if we talk?"

He had not been brought up to mind. He was putty in any adult's hands.

The boy sat up, feet dangling well off the floor, and folding his little hands, waited patiently for whatever I had in mind.

"We're going to play a game," I told him. "Won't that be fun?"

—Who's *the hypocrite?* thought a voice from my past, but which past I didn't care to think.

The boy nodded indifferently.

"Do you like to remember things?" I asked him.

He looked at me a while, and shrugged.

—*Call him by name*, suggested something within me, but I shut her up.

"Don't you remember things sometimes?" I pressed.

The boy realized I wasn't going to drop it. He thought a while, sullenly. "Rather sleep," he said at last.

I wasn't going to get away from the subject. "What's the earliest thing you can remember?" I asked him.

A long pause, as he considered his clasped hands (left on top, I noticed). Then he looked up at me. "You are?" he ventured warily.

I sighed silently. This wasn't going to be easy. All the usual methods took time. And here we were heading into what at best would be a death trauma, and at worst . . . would be much worse.

"Well, we're going to play the remembering game. Did you ever . . . "

Voice in my ear, "Blackship in orbit, Hume."

"Uh-huh." I continued my spiel with hardly a break. "You know how you remember things that happened to you?"

He wasn't being co-operative; he didn't even want to admit that much. Plump little kid, with a bland round face. The sort a mother might bring herself to love. Finally he nodded a millimeter.

I got up from the cot and paced the room slowly, considering. The soft colors passed over and over and over us. His head didn't move, but those eyes were always on me.

"Suppose I tell you something that never happened? And then *you* go on with the memory—just as if it *did* happen. But of course, it didn't."

Damn, he was old enough to feel an inconsistency somewhere. "But if it didn't *happen,* I can't *remember* it."

At least he was talking.

"Yes . . . you . . . can," I insisted firmly. Authority speaking. "All sorts of people do it. Anybody can. Didn't you know that?"

He shook his head dubiously, eyes still fastened on me.

"Well, they *can,*" I lied smoothly. "And it's a lot of fun to play that remembering game. Shall we try?"

Again he shrugged, which was all he could do when he was scared stiff to shake his head like he wanted.

"It really works," I went on. "I'll show you." I kept pacing, trying to appear as if I were just now making up a previously unthought-of scenario. "Well, suppose you were a big grown-up. You can suppose that, can't you?"

He nodded. That, at least, never fails with kids.

"Okay, you're a big grown-up. That is, you were once upon a time, long, long ago. Let's see. Let's suppose you live around here, because you already know this place pretty well, so it'll help you pretend-remember. Do you understand? You've got to remember when you were a grown-up around here, long ago. But," I leaned over, arms resting on the cot to either side of him, and looked him straight in the eye, "but it never ever *really* happened. You're just remembering a pretend. Okay?"

He nodded quickly, either because he understood or, more likely, to get me back out of close eyeball contact. I resumed my pacing.

"But we can't have it all *just* like it is now, can we? I guess some things were different, back then. Let's not have the dome, okay? then we can see that blue sun right from the compound. And we'll have wood buildings, but they'll be sort of different ones."

Voice: "Hume, the blackship just sent out a shuttle. You won't have too much time to come up with something. How's it going in there?"

I didn't answer him.

"Well, what can you remember like that?" I asked the boy.

He looked down. "Nothing," he said in a low voice.

"You must be able to remember *some* thing like that," I said sharply.

"I won't," he said dully. "Don't like it."

The strobes went round and round, and I stared at him. Drugs coursed in his veins, he was prepped to the gills with prehypnotic conditioning. And yet . . .

"I won't. I don't like it."

Had I ever expected anything different? Regression isn't meant to be easy. The psyche fights it with all it's got. And with good reason.

Something in me, ignoring my trained experience, had awaited a miracle. It wouldn't be forthcoming. I had hit enough regression resistance before to know when I had a no-chance case. Maybe not in days; certainly not in minutes.

I gave up.

And then I was on my knees in front of Herbie and my arms were around him. I felt his small body quivering wherever I touched him.

"Herbie," I was saying desperately, "oh, poor kid, I'm sorry. Forgive me, Herbie, I didn't want to do this to you."

And I was crying.

Herbie was staring off into the dim corners of the room where the lights crissed and crossed, when I dried my eyes on my arm, and looked back at him. His cheek was twitching.

"Please understand, Herbie, it's because it's so awfully important, for everybody. You've just got to try to remember when you were a big person. Or you and me and your daddy and mommy, everybody . . . we're all going to die."

Now his cheek was twitching as spasmodically as a semaphore. He looked at me. "Do I have to remember? Will you *make* me remember?"

And I said, "No, Herbie, not if you don't want to. I'd never make you if you don't want to."

And abruptly realized that I, I hadn't said a word in minutes. It had been Barbara stroking him, wooing him, calling him Herbie. Barbara crying, not me.

—*Barbara, get out of this. It's my show, you're dead.*

—*Tim, leave Barb alone. You gave up. She's doing a hell of a lot better than you were.*

That was Mike, of course.

I was losing control of my own mind, beginning to think of them as real living persons in my skull. I reached to shut them down.

My ear clicked and Caldoza's voice came in, haggardly. "The alien shuttle's landing in the clearing, Hume. I gather you haven't got an answer yet."

Mike said, "I think we'll have it very soon, Caldoza."

"Thanks for trying," said Caldoza, "but there's no more time. Better stop the regression. Spare the boy's mind . . . if any of us live through this."

One of us thumbed the speaker off. Caldoza could still contact me, but I didn't want him able to hear us at this stage. Girded up though he was to sacrifice the kid, he still might change his mind when it came to the actual slaughter. And I was going through with this, regardless. Mike's ghost had challenged me. I was trying to shuffle Mike back under where he belonged when Herbie said slowly, "I know what you want me to remember. You want me to tell you my dreams."

Damn! How else could a three-year-old interpret a demand for memories that never happened? I opened my mouth to correct him, but Barbara used it instead.

"Of course, Herbie. Did you dream of being a big man in this place?"

His voice was withdrawn. "I don't think I can remember being a big man." he said softly.

"Okay, not a man, maybe. Maybe you can remember being a woman . . . or a kid, another kid. Just tell me what you remember."

"Mister," said Herbie, reaching out and taking my hand. "Mister, I think if I start remembering I'm going to get hurt."

"I don't want you to get hurt, dear," said Barbara, pulling him to me. "I love you, Herbie."

He looked up at us, amazed.

"You . . . love me?"

We tipped his head up and Barbara kissed him gently. "I love you very much," she said, and it was true. I sat silent and let her talk. "I would never ask you to remember . . . frightening things, except it's very important. If you can remember, then maybe . . . we can stop other terrible things happening to all of us. *Really* happening."

And Mike tousled Herbie's hair. "So come on, big boy. You can do it, Herb."

Herbie looked at them a long while and then suddenly threw his arms about me and kissed Barbara. "I'll try," he said quickly. "Cause you want me to. But it's . . . bad, it's ugly."

"It can't be too bad, because it never really . . ."

Herbie looked me in the eye. "No. It really happened. I know."

Without waiting for a response, he closed his eyes and his face softened in relaxation. There was a long stretched waiting as my laced fingers tightened painfully as if I prayed. Then slowly Herbie slumped backward on the cot, his arms and legs waving meaninglessly, like reeds in an eddy.

I reached out to touch him, and Barbara stopped me with a thought. Herbie opened his eyes and looked up at us with the gently vacuous smile of an idiot angel. His mouth opened and closed slowly, voicelessly.

And that explains it, thought Mike. *Did you get it, Barb?*

And Barbara thought, *How simple, how sad. Do you think Tim can handle it?*

Not yet, returned Mike.

"Hume," came Caldoza's voice. "The aliens are emerging from their shuttle. As soon as they come within range we're opening fire. You can be more help out here now." A pause. "Is the boy all right?"

What are you two keeping from me? I thought furiously. *Damn it, I've got to know what's going on.*

Mike was snapping at Caldoza over the communicator. "If you fire on them, I'll have your ass strewn around this whole planet in little pieces!" A stray bit of me wondered what had gotten into Mike; he'd never acted like that in his own life.

He's not listening, said Barbara. *He's switched off.* She put my arm around Herbie's shoulders. *Help him up. We've got to go out and stop this craziness.*

I planted myself firmly, feeling the others tugging at my muscles, but, with concentrated stubbornness, keeping them mine. "I'm not moving a step till I know what's going on," I insisted.

Tim, listen. The aliens landed in the same clearing we did, came along the path, and met their first human by the big tamalpo tree . . .

"How do you know all this? Herbie hasn't said a thing."

I felt a hasty consultation behind walls in my mind from which I was shut out, and then Mike said, *In his last life, Herbie was a strong telepath, Tim. He sensed everything that happened that day to everyone, though he died before he could sort it out.*

"That doesn't make sense," I shouted, shouted to myself in a dark room.

Herbie's got the memories of Lashag, his previous life. Herbie himself's no telepath, but I am and I'm feeding the data to Barbara.

"And not to me!" I was outraged to my core.

Please, Tim, said Barbara. *Trust us.*

"Why should I?"

To survive! snapped Mike, but Barbara pushed him aside.

Because we need one another, she thought like a caress. *Because we know each other as well as we know ourselves. Because we love one another.*

"No!" I yelled, stepping backward as if I could avoid her that way. "You aren't people any more. You're just dead memories!"

Living memories, Mike corrected gently. *When we were alive before, we were held in life by the neuronic structure of our own brains. Now we are held in life by part of yours. Is there such a difference?*

"But I . . ." Staggering like a drunk, flinging my hands before my face, I was running scared, disgusted, finding no place to hide. I could not *let* them be living persons. How could I live with people who *knew,* knew everything about me, from every time I jacked off to how I let my father die without word from me, who knew the hate for others and myself that lay under my jacket of cold professionalism?

We know, we've always known, said Barbara. *And you can see for yourself what we think of it. You know us, don't you?*

And I saw her as she saw me, through and through, and saw she did know, and suffered with me, and loved me with and through it all.

Ted Reynolds

And this time the tears were mine.

We can do something about all that old muck, Mike was saying, *if we work together. But for now, we've got to move fast, or we're dead all over again.*

I let them lift the limp boy and carry him from the room. We emerged into the violet-lit compound and started across it at a rapid trot.

What's the story on the massacre, Mike? I thought, saving speaking breath. *I can take it.*

An accident, a misunderstanding, said Mike. *We've got to keep from repeating it. We've got to.*

Abruptly Herbie stirred on my shoulder and uttered words, slurred but intelligible. " . . . the alien, tall and thin and cunningly jointed, it travels the stars and seeks for answers as we do. But . . . it is very uneasy."

Lashag's reliving the first contact, explained Mike. *Barbara's teaching him the words through me.*

We ran towards the gate, the heavy projectors set in it, the armed men staring outward. Caldoza, glaring out through the translucent dome to where the path emerged from the trees, turned rapidly at our approach. We almost plowed into him before we could stop.

"We've got it, Caldoza," said Mike. I still didn't know what we had discovered, and hung on every word that came out of my mouth. "The aliens are strong natural telepaths. They came without hostile intent. They were just trying to communicate."

Every face turned toward us. Caldoza's was a study in hope, disbelief, and confusion. "But they murdered . . . "

"The first telepathic probes caused great mental distress in the humans." Mike hurried on. "Someone shot, and both humans and aliens panicked. The aliens . . . well, they began *shouting,* telepathically. They couldn't know that our minds are as unprotected against telepathic overstimuli as theirs against too much sound or light."

"But we can't just allow . . . "

There was a sudden collective intake of breath from the men at the gate. I looked out to see flowing shapes sliding from beneath the trees, huge shapeless purple worms.

In the sudden silence Herbie's slow voice could be heard. "They fall, they die," he was saying sadly. "Too late I realize that the stronger I call, the faster they die; my mindcalls are killing them. Now Golard is dead, and Trephanie, and I die, and scores of marvellous feeling thinking beings are dead, and we have done it. We did not mean it so, oh truth, we did not . . . " Silence.

"Not your fault, Lashag," Barbara said. "You couldn't know. We love you anyway."

The idiot angel smiled, softened and faded away, and Herbie was a three-year-old again. I set him carefully on the ground, where he clung tightly to my hand.

Caldoza was looking at Herbie in awe. He and I were coming to understand at the same time.

"Yes," said Mike. "Herbie's last life . . . well, he wasn't one of the colonists. He was one of the aliens."

I waited for myself to stiffen in fear and disgust, and became aware at once I wasn't going to. The projection of my fears onto unknown Others was gone. Mike and Barbara had touched these alien minds and trusted them. And I trusted Mike's judgement and Barbara's heart.

We looked at Caldoza, alone in himself and afraid among his men, and pitied him. Did I say we? Well, I meant we!

"We're going out there to meet them," I told him. "Herbert and I will be emissaries."

"Going *out* there!" gasped Caldoza. "Just the two of you?"

I smiled. "Five of us," I corrected gently. "Three of me, and two of Herbie. It should work out all right now. We're prepared for mental contact, we can communicate through Mike and Lashag, and we think of them as friends, not ugly killer maggots."

Caldoza looked dazed, don't blame him. "Friends!"

"We'll stay out of that telepathic panic cycle," said Mike. "I'm not about to blow it, now I got another chance to do something right."

"I want to meet them," said Herbie. "I think they're neat."

"They're an admirable people," said Barbara. "They can teach us love."

"We are looking forward to sharing lives with you," said Lashag.

"So don't worry," I said. "We've got you covered." ∎

NOVICE

James H. Schmitz

There was, Telzey Amberdon thought, someone besides TT and herself in the garden. Not, of course, Aunt Halet, who was in the house waiting for an early visitor to arrive, and not one of the servants. Someone or something else must be concealed among the thickets of magnificently flowering native Jontarou shrubs about Telzey.

She could think of no other way to account for Tick-Tock's spooked behavior—nor, to be honest about it, for the manner her own nerves were acting up without visible cause this morning.

Telzey plucked a blade of grass, slipped the end between her lips and chewed it gently, her face puzzled and concerned. She wasn't ordinarily afflicted with nervousness. Fifteen years old, genius level, brown as a berry and not at all bad-looking in her sunbriefs, she was the youngest member of one of Orado's most prominent families and a second-year law student at one of the most exclusive schools in the Federation of the Hub. Her physical, mental, and emotional health, she'd always been informed, was excellent. Aunt Halet's frequent cracks about the inherent instability of the genius level could be ignored; Halet's own stability seemed questionable at best.

But none of that made the present odd situation any less disagreeable. . .

The trouble might have begun, Telzey decided, during the night, within an hour after they arrived from the spaceport at the guest house Halet had rented in Port Nichay for their vacation on Jontarou. Telzey had retired at once to her second-story bedroom with Tick-Tock; but she barely got to sleep before something awakened her again. Turning over, she discovered TT reared up before the window, her forepaws on the sill, big cat-head outlined against the star-hazed night sky, staring fixedly down into the garden.

Telzey, only curious at that point, climbed out of bed and joined TT at the window. There was nothing in particular to be seen, and if the scents and minor night-sounds which came from the garden weren't exactly what they were used to, Jontarou was after all an unfamiliar planet. What else would one expect here?

But Tick-Tock's muscular back felt tense and rigid when Telzey laid her arm across it, and except for an absent-minded dig with her forehead against Telzey's shoulder, TT refused to let her attention be distracted from whatever had absorbed it. Now and then, a low, ominous rumble came from her furry throat, a half-angry, half-questioning sound. Telzey began to feel a little uncomfortable. She managed finally to coax Tick-

Tock away from the window, but neither of them slept well the rest of the night. At breakfast, Aunt Halet made one of her typical nasty-sweet remarks.

"You look so fatigued, dear—as if you were under some severe mental strain which, of course, you might be," Halet added musingly. With her gold-blond hair piled high on her head and her peaches and cream complexion, Halet looked fresh as a daisy herself . . . a malicious daisy. "Now wasn't I right in insisting to Jessamine that you needed a vacation away from that terribly intellectual school?" She smiled gently.

"Absolutely," Telzey agreed, restraining the impulse to fling a spoonful of egg yolk at her father's younger sister. Aunt Halet often inspired such impulses, but Telzey had promised her mother to avoid actual battles on the Jontarou trip, if possible. After breakfast, she went out into the back garden with Tick-Tock, who immediately walked into a thicket, camouflaged herself and vanished from sight. It seemed to add up to something. But what?

Telzey strolled about the garden a while, maintaining a pretense of nonchalant interest in Jontarou's flowers and colorful bug life. She experienced the most curious little chills of alarm from time to time, but discovered no signs of a lurking intruder, or of TT either. Then, for half an hour or more, she'd just sat cross-legged in the grass, waiting quietly for Tick-Tock to show up of her own accord. And the big lunkhead hadn't obliged.

Telzey scratched a tanned kneecap, scowling at Port Nichay's park trees beyond the garden wall. It seemed idiotic to feel scared when she couldn't even tell whether there was anything to be scared about! And, aside from that, another unreasonable feeling kept growing stronger by the minute now. This was to the effect that she should be doing some unstated but specific thing . . .

In fact, that Tick-tock *wanted* her to do some specific thing!

Completely idiotic!

Abruptly, Telzey closed her eyes, thought sharply, "Tick-Tock?" and waited — suddenly very angry at herself for having given in to her fancies to this extent—for whatever might happen.

She had never really established that she was able to tell, by a kind of symbolic mind-picture method, like a short waking dream, approximately what TT was thinking and feeling. Five years before, when she'd discovered Tick-Tock—an odd-looking and odder-behaved stray kitten then—in the woods near the Amberdons' summer home on Orado, Telzey had thought so. But it might never have been more than a colorful play of her imagination; and after she got into law school and grew increasingly absorbed in her studies, she almost forgot the matter again.

Today, perhaps because she was disturbed about Tick-Tock's behavior, the customary response was extraordinarily prompt. The warm glow of sunlight shining through her closed eyelids faded out quickly and was replaced by some inner darkness.

James H. Schmitz

In the darkness there appeared then an image of Tick-Tock sitting a little way off beside an open door in an old stone wall, green eyes fixed on Telzey. Telzey got the impression that TT was inviting her to go through the door, and, for some reason, the thought frightened her.

Again, there was an immediate reaction. The scene with Tick-Tock and the door vanished; and Telzey felt she was standing in a pitch-black room, knowing that if she moved even one step forward, something that was waiting there silently would reach out and grab her.

Naturally, she recoiled . . . and at once found herself sitting, eyes still closed and the sunlight bathing her lids, in the grass of the guest house garden.

She opened her eyes, looked around. Her heart was thumping rapidly. The experience couldn't have lasted more than four or five seconds, but it had been extremely vivid, a whole compact little nightmare. None of her earlier experiments at getting into mental communication with TT had been like that.

It served her right, Telzey thought, for trying such a childish stunt at the moment! What she should have done at once was to make a methodical search for the foolish beast—TT was bound to be *somewhere* nearby—locate her behind her camouflage, and hang on to her then until this nonsense in the garden was explained! Talented as Tick-Tock was at blotting herself out, it usually was possible to spot her if one directed one's attention to shadow patterns. Telzey began a surreptitious study of the flowering bushes about her.

Three minutes later, off to her right, where the ground was banked beneath a six-foot step in the garden's terraces, Tick-Tock's outline suddenly caught her eye. Flat on her belly, head lifted above her paws, quite motionless, TT seemed like a transparent wraith stretched out along the terrace, barely discernible even when stared at directly. It was a convincing illusion; but what seemed to be rocks, plant leaves, and sun-splotched earth seen through the wraith-outline was simply the camouflage pattern TT had printed for the moment on her hide. She could have changed it completely in an instant to conform to a different background.

Telzey pointed an accusing finger.

"See you!" she announced, feeling a surge of relief which seemed as unaccountable as the rest of it.

The wraith twitched one ear in acknowledgment, the head outlines shifting as the camouflaged face turned towards Telzey. Then the inwardly uncamouflaged, very substantial-looking mouth opened slowly, showing Tick-Tock's red tongue and curved white tusks. The mouth stretched in a wide yawn, snapped shut with a click of meshing teeth, became indistinguishable again. Next, a pair of camouflaged lids drew back from TT's round, brilliant-green eyes. The eyes stared across the lawn at Telzey.

Telzey said irritably, "Quit clowning around, TT!"

The eyes blinked, and Tick-Tock's natural bronze-brown color suddenly flowed over her head, down her neck and across her body into legs and tail. Against the side of the terrace, as if materializing into solidity at that moment, appeared two hundred pounds of supple, rangy, long-tailed cat . . . or catlike creature. TT's actual origin had never been established. The best guesses were that what Telzey had found playing around in the woods five years ago was either a biostructural experiment which had got away from a private laboratory on Orado, or some spaceman's lost pet, brought to the capital planet from one of the remote colonies beyond the Hub. On top of TT's head was a large, fluffy pompom of white fur, which might have looked ridiculous on another animal, but didn't on her. Even as a fat kitten, hanging head down from the side of a wall by the broad sucker pads in her paws, TT had possessed enormous dignity.

Telzey studied her, the feeling of relief fading again. Tick-Tock, ordinarily the most restful and composed of companions, definitely was still tensed up about something. That big, lazy yawn a moment ago, the attitude of stretched-out relaxation . . . all pure sham!

"What *is* eating you?" she asked in exasperation.

The green eyes stared at her, solemn, watchful, seeming for that fleeting instant quite alien. And why, Telzey thought, should the old question of what Tick-Tock really was pass through her mind just now? After her rather alarming rate of growth began to taper off last year, nobody had cared any more.

For a moment, Telzey had the uncanny certainty of having had the answer to this situation almost in her grasp. An answer which appeared to involve the world of Jontarou, Tick-Tock, and of all unlikely factors—Aunt Halet.

She shook her head. TT's impassive green eyes blinked.

Jontarou? The planet lay outside Telzey's sphere of personal interests, but she'd read up on it on the way here from Orado. Among all the worlds of the Hub, Jontarou was *the* paradise for zoologists and sportsmen, a gigantic animal preserve, its continents and seas swarming with magnificent game. Under Federation law, it was being retained deliberately in the primitive state in which it had been discovered. Port Nichay, the only city, actually the only inhabited point on Jontarou, was beautiful and quiet, a pattern of vast but elegantly slender towers, each separated from the others by four or five miles of rolling parkland and interconnected only by the threads of transparent skyways. Near the horizon, just visible from the garden, rose the tallest towers of all, the green and gold spires of the Shikaris' Club, a center of Federation affairs and of social activity. From the aircar which brought them across Port Nichay the evening before, Telzey had seen occasional strings of guest houses, similar to the one Halet had rented, nestling along the park slopes.

Nothing very sinister about Port Nichay or green Jontarou, surely!

Halet? That blonde, slinky, would-be Machiavelli? What could—?

Telzey's eyes narrowed reflectively. There'd been a minor occurrence—at least, it seemed minor—just before the spaceliner docked last night. A young woman from

James H. Schmitz

one of the newscasting services had asked for an interview with the daughter of Federation Councilwoman Jessamine Amberdon. This happened occasionally; and Telzey had no objections until the newshen's gossipy persistence in inquiring about the "unusual pet" she was bringing to Port Nichay with her began to be annoying. TT might be somewhat unusual, but that was not a matter of general interest; and Telzey said so. Then Halet moved smoothly into the act and held forth on Tick-Tock's appearance, habits, and mysterious antecedents, in considerable detail.

Telzey had assumed that Halet was simply going out of her way to be irritating, as usual. Looking back on the incident, however, it occurred to her that the chatter between her aunt and the newscast woman had sounded oddly stilted—almost like something the two might have rehearsed.

Rehearsed for what purpose? Tick-Tock . . . Jontarou.

Telzey chewed gently on her lower lip. A vacation on Jontarou for the two of them and TT had been Halet's idea, and Halet had enthused about it so much that Telzey's mother at last talked her into accepting. Halet, Jessamine explained privately to Telzey, had felt they were intruders in the Amberdon family, had bitterly resented Jessamine's political honors and, more recently, Telzey's own emerging promise of brilliance. This invitation was Halet's way of indicating a change of heart. Wouldn't Telzey oblige?

So Telzey had obliged, though she took very little stock in Halet's change of heart. She wasn't, in fact, putting it past her aunt to have some involved dirty trick up her sleeve with this trip to Jontarou. Halet's mind worked like that.

So far there had been no actual indications of purposeful mischief. But logic did seem to require a connection between the various puzzling events here . . . A newscaster's rather forced-looking interest in Tick-Tock—Halet could easily have paid for that interview. Then TT's disturbed behavior during their first night in Port Nichay, and Telzey's own formless anxieties and fancies in connection with the guest house garden.

The last remained hard to explain. But Tick-Tock . . . and Halet . . . might know something about Jontarou that she didn't know.

Her mind returned to the results of the half-serious attempt she'd made to find out whether there was something Tick-Tock "wanted her to do." An open door? A darkness where somebody waited to grab her if she took even one step forward? It couldn't have had any significance. Or could it?

So you'd like to try magic, Telzey scoffed at herself. Baby games . . . How far would you have got at law school if you'd asked TT to help with your problems?

Then why had she been thinking about it again?

She shivered, because an eerie stillness seemed to settle on the garden. From the side of the terrace, TT's green eyes watched her.

Telzey had a feeling of sinking down slowly into a sunlit dream, into something very remote from law school problems.

"Should I go through the door?" she whispered.

The bronze cat-shape raised its head slowly. TT began to purr.

Tick-Tock's name had been derived in kittenhood from the manner in which she purred—a measured, oscillating sound, shifting from high to low, as comfortable and often as continuous as the unobtrusive pulse of an old clock. It was the first time, Telzey realized now, that she'd heard the sound since their arrival on Jontarou. It went on for a dozen seconds or so, then stopped. Tick-Tock continued to look at her.

It appeared to have been an expression of definite assent. . . .

The dreamlike sensation increased, hazing over Telzey's thoughts. If there was nothing to this mind-communication thing, what harm could symbols do? This time, she wouldn't let them alarm her. And if they did mean something . . .

She closed her eyes.

The sunglow outside faded instantly. Telzey caught a fleeting picture of the door in the wall, and knew in the same moment that she'd already passed through it.

She was not in the dark room then, but poised at the edge of a brightness which seemed featureless and without limit, spread out around her with a feeling-tone like "sea" or "sky." But it was an unquiet place. There was a sense of unseen things on all sides watching her and waiting.

Was this another form of the dark room—a trap set up in her mind? Telzey's attention did a quick shift. She was seated in the grass again; the sunlight beyond her closed eyelids seemed to shine in quietly through rose-tinted curtains. Cautiously, she let her awareness return to the bright area; and *it* was still there. She had a moment of excited elation. She was controlling this! And why not, she asked herself. These things were happening in *her* mind, after all!

She would find out what they seemed to mean, but she would be in no rush to . . .

An impression as if, behind her, Tick-Tock had thought, "Now I can help again!"

Then a feeling of being swept swiftly, irresistibly forwards, thrust out and down. The brightness exploded in thundering colors around her. In fright, she made the effort to snap her eyes open, to be back in the garden; but now she couldn't make it work. The colors continued to roar about her, like a confusion of excited, laughing, triumphant voices. Telzey felt caught in the middle of it all, suspended in invisible spider webs. Tick-Tock seemed to be somewhere nearby, looking on. Faithless, treacherous TT!

Telzey's mind made another wrenching effort, and there was a change. She hadn't got back into the garden, but the noisy, swirling colors were gone and she had the feeling of reading a rapidly moving microtape now, though she didn't actually see the tape.

The tape, she realized, was another symbol for what was happening, a symbol easier for her to understand. There were voices, or what might be voices, around her; on the invisible tape she seemed to be reading what they said.

James H. Schmitz

A number of speakers, apparently involved in a fast, hot argument about what to do with her. Impressions flashed past . . .

Why waste time with her? It was clear that kitten-talk was all she was capable of! . . . Not necessarily; that was a normal first step. Give her a little time! . . . But what—exasperatedly—could *such* a small-bite *possibly* know that would be of significant value?

There was a slow, blurred, awkward-seeming interruption. Its content was not comprehensible to Telzey at all, but in some unmistakable manner it was defined as Tick-Tock's thought.

A pause as the circle of speakers stopped to consider whatever TT had thrown into the debate.

Then another impression . . . one that sent a shock of fear through Telzey as it rose heavily into her awareness. Its sheer intensity momentarily displaced the tape-reading symbolism. A savage voice seemed to rumble:

"Toss the tender small-bite to *me*"—malevolent crimson eyes fixed on Telzey from somewhere not far away—"and let's be done here!"

Startled, stammering protest from Tick-Tock, accompanied by gusts of laughter from the circle. Great sense of humor these characters had, Telzey thought bitterly. That crimson-eyed thing wasn't joking at all!

More laughter as the circle caught her thought. Then a kind of majority opinion found sudden expression:

"Small-bite *is* learning! No harm to wait—We'll find out quickly—Let's . . ."

The tape ended; the voices faded; the colors went blank. In whatever jumbled-up form she'd been getting the impressions at that point—Telzey couldn't have begun to describe it—the whole thing suddenly stopped.

She found herself sitting in the grass, shaky, scared, eyes open. Tick-Tock stood beside the terrace, looking at her. An air of hazy unreality still hung about the garden.

She might have flipped! She didn't think so; but it certainly seemed possible! Otherwise . . . Telzey made an attempt to sort over what had happened.

Something *had* been in the garden! Something had been inside her mind. Something that was at home on Jontarou.

There'd been a feeling of perhaps fifty or sixty of these . . . well, beings. Alarming beings! Reckless, wild, hard . . . and that red-eyed nightmare! Telzey shuddered.

They'd contacted Tick-Tock first, during the night. TT understood them better than she could. Why? Telzey found no immediate answer.

Then Tick-Tock had tricked her into letting her mind be invaded by these beings. There must have been a very definite reason for that.

She looked over at Tick-Tock. TT looked back. Nothing stirred in Telzey's thoughts. Between *them* there was still no direct communication.

Then how had the beings been able to get through to her?

Telzey wrinkled her nose. Assuming this was real, it seemed clear that the game of symbols she'd made up between herself and TT had provided the opening. Her whole experience just now had been in the form of symbols, translating whatever occurred into something she could consciously grasp.

"Kitten-talk" was how the beings referred to the use of symbols; they seemed contemptuous of it. Never mind, Telzey told herself; they'd agreed she was learning.

The air over the grass appeared to flicker. Again she had the impression of reading words off a quickly moving, not quite visible tape.

"You're being taught and you're learning," was what she seemed to read. "The question was whether you were capable of partial understanding as your friend insisted. Since you were, everything else that can be done will be accomplished very quickly." A pause, then with a touch of approval, "You're a well-formed mind, small-bite! Odd and with incomprehensibilities, but well-formed—"

One of the beings, and a fairly friendly one—at least not unfriendly. Telzey framed a tentative mental question. "Who are you?"

"You'll know very soon." The flickering ended; she realized she and the question had been dismissed for the moment. She looked over at Tick-Tock again.

"Can't *you* talk to me now, TT?" she asked silently.

A feeling of hesitation.

"Kitten-talk!" was the impression that formed itself with difficulty then. It was awkward, searching; but it came unquestionably from TT. "Still learning, too, Telzey!" TT seemed half anxious, half angry. "We—"

A sharp buzz-note reached Telzey's ears, wiping out the groping thought-impression. She jumped a little, glanced down. Her wrist-talker was signaling. For a moment, she seemed poised uncertainly between a world where unseen, dangerous-sounding beings referred to one as small-bite and where TT was learning to talk, and the familiar other world where wrist-communicators buzzed periodically in a matter-of-fact manner. Settling back into the more familiar world, she switched on the talker.

"Yes?" she said. Her voice sounded husky.

"Telzey, dear," Halet murmured honey-sweet from the talker, "would you come back into the house, please? The living room— We have a visitor who very much wants to meet you."

Telzey hesitated, eyes narrowing. Halet's visitor wanted to meet *her?*

"Why?" she asked.

"He has something *very* interesting to tell you, dear." The edge of triumphant malice showed for an instant, vanished in murmuring sweetness again. "So please hurry!"

"All right." Telzey stood up. "I'm coming."

"Fine, dear!" The talker went dead.

Telzey switched off the instrument, noticed that Tick-Tock had chosen to disappear meanwhile.

Flipped? She wondered, starting up towards the house. It was clear Aunt Halet had prepared some unpleasant surprise to spring on her, which was hardly more than normal behavior for Halet. The other business? She couldn't be certain of anything there. Leaving out TT's strange actions—which might have a number of causes, after all—that entire string of events could have been created inside her head. There was no contradictory evidence so far.

But it could do no harm to take what *seemed* to have happened at face value. Some pretty grim event might be shaping up, in a very real way, around here . . .

"You reason logically!" The impression now was of a voice speaking to her, a voice that made no audible sound. It was the same being who'd addressed her a minute or two ago.

The two worlds between which Telzey had felt suspended seemed to glide slowly together and become one.

"I go to law school," she explained to the being, almost absently.

Amused agreement. "So we heard."

"What do you want of me?" Telzey inquired.

"You'll know soon enough."

"Why not tell me now?" Telzey urged. It seemed about to dismiss her again.

Quick impatience flared at her. "Kitten-pictures! Kitten-thoughts! Kitten-talk! Too slow, too slow! YOUR pictures—too much YOU! Wait till the . . ."

Circuits close . . . channels open . . . Obstructions clear? What *had* it said? There'd been only the blurred image of a finicky, delicate, but perfectly normal technical operation of some kind.

". . . Minutes now!" the voice concluded. A pause, then another thought tossed carelessly at her. "This is more important to you, small-bite, than to *us!*" The voice impression ended as sharply as if a communicator had snapped off.

Not *too* friendly! Telzey walked on toward the house, a new fear growing inside her . . . a fear like the awareness of a storm gathered nearby, still quiet—deadly quiet, but ready to break.

"Kitten-pictures!" a voice seemed to jeer distantly, a whispering in the park trees beyond the garden wall.

Halet's cheeks were lightly pinked; her blue eyes sparkled. She looked downright stunning, which meant to anyone who knew her that the worst side of Halet's nature was champing at the bit again. On uninformed males it had a dazzling effect, however; and Telzey wasn't surprised to find their visitor wearing a tranced expression when she came into the living room. He was a tall, outdoorsy man with a tanned, bony face, a neatly trained black mustache, and a scar down one cheek which would have seemed dashing if it hadn't been for the stupefied look. Beside his chair stood a large, clumsy instrument which might have been some kind of telecamera.

Halet performed introductions. Their visitor was Dr. Droon, a zoologist. He had been tuned in on Telzey's newscast interview on the liner the night before, and wondered whether Telzey would care to discuss Tick-Tock with him.

"Frankly, no," Telzey said.

Dr. Droon came awake and gave Telzey a surprised look. Halet smiled easily.

"My niece doesn't intend to be discourteous, doctor," she explained.

"Of course not," the zoologist agreed doubtfully.

"It's just," Halet went on, "that Telzey is a little, oh, sensitive where Tick-Tock is concerned. In her own way, she's attached to the animal. Aren't you, dear?"

"Yes," Telzey said blandly.

"Well, we hope this isn't going to disturb you too much, dear." Halet glanced significantly at Dr. Droon. "Dr. Droon, you must understand, is simply doing . . . well, there is something very important he must tell you now."

Telzey transferred her gaze back to the zoologist. Dr. Droon cleared his throat. "I, ah, understand, Miss Amberdon, that you're unaware of what kind of creature your, ah, Tick-Tock is?"

Telzey started to speak, then checked herself, frowning. She had been about to state that she knew exactly what kind of creature TT was . . . but she didn't, of course! Or did she? She . . .

She scowled absent-mindedly at Dr. Droon, biting her lip.

"Telzey!" Halet prompted gently.

"Huh?" Telzey said. "Oh . . . please go on, doctor!"

Dr. Droon steepled his fingers. "Well," he said, "she . . . your pet . . . is, ah, a young crest cat. Nearly full grown now, apparently, and—"

"Why, yes!" Telzey cried.

The zoologist looked at her. "You knew that—"

"Well, not really," Telzey admitted. "Or sort of." She laughed, her cheeks flushed. "This is the most . . . go ahead please! Sorry I interrupted." She stared at the wall beyond Dr. Droon with a rapt expression.

The zoologist and Halet exchanged glances. Then Dr. Droon resumed cautiously. The crest cats, he said, were a species native to Jontarou. Their existence had been known for only eight years. The species appeared to have had a somewhat limited range—the Baluit mountains on the opposite side of the huge continent on which Port Nichay had been built . .

Telzey barely heard him. A very curious thing was happening. For every sentence Dr. Droon uttered, a dozen other sentences appeared in her awareness. More accurately, it was as if an instantaneous smooth flow of information relevant to whatever he said arose continuously from what might have been almost her own memory, but

James H. Schmitz

wasn't. Within a minute or two, she knew more about the crest cats of Jontarou than Dr. Droon could have told her in hours . . . much more than he'd ever known.

She realized suddenly that he'd stopped talking, that he had asked her a question. "Miss Amberdon?" he repeated now, with a note of uncertainty.

"Yar-rrr-REE!" Telzey told him softly. "I'll drink your blood!"

"Eh?"

Telzey blinked, focused on Dr. Droon, wrenching her mind away from a splendid view of the misty-blue peaks of the Baluit range.

"Sorry," she said briskly. "Just a joke!" She smiled. "Now what were you saying?"

The zoologist looked at her in a rather odd manner for a moment. "I was inquiring," he said then, "whether you were familiar with the sporting rules established by the various hunting associations of the Hub in connection with the taking of game trophies?"

Telzey shook her head. "No, I never heard of them."

The rules, Dr. Droon explained, laid down the type of equipment . . . weapons, spotting and tracking instruments, number of assistants, and so forth . . . a sportsman could legitimately use in the pursuit of any specific type of game. "Before the end of the first year after their discovery," he went on, "the Baluit crest cats had been placed in the ultra-equipment class."

"What's ultra-equipment?" Telzey asked.

"Well," Dr. Droon said thoughtfully, "it doesn't quite involve the use of full battle armor . . . not quite! And, of course, even with that classification the sporting principle of mutual accessibility must be observed."

"Mutual . . . oh, I see!" Telzey paused as another wave of silent information rose into her awareness; went on, "So the game has to be able to get at the sportsman too, eh?"

"That's correct. Except in the pursuit of various classes of flying animals, a shikari would not, for example, be permitted the use of an aircar other than as a means of simple transportation. Under these conditions, it was soon established that crest cats were being obtained by sportsmen who went after them at a rather consistent one-to-one ratio."

Telzey's eyes widened. She'd gathered something similar from her other information source but hadn't quite believed it. "One hunter killed for each cat bagged?" she said. "That's pretty rough sport, isn't it?

"Extremely rough sport!" Dr. Droon agreed dryly. "In fact, when the statistics were published, the sporting interest in winning a Baluit cat trophy appears to have suffered a sudden and sharp decline. On the other hand, a more scientific interest in these remarkable animals was coincidingly created, and many permits for their acquisition by the agents of museums, universities, public, and private collections were issued. Sporting rules, of course, do not apply to that activity."

Telzey nodded absently. "I see! *They* used aircars, didn't they? A sort of heavy knockout gun—"

"Aircars, long-range detectors and stunguns are standard equipment in such work," Dr. Droon acknowledged. "Gas and poison are employed, of course, as circumstances dictate. The collectors were relatively successful for a while.

"And then a curious thing happened. Less than two years after their existence became known, the crest cats of the Baluit range were extinct! The inroads made on their numbers by man cannot begin to account for this, so it must be assumed that a sudden plague wiped them out. At any rate, not another living member of the species has been seen on Jontarou until you landed here with your pet last night."

Telzey sat silent for some seconds. Not because of what he had said, but because the other knowledge was still flowing into her mind. On one very important point that was at variance with what the zoologist had stated; and from there a coldly logical pattern was building up. Telzey didn't grasp the pattern in complete detail yet, but what she saw of it stirred her with a half incredulous dread.

She asked, shaping the words carefully but with only a small part of her attention on what she was really saying, "Just what does all that have to do with Tick-Tock, Dr. Droon?"

Dr. Droon glanced at Halet, and returned his gaze to Telzey. Looking very uncomfortable but quite determined, he told her, "Miss Amberdon, there is a Federation law which states that when a species is threatened with extinction, any available survivors must be transferred to the Life Banks of the University League, to insure their indefinite preservation. Under the circumstances, this law applies to, ah, Tick-Tock!"

So that had been Halet's trick. She'd found out about the crest cats, might have put in as much as a few months arranging to make the discovery of TT's origin on Jontarou seem a regrettable mischance—something no one could have foreseen or prevented. In the Life Banks, from what Telzey had heard of them, TT would cease to exist as an individual awareness while scientists tinkered around with the possibilities of reconstructing her species.

Telzey studied her aunt's carefully sympathizing face for an instant, asked Dr. Droon, "What about the other crest cats you said were collected before they became extinct here? Wouldn't they be enough for what the Life Banks need?"

He shook his head. "Two immature male specimens are known to exist, and they are at present in the Life Banks. The others that were taken alive at the time have been destroyed . . . often under nearly disastrous circumstances. They are enormously cunning, enormously savage creatures, Miss Amberdon! The additional fact that they can conceal themselves to the point of being virtually undetectable except by the use of instruments makes them one of the most dangerous animals known. Since the young

James H. Schmitz

female which you raised as a pet has remained docile . . . so far . . . you may not really be able to appreciate that.''

"Perhaps I can," Telzey said. She nodded at the heavy-looking instrument standing beside his chair. "And that's—?"

"It's a life detector combined with a stungun, Miss Amberdon. I have no intention of harming your pet, but we can't take chances with an animal of that type. The gun's charge will knock it unconscious for several minutes—just long enough to let me secure it with paralysis belts.''

"You're a collector for the Life Banks, Dr. Droon?"

"That's correct."

"Dr. Droon," Halet remarked, "has obtained a permit from the Planetary Moderator, authorizing him to claim Tick-Tock for the University League and remove her from the planet, dear. So you see there is simply nothing we can do about the matter! Your mother wouldn't like us to attempt to obstruct the law, would she?" Halet paused. "The permit should have your signature, Telzey, but I can sign in your stead if necessary."

That was Halet's way of saying it would do no good to appeal to Jontarou's Planetary Moderator. She'd taken the precaution of getting his assent to the matter first.

"So now if you'll just call Tick-Tock, dear . . ." Halet went on.

Telzey barely heard the last words. She felt herself stiffening slowly, while the living room almost faded from her sight. Perhaps, in that instant, some additional new circuit had closed in her mind, or some additional new channel had opened, for TT's purpose in tricking her into contact with the reckless, mocking beings outside was suddenly and numbingly clear.

And what it meant immediately was that she'd have to get out of the house without being spotted at it, and go some place where she could be undisturbed for half an hour.

She realized that Halet and the zoologist were both staring at her.

"Are you ill, dear?"

"No." Telzey stood up. It would be worse than useless to try to tell these two anything! Her face must be pretty white at the moment—she could feel it—but they assumed, of course, that the shock of losing TT had just now sunk in on her.

"I'll have to check on that law you mentioned before I sign anything," she told Dr. Droon.

"Why, yes . . ." He started to get out of his chair. "I'm sure that can be arranged, Miss Amberdon!"

"Don't bother to call the Moderator's office," Telzey said. "I brought my law library along. I'll look it up myself." She turned to leave the room.

"My niece," Halet explained to Dr. Droon who was beginning to look puzzled, "attends law school. She's always so absorbed in her studies . . . Telzey?"

"Yes, Halet?" Telzey paused at the door.

"I'm very glad you've decided to be sensible about this, dear. But don't take too long, will you? We don't want to waste Dr. Droon's time."

"It shouldn't take more than five or ten minutes," Telzey told her agreeably. She closed the door behind her, and went directly to her bedroom on the second floor. One of her two valises was still unpacked. She locked the door behind her, opened the unpacked valise, took out a pocket edition law library and sat down at the table with it.

She clicked on the library's viewscreen, tapped the clearing and index buttons. Behind the screen, one of the multiple rows of pinhead tapes shifted slightly as the index was flicked into reading position. Half a minute later, she was glancing over the legal section on which Dr. Droon had based his claim. The library confirmed what he had said.

Very neat of Halet, Telzey thought, very nasty . . . and pretty idiotic! Even a second-year law student could think immediately of two or three ways in which a case like that could have been dragged out in the Federation's courts for a couple of decades before the question of handing Tick-Tock over to the Life Banks became too acute.

Well, Halet simply wasn't really intelligent. And the plot to shanghai TT was hardly even a side issue now.

Telzey snapped the tiny library shut, fastened it to the belt of her sunsuit and went over to the open window. A two-foot ledge passed beneath the window, leading to the roof of a patio on the right. Fifty yards beyond the patio, the garden ended in a natural-stone wall. Behind it lay one of the big wooded park areas which formed most of the ground level of Port Nichay.

Tick-Tock wasn't in sight. A sound of voices came from ground-floor windows on the left. Halet had brought her maid and chauffeur along; and a chef had showed up in time to make breakfast this morning, as part of the city's guest house service. Telzey took the empty valise to the window, set it on end against the left side of the frame, and let the window slide down until its lower edge rested on the valise. She went back to the house guard-screen panel beside the door, put her finger against the lock button, and pushed.

The sound of voices from the lower floor was cut off as outer doors and windows slid silently shut all about the house. Telzey glanced back at the window. The valise had creaked a little as the guard field drove the frame down on it, but it was supporting the thrust. She returned to the window, wriggled feet foremost through the opening, twisted around and got a footing on the ledge.

A minute later, she was scrambling quietly down a vine-covered patio trellis to the ground. Even after they discovered she was gone, the guard screen would keep everybody in the house for some little while. They'd either have to disengage the screen's main mechanisms and start poking around in them, or force open the door

James H. Schmitz

to her bedroom and get the lock unset. Either approach would involve confusion, upset tempers, and generally delay any organized pursuit.

Telzey edged around the patio and started towards the wall, keeping close to the side of the house so she couldn't be seen from the windows. The shrubbery made minor rustling noises as she threaded her way through it . . . and then there was a different stirring which might have been no more than a slow, steady current of air moving among the bushes behind her. She shivered involuntarily but didn't look back.

She came to the wall, stood still, measuring its height, jumped and got an arm across it, swung up a knee and squirmed up and over. She came down on her feet with a small thump in the grass on the other side, glanced back once at the guest house, crossed a path and went on among the park trees.

Within a few hundred yards, it became apparent that she had an escort. She didn't look around for them, but spread out to right and left like a skirmish line, keeping abreast with her, occasional shadows slid silently through patches of open, sunlit ground, disappeared again under the trees. Otherwise, there was hardly anyone in sight. Port Nichay's human residents appeared to make almost no personal use of the vast parkland spread out beneath their tower apartments; and its traffic moved over the airways, visible from the ground only as rainbow-hued ribbons which bisected the sky between the upper tower levels. An occasional private aircar went by overhead.

Wisps of thought which were not her own thoughts flicked through Telzey's mind from moment to moment as the silent line of shadows moved deeper into the park with her. She realized she was being sized up, judged, evaluated again. No more information was coming through; they had given her as much information as she needed. In the main perhaps, they were simply curious now. This was the first human mind they'd been able to make heads or tails of, and that hadn't seemed deaf and silent to their form of communication. They were taking time out to study it. They'd been assured she would have something of genuine importance to tell them; and there was some derision about that. But they were willing to wait a little, and find out. They were curious and they liked games. At the moment, Telzey and what she might try to do to change their plans was the game on which their attention was fixed.

Twelve minutes passed before the talker on Telzey's wrist began to buzz. It continued to signal off and on for another few minutes, then stopped. Back in the guest house they couldn't be sure yet whether she wasn't simply locked inside her room and refusing to answer them. But Telzey quickened her pace.

The park's trees gradually became more massive, reached higher above her, stood spaced more widely apart. She passed through the morning shadow of the residential tower nearest the guest house, and emerged from it presently on the shore of a small lake. On the other side of the lake, a number of dappled grazing animals like long-necked, tall horses lifted their heads to watch her. For some seconds they seemed only mildly interested, but then a breeze moved across the lake, crinkling the surface of the water; and as it touched the opposite shore, abrupt panic exploded among the grazers. They wheeled, went flashing away in effortless twenty-foot strides, and were gone among the trees.

Telzey felt a crawling along her spine. It was the first objective indication she'd had of the nature of the company she had brought to the lake, and while it hardly came as a surprise, for a moment her urge was to follow the example of the grazers.

"Tick-Tock?" she whispered, suddenly a little short of breath.

A single up-and-down purring note replied from the bushes on her right. TT was still around, for whatever good that might do. Not too much, Telzey thought, if it came to serious trouble. But the knowledge was somewhat reassuring . . . and this, meanwhile, appeared to be as far as she needed to get from the guest house. They'd be looking for her by aircar presently, but there was nothing to tell them in which direction to turn first.

She climbed the bank of the lake to a point where she was screened both by thick, green shrubbery and the top of a single immense tree from the sky, sat down on some dry, mossy growth, took the law library from her belt, opened it and placed it in her lap. Vague stirrings indicated that her escort was also settling down in an irregular circle about her; and apprehension shivered on Telzey's skin again. It wasn't that their attitude was hostile; they were simply overawing. And no one could predict what they might do next. Without looking up, she asked a question in her mind.

"Ready?"

Sense of multiple acknowledgment, variously tinged—sardonic; interestedly amused; attentive; doubtful. Impatience quivered through it too, only tentatively held in restraint, and Telzey's forehead was suddenly wet. Some of them seemed on the verge of expressing disapproval with what was being done here—

Her fingers quickly flicked in the index tape, and the stir of feeling about her subsided, their attention captured again for the moment. Her thoughts became to some degree detached, ready to dissect another problem in the familiar ways and present the answers to it. Not a very involved problem essentially, but this time it wasn't a school exercise. Her company waited, withdrawn, silent, aloof once more, while the index blurred, checked, blurred and checked. Within a minute and a half, she had noted a dozen reference symbols. She tapped in another of the pinhead tapes, glanced over a few paragraphs, licked salty sweat from her lip, and said in her thoughts, emphasizing the meaning of each detail of the sentence so that there would be no misunderstanding, "This is the Federation law that applies to the situation which existed originally on this planet. . . ."

There were no interruptions, no commenting thoughts, no intrusions of any kind, as she went step by step through the section, turned to another one, and another. In perhaps twelve minutes she came to the end of the last one, and stopped. Instantly, argument exploded about her.

James H. Schmitz

Telzey was not involved in the argument; in fact, she could grasp only scraps of it. Either they were excluding her deliberately, or the exchange was too swift, practiced and varied to allow her to keep up. But their vehemence was not encouraging. And was it reasonable to assume that the Federation's laws would have any meaning for minds like these? Telzey snapped the library shut with fingers that had begun to tremble, and placed it on the ground. Then she stiffened. In the sensations washing about her, a special excitement rose suddenly, a surge of almost gleeful wildness that choked away her breath. Awareness followed of a pair of malignant crimson eyes fastened on her, moving steadily closer. A kind of nightmare paralysis seized Telzey—they'd turned her over to that red-eyed horror! She sat still, feeling mouse-sized.

Something came out with a crash from a thicket behind her. Her muscles went tight. But it was TT who rubbed a hard head against her shoulder, took another three stiff-legged steps forward and stopped between Telzey and the bushes on their right, back rigid, neck fur erect, tail twisting.

Expectant silence closed in about them. The circle was waiting. In the greenery on the right something made a slow, heavy stir.

TT's lips peeled back from her teeth. Her head swung towards the motion, ears flattening, transformed to a split, snarling demon-mask. A long shriek ripped from her lungs, raw with fury, blood lust and challenge.

The sound died away. For some seconds the tension about them held; then came a sense of gradual relaxation mingled with a partly amused approval. Telzey was shaking violently. It had been, she was telling herself, a deliberate test . . . not of herself, of course, but of TT. And Tick-Tock had passed with honors. That her nerves had been half ruined in the process would seem a matter of no consequence to this rugged crew . . .

She realized next that someone here was addressing her personally.

It took a few moments to steady her jittering thoughts enough to gain a more definite impression than that. This speaker, she discovered then, was a member of the circle of whom she hadn't been aware before. The thought-impressions came hard and cold as iron—a personage who was very evidently in the habit of making major decisions and seeing them carried out. The circle, its moment of sport over, was listening with more than a suggestion of deference. Tick-Tock, far from conciliated, green eyes still blazing, nevertheless was settling down to listen, too.

Telzey began to understand.

Her suggestions, Iron Thoughts informed her, might appear without value to a number of foolish minds here, but *he* intended to see they were given a fair trial. Did he perhaps hear, he inquired next of the circle, throwing in a casual but horridly vivid impression of snapping spines and slashed shaggy throats spouting blood, any objection to that?

Dead stillness all around. There was, definitely, no objection! Tick-Tock began to grin like a pleased kitten.

That point having been settled in an orderly manner now, Iron Thoughts went on coldly to Telzey, what specifically did she propose they should do?

Halet's long, pearl-gray sportscar showed up above the park trees twenty minutes later. Telzey, face turned down towards the open law library in her lap, watched the car from the corner of her eyes. She was in plain view, sitting beside the lake, apparently absorbed in legal research. Tick-Tock, camouflaged among the bushes thirty feet higher up the bank, had spotted the car an instant before she did and announced the fact with a three-second break in her purring. Neither of them made any other move.

The car was approaching the lake but still a good distance off. Its canopy was down, and Telzey could just make out the heads of three people inside. Delquos, Halet's chauffeur, would be flying the vehicle, while Halet and Dr. Droon looked around for her from the sides. Three hundred yards away, the aircar began a turn to the right. Delquos didn't like his employer much; at a guess, he had just spotted Telzey and was trying to warn her off.

Telzey closed the library and put it down, picked up a handful of pebbles and began flicking them idly, one at a time, into the water. The aircar vanished to her left.

Three minutes later, she watched its shadow glide across the surface of the lake towards her. Her heart began to thump almost audibly, but she didn't look up. Tick-Tock's purring continued, on its regular, unhurried note. The car came to a stop almost directly overhead. After a couple of seconds, there was a clicking noise. The purring ended abruptly.

Telzey climbed to her feet as Delquos brought the car down to the bank of the lake. The chauffeur grinned ruefully at her. A side door had been opened, and Halet and Dr. Droon stood behind it. Halet watched Telzey with a small smile while the naturalist put the heavy life-detector-and-stungun device carefully down on the floorboards.

"If you're looking for Tick-Tock," Telzey said, "she isn't here."

Halet just shook her head sorrowfully.

"There's no use lying to us, dear! Dr. Droon just stunned her."

They found TT collapsed on her side among the shrubs, wearing her natural color. Her eyes were shut; her chest rose and fell in a slow breathing motion. Dr. Droon, looking rather apologetic, pointed out to Telzey that her pet was in no pain, that the stungun had simply put her comfortably to sleep. He also explained the use of the two sets of webbed paralysis belts which he fastened about TT's legs. The effect of the stun charge would wear off in a few minutes, and contact with the inner surfaces of the energized belts would then keep TT anesthetized and unable to move until the belts were removed. She would, he repeated, be suffering no pain throughout the process.

Telzey didn't comment. She watched Delquos raise TT's limp body above the level

James H. Schmitz

of the bushes with a gravity hoist belonging to Dr. Droon, and maneuver her back to the car, the others following. Delquos climbed into the car first, opened the big trunk compartment in the rear. TT was slid inside and the trunk compartment locked.

"Where are you taking her?" Telzey asked sullenly as Delquos lifted the car into the air.

"To the spaceport, dear," Halet said. "Dr. Droon and I both felt it would be better to spare your feelings by not prolonging the matter unnecessarily."

Telzey wrinkled her nose disdainfully, and walked up the aircar to stand behind Delquos' seat. The leaned against the back of the seat for an instant. Her legs felt shaky.

The chauffeur gave her a sober wink from the side.

"That's a dirty trick she's played on you, Miss Telzey!" he murmured. "I tried to warn you."

"I know." Telzey took a deep breath. "Look, Delquos, in just a minute something's going to happen! It'll look dangerous, but it won't be. Don't let it get you nervous . . . right?"

"Huh?" Delquos appeared startled, but kept his voice low. "Just *what's* going to happen?"

"No time to tell you. Remember what I said."

Telzey moved back a few steps from the driver's seat, turned around, said unsteadily, "Halet . . . Dr. Droon—"

Halet had been speaking quietly to Dr. Droon; they both looked up.

"If you don't move, and don't do anything stupid," Telzey said rapidly, "you won't get hurt. If you do . . . well, I don't know! You see, there's another crest cat in the car . . ." In her mind she added, "Now!"

It was impossible to tell in just what section of the car Iron Thoughts had been lurking. The carpeting near the rear passenger seats seemed to blur for an instant. Then he was there, camouflage dropped, sitting on the floorboards five feet from the naturalist and Halet.

Halet's mouth opened wide; she tried to scream but fainted instead. Dr. Droon's right hand started out quickly towards the big stungun device beside his seat. Then he checked himself and sat still, ashen-faced.

Telzey didn't blame him for changing his mind. She felt he must be a remarkably brave man to have moved at all. Iron Thoughts, twice as broad across the back as Tick-Tock, twice as massively muscled, looked like a devil-beast even to her. His dark-green marbled hide was criss-crossed with old scar patterns; half his tossing crimson crest appeared to have been ripped away. He reached out now in a fluid, silent motion, hooked a paw under the stungun and flicked upwards. The big instrument rose in an incredibly swift, steep arc eighty feet into the air, various parts flying away from it, before it started curving down toward the treetops below the car. Iron Thoughts lazily swung his head around and looked at Telzey with yellow fire-eyes.

"Miss Telzey! Miss Telzey!" Delquos was muttering behind her. "You're sure it won't . . ."

Telzey swallowed. At the moment, she felt barely mouse-sized again. "Just relax!" she told Delquos in a shaky voice. "He's really quite t-t-t-tame."

Iron Thoughts produced a harsh but not unamiable chuckle in her mind.

The pearl-gray sportscar, covered now by its streamlining canopy, drifted down presently to a parking platform outside the suite of offices of Jontarou's Planetary Moderator, on the fourteenth floor of the Shikaris' Club Tower. An attendant waved it on into a vacant slot.

Inside the car, Delquos set the brakes, switched off the engine, asked, "Now what?"

"I think," Telzey said reflectively, "we'd better lock you in the trunk compartment with my aunt and Dr. Droon while I talk to the Moderator."

The chauffeur shrugged. He'd regained most of his aplomb during the unhurried trip across the parklands. Iron Thoughts had done nothing but sit in the center of the car, eyes half shut, looking like instant death enjoying a dignified nap and occasionally emitting a ripsawing noise which might have been either his style of purring or a snore. And Tick-Tock, when Delquos peeled the paralysis belts off her legs at Telzey's direction, had greeted him with her usual reserved affability. What the chauffeur was suffering from at the moment was intense curiosity, which Telzey had done nothing to relieve.

"Just as you say, Miss Telzey," he agreed. "I hate to miss whatever you're going to be doing here, but if you *don't* lock me up now, Miss Halet will figure I was helping you and fire me as soon as you let her out."

Telzey nodded, then cocked her head in the direction of the rear compartment. Faint sounds coming through the door indicated that Halet had regained consciousness and was having hysterics.

"You might tell her," Telzey suggested, "that there'll be a grown-up crest cat sitting outside the compartment door." This wasn't true, but neither Delquos nor Halet could know it. "If there's too much racket before I get back, it's likely to irritate him . . ."

A minute later, she set both car doors on lock and went outside, wishing she were less informally clothed. Sunbriefs and sandals tended to make her look juvenile.

The parking attendant appeared startled when she approached him with Tick-Tock striding alongside.

"They'll never let you into the offices with that thing, miss," he informed her. "Why, it doesn't even have a collar!"

"Don't worry about it," Telzey told him aloofly.

She dropped a two-credit piece she'd taken from Halet's purse into his hand, and continued on toward the building entrance. The attendant squinted after her, trying

James H. Schmitz

unsuccessfully to dispel an odd impression that the big catlike animal with the girl was throwing a double shadow.

The Moderator's chief receptionist also had some doubts about TT, and possibly about the sunbriefs, though she seemed impressed when Telzey's identification tag informed her she was speaking to the daughter of Federation Councilwoman Jessamine Amberdon.

"You feel you can discuss this . . . emergency . . . only with the Moderator himself, Miss Amberdon?" she repeated.

"Exactly," Telzey said firmly. A buzzer sounded as she spoke. The receptionist excused herself and picked up an earphone. She listened a moment, said blandly, "Yes . . . Of course . . . Yes, I understand," replaced the earphone and stood up, smiling at Telzey.

"Would you come with me, Miss Amberdon?" she said. "I think the Moderator will see you immediately . . ."

Telzey followed her, chewing thoughtfully at her lip. This was easier than she'd expected—in fact, too easy! Halet's work? Probably. A few comments to the effect of "A highly imaginative child . . . overexcitable," while Halet was arranging to have the Moderator's office authorize Tick-Tock's transfer to the Life Banks, along with the implication that Jessamine Amberdon would appreciate a discreet handling of any disturbance Telzey might create as a result.

It was the sort of notion that would appeal to Halet—

They passed through a series of elegantly equipped offices and hallways, Telzey grasping TT's neck-fur in lieu of a leash, their appearance creating a tactfully restrained wave of surprise among secretaries and clerks. And if somebody here and there was troubled by a fleeting, uncanny impression that not one large beast but two seemed to be trailing the Moderator's visitor down the aisles, no mention was made of what could have been only a momentary visual distortion. Finally, a pair of sliding doors opened ahead, and the receptionist ushered Telzey into a large, cool balcony garden on the shaded side of the great building. A tall, gray-haired man stood up from the desk at which he was working, and bowed to Telzey. The receptionist withdrew again.

"My pleasure, Miss Amberdon," Jontarou's Planetary Moderator said, "be seated, please." He studied Tick-Tock with more than casual interest while Telzey was settling herself into a chair, added, "And what may I and my office do for you?"

Telzey hesitated. She'd observed his type on Orado in her mother's circle of acquaintances—a senior diplomat, a man not easy to impress. It was a safe bet that he'd had her brought out to his balcony office only to keep her occupied while Halet was quietly informed where the Amberdon problem child was and requested to come over and take charge.

What she had to tell him now would have sounded rather wild even if presented by a presumably responsible adult. She could provide proof, but until the Moderator was already nearly sold on her story, that would be a very unsafe thing to do. Old

Iron Thoughts was backing her up, but if it didn't look as if her plans were likely to succeed, he would be willing to ride herd on his devil's pack just so long . . .

Better start the ball rolling without any preliminaries, Telzey decided. The Moderator's picture of her must be that of a spoiled, neurotic brat in a stew about the threatened loss of a pet animal. He expected her to start arguing with him immediately about Tick-Tock.

She said, "Do you have a personal interest in keeping the Baluit crest cats from becoming extinct?"

Surprise flickered in his eyes for an instant. Then he smiled.

"I admit I do, Miss Amberdon," he said pleasantly. "I should like to see the species re-established. I count myself almost uniquely fortunate in having had the opportunity to bag two of the magnificent brutes before disease wiped them out on the planet."

The last seemed a less than fortunate statement just now. Telzey felt a sharp tingle of alarm, then sensed that in the minds which were drawing the meaning of the Moderator's speech from her mind there had been only a brief stir of interest.

She cleared her throat, said, "The point is that they weren't wiped out by disease."

He considered her quizzically, seemed to wonder what she was trying to lead up to. Telzey gathered her courage, plunged on, "Would you like to hear what did happen?"

"I should be much interested, Miss Amberdon," the Moderator said without change of expression. "But first, if you'll excuse me a moment . . ."

There had been some signal from his desk which Telzey hadn't noticed, because he picked up a small communicator now, said, "Yes?" After a few seconds, he resumed, "That's rather curious, isn't it? . . . Yes, I'd try that . . . No, that shouldn't be necessary . . . Yes, please do. Thank you." He replaced the communicator, his face very sober; then, his eyes flicking for an instant to TT, he drew one of the upper desk drawers open a few inches, and turned back to Telzey.

"Now, Miss Amberdon," he said affably, "you were about to say? About these crest cats . . ."

Telzey swallowed. She hadn't heard the other side of the conversation, but she could guess what it had been about. His office had called the guest house, had been told by Halet's maid that Halet, the chauffeur, and Dr. Droon were out looking for Miss Telzey and her pet. The Moderator's office had then checked on the sportscar's communication number and attempted to call it. And, of course, there had been no response.

To the Moderator, considering what Halet would have told him, it must add up to the grim possibility that the young lunatic he was talking to had let her three-quarters-grown crest cat slaughter her aunt and the two men when they caught up with her! The office would be notifying the police now to conduct an immediate search for the missing aircar.

James H. Schmitz

When it would occur to them to look for it on the Moderator's parking terrace was something Telzey couldn't know. But if Halet and Dr. Droon were released before the Moderator accepted her own version of what had occurred, and the two reported the presence of wild crest cats in Port Nichay, there would be almost no possibility of keeping the situation under control. Somebody was bound to make some idiotic move, and the fat would be in the fire . . .

Two things might be in her favor. The Moderator seemed to have the sort of steady nerve one would expect in a man who had bagged two Baluit crest cats. The partly opened desk drawer beside him must have a gun in it; apparently he considered that a sufficient precaution against an attack by TT. He wasn't likely to react in a panicky manner. And the mere fact that he suspected Telzey of homicidal tendencies would make him give the closest attention to what she said. Whether he believed her then was another matter, of course.

Slightly encouraged, Telzey began to talk. It did sound like a thoroughly wild story, but the Moderator listened with an appearance of intent interest. When she had told him as much as she felt he could be expected to swallow for a start, he said musingly, "So they weren't wiped out—they went into hiding! Do I understand you to say they did it to avoid being hunted?"

Telzey chewed her lip frowningly before replying. "There's something about that part I don't quite get," she admitted. "Of course I don't quite get either why you'd want to go hunting . . . twice . . . for something that's just as likely to bag you instead!"

"Well, those are, ah, merely the statistical odds," the Moderator explained. "If one has enough confidence, you see—"

"I don't really. But the crest cats seem to have felt the same way—at first. They were getting around one hunter for every cat that got shot. Humans were the most exciting game they'd ever run into.

"But then that ended, and the humans started knocking them out with stunguns from aircars where they couldn't be got at, and hauling them off while they were helpless. After it had gone on for a while, they decided to keep out of sight.

"But they're still around . . . thousands and thousands of them! Another thing nobody's known about them is that they weren't only in the Baluit mountains. There were crest cats scattered all through the big forests along the other side of the continent."

"Very interesting," the Moderator commented. "Very interesting, indeed!" He glanced towards the communicator, then returned his gaze to Telzey, drumming his fingers lightly on the desk top.

She could tell nothing at all from his expression now, but she guessed he was thinking hard. There was supposed to be no native intelligent life in the legal sense on Jontarou, and she had been careful to say nothing so far to make the Baluit cats look like more than rather exceptionally intelligent animals. The next—rather large—question should be how she'd come by such information.

If the Moderator asked her that, Telzey thought, she could feel she'd made a beginning at getting him to buy the whole story.

"Well," he said abruptly, "if the crest cats are not extinct or threatened with extinction, the Life Banks obviously have no claim on your pet." He smiled confidingly at her. "And that's the reason you're here, isn't it?"

"Well, no," Telzey began, dismayed. "I—"

"Oh, it's quite all right, Miss Amberdon! I'll simply rescind the permit which was issued for the purpose. You need feel no further concern about that." He paused. "Now, just one question . . . do you happen to know where your aunt is at present?"

Telzey had a dead, sinking feeling. So he hadn't believed a word she said. He'd been stalling her along until the aircar could be found.

She took a deep breath. "You'd better listen to the rest of it."

"Why, is there more?" the Moderator asked politely.

"Yes. The important part! The kind of creatures they are, they wouldn't go into hiding indefinitely just because someone was after them."

Was there a flicker of something beyond watchfulness in his expression. "What would they do, Miss Amberdon?" he asked quietly.

"If they couldn't get at the men in the aircars and couldn't communicate with them"—the flicker again!—"they'd start looking for the place the men came from, wouldn't they? It might take them some years to work their way across the continent and locate us here in Port Nichay. But supposing they did it finally and a few thousand of them are sitting around in the parks down there right now? They could come up the side of these towers as easily as they go up the side of a mountain. And supposing they'd decided that the only way to handle the problem was to clean out the human beings in Port Nichay?"

The Moderator stared at her in silence a few seconds. "You're saying," he observed then "that they're rational beings—above the Critical I. Q. level."

"Well," Telzey said, "legally they're rational. I checked on that. About as rational as we are, I suppose."

"Would you mind telling me now how you happen to know this?"

"They told me," Telzey said.

He was silent again, studying her face. "You mentioned, Miss Amberdon, that they have been unable to communicate with other human beings. This suggests then that you are a xenotelepath . . ."

"I am?" Telzey hadn't heard the term before. "If it means that I can tell what the cats are thinking, and they can tell what I'm thinking, I guess that's the word for it." She considered him, decided she had him almost on the ropes, went on quickly.

"I looked up the laws, and told them they could conclude a treaty with the Federation which would establish them as an Affiliated Species . . . and that would settle everything the way they would want it settled, without trouble. Some of them believed me. They decided to wait until I could talk to you. If it works out, fine! If it doesn't"—she felt her voice falter for an instant—"they're going to cut loose fast!"

The Moderator seemed undisturbed. "What am I supposed to do?"

"I told them you'd contact the Council of the Federation on Orado."

"Contact the Council?" he repeated coolly. "With no more proof for this story than your word, Miss Amberdon?"

Telzey felt a quick, angry stirring begin about her, felt her face whiten.

"All right," she said. "I'll give you proof! I'll have to now. But that'll be it. Once they've tipped their hand all the way, you'll have about thirty seconds left to make the right move. I hope you remember that!"

He cleared his throat. "I—"

"NOW!" Telzey said.

Along the walls of the balcony garden, beside the ornamental flower stands, against the edges of the rock pool, the crest cats appeared. Perhaps thirty of them. None quite as physically impressive as Iron Thoughts, who stood closest to the Moderator; but none very far from it. Motionless as rocks, frightening as gargoyles, they waited, eyes glowing with hellish excitement.

"This is *their* council, you see," Telzey heard herself saying.

The Moderator's face had also paled. But he was, after all, an old shikari and a senior diplomat. He took an unhurried look around the circle, said quietly, "Accept my profound apologies for doubting you, Miss Amberdon!" and reached for the desk communicator.

Iron Thoughts swung his demon head in Telzey's direction. For an instant, she picked up the mental impression of a fierce yellow eye closing in an approving wink.

"An open transmitter line to Orado," the Moderator was saying into the communicator. "The Council. And snap it up! Some very important visitors are waiting."

The offices of Jontarou's Planetary Moderator became an extremely busy and interesting area then. Quite two hours passed before it occurred to anyone to ask Telzey again whether she knew where her aunt was at present.

Telzey smote her forehead.

"Forgot all about that!" she admitted, fishing the sportscar's keys out of the pocket of her sunbriefs. "They're out on the parking platform . . ."

The preliminary treaty arrangements between the Federation of the Hub and the new Affiliated Species of the Planet of Jontarou were formally ratified two weeks later, the ceremony taking place on Jontarou, in the Champagne Hall of the Shikaris' Club.

Telzey was able to follow the event only by news viewer in her ship-cabin, she and Halet being on the return trip to Orado by then. She wasn't too interested in the treaty's details—they conformed almost exactly to what she had read out to Iron

Thoughts and his co-chiefs and companions in the park. It was the smooth bridging of the wide language gap between the contracting parties by a row of interpreting machines and a handful of human xenotelepaths which held her attention.

As she switched off the viewer, Halet came wandering in from the adjoining cabin.

"I was watching it, too!" Halet observed. She smiled. "I was hoping to see dear Tick-Tock."

Telzey looked over at her. "Well, TT would hardly be likely to show up in Port Nichay," she said. "She's having too good a time now finding out what life in the Baluit range is like."

"I suppose so," Halet agreed doubtfully, sitting down on a hassock. "But I'm glad she promised to get in touch with us again in a few years. I'll miss her."

Telzey regarded her aunt with a reflective frown. Halet meant it quite sincerely, of course; she had undergone a profound change of heart during the past two weeks. But Telzey wasn't without some doubts about the actual value of a change of heart brought on by telepathic means. The learning process the crest cats had started in her mind appeared to have continued automatically several days longer than her rugged teachers had really intended; and Telzey had reason to believe that by the end of that time she'd developed associated latent abilities of which the crest cats had never heard. She'd barely begun to get it all sorted out yet, but . . . as an example . . . she'd found it remarkably easy to turn Halet's more obnoxious attitudes virtually upside down. It had taken her a couple of days to get the hang of her aunt's personal symbolism, but after that there had been no problem.

She was reasonably certain she'd broken no laws so far, though the sections in the law library covering the use and abuse of psionic abilities were veiled in such intricate and downright obscuring phrasing—deliberately, Telzey suspected—that it was really difficult to say what they did mean. But even aside from that, there were a number of arguments in favor of exercising great caution.

Jessamine, for one thing, was bound to start worrying about her sister-in-law's health if Halet turned up on Orado in her present state of mind, even though it would make for a far more agreeable atmosphere in the Amberdon household.

"Halet," Telzey inquired mentally, "do you remember what an all-out stinker you used to be?"

"Of course, dear," Halet said aloud. "I can hardly wait to tell dear Jessamine how much I regret the many times I . . ."

"Well," Telzey went on, still verbalizing it silently, "I think you'd really enjoy life more if you were, let's say, about halfway between your old nasty self and the sort of sickening-good kind you are now."

"Why, Telzey!" Halet cried out with dopey amiability. "What a delightful idea!"

"Let's try it," Telzey said.

There was silence in the cabin for some twenty minutes then while she went painstakingly about remolding a number of Halet's character traits for the second time.

James H. Schmitz

She still felt some misgiving about it; but if it became necessary, she probably could always restore the old Halet *in toto*.

These, she told herself, definitely were powers one should treat with respect! Better rattle through law school first; then, with that out of the way, she could start hunting around to see who in the Federation was qualified to instruct a genius-level novice in the proper handling of psionics. . . . ■

CHILD OF ALL AGES
P. J. Plauger

The child sat in the waiting room with her hands folded neatly on her lap. She wore a gay print dress made of one of those materials that would have quickly revealed its cheapness had it not been carefully pressed. Her matching shoes had received the same meticulous care. She sat prim and erect, no fidgeting, no scuffing of shoes against chair legs, exhibiting a patience that legions of nuns have striven, in vain, to instill in other children. This one looked as if she had done a lot of waiting.

May Foster drew back from the two-way mirror through which she had been studying her newest problem. She always felt a little guilty about spying on children like this before an interview, but she readily conceded to herself that it helped her handle cases better. By sizing up an interviewee in advance, she saved precious minutes of sparring and could usually gain the upper hand right at the start. Dealing with "problem" children was a no-holds-barred proposition, if you wanted to survive in the job without ulcers.

That patience could be part of her act, May thought for a moment. But no, that didn't make sense. Superb actors that they were, these kids always reserved their performances for an audience; there was no reason for the girl to suspect the special mirror on this, her first visit to Mrs. Foster's office. One of the best advantages to be gained from the mirror, in fact, was the knowledge of how the child behaved when a social worker wasn't in the room. Jekyll and Hyde looked like twins compared to the personality changes May had witnessed in fifteen years of counseling.

May stepped out of the darkened closet, turned on the room lights and returned to her desk. She scanned the folder one last time, closed it in front of her and depressed the intercom button.

"Louise, you can bring the child in now."

There was a slight delay, then the office door opened and the child stepped in. For all her preparation, May was taken aback. The girl was thin, much thinner than she looked sitting down, but not to the point of being unhealthy. Rather, it was the kind of thinness one finds in people who are still active in their nineties. Not wiry, but enduring. And those eyes.

May was one of the first Peace Corps volunteers to go into central Africa. For two years she fought famine and malnutrition with every weapon, save money, that modern technology could bring to bear. In the end it was a losing battle, because politics and tribal hatred dictated that thousands upon thousands must die the slow death of starvation. That was where she had seen eyes like that before.

Children could endure pain and hunger, forced marches, even the loss of their parents, and still recover eventually with the elasticity of youth. But when their flesh melted down to the bone, their bellies distended, then a look came into their eyes that remained ever with them for their few remaining days. It was the lesson learned much too young that the adult world was not worthy of their trust, the realization that death was a real and imminent force in their world. For ten years after, May's nightmares were haunted by children staring at her with those eyes.

Now this one stood before her and stared into her soul with eyes that had looked too intimately upon death.

As quickly as she had been captured, May felt herself freed. The girl glanced about the room, as if checking for fire exits, took in the contents of May's desk with one quick sweep, then marched up to the visitor's chair and planted herself in it with a thump.

"My name is Melissa," she said, adding a nervous grin. "You must be Mrs. Foster." She was all little girl now, squirming the least little bit and kicking one shoe against another. The eyes shone with carefree youth.

May shook herself, slowly recovered. She thought she had seen everything before, until now. The guileless bit was perfect—Melissa looked more like a model eight-year-old than a chronic trouble-maker going on, what was it? Fourteen. *Fourteen?*

"You've been suspended from school for the third time this year, Melissa," she said with professional sternness. May turned on her best Authoritarian Glare, force three.

"Yep," the child said with no trace of contrition. The Glare faded, switched to Sympathetic Understanding.

"Do you want to tell me about it?" May asked softly.

Melissa shrugged.

"What's to say? Old Man M—uh, Mr. Morrisey and I got into an argument again in history class." She giggled. "He had to pull rank on me to win." Straight face.

"Mr. Morrisey has been teaching history for many years," May placated. "Perhaps he felt that he knows more about the subject than you do."

"Morrisey has his head wedged!" May's eyebrows skyrocketed, but the girl ignored the reproach, in her irritation. "Do you know what he was trying to palm off on the class? He was trying to say that the Industrial Revolution in England was a step backward.

"Kids working six, seven days a week in the factories, going fourteen hours at a stretch, all to earn a few pennies a week. That's all he could see! He never thought to ask *why* they did it if conditions were so bad."

"Well, why did they?" May asked reflexively. She was caught up in the child's enthusiasm.

The girl looked at her pityingly.

"Because it was the best game in town, that's why. If you didn't like the factory, you could try your hand at begging, stealing, or working on a farm. If you got caught begging or stealing in those days they boiled you in oil. No joke. And farm work." She made a face.

"That was seven days a week of busting your tail from *before* sunup to *after* sundown. And what did you have to show for it? In a good year, you got all you could eat; in a bad year you starved. But you worked just as hard on an empty gut as on a full one. Harder.

"At least with a factory job you had money to buy what food there was when the crops failed. That's progress, no matter how you look at it."

May thought for a moment.

"But what about all the children maimed by machinery?" she asked. "What about all the kids whose health was destroyed from breathing dust or stoking fires or not getting enough sun?"

"Ever seen a plowboy after a team of horses walked over him? Ever had sunstroke?" She snorted. "Sure those factories were bad, but everything else was *worse*. Try to tell that to Old Man Morrisey, though."

"You talk as if you were there," May said with a hint of amusement.

Flatly. "I read a lot."

May recalled herself to the business at hand.

"Even if you were right, you still could have been more tactful, you know." The girl simply glowered and hunkered down in her chair. "You've disrupted his class twice, now, and Miss Randolph's class too."

May paused, turned up Sympathetic Understanding another notch.

"I suspect your problem isn't just with school. How are things going at home?"

Melissa shrugged again. It was a very adult gesture.

"Home." Her tone eliminated every good connotation the word possessed. "My fa—my foster father died last year. Heart attack. Bam! Mrs. Stuart still hasn't gotten over it." A pause.

"Have you?"

The girl darted a quick glance.

"Everybody dies, sooner or later." Another pause. "I wish Mr. Stuart had hung around a while longer, though. He was OK."

"And your mother?" May prodded delicately.

"My *foster* mother can't wait for me to grow up and let her off the hook. Jeez, she'd marry me off next month if the law allowed." She stirred uncomfortably. "She keeps dragging boys home to take me out."

"Do you like going out with boys?"

A calculating glance.

"Some. I mean boys are OK, but I'm not ready to settle down quite yet." A nervous laugh. "I mean I don't *hate* boys or anything. I mean I've still got lots of time for that sort of stuff when I grow up."

"You're nearly fourteen."

"I'm small for my age."

Another tack.

"Does Mrs. Stuart feed you well?"

"Sure."

"Do you make sure you eat a balanced diet?"

"Of course. Look, I'm just naturally thin, is all. Mrs. Stuart may be a pain in the neck, but she's not trying to kill me off or anything. It's just that—" a sly smile crossed her face. "Oh, I get it."

Melissa shifted to a pedantic false baritone.

"A frequent syndrome in modern urban society is the apparently nutrition-deficient early pubescent female. Although in an economic environment that speaks against a lack of financial resources or dietary education, said subject nevertheless exhibits a seeming inability to acquire adequate sustenance for growth.

"Subject is often found in an environment lacking in one or more vital male supportive roles and, on close examination, reveals a morbid preoccupation with functional changes incident to the onset of womanhood. Dietary insufficiency is clearly a tacit vehicle for avoiding responsibilities associated with such changes."

She took an exaggerated deep breath.

"Whew! That Anderson is a long-winded son of a gun. So they stuck you with his book in Behav. Psych. too, huh?" She smiled sweetly.

"Why, yes. That is, we read it. How did you know?"

"Saw it on your bookshelf. Do you have any candy?"

"Uh, no."

"Too bad. The last social worker I dealt with always kept some on hand. You ought to, too. Good for public relations." Melissa looked aimlessly around the room.

May shook herself again. She hadn't felt so out of control in years. Not since they tried her out on the black ghetto kids. She dug in her heels.

"That was a very pretty performance, Melissa. I see you do read a lot. But did it ever occur to you that what Anderson said might still apply to you? Even if you do make a joke out of it."

"You mean, do I watch what I eat, because I'm afraid to grow up?" A nod. "You'd better believe it. But not because of that guff Anderson propagates."

The girl glanced at the photographs on the desk. looked keenly into May's eyes.

"Mrs. Foster, how open-minded are you? No, strike that. I've yet to meet a bigot who didn't think of himself as Blind Justice, Incarnate. Let's try a more pragmatic test. Do you read science fiction?"

"Uh, some."

"Fantasy?"

"A little."

"Well, what do you think of it? I mean, do you enjoy it?" Her eyes bored.

"Well, uh, I guess I like some of it. Quite a bit of it leaves me cold." She hesitated. "My husband reads it mostly. And my father-in-law. He's a biochemist," she added lamely, as though that excused something.

Melissa shrugged her adult shrug, made up her mind.

"What would you say if I told you my father was a wizard?"

"Frankly, I'd say you've built up an elaborate delusional system about your unknown parents. Orphans often do, you know."

"Yeah, Anderson again. But thanks for being honest; it was the right answer for you. I suspect, however," she paused, fixed the woman with an unwavering sidelong glance, "you're willing to believe that I might be more than your average maladjusted foster child."

Under that stare, May could do nothing but nod. Once. Slowly.

"What would you say if I told you that I am over twenty-four hundred years old?"

May felt surprise, fear, elation, an emotion that had no name.

"I'd say that you ought to meet my husband."

The child sat at the dinner table with her hands folded neatly on her lap. The three adults toyed with their aperitifs and made small talk. Melissa responded to each effort to bring her into the conversation with a few polite words, just the right number of just the right words for a well-behaved child to speak when she is a first-time dinner guest among people who hardly know her. But she never volunteered any small talk of her own.

George Foster, Jr., sensed that the seemingly innocent child sitting across from him was waiting them out, but he couldn't be sure. One thing he was sure of was that if this child were indeed older than Christendom he didn't have much chance against her in intellectual games. That much decided, he was perfectly willing to play out the evening in a straightforward manner. But in his own good time.

"Would you start the salad around, Dad?" he prompted. "I hope you like endive, Melissa. Or is that also a taste acquired in adulthood, like alcohol?" The girl had refused a dry sherry, politely but firmly.

"I'm sure I'll enjoy the salad, thank you. The dressing smells delicious. It's a personal recipe, isn't it?"

"Yes, as a matter of fact it is," George said in mild surprise. He suddenly realized that he habitually classified all thin people as picky, indifferent eaters. A gastronome didn't have to be overweight.

"Being a history professor gives me more freedom to schedule my time than May has," he found himself explaining. "It is an easy step from cooking because you must, to cooking because you enjoy it. That mustard dressing is one of my earliest inventions. Would you like the recipe?"

"Yes, thank you. I don't cook often, but when I do I like to produce something better than average." She delivered the pretty compliment with a seeming lack of guile. She also avoided, George noted, responding to the veiled probe about her age. He was becoming more and more impressed.

They broke bread and munched greens.

How do I handle this? By the way, May tells me you're twenty-four hundred years old. He met his father's eye, caught the faintest of shrugs. *Thanks for the help.*

"By the way, May tells me you were in England for a while." Now why in hell did he say that?

"I didn't actually say so, but yes, I was. Actually, we discussed the Industrial Revolution, briefly."

Were you there?

"I'm a medievalist, actually, but I'm also a bit of an Anglophile." George caught himself before he could lapse into the clipped, pseudo-British accent that phrase always triggered in him. He felt particularly vulnerable to making an ass of himself under that innocent gaze.

"Do you know much about English royalty?" He was about as subtle as a tonsillectomy.

"We studied it in school some."

"I always wanted to be another Admiral Nelson. Damned shame the way he died. What was it the king said after his funeral, it was Edward, I think—"

Melissa put her fork down.

"It was King George, and you know it. Look, before I came here I lived in Berkeley for a while." She caught May's look. "I know what my records say. After all, I wrote them . . . as I was saying, I was in Berkeley a few years back. It was right in the middle of the worst of the student unrest and we lived not three blocks from campus. Every day I walked those streets and every night we'd watch the riots and the thrashing on TV. Yet not once did I ever see one of those events with my own eyes."

She looked at them each in turn.

"Something could be happening a block away, something that attracted network television coverage and carloads of police, and I wouldn't know about it until I got home and turned on Cronkite. I think I may have smelled tear gas, once."

She picked up her fork.

"You can quiz me all you want to, Dr. Foster, about admirals and kings and dates. I guess that's what history is all about. But don't expect me to tell you about anything I didn't learn in school. Or see on television."

She stabbed viciously at a last scrap of endive. They watched her as she ate.

"Kids don't get invited to the events that make history. Until very recently all they ever did was work. Worked until they grew old or worked until they starved or worked until they were killed by a passing war. That's as close as most kids get to history, outside the classroom. Dates don't mean much when every day looks like every other.''

George was at a loss for something to say after that, so he got up and went to the sideboard where the main dishes were being kept warm. He made an elaborate exercise out of removing lids and collecting hot pads.

"Are you really twenty-four hundred years old?" asked George Foster, Sr. There, it was out in the open.

"Near as I can tell," spooning chicken and dumplings onto her plate. "Like I said, dates don't mean much to a kid. It was two or three hundred years before I gave much thought to when everything started. By then, it was a little hard to reconstruct. I make it twenty-four hundred and thirty-three years, now. Give or take a decade.''

Give or take a decade!

"And your father was a magician?" May pursued.

"Not a magician, a wizard." A little exasperated. "He didn't practice magic or cast spells; he was a wise man, a scholar. You could call him a scientist, except there wasn't too much science back then. Not that he didn't know a lot about some things—obviously he did—but he didn't work with an *organized* body of knowledge the way people do now.''

Somehow she had contrived to fill her plate and make a noticeable dent in her chicken without interrupting her narrative. George marveled at the girl's varied social talents.

"Anyway, he was working on a method of restoring youth. Everybody was, in those days. Very stylish. There was actually quite a bit of progress being made. I remember one old geezer actually renewed his sex life for about thirty years.''

"You mean, you know how to reverse aging?" George, Sr. asked intently. The candlelight couldn't erase all the lines in his face.

"Sorry, no, I didn't say that.'' She watched the elder Foster's expression closely, her tone earnestly entreating him to believe her. "I just said I know of one man who did that once. For a while. But he didn't tell anyone else how he did it, as far as I know. The knowledge died with him.''

Melissa turned to the others, looking for supporting belief.

"Look, that's the way people were, up until the last few centuries. Secrecy was what kept science from blossoming for so long. I saw digitalis appear and disappear at least three times before it became common knowledge . . . I really can't help you.'' Gently.

"I believe you, child." George, Sr. reached for the wine bottle.

"My father spend most of his time trying to second-guess the competition. I suppose they were doing the same thing. His only real success story was me. He found a way to stop the aging process just before puberty, and it's worked for me all this time.''

"He told you how he did it?" George, Sr. asked.

"I know what to do. I don't understand the mechanism, yet. I know it's of no use to adults."

"You've tried it?"

"Extensively." An iron door of finality clanged in that word.

"Could you describe the method?"

"I could. I won't. Perhaps I am just a product of my age, but secrecy seems to be the only safe haven in this matter. I've had a few painful experiences." They waited, but she did not elaborate.

George, Jr. got up to clear the table. He reached to pick up a plate and stopped.

"Why have you told us all this, Melissa?"

"Isn't it obvious?" She folded her hands on her lap in that posture of infinite patience. "No, I suppose it isn't unless you've lived as I have.

"After my father died, I hung around Athens for a while—did I mention, that's where we lived? But too many people knew me and began to wonder out loud about why I wasn't growing up. Some of the other wizards began to eye me speculatively, before I wised up and got out of town. I didn't want to die a prisoner before anyone figured out I had nothing useful to divulge.

"I soon found that I couldn't escape from my basic problem. There's always someone happy to take in a child, particularly a healthy one that's willing to do more than her share of the work. But after a few years, it would become obvious that I was not growing up like other children. Suspicion would lead to fear, and fear always leads to trouble. I've learned to judge to a nicety when it's time to move on."

George, Jr. placed a covered server on the table and unveiled a chocolate layer cake. Like all children throughout time, Melissa grinned in delight.

"It's a decided nuisance looking like a child—*being* a child—particularly now. You can't just go get a job and rent your own apartment. You can't apply for a driver's license. You have to *belong* to someone and be in school, or some government busybody will be causing trouble. And with modern record-keeping, you have to build a believable existence on paper too. That's getting harder all the time."

"It would seem to me," interposed George, Jr., "that your best bet would be to move to one of the less developed countries. In Africa, or South America. There'd be a lot less hassle."

Melissa made a face.

"No, thank you. I learned a long time ago to stick with the people who have the highest standard of living around. It's worth the trouble . . . *Nur wer in Wohlstand lebt, lebt angenehm.* You know Brecht? Good."

The girl gave up all pretense of conversation long enough to demolish a wedge of cake.

"That was an excellent dinner. Thank you." She dabbed her lips daintily with her napkin. "I haven't answered your question completely.

"I'm telling you all about myself because it's time to move on again. I've overstayed my welcome with the Stuarts. My records are useless to me now—in fact they're an embarrassment. To keep on the way I've been, I'll have to manufacture a whole new set and insinuate them into someone's files, somewhere. I thought it might be easier this time to take the honest approach."

She looked at them expectantly.

"You mean, you want us to help you get into a new foster home?" George, Jr. strained to keep the incredulity out of his voice.

Melissa looked down at her empty dessert plate.

"George, you are an insensitive lout," May said with surprising fervor. "Don't you understand? She's asking us to take her in."

George was thunderstruck.

"Us? Well, ah. But we don't have any children for her to play with. I mean—" He shut his mouth before he started to gibber. Melissa would not look up. George looked at his wife, his father. It was clear that they had completely outpaced him and had already made up their minds.

"I suppose it's possible," he muttered lamely.

The girl looked up at last, tears lurking in the corners of her eyes.

"Oh, please. I'm good at housework and I don't make any noise. And I've been thinking—maybe I don't know much history, but I do know a lot about how people lived in a lot of different times and places. And I can read all sorts of languages. Maybe I could help you with your medieval studies." The words tumbled over each other.

"And I remember some of the things my father tried," she said to George, Sr. "Maybe your training in biochemistry will let you see where he went wrong. I know he had some success." The girl was very close to begging, George knew. He couldn't bear that.

"Dad?" he asked, mustering what aplomb he could.

"I think it would work out," George, Sr. said slowly. "Yes. I think it would work out quite well."

"May?"

"You know my answer, George."

"Well, then." Still half bewildered. "I guess it's settled. When can you move in, Melissa?"

The answer, if there was one, was lost amidst scraping of chairs and happy bawling noises from May and the girl. *May always wanted a child,* George rationalized, *perhaps this will be good for her.* He exchanged a tentative smile with his father.

May was still hugging Melissa enthusiastically. Over his wife's shoulder, George could see the child's tear-streaked face. For just one brief moment, he thought he detected an abstracted expression there, as though the child was already calculating how long this particular episode would last. But then the look was drowned in another flood of happy tears and George found himself smiling at his new daughter.

The child sat under the tree with her hands folded neatly on her lap. She looked up as George, Sr. approached. His gait had grown noticeably less confident in the last year; the stiffness and teetery uncertainly of age could no longer be ignored. George, Sr. was a proud man, but he was no fool. He lowered himself carefully onto a tree stump.

"Hello, Grandpa," Melissa said with just a hint of warmth. She sensed his mood, George, Sr. realized, and was being carefully disarming.

"Mortimer died," was all he said.

"I was afraid he might. He'd lived a long time, for a white rat. Did you learn anything from the last blood sample?"

"No." Wearily. "Usual decay products. He died of old age. I could put it fancier, but that's what it amounts to. And I don't know why he suddenly started losing ground, after all these months. So I don't know where to go from here."

They sat in silence, Melissa patient as ever.

"You could give me some of your potion."

"No."

"I know you have some to spare—you're cautious. That's why you spend so much time back in the woods, isn't it? You're making the stuff your father told you about."

"I told you it wouldn't help you any and you promised not to ask." There was no accusation in her voice, it was a simple statement.

"Wouldn't you like to grow up, sometime?" he asked at length.

"Would you choose to be Emperor of the World if you knew you would be assassinated in two weeks? No, thank you. I'll stick with what I've got."

"If we studied the makeup of your potion, we might figure out a way to let you grow up and still remain immortal."

"I'm not at all immortal. Which is why I don't want too many people to know about me or my methods. Some jealous fool might decide to put a bullet through my head out of spite . . . I can endure diseases. I even regrew a finger once—took forty years. But I couldn't survive massive trauma." She drew her knees up and hugged them protectively.

"You have to realize that most of my defenses are prophylactic. I've learned to anticipate damage and avoid it as much as possible. But my body's defenses are just extensions of a child's basic resource, growth. It's a tricky business to grow out of an injury without growing up in the process. Once certain glands take over, there's no stopping them.

"Take teeth, for instance. They were designed for a finite lifetime, maybe half a century of gnawing on bones. When mine wear down, all I can do is pull them and wait what seems like forever for replacements to grow in. Painful, too. So I brush after meals and avoid abrasives. I stay well clear of dentists and their drills. That way I only have to suffer every couple of hundred years."

George, Sr. felt dizzy at the thought of planning centuries the way one might lay out semesters. Such incongruous words from the mouth of a little girl sitting under a tree hugging her knees. He began to understand why she almost never spoke of her age or her past unless directly asked.

"I know a lot of biochemistry, too," she went on. "You must have recognized that by now." He nodded, reluctantly. "Well, I've studied what you call my 'potion' and I don't think we know enough biology or chemistry yet to understand it. Certainly not enough to make changes.

"I know how to hold onto childhood. That's not the same problem as restoring youth."

"But don't you want badly to be able to grow up? You said yourself what a nuisance it is being a child in the Twentieth Century."

"Sure, it's a nuisance. But it's what I've got and I don't want to risk it." She leaned forward, chin resting on kneecaps.

"Look, I've recruited other kids in the past. Ones I liked, ones I thought I could spend a long time with. But sooner or later, every one of them snatched at the bait you're dangling. They all decided to grow up "just a little bit." Well, they did. And now they're dead. I'll stick with my children's games, if it please you."

"You don't mind wasting all that time in school? Learning the same things over and over again? Surrounded by nothing but children? *Real* children?" He put a twist of malice in the emphasis.

"What waste? Time? Got lots of that. How much of your life have you spent actually doing research, compared to the time spent writing reports and driving to work? How much time does Mrs. Foster get to spend talking to troubled kids? She's lucky if she averages five minutes a day. We all spend most of our time doing routine chores. It would be unusual if any of us did not.

"And I don't mind being around kids. I like them."

"I never have understood that," George, Sr. said half abstractedly. "How well you can mix with children so much younger than you. How you can act like them."

"You've got it backwards," she said softly. "They act like me. All children are immortal, until they grow up."

She let that sink in for a minute.

"Now I ask you, Grandpa, you tell me why I should want to grow up."

"There are other pleasures," he said eventually, "far deeper than the joys of childhood."

"You mean sex? Yes, I'm sure that's what you're referring to. Well, what makes you think a girl my age is a virgin?"

He raised his arms in embarrassed protest, as if to ward such matters from his ears.

"No, wait a minute. You brought this up," she persisted, "look at me. Am I unattractive? Good teeth, no pock marks. No visible deformities. Why, a girl like me would make first-rate wife material in some circles. Particularly where the average life expectancy is, say, under thirty-five years—as it has been throughout much of history. Teen-age celibacy and late marriage are conceits that society has only recently come to afford."

She looked at him haughtily.

"I have had my share of lovers, and you can bet I've enjoyed them as much as they've enjoyed me. You don't need glands for that sort of thing so much as sensitive nerve endings—and a little understanding. Of course, my boyfriends were all a little disappointed when I failed to ripen up, but it was fun while it lasted.

"Sure, it would be nice to live in a woman's body, to feel all those hormones making you do wild things. But to me, sex isn't a drive, it's just another way of relating to *people*. I already recognize my need to be around people, uncomplicated by any itches that need scratching. My life would be a lot simpler if I could do without others, heaven knows. I certainly don't have to be forced by glandular pressure to go in search of company. What else is there to life?"

What else, indeed? George, Sr. thought bitterly. One last try.

"Do you know about May?" he asked.

"That she can't have children? Sure, that was pretty obvious from the start. Do you think I can help her? You do, yes. Well, I can't. I know even less about that than I do about what killed Mortimer."

Pause.

"I'm sorry, Grandpa."

Silence.

"I really am."

Silence.

Distantly, a car could be heard approaching the house. George, Jr. was coming home. The old man got up from the stump slowly and stiffly.

"Dinner will be ready soon." He turned toward the house. "Don't be late. You know your mother doesn't like you to play in the woods."

The child sat in the pew with her hands folded neatly on her lap. She could hear the cold rain lash against the stained glass windows, their scenes of martyrdom muted by the night lurking outside. Melissa had always liked churches. In a world filled with change and death, church was a familiar haven, a resting place for embattled innocents to prepare for fresh encounters with a hostile world.

Her time with the Fosters was over. Even with the inevitable discord at the end, she was already able to look back over her stay with fond remembrance. What saddened her most was that her prediction that first evening she came to dinner had been so accurate. She kept hoping that just once her cynical assessment of human nature would prove wrong and she would be granted an extra year, even an extra month, of happiness before she was forced to move on.

Things began to go really sour after George, Sr. had his first mild stroke. It was

George, Jr. who became the most accusatory then. (The old man had given up on Melissa; perhaps that was what angered George, Jr. the most.) There was nothing she could say or do to lessen the tension. Just being there, healthy and still a prepubescent child unchanged in five years of photographs and memories—her very presence made a mockery of the old man's steady retreat in the face of mortality.

Had George, Jr. understood himself better, perhaps he would not have been so hard on the girl. (But then, she had figured that in her calculations.) He thought it was May who wanted children so badly, when in actuality it was his own subconscious striving for that lesser form of immortality that made their childless home ring with such hollowness. All May begrudged the child was a second chance at the beauty she fancied lost with the passing of youth. Naturally May fulfilled her own prophecy, as so many women do, by discarding a little more glow with each passing year.

George, Jr. took to following Melissa on her trips into the woods. Anger and desperation gave him a stealth she never would have otherwise ascribed to him. He found all her hidden caches and stole minute samples from each. It did him no good, of course, nor his father, for the potion was extremely photoreactant (her father's great discovery and Melissa's most closely guarded secret). The delicate long chain molecules were smashed to a meaningless soup of common organic substances long before any of the samples reached the analytical laboratory.

But that thievery was almost her undoing. She did not suspect anything until the abdominal cramps started. Only twice before in her long history—both times of severe famine—had that happened. In a pure panic, Melissa plunged deep into the forest, to collect her herbs and mix her brews and sleep beside them in a darkened burrow for the two days it took them to ripen. The cramps abated, along with her panic, and she returned home to find that George, Sr. had suffered a second stroke.

May was furious—at what, she could not say precisely—there was no talking to her. George, Jr. had long been a lost cause. Melissa went to her room, thought things over a while, and prepared to leave. As she crept out the back door, she heard George, Jr. talking quietly on the telephone.

She hot-wired a neighbor's car and set off for town. Cars were pulling into the Foster's drive as she went past, hard-eyed men climbing out. Melissa had cowered in alleyways more than once to avoid the gaze of Roman centurions. These may have been CIA, FBI, some other alphabet name to disguise their true purpose in life, but she knew them for what they were. She had not left a minute too soon.

No one thinks to look for stolen cars when a child disappears; Melissa had some time to maneuver. She abandoned the sedan in town less than a block away from the bus depot. At the depot, she openly bought a one-way ticket to Berkeley. She was one of the first aboard and made a point of asking the driver, in nervous little-girl fashion, whether this was really the bus to Berkeley, She slipped out while he was juggling paperwork with the dispatcher.

With one false trail laid, she was careful not to go running off too quickly in another

　　　　　　　　　　　　　　　　　　　　　　　　P.J. Plauger

direction. Best to lay low until morning, at least, then rely more on walking than riding to get somewhere else. Few people thought to walk a thousand miles these days; Melissa had done it more times than she could remember.

"We have to close up, son," a soft voice said behind her. She suddenly remembered her disguise and realized the remark was addressed to her. She turned to see the priest drifting toward her, his robes rustling almost imperceptibly. "It's nearly midnight," the man said with a smile, "you should be getting home."

"Oh, hello, Father. I didn't hear you come in."

"Is everything all right? You're out very late."

"My sister works as a waitress, down the block. Dad likes me to walk her home. I should go meet her now. Just came in to get out of the rain for a bit. Thanks."

Melissa smiled her sincerest smile. She disliked lying, but it was important not to appear out of place. No telling how big a manhunt might be mounted to find her. She had no way of knowing how much the Fosters would be believed. The priest returned her smile.

"Very good. But you be careful too, son. The streets aren't safe for anyone, these days."

They never have been, Father.

Melissa had passed as a boy often enough in the past to know that safety, from anything, depended little on sex. At least not for children.

That business with the centurions worried her more than she cared to admit. The very fact that they turned out in such numbers indicated that George, Jr. had at least partially convinced someone important.

Luckily, there was no hard evidence that she was really what she said she was. The samples George, Jr. stole were meaningless and the pictures and records May could produce on her only covered about an eight-year period. That was a long time for a little girl to remain looking like a little girl, but not frighteningly out of the ordinary.

If she was lucky, the rationalizations had already begun. Melissa was just a freak of some kind, a late maturer and a con artist. The Fosters were upset—that much was obvious—because of George, Sr. They should not be believed too literally.

Melissa could hope. Most of all she hoped that they didn't have a good set of her fingerprints. (She had polished everything in her room before leaving.) Bureaucracies were the only creatures she could not outlive—it would be very bad if the U.S. Government carried a grudge against her.

Oh well, that was the last time she would try the honest approach for quite some time.

The rain had backed off to a steady drizzle. That was an improvement, she decided, but it was still imperative that she find some shelter for the night. The rain matted her freshly cropped hair and soaked through her thin baseball jacket. She was cold and tired.

Melissa dredged up the memories, nurtured over the centuries, of her first, real childhood. She remembered her mother, plump and golden-haired, and how safe and warm it was curled up in her lap. That one was gone now, along with millions of other mothers out of time. There was no going back.

Up ahead, on the other side of the street, a movie marquee splashed light through the drizzle. Black letters spelled out a greeting:

WALT DISNEY TRIPLE FEATURE

CONTINUOUS PERFORMANCES FOR CHILDREN OF ALL AGES

That's me, Melissa decided, and skipped nimbly over the rainchoked gutter. She crossed the street on a long diagonal, ever on the lookout for cars, and tendered up her money at the ticket window. Leaving rain and cold behind for a time, she plunged gratefully into the warm darkness. ∎

EMERGENCE
David R. Palmer

Nothing to do? Nowhere to go? Time hangs heavy? Bored? Depressed? Also badly scared? Causal factors beyond control?

Unfortunate. Regrettable. Vicious cycle—snake swallowing own tail. Mind dwells on problems; problems fester, assume ever greater importance for mind to dwell on. Etc. Bad enough where problems minor.

Mine aren't.

Psychology text offers varied solutions: recommends keeping occupied, busywork if necessary; keep mind distracted. Better if busywork offers challenge, degree of frustration. Still better that I have responsibility. All helps.

Perhaps.

Anyway, keeping busy difficult. Granted, more books in shelter than public library; more tools, equipment, supplies, etc., than Swiss Family Robinson's wrecked ship—all latest developments: lightest, simplest, cleverest, most reliable, non-rusting, Sanforized. All useless unless—correction, *until* I get out (and of lot, know uses of maybe half dozen: screwdriver for opening stuck drawer; hammer to tenderize steak, break ice cubes; hacksaw for cutting frozen meat . . .).

Oh, well, surely must be books explaining selection, use.

Truly, surely are books—thousands! Plus microfilm library—even bigger. Much deep stuff: classics, contemporary; comprehensive museum of man's finest works: words, canvas, 3-D and multi-view reproductions of statuary. Also scientific: medical, dental, veterinary, entomology, genetics, marine biology; engineering, electronics, physics (both nuclear and garden variety), meteorology, astronomy; carpentry, agriculture, welding (equipment, too), woodcraft, survival, etc., etc., etc.; poetry, fiction, biographies of great, near-great; philosophy—even complete selection of world's fantasy, new and old. Complete Oz books, etc., Happy surprise, that.

Daddy was determined man's highest achievements not vanish in Fireworks; also positive same just around corner. Confession: Wondered sometimes if was playing with complete deck; spent incalculable sums on shelter and contents. Turns out was right; is probably having last laugh Somewhere. Wish were here to needle me about it—but wouldn't if could; was too nice. Miss him. Very much.

Growing maudlin. Above definitely constitutes "dwelling" in pathological sense as defined by psychology text. Time to click heels, clap hands, smile, Shuffle Off to Buffalo.

Anyhow, mountains of books, microfilm of limited benefit; too deep. Take classics: Can tolerate just so long; then side effects set in. Resembles obtaining manicure by scratching fingernails on blackboard—can, but would rather suffer long fingernails. Same with classics as sole remedy for "dwelling": Not sure which is worse. May be that too much culture in sudden doses harmful to health; perhaps must build up immunity progressively.

And technical is worse. Thought I had good foundation in math, basic sciences. Wrong—background good, considering age; but here haven't found anything elementary enough to form opening wedge. Of course, haven't gotten organized yet; haven't assimilated catalog, planned orderly approach to subjects of interest. Shall; but for now, can get almost as bored looking at horrid pictures of results of endocrine misfunctions as by wading through classics.

And am rationing fantasy, of course. Thousands of titles, but dasn't lose head. Speedreader, you know; breach discipline, well runs dry in matter of days.

Then found book on Pitman Shorthand. Changed everything. Told once by unimpeachable source (Mrs. Hartman, Daddy's secretary and receptionist) was best, potentially fastest, most versatile of various pen systems. Also most difficult to learn well. (Footnote, concession to historical accuracy: Was also her system; source possibly contaminated by tinge of bias.) However, seemed promising; offered challenge, frustration. Besides, pothook patterns quite pretty, art form of sorts. Hoped would be entertaining.

Was—for about two days. Then memory finished absorbing principles of shorthand theory, guidelines for briefing and phrasing; transferred same to cortex—end of challenge. Tiresome being genius sometimes.

Well, even if no longer entertaining for own sake, still useful, much more practical than longhand; ideal for keeping journal, writing biography for archeologists. Probably not bother if limited to longhand; too slow, cumbersome. Effort involved would dull enthusiasm (of which little present anyway), wipe out paper supply in short order. Pitman fits entire life story on line and a half. (Of course, helps I had short life—correction: Helps brevity; does nothing for spirits.)

Problem with spirits serious business. Body trapped far underground; emotional index substantially lower. Prospects not good for body getting out alive, but odds not improved by emotional state. Depression renders intelligent option assessment improbable. In present condition would likely overlook ten good bets, flip coin over dregs. Situation probably not hopeless as seems, but lacking data, useful education, specialized knowledge (and guts), can't form viable conclusion suggesting happy ending. And lacking same, tend to assume worst.

So journal not just for archeologists; is therapeutic. Catharsis: Spill guts on paper, feel better. Must be true—psychology text says so (though cautions is better to pay Ph.D.-equipped voyeur week's salary per hour to listen. However, none such included in shelter inventory; will have to make do).

David R. Palmer

First step: Bring journal up to date. Never kept one; not conversant with format requirements, Right Thing To Do. Therefore will use own judgment. One thing certain: Sentence structure throughout will have English teachers spinning in graves (those fortunate enough to have one).

English 60-percent flab, null symbols, waste. Suspect massive inefficiency stems from subconsciously recognized need to stall, give inferior intellects chance to collect thoughts into semblance of coherence (usually without success), and to show off (my $12-word can lick your $10-word). Will not adhere to precedent; makes little sense to write shorthand, then cancel advantage by employment of rambling academese.

Keep getting sidetracked into social criticism. Probably symptom of condition. Stupid; all evidence says no society left. Was saying:

First step: Bring journal up to present; purge self of neuroses, sundry hangups. Then record daily orderly progress in study of situation, subsequent systematic (brilliant) self-extrication from dire straits. Benefits twofold:

First, will wash, dry, fold, put away psyche; restore mind to customary genius; enhance prospects for successful escape, subsequent survival. Second, will give archeologists details on cause of untimely demise amidst confusing mass of artifacts in shelter should anticipated first benefit lose rosy glow. (Must confess solicitude for bone gropers forced; bones in question *mine!*)

Enough maundering. Time to bear down, flay soul for own good. Being neurotic almost as tiresome as being genius. (Attention archeologists: Clear room of impressionable youths and/or mixed company—torrid details follow:)

Born 11 years ago in small Wisconsin town, only child of normal parents. Named Candidia Maria Smith; reduced to Candy before ink dried on certificate. Early indications of atypicality: Eyes focused, tracked at birth; cause-effect association evident by six weeks; first words at four months; sentences at six months.

Orphaned at ten months. Parents killed in car accident.

No relatives—created dilemma for baby-sitter. Solved when social worker took charge. Was awfully cute baby: adopted in record time.

Doctor Foster and wife good parents: loving, attentive: very fond of each other, showed it. Provided good environment for formative years. Then Momma died. Left just Daddy and me; drew us very close. Was probably shamelessly spoiled, but also stifled.

Barely five then, but wanted to *learn*—only Daddy had firm notions concerning appropriate learning pace, direction for "normal" upbringing. Did not approve of precocity; felt was unhealthy, would lead to future maladjustment, unhappiness. Also paternalistic sexist: had bad case of ingrown stereotypitis. Censored activities, reading; dragged heels at slightest suggestion of precocious behavior, atypical interests.

Momma disagreed; aided, indulged. With her help I learned to read by age two; understood basic numerical relationships by three: could add, subtract, multiply, divide. Big help until she had to leave.

So sneaked most of education. Had to—certainly not available in small-town class-room. Not difficult; developed speedreading habit, could finish high school text in 10, 20 minutes; digest typical best-seller in half, three-quarters of hour. Haunted school, local libraries every opportunity (visits only; couldn't bring choices home). But town small; exhausted obvious resources three years ago. Have existed since on meager fruits of covert operations in friends' homes, bookstores, occasional raids on neighboring towns' libraries, schools. Of course not all such forays profitable; small-town resources tend to run same direction: slowly, in circles. Catalogs mostly shallow, duplicated; originality lacking.

Frustrating. Made more so by knowledge that Daddy's personal in-house library rivaled volume count of local school, public libraries put together (not counting shelter collection, but didn't know about that then)—and couldn't get halfway down first page of 95 percent of contents.

Daddy pathologist; books imperviously technical. So far over head, couldn't even tell where gap lay (ask cannibal fresh off plane from Amazon for analysis of educational deficiencies causing noncomprehension of commercial banking structure). Texts dense; assumed reader already possessing high-level competency. Sadly lacking in own case—result of conspiracy. So languished, fed in dribbles as tireless prospecting uncovered new sources.

Single bright exception: Soo Kim McDivott, son of American missionary in Boxer Rebellion days, product of early East-West alliance. Was 73 when retired, moved next door two years ago. Apparently had been teacher whole life but never achieved tenure; tended to get fired over views. Didn't appear to mind.

Strange old man. Gentle, soft-spoken, very polite; small, seemed almost frail. Oriental flavoring lent elf-like quality to wizened features; effect not reduced by mischief sparkling from eyes.

Within two weeks became juvenile activity focus for most of town. Cannot speak for bulk of kids, but motivation obvious in own case: Aside from intrinsic personal warmth, knew everything—and if exception turned up would gleefully drop every-thing, help find out—and had *books*. House undoubtedly in violation of Fire Code; often wondered how structural members took load.

Fascinating man: could, would discuss anything. But wondered for a time how managed as teacher; never answered questions but with questions. Seemed whenever I had question, ended up doing own research, telling *him* answer. Took a while to catch on, longer before truly appreciated: Had no interest in teaching knowledge, factual information—taught learning. Difference important; seldom understood, even more rarely appreciated. Don't doubt was reason for low retirement income.

Oh, almost forgot: Could split bricks with sidelong glance, wreak untold destruction with twitch of muscle. Any muscle. Was Tenth Degree Master of Karate. Didn't know were such; thought ratings stopped at Eighth—and heard rumors *they* could walk on

David R. Palmer

water. (But doubt Master Mac would bother. Should need arise, would politely ask waters to part—but more likely request anticipated, unnecessary.)

Second day after moving in, Master was strolling down Main Street when happened upon four young men, early 20s, drunk, unkempt—Summer People (sorry, my single ineradicable prejudice)—engaged in self-expression at Miller's Drugstore. Activities consisted of inverting furniture, displays; dumping soda-fountain containers (milk, syrup, etc.) on floor; throwing merchandise through display windows. Were discussing also throwing Mr. Miller when Master Mac arrived on scene.

Assessed situation; politely requested cease, desist, await authorities' arrival. Disbelieving onlookers closed, averted eyes; didn't want to watch expected carnage. Filthy Four dropped Mr. Miller, converged on frail-looking old Chinese. Then all fell down, had subsequent difficulty arising. Sitatuion remained static until police arrived.

Filthies taken into custody, then to hospital. Attempted investigation of altercation unrewarding: Too many eyewitness accounts—all contradictory, disbelieving, unlikely. However, recurring similarities in stories suggested simultaneous stumble as Filthies reached for Master; then all fell, accumulating severe injuries therefrom: four broken jaws, two arms, two legs, two wrists; two dislocated hips; two ruptured spleens. Plus bruises in astonishing places.

Single point of unanimity—ask *anyone:* Master Mac never moved throughout.

Police took notes in visibly strained silence. Also took statement from Master Mac. But of dubious help: Consisted mostly of questions.

Following week YMCA announced Master Mac to teach karate classes. Resulted in near riot (by small-town standards). Standing room only at registration; near fistfights over positions in line.

Was 16th on list to start first classes but deserve no credit for inclusion: Daddy's doing. Wanted badly—considering sociological trends, self-defense skills looked ever more like required social graces for future survival—but hesitated to broach subject; seemed probable conflict with "normal upbringing" dictum.

So finally asked. Surprise! Agreed—granted dispensation! Was still in shock when Daddy asked time, date of registration. Showed article in paper: noon tomorrow. Looked thoughtful maybe five seconds; then rushed us outdoors, down street to Y. Already 15 ahead of us, equipped to stay duration.

Daddy common as old slipper: warm, comfortable, folksy. But shared aspects with iceberg: Nine-tenths of brains not evident in everyday life. Knew was very smart, of course. Implicit from job: pathologist knows everything any other specialist does, plus own job. Obviously not career for cretin—and was *good* pathologist. Renowned.

But not show-off; was easy to forget; reminders few, far between. Scope, foresight, quick reactions, Command Presence demonstrated only in time of need.

Such occurred now: While I stood in line with mouth open (and 20 more hopefuls piled up behind like Keystone Cops), Daddy organized friends to bring chairs, cot, food, drink, warm clothing, blankets, rainproofs, etc. Took three minutes on phone.

Was impressed. Then astounded—spent whole night on sidewalk with me, splitting watches, trading off visits to Little Persons' room when need arose.

Got all choked up when he announced intention. Hugged him breathless; told him Kismet had provided better father than most workings of genetic coincidence. Did not reply, but got hugged back harder than usual; caught glimpse of extra reflections in corners of eyes from streetlight. Special night; full of warmth, feelings of belonging, togetherness.

After Daddy's magnificent contribution, effort to get me into class, felt slight pangs of guilt over my subsequent misdirection, concealment of true motivation. True, attended classes, worked hard; became, in fact, star pupil. But had to—star pupils qualified for private instruction—yup!—at Master's home, surrounded by what appeared to be 90 percent of books in Creation.

Earned way though. Devoted great effort to maintain favored status; achieved Black Belt in ten months, state championship (for age/weight group) six months later. Was considered probable national championship material, possibly world. Enjoyed; great fun, terrific physical conditioning, obvious potential value (ask Filthy Four), good for ego due to adulation over ever-lengthening string of successes, capture of state loving cup (ironic misnomer—contest was mock combat: "killed" seven opponents, "maimed" 22 others for life or longer).

But purely incidental in no way distracted from main purpose:

With aid of Master (addressed as Teacher away from *dojo*) had absorbed equivalent of advanced high school education, some college by time world ended: Math through calculus, chemistry, beginnings of physics; good start on college biology, life sciences—doing well.

Occasionally caught Teacher regarding me as hen puzzles over product of swan egg slipped into nest; making notes in "Tarzan File" (unresolved enigma: huge file, never explained; partially concerned me, as achievements frequently resulted in entries, but was 36 inches thick before I entered picture), but definitely approved—and his approval better for ego than state cup.

Regarding which, had by then achieved Fifth Degree; could break brick with edge of hand, knee, foot. But didn't after learned could. Prospect distressed Daddy. Poor dear could visualize with professional exactitude pathological consequences of attempt by untrained; knew just what each bone splinter would look like, where would be driven; which tendons torn from what insertions; which nerves destroyed forever, etc. Had wistful ambition I might follow into medicine; considered prospects bleak for applicant with deformed, calloused hammers dangling from wrists.

Needless concern; callouses unnecessary. With proper control, body delivers blow through normal hands without discomfort, damage. Is possible, of course, to abuse nature to point where fingers, knuckles, edge of hands, etc., all turn to flint, but never seen outside exhibitions. Serves no purpose in practice of art; regarded with disdain by serious student, Master alike.

So much for happy memories.

Not long ago world situation took turn for worse. Considering character of usual headlines when change began, outlook became downright grim. Daddy tried to hide concern but spent long hours reading reports from Washington (appreciated for first time just how renowned was when saw whom from), watching news; consulting variety of foreign, domestic officials by phone. Seemed cheerful enough, but when thought I wasn't looking, mask slipped.

Finally called me into study. Sat me down; gave long, serious lecture on how bad things were. Made me lead through house, point out entrances to emergency chute leading down to shelter (dreadful thing—200 foot vertical drop in pitch dark, cushioned at bottom only by gradual curve as polished sides swing to horizontal, enter shelter). Then insisted we take plunge for practice. Although considered "practice" more likely to induce psychic block, make subsequent use impossible — even in time of need — performed as requested. Not as bad as expected; terror index fell perhaps five percent short of anticipation. But not fun.

However, first time in shelter since age three. Scenic attractions quickly distracted from momentary cardiac arrest incurred in transit. Concealed below modest small-town frame house of unassuming doctor was Eighth Wonder of World. Shelter is three-story structure carved from bedrock, 100 feet by 50; five-eighths shelves, storage compartments. Recognized microfilm viewer immediately; identical to one used at big hospital over in next county. Film storage file cabinets same, too—only occupied full length of two long walls, plus four free-standing files ran almost full length of room. Rest bookshelves, as is whole of second floor. Basement seems mostly tools, machinery, instrumentation.

Hardly heard basic life-support function operation lecture: air regeneration, waste reclamation, power production, etc. Was all could do to look attentive—books drew me like magnet. However, managed to keep head; paid sufficient attention to ask intelligent-sounding questions. Actually learned basics of how to work shelter's vital components.

. . . Because occurred to me: Could read undisturbed down here if knew how to make habitable. (Feel bad about that, too; here Daddy worried sick over my survival In The Event Of—and object of concern scheming about continuing selfish pursuit of printed word.)

Tour, lecture ended. Endless spiral staircase up tube five feet in diameter led back to comfortable world of small-town reality. Life resumed where interrupted.

With exception: Was now alert for suitable opportunity to begin exploration of shelter.

Not readily available. As Fifth was qualified assistant instructor at formal classes; took up appreciable portion of time. Much of rest devoted to own study—both Art (wanted to attain Sixth; would have been youngest in world) and academics, both under approving eye of Master. Plus null time spent occupying space in grammar school classroom, trying not to look too obviously bored while maintaining straight-A average (only amusement consisted of correcting teachers, textbooks—usually involved digging up proof, confrontations in principal's office). Plus sundry activities rounding out image of "normally well-rounded" 11-year-old.

But patience always rewarded. If of sufficient duration. Daddy called to Washington; agreed was adult enough to take care of self, house, Terry during three days' expected absence. Managed not to drool at prospect.

Terry? True, didn't mention before, by name; just that had responsibility. Remember? First page, fourth paragraph. Pay attention—may spring quiz.

Terry is retarded, adoptive twin brother. Saw light of day virtually same moment I emerged—or would have had opened eyes. Early on showed more promise than I: Walked at nine weeks, first words at three months, could fly at 14 weeks. Achieved fairly complex phrases by six months but never managed complete sentences. Peaked early but low.

Not fair description. Actually Terry is brilliant—for macaw. Also beautiful. Hyacinthine Macaw, known to low-brows as Hyacinth, pseudo-intellectuals as *Anodorhynchus hyacinthinus*—terrible thing to say about sweet baby bird. Full name Terry D. Foster (initial stands for Dactyll). Length perhaps 36 inches (half of which is tail feathers); basic color rich, glowing hyacinth blue (positively electric in sunlight), with bright yellow eye patches like clown, black feet and bill. Features permanently arranged in jolly Alfred E. Newman, village-idiot smile. Diet is anything within reach, but ideally consists of properly mixed seeds, assorted fruits, nut, sprinkling of meat, etc.

Hobbies include getting head and neck scratched (serious business, this), art of conversation, destruction of world. Talent for latter avocation truly awe-inspiring: 1,500 pounds pressure available at business end of huge, hooked beak. Firmly believe if left Terry with four-inch cube of solid tungsten carbide, would return in two hours to find equivalent mass of metal dust, undimmed enthusiasm.

Was really convinced were siblings when very young. First deep childhood trauma (not affected by loss of blood parents; too young at time, too many interesting things happening) induced by realization was built wrong, would never learn to fly. Had stubbornly mastered perching on playpen rail shortly after began walking (though never did get to point of preferring nonchalant one-legged stance twin affected—toes deformed: stunted, too short for reliable grip), but subsequent step simply beyond talents.

Suspect this phase of youth contributed to appearance of symptoms leading to early demise of Momma Foster. Remember clearly first time she entered room, found us perched together on rail, furiously "exercising wings." Viewed in retrospect, is amazing didn't expire on spot.

(Sounds cold, unfeeling; is not. Momma given long advance notice; knew almost to day when could expect to leave. Prepared me with wisdom, understanding, love. Saw departure as unavoidable but wonderful opportunity, adventure; stated was prepared to accept, even excuse reasonable regret over plans spoiled, things undone—but not grief. Compared grief over death of friend to envy of friend's good fortune: selfish reaction—feeling sorry for self, not friend. Compared own going to taking wonderful trip; "spoiled plans" to giving up conflicting movie, picnic, swim in lake. Besides, was given big responsibility—charged me with "looking after Daddy." Explained he had formed many elaborate plans involving three of us—many more than she or I had. Would doubtless be appreciably more disappointed, feel more regret over inability to carry out. Would need love, understanding during period it took him to reform plans around two remaining behind. Did such a job on me that truly did not suffer loss, grief; just missed her when gone, hoped was having good time.)

Awoke morning of Daddy's trip to startling realization—didn't want him to go. Didn't like prospect of being alone three days: didn't like idea of *him* alone three days. Lay abed trying to resolve disquieting feeling. Or at least identify. Could do neither; had never forebode before. Subliminal sensation: below conscious level but intrusive. Multiplied by substantial factor could be mistaken for fear—no, not fear, exactly; more like mindless, screaming terror.

But silly; nothing to be scared about. Mrs. Hartman would be working in office in front part of house during day; house locked tight at night—with additional security provided by certain distinctly non-small-town devices Daddy recently caused installed. Plus good neighbors on all sides, available through telephone right at bedside or single loud scream.

Besides, was I not Candy Smith-Foster, State Champion, Scourge of Twelve-and-Under Class, second most dangerous mortal within 200-mile radius? (By now knew details of Filthy Four's "stumble," and doubt would have gotten off so lightly had I been intercessor.)

Was. So told feeling to shut up. Washed, dressed, went down to breakfast with Daddy and Terry.

Conduct during send-off admirable; performance qualified for finals in stiff-upper-lip-of-year award contest. Merely gave big hug, kiss; cautioned stay out of trouble in capital, but if occurred, call me soonest—would come to rescue: split skulls, break bones, mess up adversaries something awful. Sentiment rewarded by lingering return hug, similar caution about self during absence (but expressed with more dignity). Then door of government-supplied, chauffeur-driven, police-escorted limousine closed; vehicle made its long, black way down street, out of sight around corner.

Spent morning at school, afternoon teaching at Y, followed by own class with Master. Finally found self home, now empty except Terry (voicing disapproval of day's isolation at top of ample lungs): Mrs. Hartman done for day, had gone home. Silenced twin by scratching head, transferring to shoulder (loves assisting with household chores, but acceptance means about three times as much work as doing by self—requires everything done at arms' length, out of reach).

Made supper, ate, gave Terry whole tablespoon of peanut butter as compensation for boring day (expressed appreciation by crimping spoon double). Did dishes, cleaned house in aimless fashion; started over.

Finally realized was dithering, engaging in busywork; afraid to admit was really home alone, actually had opportunity for unhindered investigation of shelter. Took hard look at conflict; decided was rooted in guilt over intent to take advantage of Daddy's absence to violate known wishes. Reminded self that existence of violation hinged upon accuracy of opinion concerning unvocalized desires; "known wishes" question-begging terminology if ever was one. Also told self firmly analysis of guilt feeling same as elimination. Almost believed.

Impatiently stood, started toward basement door. Terry recognized signs, set up protest against prospect of evening's abandonment. Sighed, went back, transferred to shoulder. Brother rubbed head on cheek in gratitude, gently bit end of nose, said, "You're so bad," in relieved tones. Gagged slightly; peanut-butter breath from bird is rare treat.

Descended long spiral stairs down tube to shelter. Ran through power-up routine, activated systems. Then began exploration.

Proceeded slowly. Terry's first time below; found entertaining. Said, "How '*bout* that!" every ten seconds. Also stretched neck, bobbed head, expressed passionate desire to sample every book as pulled from shelf. Sternly warned of brief future as giblet dressing if so much as touched single page. Apparently thought prospect sounded fun, redoubled efforts. But was used to idiot twin's antisocial behavior; spoiled fun almost without conscious thought as proceeded with exploration.

Soon realized random peeking useless; was in position of hungry kid dropped in middle Willy Wonka's Chocolate Factory: Too much choice. Example: Whole cabinet next to micro-film viewer was *catalog!*

Three feet wide, eight high; drawers three feet deep, six inches wide (rows of six); ten titles per card (*thin* cards)—72 cubic feet of solid catalog.

Took breath away to contemplate. Also depressed; likelihood of mapping orderly campaign to augment education not good. Didn't know where to start; which books, films within present capacity; where to go from there. Only thing more tiresome than being repressed genius is being ignorant genius recognizing own status.

Decided to consult Teacher; try to get him to list books he considered ideal to further education most rapidly from present point, cost no object. (Was giving consideration to Daddy's ambition to see me become doctor; but regardless, no education wasted. Knowledge worthwhile for own sake.) Didn't feel should report discovery—would be breach of confidence—but could use indirect approach. Not lie; just not mention that any book suggested undoubtedly available on moment's notice. Ought to fool him all of ten seconds.

Started toward switchboard to power-down shelter. Hand touching first switch in sequence when row of red lights began flashing, three large bells on wall next to panel commenced deafening clangor. Snatched hand back as if from hot stove; thought had

David R. Palmer

activated burglar alarm (if reaction included thought at all). Feverish inspection of panel disclosed no hint of such, but found switch marked "Alarm Bells, North American Air Defense Command Alert." Opened quickly; relieved to note cessation of din, but lights continued flashing. Then, as watched, second row, labeled, "Attack Detected," began flashing.

Problem with being genius is tendency to think deep, mull hidden significance, overlook obvious. Retrieved Terry (as usual, had gone for help at first loud noise), scratched head to soothe nerves. Twin replied, "That's *bad!*" several times; dug claws into shoulder, flapped wings to show had not really been scared. Requested settle down, shut up; wished to contemplate implications of board.

Impressive. Daddy must be truly high-closet VIP to rate such inside data supplied to home shelter. As considered this, another row flashed on, this labeled, "Retaliation Initiated." Imagine—blow-by-blow nuclear war info updates supplied to own home! Wonderful to be so important. Amazing man. And so modest—all these years never let on. Wondered about real function in government. With such brains was probably head of super-secret spy bureau in charge of dozens of James Bond types.

Don't know how long mindless rumination went on; finally something clicked in head: Attack? Retaliation? *Hey . . . !* Bolted for steps. Terry dug in claws, voiced protest over sudden movements.

Stopped like statue. Daddy's voice, tinny, obviously recording: "Red alert, radiation detected. Level above danger limit. Shelter will seal in 30 seconds—29, 28, 27 . . . " Stood frozen; listened as familiar voice delivered requiem for everything known and loved—including probably self. Interrupted count once at 15-second mark to repeat radiation warning, again at five seconds.

Then came deep-toned humming; powerful motors slid blocks of concrete, steel, asbestos across top of stairwell, did same for emergency-entry chute. Sealing process terminated with solidly mechanical clunks, thuds. Motors whined in momentary overload as program ensured was tight.

Then truly alone. Stood staring at nothing for long minutes. Did not know when silent tears began; noticed wet face when Terry sampled, found too salty. Shook head; said softly, "Poooor bay-bee-ee . . . "

Presently found self sitting in chair. Radio on; could not remember turning switch, locating CONELRAD frequency. Just sat, listened to reports. Only time stirred was to feed, water Terry; use potty. Station on air yet, but manned only first three days.

Was enough, told story: Mankind eliminated. Radiation, man-made disease. International quick-draw ended in tie.

Final voice on air weakly complained situation didn't make sense: Was speaking from defense headquarters near Denver—miles underground, utterly bombproof, airtight; self-contained air, water—so why dying? Why last alive in entire installation? Didn't make sense. . . .

Agreed, but thought objection too limited in scope. Also wondered why *we* were still alive. Likewise didn't make sense.

If invulnerability of NORAD headquarters—located just this side of Earth's core under Cheyenne Mountain—proving ineffective, how come fancy sub-cellar hidey-hole under house in small town still keeping occupants alive? And for how long? Figured had to be just matter of time.

Therefore became obsessed with worry over fate of retarded brother. Were safe from radiation (it seemed), but plague another matter. Doubted would affect avian biochemistry; would kill me, leave poor baby to starve, die of thirst. Agonized over dilemma for days. Finally went downstairs; hoped might turn up something in stores could use as Terry's Final Friend.

Did. Found armory. Thought of what might have to do almost triggered catatonia; but knew twin's escape from suffering dependent on me, so mechanically went ahead with selection of shotgun. Found shells, loaded gun. Carried upstairs, placed on table. Then waited for cue.

Knew symptoms; various CONELRAD voices had described own, those of friends. Were six to syndrome. Order in which appeared reported variable; number present at onset of final unconsciousness not. Four symptoms always; then fifth: period of extreme dizziness—clue to beginning of final decline. Was important, critical to timing with regard to Terry. Desperately afraid might wait too long; condemn poor incompetent to agonizing last days. And almost more afraid might react to false alarm, proceed with euthanasia; then fail to die—have to face scattered, blood-spattered feathers, headless body of sweetest, jolliest, most devoted, undemandingly loving friend had ever known.

Which was prospect if acted too soon—intended to stand 20 feet away, blow off head while engrossed in peanut butter. Pellet expansion sufficient at that distance to ensure virtually instantaneous vaporization of entire head, instant kill before possibility of realization, pain. Would rather suffer own dismemberment, boiling in oil than see innocent baby suffer, know was me causing.

Thus, very important to judge own condition accurately when plague sets in.

Only hasn't yet. Been waiting three weeks, paralyzed with grief, fear, apprehension, indecision. But such emotions wearisome when protracted; eventually lose grip on victim. I think perhaps might have—particularly now that journal up to date, catharsis finished. Book says therapy requires good night's sleep after spilling guts; then feel better in morning. Suspect may be right; do feel better.

Okay. Tomorrow will get *organized . . . !*

Good morning, Posterity! Happy to report I spent good night. Slept as if already dead—first time since trouble began. No dreams; if tossed, turned, did so without noticing. Appears writer of psychology text knew stuff (certainly should have: more letters following name than in). Catharsis worked—at least would seem; felt good on waking. Wounds obviously not healed yet, but closed. A beginning—scabs on soul much better than hemorrhage.

Situation unchanged; obviously not happy about fact (if were would know had slipped cams), but this morning can look at Terry without bursting into tears; can face possibility might have to speed birdbrained twin to Reward before own condition renders unable. Thought produces entirely reasonable antipathy, sincere hope will prove unnecessary—but nothing more.

Despairing paralysis gone; mind no longer locked into hopeless inverse logarithmic spiral, following own tail around ever-closer, all-enveloping fear of ugly possibility.

Seems have regained practical outlook held prior to Armageddon; i.e., regard worry as wasteful, contra-productive if continued after recognition, analysis of impending problem, covering bases to extent resources permit. Endless bone-worrying not constructive exercise; if anything, diminishes odds for favorable outcome by limiting scope of mind's operation, cuts down opportunities for serendipity to lend hand. Besides, takes fun out of life—especially important when little enough to be had.

Time I rejoined world of living (possibly not most apt choice of words—hope do not find am in exclusive possession). First step: consider physical well-being. Have sadly neglected state of health past three weeks; mostly just sat in chair, lay abed listening to airwaves hiss.

And speaking of physical well-being—has just occurred: am ravenous! Have nibbled intermittently without attention to frequency, content—mostly when feeding, watering Terry. (Regardless of own condition, did *not* neglect jovial imbecile during course of depression. Even cobbled up makeshift stand from chair, hardwood implement handle; found sturdy dishes, secured firmly to discourage potential hilarity. Granted, diet not ideal—canned vegetables, fruits, meat, etc.—but heard no complaints from clientele, and would be no doubt if existed: Dissatisfaction with offerings usually first indicated by throwing on floor; if prompt improvement not forthcoming, abandons subtlety.)

Have also noticed am *filthy!* Wearing same clothes came downstairs in three weeks ago. Neither garments nor underlying smelly germ farm exposed to water, soap, deodorant since. (Can be same fastidious Candy Smith-Foster who insists upon shower, complete change of clothing following any hint of physical exertion, contact with even potentially soiled environment? Regrettably is.) And now that am in condition to notice—*have!* Self-respecting maggot would take trade elsewhere.

So please excuse. Must rectify immediately. Bath (probably take three, four complete water changes to do job); then proper meal, clean clothes. Then get down to business. Time to find out about contents of shelter—availability of resources relevant to problems.

Be back later . . . .

Apologies for delay, neglect. But have been so *busy!*

Bath, resumption of proper nutrition completed cure. Spirits restored; likewise determination, resourcefulness, curiosity (intellectual variety; am not snoop—rumors to contrary). Also resumed exercises, drills (paid immediate penalty for three-week neglect of Art—first attempt at usual *kata* nearly broke important places, left numerous sore muscles.)

Have systematically charted shelter. Took pen, pad downstairs to stores, took inventory. Then went through bookshelves in slow, painstaking manner; recorded titles, locations of volumes applicable to problems. Project took best part of three days. Worth effort; variety, volume of equipment simply awesome. Together with library probably represents everything necessary for singlehanded founding of bright new civilization—from scratch, if necessary. (Not keen on singlehanded part, however; sounds lonely. Besides, know nothing about Applied Parthogenesis; not merit badge topic in scouts. Only memory of subject's discussion concerned related research—was no-no; leader claimed caused myopia, acne, nonspecific psychoses. Oh, well, considering age, prospects for achieving functional puberty, seems less than pressing issue.)

Speaking of pressing issues, however—found *food*. Founder of civilization will certainly eat well in interim. Must be five-year supply of frozen meat, fruit, fresh vegetables in deep-freeze locker adjoining lower level (huge things—50 feet square). Stumbled upon by accident; door wasn't labeled. Opened during routine exploration expecting just another bin. Light came on illuminating scenery—almost froze tip of nose admiring contents before realized was standing in 50-degree-below-zero draft. Also good news for Terry: Daddy anticipated presence; lifetime supply of proper seed mix in corner bin. Will keep forever; too cold to hatch inevitable weevil eggs, etc.

Actually haven't minded canned diet; good variety available—but sure was nice to drop mortally-peppered steak onto near-incandescent griddle, inhale fumes as cooked: then cut with fork while still bleeding inside charred exterior. Of course had to fight Terry for share; may be something likes better, but doesn't come readily to mind.

Is regrettable this could be part of Last Words; means must exercise honesty in setting down account. Bulk of organized theologies I've read opine dying with lie upon lips bodes ill for direction of departure. Since can be no doubt of Terry's final Destination, must keep own power dry. Twin would be lonely if got There without me—besides, without watching would announce presence by eating pearls out of Gate.

So despite self-serving impulses, must record faithfully shameful details of final phase in monumental inventory: assault upon card file. Intended to make painstaking, card-by-card inspection of microfilm catalog (vastly more extensive than bound collection), recording titles suggesting relevance to problems. Grim prospect; 72 cubic feet holds dreadful quantity of cards—each with ten titles. Even considering own formidable reading speed, use of Pitman for notes, seemed likely project would account for substantial slice of remaining lifespan—even assuming can count upon normal duration.

David R. Palmer

However, could see no other way; needed information. So took down first drawer (from just below ceiling, of course; but thoughtful Daddy provided rolling ladder as in public stacks), set on table next to notepad. Sighed, took out first card, scanned—stopped, looked again. Pulled out next 20, 30; checked quickly. Made unladylike observation regarding own brains (genius, remember?). Reflected (after exhausted self-descriptive talents) had again underestimated Daddy.

Humble healer, gentle father was embodiment of patience—but had none with unnecessary inefficiency. Obviously would have devised system to locate specifics in such huge collection. Useless otherwise; researcher could spend most of life looking for data instead of using.

First 200 cards index of *index*. Alphabetically categorized, cross-referenced to numbered file locations. Pick category, look up location in main file; check main file for specific titles, authors; find films from specific location number on individual card. Just like downtown.

So after settled feathers from self-inflicted wounds (ten well-deserved lashes with sharp tongue), got organized. Selected categories dealing with situation; referred to main index; decided upon specific films, books. Cautioned Terry again about giblet shortage, dug out selections. Settled down to become expert in nuclear warfare, viral genocide; construction details, complete operation of shelter systems.

Have done so. Now know exactly what happened. Every ugly detail. Know which fissionables used, half-life durations; viral, bacterial agents employed; how deployed, how long remain viable threats without suitable living hosts. Know what they used on us—vice versa. Found Daddy's papers dealing with secret life.

Turns out was heavyweight government consultant. Specialty was countering biological warfare. Privy to highest secrets; Knew all about baddest bugs on both sides. Knew how used, countermeasures most effective—personally responsible for development programs aimed at wide-spectrum etiotropic counteragents. Also knew intimate details of nuclear hardware poised on both sides of face-off. Seems had to: radiation level often key factor: In many cases benign virus, bacteria turned instantaneously inimical upon exposure to critical wavelengths. Only difference between harmless tourist and pathogen: Soothing counsel transmitted from pacific gene in DNA helix to cytoplasmic arsenal by radiation-vulnerable RNA messenger. Enter energy particle flood, exit restraint; hello Attila the Germ. Clever these mad scientists.

Undoubtedly how attack conducted—explains, too, fall of hermetically sealed NORAD citadel. Entire country seeded over period of time with innocuous first-stage organisms until sufficiently wide-spread. Then special warheads—carefully spaced to irradiate every inch of target with critical wavelength—simultaneously detonated at high altitude across whole country. Bombs dropping vertically from space remained undetected until betrayed by flash—by which time too late; radiation front travels just behind visible light. Not a window broken but war already over: Everybody running for shelter already infected, infectious with at least one form of now-activated, utterly lethal second-stage plague. Two, three days later—all of them dead.

Supposed to be another file someplace down here detailing frightful consequences to attackers: haven't found yet. Only mention in this one suggests annihilation even sure, more complete among bad guys—and included broken windows.

Tone of comment regretful. Not sure can agree. True, most dead on both sides civilians—but are truly innocent? Who permitted continuing rule by megalomaniacs? Granted, would have been costly for populace to throw incumbent rascals out, put own rascals in—but considering cost of failure in present light . . .

Must give thought before passing judgment.

Enough philosophy.

Have learned own tactical situation not bad. No radiation detectable on surface, immediate area (instrumentation in shelter; sensors upstairs on roof of house—part of TV antenna). Not surprising: According to thesis, nuclear stuff to be used almost exclusively as catalyst for viral, bacterial invaders. Bursts completely clean—no fallout at all—high enough to preclude physical damage. Exception: Direct hits anticipated on known ICBM silos, SAC bases, Polaris submarines, bomber-carrying carriers, overseas installations—and Washington.

Where Daddy went. Hope was quick, clean.

Plague another question entirely. Daddy holds opinion infection of target country self-curing. No known strain in arsenals of either side capable of more than month's survival outside proper culture media; i.e., living human tissue (shudder to contemplate where, how media obtained for experimentation leading to conclusion). Odds very poor such available longer than two, three days after initial attack; therefore should be only another week before is safe to venture outside, see what remains of world. However, wording, " . . . should be . . . " erodes confidence in prediction; implies incomplete date, guesswork—*gamble*. Considering stake involved is own highly regarded life, placing absolute reliance on stated maximum contagion parameters not entirely shrewd policy.

So shan't. Now that can get out whenever wish, no longer have such pressing need to; claustrophobic tendencies gone. Shelter quite cozy (considering): Dry, warm, plumbing, furniture; great food (brilliantly prepared), safe water; good company, stimulating conversation ("Hello, baby! What'cha doin'? You're so bad! Icky *pooh!*"); plus endless supply of knowledge. Delay amidst such luxury seems small price for improved odds. So will invest extra two months as insurance.

Figure arbitrary; based on theory that treble safety factor was good enough for NASA, should be good enough for me. (Of course theory includes words "should be" again, but must draw line somewhere.)

And *can* get out when ready. Easy: Just throw proper switches. All spelled out in detailed manual on shelter's systems, operation. Nothing to it. Just pick up book, read. After finding. After learning exists in first place. (Daddy could have reduced first three weeks' trauma had bothered to mention, point out where kept—on other hand, had learned how to get out prior to absorbing details on attack, would doubtless be dead now.)

Makes fascinating reading. Shelter eloquent testimonial to wisdom of designer. Foresight, engineering brilliance embodied in every detail. Plus appalling amount of money, shameless level of political clout. Further I got into manual, more impressed became. Is NORAD headquarters miniaturized, improved: hermetically sealed; air, water, wastes recycled; elaborate communications equipment; sophisticated sensory complex for radiation, electronics, detection, seismology, medicine. Power furnished by nuclear device about size of Volkswagen—classified, of course (talk about clout?). Don't know if works; supposed to come on automatically when municipal current fails. But according to instruments am still running on outside power.

Let's see—nope; seems to be about everything for now. Will update journal as breathtaking developments transpire.

Hi. One-month mark today. Breathless developments to date:

1. Found stock of powdered milk; awful. Okay in soup, chocolate, cooking, etc., but alone tastes boiled.

2. Discovered unplugged phone in hitherto-unnoticed cabinet. Also found jack. Plugged in, found system still working. Amused self by ringing phones about country—random area codes, number. But no answers, of course; and presently noticed tears streaming down face. Decided not emotionally healthy practice. Discontinued.

3. Employed carpentry tools, pieces of existing makeshift accommodation to fabricate proper stand for brother. Promptly demonstrated gratitude by chewing through perch (which had not bothered for whole *month!*). Replaced with thick, hardwood sledge handle; sneered, dared him try again. Have thereby gained temporary victory: Fiend immediately resumed game but achieving little progress. Wish had stands from upstairs in house. Are three, all 11 years old—still undamaged (of course, perches consist of hard-cured, smoothcast concrete—detail possibly relevant to longevity).

Guess that's it for now. Watch this space for further stirring details.

Two months—hard to believe not millennia. Einstein correct: Time *is* relative. Hope doesn't get more so; probably stop altogether. Have wondered occasionally if already hasn't.

Not to imply boredom. Gracious, how could be bored amidst unremitting pressure from giddy round of social activities? For instance, just threw gala party to celebrate passing of second month. Was smash, high point of entombment, sensation of sepulchral social schedule. Went all out—even invited Terry (desperately relieved to find invitee able to squeeze event into already busy whirl of commitments).

First class event: Made cake, fried chicken thighs, broiled small steak; even found ice cream. All turned out well. Preferred steak, cake myself; honored guest chose ice cream (to eyebrows), chicken bones (splits shafts, devours marrow—possibly favoritest treat of all). No noisemakers in inventory (gross oversight), but assemblage combined efforts to compensate. At peak of revelry birdbrain completed chewing through perch. Was standing on end at time, of course; accepted downfall with pride, air of righteous triumph. Then waddled purposefully in direction of nearest chair leg. Had to move fast to dissuade.

Replaced perch.

Also have read 104 microfilmed books, regular volumes. Am possibly world's foremost living authority on everything.

As if matters.

Later.

Ever wanted something so bad could almost taste, needed so long seemed life's main ambition? Finally got—wished hadn't?

You guessed: Three months up—*finally!*

Went upstairs, outside. Stayed maybe two hours. Wandered old haunts: familiar neighborhood, Main Street shopping area, Quarry Lake Park, school, Y, etc.

Should have quit sooner: would, had understood nature of penalty accruing. By time got back was already too late; trembling all over, tears running down face. Scabs all scraped from wounds: worms awake, gnawing soul. In parlance of contemporaries-past: Was bad trip.

However, conditions outside are fact of life, something must face. Must overcome reaction unless intend to spend balance of years simulating well-read mole. Nature works slowly, methods unesthetic; tidying up takes years. Inescapable; must accept as is; develop blind spot, immunity. Meanwhile will just have to cope best I can with resulting trauma each time crops up until quits cropping.

Well, coping ought to be no problem. Catharsis worked before, should again. But wish were some other way. No fun; hurts almost as much second time around. But works—and already learned cannot function with psyche tied in knots. So time to quit stalling. "Sooner started, sooner done; sooner outside, having fun."—Anon. (Understandably.)

Only just *can't* right now. Not in mood; still hurting from initial trauma, Guess I'll go read some more. Or pound something together with hammer.

Or apart.

Later.

Okay. Feel no better yet, but feel less bad. Is time got on with therapy.

Suspect current problems complicated by *déjà vu*. Still retain vivid mental picture of body of Momma Foster minutes after pronounced dead. Bore physical resemblance to warm, wise, vital woman whose limitless interests, avid curiosity, ready wonderment, hearty enjoyment of existence had so enriched early years.

David R. Palmer

But body not person—person *gone*. Resemblance only underscored absence.

So too with village: Look quick, see no difference. Bears resemblance to contentedly industrious, unassuming, small farm town of happy childhood. Same tall, spreading trees shade same narrow streets; well-kept, comfortably ageless old homes. Old-fashioned street lights line Main Street's storefront downtown business district, unchanged for 50 years, fronting on classic village square. Hundred-year-old township building centered in square amidst collection of heroic statues, World War One mementos, playground equipment; brightly-painted, elevated gazebo for public speakers. Look other direction down street, see own ivy-covered, redbrick school at far end, just across from Y. Next door, Teacher's house looks bright, friendly, inviting as ever in summer-afternoon sunshine.

But open door, step out onto porch—illusion fades. Popular fallacy attends mystique of small towns: Everyone knows are "quiet." Not so; plenty of noise, but right kind—comfortable, unnoticed.

Until gone.

Silence is shock. Is wrong, but takes whole minutes to analyze *why* wrong; identify anomalous sensation, missing input.

Strain ears for hint of familiar sound: Should be faint miasma of voices, traffic sounds drifting up from direction of Main Street; chatter, squeals, laughter from schoolyard. Too, is truly small town, farmlands close at hand; should hear tractors chugging in fields, stock calling from pastures. Should catch frequent hollow mutter as distant semi snores down highway past town; occasional, barely-perceptible rumble from jet, visible only as fleecy tracing against indigo sky. Should be all manner of familiar sounds.

But as well could be heart of North Woods; sounds reaching ear limited to insect noises, bird calls, wind sighing through leaves.

Visual illusion fades quickly, too. Knee-deep grass flourishes where had been immaculately groomed yards; straggly new growth bewhiskers hedges, softening precious mathematically-exact outlines. Houses up and down street show first signs of neglect: Isolated broken windows, doors standing open, missing shingles. Partially uprooted tree leans on Potter's house, cracking mortar, crushing eaves, sagging roof. Street itself blocked by car abandoned at crazy angle; tire flat, rear window broken, driver's door hanging open. Closer inspection shows Swensens' pretty yellow-brick Cape Cod nothing but fire-gutted shell; roof mostly gone, few panes of glass remain, dirty smudge marks above half-consumed doors and windows; nearby trees singed.

And the *smell . . . !* Had not spent last three months sealed in own atmosphere, doubt could have remained in vicinity. Still strong enough outside to dislodge breakfast within moments of first encounter. And did. Happily, human constitution can learn to tolerate almost anything if must. By time returned to shelter, stench faded from forefront of consciousness—had other problems more pressing:

Learned what knee-deep lawns conceal. Three months' exposure to Wisconsin summer does little to enhance cosmetic aspects of Nature's embalming methods: Sun, rain, insects, birds, probably dogs, too, have disposed of bulk of soft tissues. What remains is skeletons (mostly scattered, incomplete, partially covered by semi-cured meat, some clothing). Doubtless would have mummified completely by now in dry climate, but Wisconsin summers aren't. At best, results unappealing: at worst (first stumbled over in own front yard), dreadful shock.

Yes, I know; should have anticipated. Possibly did, in distant, nonpersonally-involved sort of way—but didn't expect to find three bodies within ten feet of own front door! Didn't expect to confront dead neighbors within three minutes after left burrow. Didn't expect so *many!* Thought most would be respectably tucked away indoors, perhaps in bed. That's where I'd be. I think.

Well, lived through initial shock, continued foray. Was not systematic exploration; just wandered streets, let feet carry us at random. Didn't seem to matter; same conditions everywhere. Peeked into houses, stores, cars; knocked on doors, hollered a lot.

Wasn't until noticed twin digging in claws, flapping wings, protesting audibly that realized was running blindly, screaming for somebody—*anybody!*

Stopped then, streaming tears, trembling, panting (must have run some distance); made desperate attempt to regain semblance of control. Dropped where stood, landed in lotus. Channeled thoughts into relaxation of body, achievement of physical serenity; hoped psyche would heed good example.

Did—sort of. Worked well enough, at least, to permit deliberate progress back to shelter, deliberate closing door, deliberate descent of stairs, deliberate placing of Terry on stand—all before threw screaming fit.

Discharged lots of tension in process, amused Terry hugely. By end of performance fink sibling was emulating noises. Ended hysteria in laughter. Backwards, true, but effective.

Recovered enough to make previous journal entry. Granted, present (therapeutic) entries beyond capacity at that point; but after spent balance of day licking wounds, night's rest, was fit enough to make present update, discharge residual pain onto paper.

Amazing stuff, therapy; still not exactly looking forward to going outside again, but seem to have absorbed trauma of dead-body/deserted-city shock; adjusted to prospect of facing again. Forewarned, should be able to go about affairs, function effectively in spite of surroundings.

Which brings up entirely relevant question: Exactly what *are* my affairs, functions . . . ? Now that am out, what to do? Where to go? What to do when get there? Why bother go at all?

Okay, fair questions. Obviously prime objective is find Somebody Else. Preferably somebody knowing awful lot about Civilizations, Founding & Maintenance Of—to say nothing of where to find next meal when supplies run out.

David R. Palmer

Certainly other survivors. Somewhere. So must put together reasonable plan of action based on logical extension of available data. Sounds good—uh, except, what *is* available data?

Available data: Everybody exposed to flash, to air at time of flash, to anybody else exposed to flash or air exposed to flash or to anybody exposed to anybody, etc., either at time of flash or during subsequent month, anywhere on planet, is dead. Period.

Shucks. Had me worried; thought for moment I had problem. Ought be plenty survivors; modern civilization replete with airtight refuges: nuclear submarines, hyperbaric chambers, space labs, jet transports, "clean assembly" facilities, many others (not to forget early-model VW beetles, so long as windows closed). Ought be many survivors of flash, initial contagion phase.

But—loaded question—how many knew enough; stayed tight throughout required month? Or got lucky, couldn't get out too soon despite best efforts? Or with best intentions, had supplies, air for duration? Or survived emotional ravages; resisted impulse to open window, take big, deliberate breath?

Could employ magnet to find needle in haystack; easy by comparison. Real problem is: *Is needle in there at all?*

Well, never mind; leave for subconscious to mull. Good track record heretofore; probably come up with solution, given time.

Other, more immediate problems confronting: For one, must think about homestead. Can't spend balance of years living underground. Unhealthy; leads to pallor. Besides, doubt is good for psyche; too many ghosts.

Where—no problem for short term; can live just about anywhere warm, dry. Adequate food supplies available in shelter, stores, home pantries, etc.; same with clothing, sundry necessities. Can scavenge for years if so inclined.

However, assuming residential exclusivity continues (and must take pessimistic view when planning), must eventually produce own food, necessities; become self-sufficient. Question is: Should start now or wait; hope won't prove necessary?

Not truly difficult decision: longer delayed, more difficult transition becomes. Livestock factor alone demands prompt attention. Doubtless was big die-off over summer. Too stupid to break out of farms, pastures, search for water, feed, most perished—"domestic" synonym for "dependent." But of survivors, doubt one in thousand makes it through winter unaided. Means if plan to farm, must round up beginning inventory before weather changes. Also means must have food, water, physical accommodations ready for inductees beforehand.

Means must have farm.

However, logic dictates commandeering farm relatively nearby. Too much of value in shelter; must maintain reasonable access. Availability of tools, books, etc., beneficial in coming project: provisioning, repairing fences, overhaul well-pumps, etc.

Plus work needed to put house in shape for winter. Wisconsin seasons rough on structures; characteristic swayback rooflines usually not included in builder's plan, zoning regulations. After summer's neglect, buildings of farm selected apt to need much work—none of which am qualified to do. Expect will find remainder of summer, fall highly educational, very busy.

So perhaps should quit reflecting on plans, get move on. Best reconnoiter nearby farms. Be nice to find one with buildings solid, wells pumping, fences intact, etc.; be equally nice to meet jolly red-dressed, white-bearded gentleman cruising down road in sleigh pulled by reindeer.

Hi, again. Surprised to see me? Me too. Thinking of changing name to Pauline, serializing journal. Or maybe just stay home, take up needlepoint. Seems during entombment character of neighborhood changed; deteriorated, gotten rough—literally gone to dogs. Stepped out of A&P right into—nope, this won't do. Better stick to chronology; otherwise sure to miss something. Might even be important someday. So:

Awoke fully recovered—again (truly growing tired of yo-yo psychology). Since planned to be out full day, collected small pile of equipment, provisions: canteen, jerky, dried apricots, bag of parrot mix; hammer, pry bar (in case forcible investigation indicated). Went upstairs, outside.

Retained breakfast by force of will until accustomed to aroma.

Took bike from garage, rode downtown (first ride in three months; almost deafened by twin's manic approval). After three months' neglect, tires a tad soft (ten-speed requires 85 pounds); stopped at Olly's Standard, reinflated. And marveled: Utilities still on, compressor, pumps, etc., still working—even bell still rang when rode across hose.

Started to go on way; stopped—had thought. Returned, bled air tanks as had seen Big Olly do. Had explained: Compression, expansion of air in tanks "made water" through condensation; accumulation bad for equipment. Found was starting to think in terms of preserving everything potentially useful against future need. (Hope doesn't develop into full-blown neurosis; maintaining whole world could cramp schedule.)

Set about conducting check of above-ground resources: Eyeball-inventoried grocery stores, hardware, seed dealers; took ride down to rail depot, grain elevators. Found supplies up everywhere; highly satisfactory results. Apparently business conducted as usual after flash until first symptoms emerged. No evidence of looting; probably all too sick to bother.

And since power still on, freezers in meat markets maintaining temperature; quantity available probably triple that in shelter. If conditions similar in nearby towns, undoubtedly have lifetime supply of everything—or until current stops. (Personally, am somewhat surprised still working; summer thunderstorms habitually drop lines, blow transformers twice, three times a year—and *winter* . . ! One good ice storm brings out candles for days; prime reason why even new houses, designed with latest heating systems, all have old-fashioned Franklin-type oil stoves in major rooms, usually multiple fireplaces. Doubt will have electricity by spring.)

OH HELL! Beg pardon; unladylike outburst—but just realized: Bet every single farm well in state *electrically* operated. I got *troubles. . . !*

Well, just one more problem for subconscious to worry about. Can't do anything about it now—but must devote serious thought.

Back to chronology: Emerged from A&P around ten; kicked up stand, prepared to swing leg over bike. Suddenly Terry squawked, gripped shoulder so hard felt like claws met in middle. Dropped bike, spun.

Six dogs: Big, lean, hungry; visibly exempt from "Best Friend" category.

Given no time to consider strategy; moment discovered, pack abandoned stealth, charged. Had barely time to toss twin into air, general direction of store roof, wish Godspeed. Then became very busy.

Had not fought in three months but continued *kata:* was in good shape. Fortunate.

First two (Shepherd, Malamute) left ground in formation, Doberman close behind. Met Malamute (bigger of two) in air with clockwise spin-kick to lower mandible attachment. Felt bones crunch, saw without watching as big dog windmilled past, knocking Shepherd sprawling. Took firm stance, drove forward front-fist blow under Doberman's jaw, impacting high on chest, left of center. Fist buried to wrist; felt scapula, clavicle, possibly also humerus crumble; attacker bounced five feet backwards, landed in tangle. Spun, side-kicked Shepherd behind ear as scrambled to rise; felt vertebrae give. Took fast step, broke Malamute's neck with edge-hand chop. Spun again, jumped for Doberman; broke neck before could rise.

Glanced up, body coiling for further combinations—relaxed; remaining three had revised schedule; were halfway across parking lot.

Looked wildly about for Terry; spotted twin just putting on brakes for touchdown on shopping cart handle 20 feet away. Wondered what had been doing in interim; seemed could have flown home, had dinner, returned to watch outcome.

Retrieved; lectured about stupidity, not following orders—suppose had been flankers? Would have been lunch before I got there.

Birdbrain accepted rebuke; nuzzled cheek in agreement, murmured, "You're so icky-poo!"

Gave up; continued sortie.

Wondered briefly at own calmness. First blows ever struck in earnest; halfway expected emotional side-effects. But none; only mild regret had not met attackers under favorable circumstances. Doberman in particular was beautiful specimen, if could disregard gauntness.

Decided, in view of events, might be best if continued explorations in less vulnerable mode. Decided was time I soloed. Had driven cars before, of course; country kids all learn vehicular operation basics soonest moment eyes (augmented by cushions) clear dashboard, feet reach pedals.

Question of which car to appropriate gave pause. Have no particular hangups: familiar (for nondriver) with automatics, three-, four-speed manuals, etc. But would be poking nose down vestigial country roads, venturing up driveways more accustomed (suitable) to passage of tractor, horses; squeezing in, out of tight places; doubtless trying hard to get very stuck. Granted, had been relatively dry recently; ground firm most places, but—considering potential operating conditions, physical demands . . .

Would take Daddy's old VW. Happy selection: Answered physical criteria (maneuverable, good traction, reliable, etc.); besides, had already driven—for sure could reach pedals, see out. Did give thought to Emerson's Jeep, but never had opportunity to check out under controlled conditions. Further, has plethora of shift levers (three!). True, might be more capable vehicle, but sober reflection suggested unfamiliar advantages might prove trap; seemed simpler, more familiar toy offered better odds of getting back.

Pedaled home quickly, keeping weather eye out for predators (can take hint). Arrived without incident. Found key, established blithe sibling on passenger's seatback: adjusted own seat for four-foot-ten-inch stature, turned key.

Results would have warmed ad-writer's heart: After standing idle three months, Beetle cranked industriously about two seconds; started.

Gauge showed better than three-quarters full, but wanted to make sure; lonely country road frequented by hungry dog packs wrong place to discover faulty gauge. So backed gingerly down drive (killed only twice), navigated cautiously to Olly's. Stuck in hose, got two gallons in before spit back. Beetle's expression seemed to say, " . . . *told* you so," as capped tank, hung up hose.

Went about tracking down suitable farm in workmanlike fashion, for beginner. Picked up area USGS Section Map from Sheriff's office. Methodically plotted progress as went; avoided circling, repetition. Drove 150 miles; visited 30, 35 farms; marked off on map as left, graded on one-to-ten basis. Were many nice places; some could make do in pinch. But none rated above seven; nothing rang bell until almost dark.

Found self at terminus of cowpath road. Had wound through patchy woods, hills; felt must go somewhere so persevered to end, where found mailbox, driveway. Turned in; shortly encountered closed gate. Opened, drove through; resecured. Followed drive through woods, over small rise, out into clearing, farmyard. Stopped abruptly.

Knew at once was *home* . . .

To right stood pretty, almost new, red-brick house; to left, brand-new, modern steel barn, hen house; twin silos (one new), three corn cribs—all full.

Got out, walked slowly around house, mouth open, heart pounding. No broken windows, doors closed, shingles all in place—*grass cut!* For glorious moment heart stopped altogether; thought had stumbled on nest of survivors. Then rounded corner, bumped into groundskeepers—sheep.

Owners quite dead. Found remains of man in chair on porch. Apparently spent last conscious moments reflecting upon happy memories. Picture album in lap suggested four impromptu graves short distance from house were wife, three children; markers

David R. Palmer

confirmed. Fine-looking people; faces showed confidence, contentment, love; condition of farm corroborated, evidenced care, pride.

Grew misty-eyed looking through album. Resolved to operate farm in manner founders would approve. Had handed me virtual "turn-key" homestead; immeasurably advanced schedule, boosted odds for self-sufficiency, survival. Least I could do in return.

Farm nestles snugly in valley amidst gently rolling, wooded countryside. Clean, cold, fast-running brook meanders generally through middle, passes within hundred yards of house; and by clever fence placement, zigs, zags, or loops through all pastures. Perimeter fence intact; strong, heavy-gauge, small-mesh fabric. Probably not entirely dog-proof, but highly resistant; with slight additional work should be adequate.

Contents of silos, cribs, loft product of season's first planting; second crop still in fields—primary reason stock alive, healthy. Internal gates open throughout; allowed access to water, varied grazing (including nibbling minor leakages from cribs, silos). Beasties spent summer literally eating "fat of land"; look it.

Besides five sheep are nine cows (two calves, one a *bull),* two mares, one gelding, sundry poultry (rooster, two dozen chickens. motley half-dozen ducks, geese). No pigs, but no tears; don't like pigs, not wild about pork either.

From evidence, losses over summer low: Found only two carcasses: two cows, one horse. Bones not scattered, doubt caused by dogs; more likely disease, injury, stupidity—salient characteristic of domestic ruminants: Given opportunity, will gorge on no-no, pay dearly later.

Wandered grounds, poked through buildings until light gone. Found good news everywhere looked. Nothing I can't use as is, put right with minor work.

Clocked distance on return: 17 miles by road. Not too bad; can walk if necessary—should breakdown occur while commuting—but perhaps wiser to hang bike on bumper. Still, machines can't last forever; only matter of time before forced back to horseback technology. Will still have occasion to visit shelter often. Map shows straightline distance only nine miles; guess better learn bulldozer operation, add road-building to skills. (Goodness—future promises such varied experiences; may vary me to death. . . .)

Was late when finally got back to shelter, tired but glowing all over at prospect. Can hardly wait for morning, start packing, moving in; start of new life.

Demented twin shares view; hardly shut up whole time were at farm. Or since. Lectured stock, dictated to poultry, narrated inspection tour throughout. Hardly took time out for snack, drink. Must be country boy at heart. So urbane, never suspected.

Hey—am really *tired!*

Good night.

Oh! Hurt places didn't even know I had. Suspect must have come into being just for occasion.

Six trips to farm. Count 'em.

Light failed just before self. Packing stuff from house no problem: Eight, ten trips to car; all done. Stuff in shelter is rub. Aye.

Two hundred feet straight up, arms loaded. Repeatedly.

Must be better way.

Good night.

This is embarrassing; guess in time quit posing as genius. Proof in pudding. What matter 200-plus IQ if actions compatible with mobile vegetable?

Occurred this morning to ponder (after third trip up stairs) how excavated material removed during construction. Hand-carried in buckets? Counting stairwell, material involved amounts to 200,000 cubic feet plus. At half cube per bucket, assuming husky lad carrying doubles, 15-minute round trips, that's 32 cubic feet every eight hours. Would take ten-man crew 625 days—not counting down time due to heart attacks, hernias, fallen arches. . . .

And what about heavy stuff? Doubt nuclear generator carried down by hand—must weigh couple tons.

Okay. Obviously done some other way. But how? Oh—shelter manual; had forgotten. Thumbed through quickly, found answer; *elevator!* Of course. Missed significance of small, odd-shaped, empty storeroom during first inspection. Other things on mind; didn't notice controls.

Balance of day much easier. Still tired tonight but not basket case.

Tomorrow is another day. . . !

STOP THE PRESSES! Strike the front page! Scoop! I'm not me—I'm something else. No—we're not us—no—oh, bother; not making *any* sense. But can't help it; hard to organize thought—so DAMNED excited. . . ! Will try, *must* try. Otherwise will end up leaving out best parts, most important stuff. Then, by time get feathers settled, blood pressure reduced, will have forgotten *everything! Oh,* must stop this *blithering!* Must get back to chronology. So . . .

Deep breath . . . release slow-oo-ow-ly . . . heart slowed to normal, physical tranquility . . . serenity . . . ohm-m-m . . .

Amazing, worked again.

Okay, resumed packing this morning. Took two loads over, returned for third. Finished; everything in car, at farm that felt would need. But still fidgeting; couldn't decide why. No question of something forgotten; farm only short drive away, omission not crisis.

Finally recognized source of unscratchable itch: Was time I did duty. Had avoided at first; knew couldn't face prospect. Then got so busy, slipped mind. But now remembered: Soo Kim McDivott. Teacher. Friend.

To friend falls duty of seeing to final resting place.

Generally inured now to face of death *per se*; unaffected last few days by myriad corpses have stepped over during course of running errands. Had no problem, for instance, removing Mr. Haralsen from porch to proper place beside wife, children; even finished job with warm feeling inside. (Suspect original trauma caused by sudden shock of events; enormity, completeness of isolation.) Condition improved now; felt could perform final service for old friend—more, felt need to.

Went next door, looked for body. Checked entire house: upstairs, downstairs, basement—even stuck head in attic.

Finally returned to library. Teacher had used as study; desk located there, most of favorite dog-eared references close at hand. Hoped might find clue regarding where-abouts amidst clutter.

First thing to catch was "Tarzan File" standing on desk. Large envelope taped to top, printing on face. Glanced at wording. Blood froze.

Was addressed to me!

Pulled loose, opened with suddenly shaking fingers. Teacher's meticulous script legible, beautiful as Jefferson's on Declaration, read:

Dearest Candidia,

It is the considered opinion of several learned men familiar with your situation among them Dr. Foster and myself, that you will survive the plague to find and read this. The viral complex employed by the enemy cannot harm you, we know; it was created as a specific against Homo sapiens.

Almost dropped letter. Surely required no genius to note implications. Took deep breath, read on:

I know, my child, that that statement must sound like the ramblings of an old man in extremis . . .

Ramble? *Teacher!* Ha! True, was old; condition intrinsic to amount of water over dam—of which lots (all deep, too). Probably also in extremis; lot of that going around when wrote this. But ramble? *Teacher?* Comes the day Teacher rambles, Old Nick announces cooling trend, New Deal, takes up post as skiing instructor on glorious powder slopes of Alternate Destination. *I* ramble; Teacher's every word precise, correct.

Precise, correct letter went on:

. . . but please, before forming an opinion, humor me to the extent of reading the balance of this letter and reviewing the supporting evidence which documents 25 years of painstaking investigation by me and others.

Note that of 1,284 incidents wherein wild animals of varying descriptions "adopted" human children, none (with the exception of the very youngest—those recovered from the wild below age three) developed significantly beyond the adoptive parents. They could not be taught to communicate; they evinced no abstract reasoning; they could not be educated. IQ testing, where applicable, produced results indistinguishable from similar tests performed on random members of the "parents" species. Further, except for the 29 cases where the adoptive parents were of a species possessing rudimentary hands (apes, monkeys, the two raccoon incidents; to a lesser degree the badger and the wolverine), the children possessed no awareness of the concept of grasping, nor did it prove possible to teach them any manual skills whatever.

Finally, most authorities (note the citations in the file) are agreed that Man is born devoid of instincts, save (a point still in contention) suckling; therefore, unlike lesser animals, human development is entirely dependent upon learning and, therefore, environment.

This principle was deeply impressed upon me during the years I spent studying a number of these children; and it occurred to me to wonder what effect this mechanism might have within human society—whether average parents, for instance, upon producing a child possessing markedly superior genetic potential, might raise such a child (whether through ignorance, unconscious resentment or envy, deliberate malice, or some unknown reason) in such a manner as to prevent his development from exceeding their own attainments; and if such efforts took place, to what extent the child would in fact be limited.

Then followed narrative of early stages of investigation, solo at first, but producing preliminary findings so startling that shortly was directing efforts of brilliant group of associates (including *Daddy!*), whole project funded by bottomless government grant. Object of search: reliable clues, indicators upon which testing program could be based enabling identification of gifted children (potential geniuses) shortly after birth, before retardation (if such truly existed) began operation.

Efforts rewarded: Various factors pinpointed which, encountered as group, were intrinsic to genetically superior children. Whereupon study shifted to second phase. As fast as "positives" found, identified, were assigned to study group. Were four:

AA (positive/advantaged), potentially gifted kids whose parents were in on experiment; guided, subsidized, assisted every way possible to provide optimum environment for learning, development. AB (positive/nonadvantaged), potential geniuses whose parents weren't let in on secret; would have to bloom or wither, depending on qualities of vine. BA (negative/advantaged), ordinary babies, random selection, whose parents were encouraged (for which read "conned") to think offspring were geniuses; also received benefit of AA-type parental coaching (and coaches didn't know whether were dealing with AA or BA parents), financial assistance. And BB (negative / nonadvantaged), control group: ordinary babies raised ordinary way. Whatever that is.

As expected, AAs did well in school; average progress tripled national norm. Further, personality development also remarkable: AA kids almost offensively well adjusted; happy, well-integrated personalities. BAs did well, too, but beat national figures by only 15 percent. Were also generally happy, but isolated individuals dem-

David R. Palmer

onstrated symptoms suggesting insecurity; perhaps being pushed close to, even beyond capabilities.

ABs also produced spotty results: Goods very good, equaling AA figures in certain cases; however, bads *very* bad; ABs had highest proportion of academic failures, behavioral problems, perceptibly maladjusted personalities.

BBs, of course, showed no variation at all from national curves; were just kids.

Study progressed cozily; all content as confirming evidence of own cleverness emerged from statistical analysis, continued to accumulate (Teacher, in particular, basking in glow emanating from vindication of theory), when suddenly Joker popped from deck;

It became obvious that AA and AB children lost vastly less time from school through illness. Further breakdown, however, showed that approximately one third of the positives had never lost any time, while the balance had attendance records indistinguishable from the norm. Detailed personal inquiry revealed that these particular children had never been sick from any cause, while the balance had had the usual random selection of childhood illnesses. It was also determined that these unfailingly healthy positives were far and away the highest group of achievers in the AA group and constituted the best, worst, and most maladjusted of the AB group.

At that time study blessed by convenient tragedy: healthy child died in traffic accident. Body secured for autopsy.

Every organ was examined minutely, every tissue sample was scrutinized microscopically and chemically, and chromosome examination was performed. Every test known to the science of pathology was performed, most three, four, and five times, because no one was willing to believe the results.

And thereafter, quickly and by various subterfuges, complete physicals, including x-rays, and biopsy samples of blood, bone, skin, hair, and a number of organs were obtained from the full test group and compared.

The differences between "healthy" positives and the balance proved uniform throughout the sample, and were unmistakeable to an anthropologist . . .

Shock upon shock: Folksy, humble, simple Teacher was Ph.D.—three times over! Was physician (double-barreled—pediatrician, psychiatrist) plus anthropologist. Predictably, renowned in all three—qualities leading to Tenth Degree not confined to Art.

. . . but none of themselves were of a character to attract the notice of a physician not specifically and methodically hunting for an unknown "common denominator," using mass sampling techniques and a very open mind; nor would they attract notice by affecting the outcome of any known medical test or procedure. The single most dramatic difference is the undisputed fact, still unexplained, that "healthy" positives are totally immune to the full spectrum of human disease.

Differences proved independent of race, sex: Makeup of AA, AB "healthy" kids

52 percent female; half Caucasoid, one third Negroid, balance apportioned between Oriental, Hispanic, Indian, other unidentifiable fractions. Breakdown matched precisely population area from which emerged.

The conclusion is indisputable: Although clearly of the genus Homo, AA and AB "healthy" children are not human beings; they are a species distinct unto themselves.

Quite aside from the obvious aspect of immunity and the less obvious anatomical characteristics which identify them, these children possess clear physical superiority over Homo sapiens children of like size and weight. They are stronger, faster, more resistant to trauma, and demonstrate markedly quicker reflexive responses. Visual, aural, and olfactory functions operate over a broader range and at higher levels of sensitivity than in humans. We have no data upon which to base even a guess as to the magnitude, but all evidence points toward a substantially longer lifespan.

A study was begun immediately, a search for clues which might help to explain this phenomenon of uniformly mutated children being born to otherwise normal, healthy human couples. And these couples were normal: To the limits of our clinical capabilities to determine, they were indistinguishable from any other Homo sapiens.

However, it was only very recently, after years of the most exhaustive background investigation and analysis, that a possible link was noticed. It was an obvious connection, but so removed in time that we almost missed its significance, due to the usual scientific tendency to probe for the abstruse while ignoring the commonplace.

The grandmothers of these children were all of a similar age, born within a two-year span: All were conceived during the rampage of the great influenza pandemic of 1918-19.

This "coincidence" fairly shouts its implications: Sweeping genetic recombination, due to specific viral invasion, affecting either of the gametes before, or both during, formation of the zygotes which became the grandmothers, creating in each half of the matrix which fitted together two generations later to become the AA and AB "healthy" children.

Personally I have no doubt that this is the explanation: however, so recently has this information come to light, that we have not had time to study the question in detail. And suspecting that something may be true—even a profound inner conviction—is not the same as proving it. I hope you will one day have the opportunity to add this question to your own studies. It needs answering.

After much reflection we named this new species Homo post hominem, meaning 'Man Who Follows Man,' for it would appear that this mutation is evolutionary in character; and that, given time and assuming it breeds true (there is no reason to suspect otherwise—in fact, chromosome examination suggests that the mutation is dominant; i.e., a sapiens/hominem pairing should unfailingly produce a hominem) it will entirely supplant Homo sapiens.

Wonderful thing, the human nervous system; accustoms quickly to mortal shocks.

David R. Palmer

Didn't even twitch as other shoe landed—or perhaps had anticipated from buildup; just wondering how would be worded:

Very nice; no fanfare, just matter-of-fact statement:

You, my child, are a Homo post hominem. You are considerably younger than your fellows among the study group, and were never involved in the study itself. Your identification and inclusion in our sample came about late and through rather involved and amusing circumstances.

The Fosters, as you know, had long desired a child and had known equally long that they could never have one. When your natural parents died, it was entirely predictable that they lost no time securing your adoption (which is certainly understandable; you were a most winning baby).

Neither Daddy nor rest of staff thought to have me tested: had been exposed to ten months' "unmonitored parentage"; was "compromised subject." Besides, Daddy wasn't interested in studying me; wanted to enjoy raising "his little girl." Professional competence crumbled before gush of atavistic paternalism. Most reprehensible.

Momma disagreed; felt determination of potential would provide useful child-rearing information. In keeping with formula long established for maintaining smooth marriage, kept disagreement to self; however, took steps: Prevailed upon staff to test me—all unbeknownst to Daddy.

Tests proved positive, but follow-up determination as to "healthy" status not performed—didn't occur to discipline-blinkered scientists, and Momma didn't know any better so didn't insist.

You were a genius; she was content. And she thereupon took it upon herself to see that you were raised in the same "advantaged" manner as the rest of the AAs—with the exception of the fact that the doctor did not know this was taking place. He continued to enjoy his "daddy's little girl" as before, prating endlessly about the advantages of "sugar and spice," etc. And as for the rest of us, after swearing each other to secrecy about your test results and our involvement, we forgot you. You were, after all, a "compromised subject."

Was almost five when next came to their attention. Had soured "sugar and spice" by glancing up, commenting living room wall " . . . looks awful hot." Was, too—result of electrical fault. Would have burned down house shortly.

Remember incident clearly. Not that caused any particular, immediate fuss, but Daddy spent balance of evening trying not to show was staring at me.

The doctor had spent much time during the previous few years observing children whose visual perception extended into the infrared and ultraviolet; and as shortly thereafter as possible, without letting Mrs. Foster know, he had you examined and tested.

Oho! Finally—explanation what triggered Daddy's reaction that day—and of friends' inexplicable night-blindness, even during summer. Of course, could understand difficulty seeing at night during winter; is *dark* outside on cold night. Only perceptible glow comes from faces, hands; and after short exposure to cold, cheeks, noses dim perceptibly.

And remember also that testing session. Salient feature was expressions of other staff as repeated tests done on previous (conspicuously unmentioned) occasion: utterly deadpan.

It was only after the tests (performed fully this time) identified you as a Homo post hominem; after the doctor had diffidently broached this fact to Mrs. Foster and she, giggling helplessly, confessed to him and, finally, we also came clean, that further testing demonstrated that you were substantially more advanced in intellectual development than the profile developed by our studies suggested you should be at that age.

How nice. Even as superkid can't be normal: still genius. Is no justice.

Detailed analysis of this phenomenon brought forth two unassessable factors: One, you had experienced ten months of unmonitored BB parentage; and two, your subsequent upbringing had been AA from your mother but BB from your father. Since we could neither analyze nor affect the first of these, we chose to continue the second factor unaltered, observing you closely and hoping that in some way, then unknown, the whipsaw combination of indulgent spoiling and accelerated, motivational education you had received to this point would continue to produce these outstanding results.

Momma's death terminated experiment; but before she left, made Teacher promise would take over overt management of education, keep pushing me hard as would accept while Daddy (apparently) continued classic BB father role. Momma felt hunger for knowledge already implanted; abetted by Daddy's careful negative psychology, seeding of environment with selected books (*Ha!* Always suspected something fishy about circumstances surrounding steady discovery of wanted, needed study materials, always just in time, just as finishing previous volume—not complaining; just wish planting had gone faster), would carry on through interim without lost momentum. Was right, too—but now know how puppet must feel when wires too thin to discern.

Phase Two of scheme hit snag, though; was not anticipated would take four years for Teacher to extricate self from complications attendant profession(s), "retire."

Fortunately the delay appeared to be without consequences. Mrs. Foster's opinion of you was borne out; Dr. Foster reported that you located every book he planted—and not a few that he didn't. He said it was rarely necessary to "steer" you; that you were quite self-motivated, distinctly tenacious, and could be quite devious when it came to tracking down knowledge in spite of the "barriers" he placed in your way.

By the time I managed to delegate all my other responsibilities to my successors and devote my entire attention to you, your advantage over other AAs had increased impressively. There were only a very few individuals showing anywhere near as much promise. And by the time the blunderings of our late friends behind the Iron Curtain put an end to all such research, you were—for your age—quite the most advanced of our hominems.

If I seem to harp on that point, it is because you must remember that this study was initiated some 20 years ago. You are ten years younger than the next youngest in our group; and as advanced as you are for your age, you still have considerable catching up to do—see that you keep at it.

Yes, I know; the exigencies of solo survival will occupy much of your time, but do not neglect your studies entirely. Cut back if you must, but do not terminate them.

Now, if I may presume to advise a singularly gifted member of an advanced species, there is security and comfort in numbers. You will doubtless find the preservation and extension of knowledge more convenient once a group of you have been assembled. Within the body of the Tarzan File you will find a complete listing of known Homo post hominems. I can anticipate no logical reason why most should not be alive and in good health.

Pawed through file with shaking hands. Found listing referred to: collection of mini-dossiers. One had small note attached. Read:

Dear Candy,

It is now almost time for me to leave, and a number of things still remain undone, so I must be brief.

The subject of this dossier, Peter Bell, is the direct, almost line-bred descendant of Alexander Graham Bell (would that I could have tested him). A measure of his intellect is the fact that he, alone of our hominems, deduced the existence and purpose of our study, the implications regarding himself, and most of the characteristics of his and your species.

To him, not long ago, I confided your existence, as well as my impressions of your potential.

As well as probably being your equal (after you reach maturity, of course), he is also nearest to your own age, at 21; and of all our subjects, I predict he is the most likely to prove compatible with you as you continue your unrelenting search for knowledge in the future—in fact, he may give you quite a run for it; he is a most motivated young man.

However, I was unable to reach him following the attack; therefore he does not know that you are alive and well in the shelter. The burden is upon you to establish contact, if such is possible—and I do urge you to make the attempt; I feel that a partnership consisting of you two would be most difficult to oppose, whatever the future may bring you.

> *Love,*
> *Teacher*

Hands shook, blood pounded in head as turned back to first letter. Balance consisted of advice on contacting other hominems—AAs from study.

Cautioned that, based on (terribly loose) extrapolation of known data, should be perhaps 150,000 of us on North American continent—but virtually *all* must be considered ABs replete with implications: High proportion of maladjusteds, discontents, rebels, borderline (or worse after shock of de-population) psychotics, plus occasional genius. Plus rare occurrences of surviving Homo sapiens.

Teacher suggested moving very deliberately when meeting strangers: Evaluate carefully, rapidly, selfishly. If decide is not sort would like for neighbor, hit first; kill without hesitation, warning. No place in consideration for racial altruism. Elimination of occasional bad apple won't affect overall chances for lifting species from endangered list; are enough of us to fill ranks after culling stock—but only one *me*. Point well taken.

Well, time grows short. So much remains to be accomplished before I leave, so I had best hurry.

I leave with confidence; I know the future of the race is in hands such as yours and Peter's. You will prosper and attain levels of development I cannot even envision; of that I am certain. I hope those heights will include much joy and contentment.

I might add this in parting: When your historians tell future generations about us, I hope they will not be unduly severe. True, we did not last the distance; also true, we did exterminate ourselves, apparently in a display of senseless, uncontrolled aggression; equally true, we did many other things that were utterly wrong.

But we did create a mighty civilization; we did accumulate a fund of knowledge vast beyond our capacity to absorb or control; we did conceive and aspire to a morality unique in history, which placed the welfare of others ahead of our own self-interest—even if most of us didn't practice it.

And we did produce you!

It may well be that we were not intended to last more than this distance. It may even be that your coming triggered seeds of self-destruction already implanted in us for that purpose; that our passing is as necessary to your emergence as a species as was our existence to your genesis.

But whatever the mechanism or its purpose, I think that when all are judged at the end of Time, Homo sapiens will be adjudged, if not actually a triumph, then at least a success, according to the standards imposed by the conditions we faced and the purposes for which we were created; just as the Cro-Magnon, Neanderthal, and Pithecanthropus—and even the brontosaur—were successful in their time when judged in light of the challenges they overcame and the purposes they served.

Single page remained. Hesitated; was final link with living past. Once read, experienced, would become just another memory. Sighed, forced eyes to focus:

Candy, my beloved daughter-in-spirit, this is most difficult to bring to a close. Irrationally I find myself grieving over losing you; "irrationally," I say, because it is obvious I who must leave. But leave I must, and there is no denying and little delaying of it.

It will be well with you and yours. Your growth has been sound, your direction

David R. Palmer

right and healthy; you cannot fail to live a life that must make us, who discovered and attempted to guide you this far, proud of our small part in your destiny, even though we are not to be permitted to observe its fulfillment. I think I understand something of how Moses must have felt as he stood looking down that last day on Nebo.

Always know that I, the doctor, and Mrs. Foster could not have loved you more had you sprung from our own flesh. Remember us fondly, but see that you waste no time grieving after us.

The future is yours, my child; go mold it as you see the need.

Goodbye, my best and best-loved pupil.

Love forever,
Soo Kim McDivott

P.S.: By the authority vested in me as the senior surviving official of the United States Karate Association, I herewith promote you to Sixth Degree. You are more than qualified; see to it that you practice faithfully and remain so.

Read, reread final page until tears deteriorated vision, made individual word resolution impossible. Placed letter reverently on desk, went upstairs, outside onto balcony porch. Was Teacher's favorite meditation setting. Settled onto veranda swing, eased legs into lotus.

Terry understood; moved silently from shoulder to lap, pressed close, started random-numbers recitation of vocabulary in barely audible, tiny baby-girl voice. Held twin nestled in arms as pain escalated, tears progressed to silent, painful, wracking sobs. Sibling's uncritical companionship, unquestioning love all that stood between me and all-engulfing blackness, fresh awareness of extent of losses threatening to overwhelm soul.

Together we watched early-afternoon cumulonimbus form up, mount into towering thunderheads, roil and churn, finally develop lightning flickers in gloom at bases, arch dark shafts of rain downward to western horizon; watched until fading light brought realization how long had sat there. Brighter stars already visible in east.

Reviewed condition with mounting surprise: Eyes dry, pain gone from throat, heart; blackness hovering over soul mere memory. Apparently had transcendentalized without conscious intent, resolved residual grief. All that remained was sweet sadness when contemplated Daddy, Momma, Teacher; were gone along with everything, everybody else, leaving only memories. Suddenly realized was grateful being permitted to keep those.

Cautiously moved exploratory muscle, first in hours. Terry twitched, fretted; then woke, set up justifiable protest over starved condition. Arose, shifted twin to shoulder; went inside, downstairs.

Picked up Tarzan File, Teacher's letter, went back to Daddy's house. Fed birdbrain, self; settled down, skimmed file's contents.

Presently concluded Teacher correct (profound shock, that): Peter Bell doubtless best prospective soulmate of lot. Very smart, very interested, very conscious: educational credits to date sound like spoof (*nobody* that young could have learned that much, except, uh . . . perhaps me—okay); very strong, quick, very advanced in study of Art (Eighth Degree!); plus (in words of Teacher): "Delightfully unconcerned about his own accomplishments; interested primarily in what he will do *next*." And, " . . . Possessed of a wry sense of humor." Sounds like my kind of guy. Hope turns out can stand him.

Sat for long moments working up nerve. Then picked up phone, deliberately dialed area code, number. Got stranded after a few moments' clicking, hissing when relay somewhere Out There stuck. Tried again: hit busy circuit (distinct from busy number: difference audible—also caused by sticky relay). Tried again muttering in beard. Stranded again. Tried again. Failed again.

"That's *bad*," offered Terry enthusiastically, bobbing head cheerfully.

Took deep breath, said very bad word, tried again.

Got ring tone! Once, twice, three times; then: Click. "Hello, is that you, Candy? Sure took you long enough. This is Peter Bell. I can't come to the phone right now, I'm outside taking care of the stock. But I've set up this telephone answering machine to guard my back. It's got an alarm on it that'll let me know you've called so I can check the tape.

"When you hear the tone at the end of my message, give me your phone number if you're not at home—*don't forget the area code* if it's different from your home—and I'll call you back the moment I get back and find your message. Boy, am I glad you're all right.

"Beep!"

Caught agape by recording. Barely managed regroupment in time to stutter out would be home; add if not, would be at farm, gave number before machine hung up, dial tone resumed.

Repeated bad word. Added frills tailored specifically for answering machine.

Did dishes, put away. Refilled twin's food dish, changed water: moved stand into study, placed next to desk, within convenient head-scratching range.

Settled into Daddy's big chair, opened journal, brought record up to date. Have done so, now up to date. Current. Completely. Nothing further to enter. So haven't entered anything else. For quite a while.

Midnight. Might as well read book.

Stupid phone.

Awoke to would-be rooster's salute to dawn's early light. Found self standing unsteadily in middle of study, blinking sleep from eyes, listening to echoes die away. Glared at twin; received smug snicker in return.

Took several moments to establish location, circumstances leading to night spent

David R. Palmer

in chair with clothes on. When succeeded, opened mouth, then didn't bother—realized bad word wouldn't help; no longer offered relief adequate to situation.

Casual approach had worn out about one A.M.—by which time had read possibly ten pages (of which couldn't remember single word). Featherhead snored on stand; nothing within reach to disassemble, had lost interest.

Yawning prodigiously myself by time abandoned pretense, grabbed phone, dialed number.

Got through first try. But was *busy!*

Repeated attempt at five-minute intervals for two hours or until fell asleep—whichever came first.

Have just tried line again. Still busy. Better go make breakfast.

Contact problem no longer funny. In two months since last entry have averaged five tries daily. Result: Either (usually) busy signal or transistorized moron spouts same message. One possible explanation (among many): Recorded message mentions no dates; could have been recorded day after Armageddon, yesterday—anytime.

Not that am languishing, sitting wringing hands by phone, however; have been *busy*. Completed move to farm; padded supply reserves; shored weaknesses; collected additional livestock, poultry. Have electrified fences, augmented where appeared marginally dogproof; trucked in additional grain (learned to drive semi, re-re-re-replete with 16-speed transmission—truly sorry about grain company's gatepost, but was in way; should have been moved long ago); located, trucked in two automatic diesel generators, connected through clever relay system so first comes on line (self-starting) if power fails, second kicks in if first quits. So far has worked every time tested, just as book said.

Have accumulated adequate fuel for operation: Brought in four tankers brim full of diesel (6,000 gallons each); rigged up interconnecting hose system guaranteeing gravity feed to generators—whichever needs, gets. At eight gallons hourly (maximum load) should provide over four months' operation if needed. (However, farm rapidly taking on aspect of truck lot. Must think about disposing of empties soon; otherwise won't be able to walk through yard.)

Overkill preparations not result of paranoia. Attempting to make place secure in absence; improve odds of finding habitable, viable farm on return, even if sortie takes longer than expected. Which could; is over 900 miles (straight-line) to file's address on Peter Bell. And he's only first on AA list; others are scattered all over.

Have attempted to cover all bets, both home and for self on trip. Chose vehicle with care: Four-wheel-drive Chevy van. Huge snow tires bulge from fenders on all four wheels, provide six inches extra ground clearance, awesome traction. Front bumper mounts electric winch probably capable of hoisting vehicle bodily up sheer cliff. Interior has bed, potty, sink, stove, sundry cabinets—and exterior boasts dreadful baroque murals on sides.

Though might appear was built specifically to fill own needs (except for murals—and need for build-ups on pedals), was beloved toy of town banker. When not pinching pennies, frittered time away boonies-crawling in endless quest for inaccessible, impassable terrain. Bragged hadn't found any. Hope so; bodes well for own venture.

Personal necessities, effects aboard. Include: Ample food, water for self, Terry; bedding, clothing, toiletries; diverse tools, including axe, bolt cutters, etc.; spares for van; siphon, pump, hose for securing gas; small, very nasty armory, including police chief's sawed-off riot gun, two Magnum revolvers, M-16 with numerous clips and scope. Not expecting trouble, but incline toward theory that probably won't rain if carry umbrella.

Leaving this journal here in shelter for benefit of archeologists: keep separate book on trip. Can consolidate on return, but if plans go awry this account still available for posterity.

Well, time to go: unknown beckons.

But have never felt so small. Awfully oig world waiting out there.

For me. ■